MURDER AT THE CHRISTMAS COOKIE BAKE-OFF

MURDER AT THE CHRISTMAS COOKIE BAKE-OFF

DARCI HANNAH

THORNDIKE PRESS
A part of Gale, a Cengage Company

© 2021 by Darci Hannah.
A Beacon Bakeshop Mystery #2.
Thorndike Press, a part of Gale, a Cengage Company.

ALL RIGHTS RESERVED

Thorndike Press® Large Print Clean Reads.
The text of this Large Print edition is unabridged.
Other aspects of the book may vary from the original edition.
Set in 16 pt. Plantin.

LIBRARY OF CONGRESS CIP DATA ON FILE.
CATALOGUING IN PUBLICATION FOR THIS BOOK
IS AVAILABLE FROM THE LIBRARY OF CONGRESS.

ISBN-13: 978-1-4328-9288-3 (hardcover alk. paper)

Published in 2021 by arrangement with Kensington Books, an imprint of Kensington Publishing Corp.

Printed in Mexico
Print Number: 01   Print Year: 2022

For Ron Hilgers

Because of you, I embrace the ridiculous, believe in the unknown, marvel at everything around me, and attempt in my own small way to share our love of baked goods with the world.

Our childhood was magical.

Until we meet again, my brother, God bless.

ACKNOWLEDGMENTS

Years ago, when I started out on this fickle career path, I never thought I'd end up writing cozy mysteries. Yet somewhere along the line I got the bug and attempted to write one. Although it was a new genre for me, I was enchanted with the process. Then divine providence directed me to Sandy Harding. Sandy, who is not only a great agent but a brilliant editor, saw something in that first manuscript and believed that she could make a cozy mystery writer out of me. Well, I think she has. For her devotion and unwavering belief, I am forever grateful. I would also like to thank my wonderful editor, John Scognamiglio, for taking a chance on the Beacon Bakeshop and working his magic. And to Rebecca Cremonese, Larissa Ackerman, and the entire team at Kensington, you guys are the very best!

I would also like to thank my talented

friend Robin Taylor, who has never wavered in her support for the books I write. And a huge thanks to my friend Tanya Holda for her incredible wisdom and for all the long walks during a difficult time; you are a godsend. And to Tanya, Sue Hanson, and Margaret Bingham, for raising a mug of coffee with me around a campfire and sharing your incredible handmade gifts during the lockdown. We shall never forget how much friendship matters. And to Jane Boundy, my dear friend who never fails to make me laugh.

This book could not have been written without the support and encouragement of my wonderful family. To my dear husband, John, and our boys, Jim, Dan, and Matt, you are my everything. To Jan and Dave Hilgers, my wonderful parents, your love and encouragement made me who I am today. And to my brother, Randy, thank you for all the phone calls and for being amazing. Love you!

And to my late brother Ron, who once bought a bakery on a whim and taught me what it meant to be a real baker. Those few short years in our late twenties live on in my memory. Such adventures! Such hard work! And those smiles of genuine delight when a customer took their first bite of a delectable baked good! Those crazy times were the inspiration for the Beacon Bakeshop Series. I hope I have done it justice. Although I miss you, every time I visit Beacon Harbor I know I am not alone. That is a true gift.

And to you, dear reader, thank you for joining me on this adventure. I am truly grateful.

CHAPTER 1

Sugarplum visions. Mine tormented me every year in the form of a ludicrous yet tantalizing belief that I could actually pull off the perfect Christmas. From past experience I had begun to doubt there really was such a thing. Sure, I'd heard tales of others having done it. Heck, the seasonal books, magazines, and movies made an industry of selling the idea and making us believe that the perfect Christmas was within our grasp. But we Bakewells were a special brand of idealists. We have a reputation of being risk takers with grand visions. Some risks, admittedly, look better on paper — like the year Dad bought Mom a real partridge in a pear tree. The moment she unveiled it in front of a room full of company, the poor bird startled and flew off in the direction of the kitchen. There it flopped around leaving no morsel of food unscathed. By the time Dad caught it, our only option had been to order Chinese takeout for fifty.

Our holidays were synonymous with chaos. My own had been no better. The first year I hosted Christmas Eve, my oven went out before the roast went in. The next year my Christmas tree fell over, breaking every glass ornament and causing a small fire. One year I'd been so busy that I hadn't realized Mom (a former eighties fashion model) had gained weight. I had bought her a skirt two sizes too small. Her silent tears still haunt me to this day! My annual Christmas party had been thwarted by ice storms and snowstorms, and once it had even been the scene of my best friend Kennedy's nastiest breakup to date. And just last year, Wellington, my giant Newfoundland dog, had done a little counter surfing when my back was turned and ate half the Christmas cake that had taken me two days to make.

And yet there was just something about Christmas — the smell of fresh-cut pine, the lights, the decorations, the presents, the food, the cravings for cookies, and the gathering of family and friends — that inspired me to reach for the sugarplums.

It might have been helpful if I actually knew what a sugarplum was.

The idea of them had been with me since

childhood, when I had learned that children of yore had visions of them dancing in their heads. I remember thinking that I liked plums, and that I *really* liked sugar, so they must be the pinnacle of Christmas delights.

Even in my adult life they had gotten the best of me, and not just at Christmas. They had given me the courage to walk away from a lucrative Wall Street career to open a bakery in an old lighthouse on the shores of Lake Michigan. It was risky, and it hadn't even looked sane on paper. But it was my sugarplum vision, and I wasn't at all sorry I had embraced it.

This year, I silently thought as I watched the UPS truck rumble up the lighthouse drive, my sugarplum Christmas was within my grasp. Manhattan and Christmas pasts were behind me. I was now the proud owner of the Beacon Bakeshop. Although our grand opening had been a little rough, the Beacon had swiftly become the heart of Beacon Harbor.

I was hosting Christmas this year at the lighthouse, and I couldn't have been more excited. My folks were flying in a week early for the town Christmas festival, and my best friend, Kennedy, was coming as well. I had made lots of new friends in the village and was even dating my hunky neighbor, Rory

Campbell. All the stars were aligning. Clutching the bright red mug between my hands, I took a sip of my gingerbread latte and smiled. Sugarplum delicious!

My latte bliss was momentarily broken by a series of loud barks coming from the other side of the lighthouse door. The Beacon Harbor Lighthouse was a large structure, housing both my spacious living quarters and the Beacon Bakeshop. The door that separated the two was a historic wonder of six-paneled oak. Although original to the lighthouse and beautiful, it wasn't entirely soundproof. Welly had heard the UPS truck, which meant that Hank was visiting. And whenever Hank appeared at the lighthouse, it meant a treat for Welly. It was five minutes until closing, and the last customers had left ten minutes ago.

For obvious reasons, drool being a close second to shedding fur, my giant, loveable pup wasn't allowed in the bakeshop during business hours and was permanently banned from the kitchen. However, during the warmer weather, all dogs were allowed in the Beacon's outdoor pup café. Warmer weather was a far-off dream, and Welly was whining.

"Does anyone mind if I release the hound?" I looked at the two young people working behind the counter.

"Not at all," Elizabeth replied. She poured another measure of milk in the steam pitcher and glanced out the window. "Poor Hank. He's got to be the busiest man in Beacon Harbor this time of the year."

"I agree. Why don't you two make him one of these." I raised my mug, then set it back on the counter as I opened the door for Welly.

"Wow, why so many boxes?" Tom, measuring espresso for another latte, lifted his brows in question.

Tom Porter was one of my full-time baristas. After a rocky opening last May, I realized that I was going to need more help with the bakery. I had already hired two fabulous young ladies, Elizabeth and Wendy. Both grew up in the town and were recent high school grads. Alaina, their friend, was hired shortly thereafter, completing what I commonly referred to as *the three amigos*. Then, just to spice things up, I hired two young men in late summer, Ryan and Tom. Ryan, who was taking online classes at a local college, had a passion for computers and making sandwiches. Tom, on the other hand, was a college grad with a degree in history and a passion for coffee. He also knew his way around an espresso machine.

Another remarkable fact was that on the days Tom opened, the girls were never late. Similarly, on the days Tom opened, there was a steady stream of young female customers who lingered a bit longer than usual in the café. His tawny good looks, easy smile, and genuine sincerity were a winning combination. The truth was, all my staff at the Beacon got along exceptionally well, which made for a happy workplace. The only thing I was sorely in need of was an assistant baker. I had hired and lost three already, never realizing it would be such a hard position to keep filled.

"They're either Christmas decorations or presents for us," Elizabeth teased, adding a grin. Tom didn't smile. He appeared troubled by all the boxes Hank was unloading.

"Elizabeth is partially correct. All those boxes contain my new Christmas lights."

"What?" Tom looked up from the gingerbread latte he was making. "How many did you order?"

"Enough to cover the lighthouse. It's a big building."

"Not that big."

While Wellington waited patiently at the door, I went to retrieve my latte. Taking a sip, I asked, "Have either of you two ever seen the movie *Christmas Vacation*?" Trying

16

to make a joke, I was greeted by a pair of blank stares. "No? Well, it's a classic. I'm no Clark Griswold, mind you, but these boxes represent my first attempt at exterior illumination." Again, they had no idea what I was talking about. I was in my mid-thirties, but their clueless stares were making me feel much older. Obviously, we were going to have to have an after-work viewing of my favorite Christmas movie.

"I get it," Elizabeth chimed in. "Not the old movie," she clarified, "but what you're doing. You're trying to outshine the competition during the Christmas festival."

"It's not about lights," Tom reminded her. "The theme this year is Christmas cookies."

"Exactly! But it's hard to find lights that look like Christmas cookies. I'm going with a candy shop theme." Apparently, they both thought I was crazy. But I wasn't. I was simply creating my sugarplum vision.

"I want to spread holiday cheer," I continued. "I want this old place to shine brighter than it ever has!" Grinning, I left the counter and joined Welly at the door, opening it for the delivery.

Tom and Elizabeth came with me. "That's ambitious," Tom remarked with an anxious glance at my delivery. "You're going to wait for Mr. Campbell, right?" He took hold of a box, helping Hank unload his hand truck.

He was referring to my boyfriend. Truthfully, I was a little offended that he assumed I needed help. Rory had his own charming log home to take care of.

"What makes you think I need Rory to help me with these? They're lights. You hang them up and plug them in. I have plenty of extension cords, light hooks, and timers. I watched a video on YouTube. I should be fine." As I spoke, I caught the grin Hank exchanged with Tom.

Tom paused. His face was flushed, whether from exertion or embarrassment I couldn't tell. "It's just that . . . well, there's a lot of lights here, and Mr. Campbell has —"

"Military experience?" I offered, placing my hands on my hips. "These are Christmas lights, not guns."

"No, a ladder . . . and coordination." This last remark he slipped in, like an extra comma in a confusing sentence. And, like that extra comma, it wasn't going to help him. My inner New Yorker was threatening to pounce. Thankfully, Elizabeth pounced instead.

"Whoa, fella. You should have stopped at ladder."

"I'm staying out of this," Hank declared,

raising a hand. He then slipped Welly a dog cookie. After ruffling my pup's head, he handed me his clipboard to sign. "Anyhow, isn't Rory in the Upper Peninsula ice fishing?"

I penned my signature and returned the clipboard. "He is. I'm planning on surprising him."

Tom cast a wary eye over all the boxes littering the café floor. "Oh, he'll be surprised, alright."

"Be back with another load." Hank flashed a conspiratorial wink and headed out the door with Welly leading the way.

Elizabeth turned to Tom. "Maybe you'd better stay and help. I'll finish making the latte then clean up."

"Look, stop worrying, you two. I'm not doing the entire lighthouse myself. I've hired Bill Morgan and his son to wrap the light tower in red and white lights. With any luck it'll look like a giant candy cane when they're done. They're also framing the roofline in white lights. I'm doing the rest." I cut open one of the boxes and pulled out a three-foot red-and-white-striped candy cane. "Isn't this darling? I'm lining the walkway with these. There are wreaths for the windows and net lights for the bushes. And that big box over there should be a giant blow-up gingerbread man. Sure, it's a lot of work, but I don't think it requires Herculean amounts of coordination."

Elizabeth folded her hands and pressed them to her lips in an effort, I suspected, to keep from bursting out in giggles. "Oh my. The Beacon is sure going to turn some heads."

Before closing for the day, Elizabeth reminded me about the bakery orders for tomorrow.

There were six coffee cakes, eight fruit pies, two French silk pies, and fifteen lunch boxes to be made along with the bakery's staple items. I'd put Ryan on the lunch boxes when he came in tomorrow. Wendy could help me frost donuts and prep mini quiches. The rest was up to me. I looked at the boxes of lights and sighed. It was going to be another long night.

CHAPTER 2

Dressed in the warmest snow gear money could buy, I convinced myself that there was still a good hour or two of daylight left. Wellington, covered in a double layer of long, silky black fur, loved the snow nearly as much as he loved lake water. It made him the perfect outdoor companion. With his bushy tail wagging happily, he followed me to the boathouse to retrieve a ladder. Yes, I had one. No, I had never used it. Then, with ladder in tow, we were ready to illuminate.

The candy cane lights went in without a hitch. After they were all connected, I added an extension cord, set the timer, and plugged the line into the industrial outdoor power strip hidden behind a bush near the bakery entrance. Although I was summoning my inner Clark Griswold, I had no wish to blow a fuse or overload the power grid.

I took a step back and marveled at how pretty the candy cane walkway looked.

"See? I can do this," I told Wellington, filling with pride. I gave him a pat on the head, then set to work on the bushes.

The old lighthouse had been landscaped with hardy boxwoods and thick bushy yews. Although they looked battered, as if they had weathered many storms as they stood firm against the length of the lighthouse, a cape of sparkling net lights transformed them into a vision of wonder.

"Wow," I breathed aloud, clapping my near-frozen hands in delight. "What do you think? Magical, right?" But Welly wasn't there. He was down by the walkway chewing on a giant candy cane light. Fear shot through me. They were plugged in! Seized by visions of an electrical explosion and singed dog fur, I let out a cry and ran after him.

"No! Bad dog!"

Wellington looked my way, thought it was a game, and ran with his prized candy cane clenched between his teeth. As he dashed for the light tower, the candy canes burst from the snow one by one, trailing in his wake.

After a stern talking-to, and after trying to make the chewed candy cane look a little less eaten, I painstakingly set them up again along the walkway. Clearly, Wellington couldn't be trusted near them. He was put on a leash for safekeeping.

My fingers were beginning to freeze by the time I tackled the bright red awning that hung over the bakery window. Using the ladder for the first time, I was determined to finish the lights. Daylight had faded, the lights were rebelling, and Welly was whining at the end of his leash. I ignored it all to hang a strand of colorful lights in the shape of hard candies. I was nearly done when I began to hear things.

Unbeknownst to me when I had purchased the historic building, it was rumored to be haunted. I didn't believe in ghosts at the time, feeling there was always a logical explanation for peculiar happenings. However, last spring I had a personal encounter with the lighthouse ghost, Captain Willy Riggs. He was the first light keeper of the Beacon Harbor Lighthouse, and, for reasons of his own, he never left. Some might find that unsettling, but Wellington and I rather liked the fact that the captain was still on duty, guarding the old lighthouse he loved.

Cold and exhausted as I was, I thought the captain might be speaking to me. On closer inspection, however, it was just the wind coming off the lake. Although Lake Michigan never froze completely, the shoreline was covered in wave-spume icicles. The ice tinkled and chimed with the undulating movement of the waves. The sing-song cadence sounded more like a woman's voice and not a man's.

Ignoring everything, I reached out as far as I could, gingerly trying to secure the strand of lights at the corner of the awning. They kept falling off. Infuriated, I reached out again, hanging on with the tips of my frozen glove. That's when the voice spoke loud and clear.

"Oooo, how lovely!"

Wellington barked. It wasn't until the ladder toppled and I found myself trapped in a snow-covered bush that I realized tying Welly's leash to the ladder might have been a mistake.

The concerned face of my dear friend, Betty Vanhoosen, peered down at me. Hers had been the voice I'd mistaken for the tinkling ice. And, quite frankly, I was happy to see her. Betty, in her early sixties, was one of Beacon Harbor's most vivacious residents. She owned Harbor Realty, was president of the Chamber of Commerce, and was a shameless town gossip. She came to the bakeshop every morning before heading off to work, keeping me apprised of all the latest news. I reached out a gloved hand

24

to her then I realized she hadn't come alone. Giggling erupted before another face appeared, this one belonging to Felicity Stewart.

Embarrassed, I waved. "Mind helping me out?"

Felicity was another shop owner in Beacon Harbor. She was tall, willowy, married, and in her mid-forties. She also owned the first shop one saw when entering the town, a year-round Christmas shop called The Tannenbaum Shoppe. How she could summon Christmas cheer all year long was a mystery to me, but she did. My lighthouse bakery was on the opposite end of town, sitting watch over the harbor and the public beach. Between us were four whole blocks of shops and eateries, hotels and summer guesthouses.

She kept giggling. "You're in a bush!"

My inner New Yorker would have sneered at her, snapping, "No duh, Sherlock!" But the new Lindsey, the kinder, bakery-owning Lindsey, choked down the insult. Instead I offered, "Thanks for noticing. Care to lend a hand?" Because I realized that I was stuck.

"Why would you tie Wellington's leash to the ladder? Are you hurt? Have you hung all these lights yourself? You really should have waited for Rory to help you with these." Betty, true to form, shot out every question sitting on her tongue before making a move to help me. Honestly, the fact that she thought I needed Rory's help was a tad more annoying than the woodsy branches stabbing my ribs. Why did everybody feel I needed his help?

I propped myself up and tried to smile but grimaced instead. With labored breath, I offered, "He's . . . ice fishing. In the U.P. I'll make you both a steaming mug of cocoa if you get me out of here."

CHAPTER 3

While Betty and Felicity settled at a café table, I shrugged off my coat and jumped to the kitchen. There I took out a saucepan, fired up the stove, and measured out the right amount of cocoa and sugar. Next, I went to the fridge and took out a gallon of whole milk. I added three cups of the milk to the sugar/cocoa mix, stirring over a medium flame until everything was blended. While the cocoa was heating, I poured heavy whipping cream into the mixer, added a quarter cup of confectioners' sugar and a teaspoon of vanilla, and turned it on. While the sweet cream was whipping up nicely, I pulled a bar of milk chocolate out of the cupboard and shaved a handful of chocolate curls. Adding a dash of cinnamon to the cocoa to boost the chocolate flavor, I was ready to divide the rich mixture into three mugs. Each was then topped with thick whipped cream and chocolate curls. Welly, although no help with the lights, got a dollop of whipped cream in a dish nonetheless.

"You really should have waited for Rory," Betty remarked again, taking her mug. I had just shooed Welly into our living quarters, where I knew he'd curl up beside the fireplace until I locked up for the night. Betty continued, "You wouldn't have landed in a bush if you had." After a cautionary look, she took a sip of her cocoa. A smile of ecstasy came to her lips.

I felt like growling at her remark but refrained. Instead, I took a seat and followed suit, soothing my vitriol with a whipped cream–filled swig of warm cocoa. Waiting for my limbs to thaw and the sugar to take hold, I finally replied, "I have a lot of lights to hang and thought I'd get a jump on it, but point taken. Hanging them is definitely not as much fun as throwing the switch and watching them shine."

Felicity, sporting a whipped cream mustache, set down her mug. "As your local Christmas aficionado, I approve your efforts. It's about time this old lighthouse got a splash of holiday cheer. Imagine our surprise when we saw you fall into that bush!" She began to laugh again.

I didn't need to imagine; I had lived it. Then, watching her ridiculous whipped cream mustache quiver on her upper lip, I began to laugh as well.

Betty was laughing at us both. Finally, she picked up her napkin. "Your lip, dear." She pretended to dab her own lip.

"What?" Felicity brought a finger to the area in question, touched whipped cream, and stopped laughing. Embarrassed, she grabbed her napkin. "You put far too much whipped cream on your cocoa, Lindsey. At the Tannenbaum Shoppe, we serve our cocoa with marshmallows, which is the correct way. But I don't expect you to know that. You own a bakery. You're hardly a Christmas aficionado like me." She curled her Christmas-red lips into a condescending smile.

I sat back in my chair and crossed my arms. I didn't know Felicity well, but I did know that she had a tendency to be tightly wound and was a bit full of herself. But did she really think she owned Christmas? Before I could chime in, defending my cocoa and my exterior illumination, Betty piped up.

"Why, there's no right way to make hot cocoa, just as there's no right way to celebrate Christmas. It's a matter of traditions and preferences. Oooo, and speaking of Christmas traditions, have we got a surprise for you. Felicity and I were at the chamber meeting this afternoon."

With all the excitement of the Christmas lights, I had forgotten all about the chamber meeting. The town was putting the finishing touches on the Christmas festival. It was a town-wide tradition and the largest Christmas celebration in the area. This year the theme was Christmas cookies, something I could really get behind. And, being new to the town, I had already volunteered to donate sixteen dozen for the celebration.

"We figured you were busy with the bakery." Betty waved her hand at the empty bakery cases. "Without the help of an assistant baker, I really don't know how you're managing. That's why we've come."

Felicity pushed her mug of cocoa away and flashed a toothy smile. "It's the best news. I went ahead and spearheaded a little campaign of my own to get even more foot traffic in our charming downtown shops and restaurants. And tonight, it was not only approved, it was applauded."

Gripping my cocoa with both hands to get them warm, I tilted my head and looked at her. Without enthusiasm I uttered, "Wow. Applauded. So, what did you propose?"

"A Christmas cookie bake-off!" Betty's excitement was barely containable. Obvi-

30

ously, due to a scathing look from Felicity, Betty wasn't supposed to have dropped the news. But this was Betty's town. Oblivious that she had stepped on Felicity's toes, Betty added, "And we're calling it The Great Beacon Harbor Christmas Cookie Bake-Off." She waved her hand in a lofty arc as she said this. "Do you get it? It's a parody of that delightful British baking show on television. Isn't it brilliant? The press release has already gone out, and the banners are being printed as we speak."

My jaw dropped in question. Was I missing something? The Christmas Festival was only nine days away. "I understand that Christmas cookies are the theme this year, but when is this bake-off supposed to happen?"

"At the festival. I know it's short notice," Felicity soothed, patting my hand with her finely manicured one. Her nails were Christmas red, and her diamond ring was spectacular. She was obviously on Santa's nice list, I mused a bit darkly. She gave my hand a firm squeeze. "You're a baker, so I'm counting on you to enter the bake-off and help spread enthusiasm about this event."

The mere thought of a Christmas cookie bake-off sent a new wave of sugarplum visions dancing through my head. My small

31

exterior illumination blunder aside, which I blamed entirely on Wellington, I could almost taste victory. My family would be here to see me win. Rory would be here as well. I was positively electrified by the thought of pulling off a double holiday whammy — winning the first ever Beacon Harbor Christmas cookie bake-off, while hosting a postcard-perfect Christmas. I looked at Felicity with a whole new wave of admiration. "What a brilliant idea. Where's the entry form?"

Felicity forced a smile. "There is no entry form."

I turned my palms toward the ceiling in a look of extreme confusion. "Then how do I enter?"

"Oh, oh, let me explain!" Betty, in the grip of a sugar buzz or simply sporting her genuine enthusiasm for the town, launched right in with the details.

According to her, The Great Beacon Harbor Christmas Cookie Bake-Off was a town-wide affair. Every shop owner in town was encouraged to offer a signature cookie for shoppers to sample as they wandered up and down the quaint, artfully decorated streets of the village. The shoppers would then cast their votes for their top four favorite cookies. On Friday night the votes would be tallied and the four winning cookie-bakers would get to compete in a live bake-off, to be held during the Christmas festival on Sunday. It was a lot to take in.

"Lindsey, dear, you look a little pale," Betty remarked. Before I could reply, she gave my cheek a quick and unexpected pinch.

"Ouch!" I rubbed my cheek as I looked at her. "I'm fine."

"Maybe you're not. You did fall off that ladder." She held me in a look of motherly concern.

"I was cushioned by a layer of outerwear and two feet of snow. No, what I'm stuck on is this Christmas cookie bake-off. You want every shop owner to provide free homemade cookies during the busiest week of holiday shopping?"

"Of course." Felicity grinned. "It'll inspire Christmas cheer. I thought you, a baker, would be up for this." With both red-nailed hands, she fluffed up her curls, then pulled her lips into a clownish frown. In an odd sort of way, that frown was a challenge.

"Ooo! Ooo, and here's the best part!" Betty, oblivious to the silent challenge that passed between Felicity and me, announced, "Felicity has secured Chicago celebrity food critic Chevy Chambers to judge our live bake-off. Can you believe our good fortune? Chevy Chambers is coming here — to judge us!"

Unfortunately, that didn't sound as good as Betty had meant it to. Or maybe it was just me and my jaded view of celebrity foodies. After all, the reason I had bought a rundown lighthouse on the shores of Lake Michigan to begin with was because of an up-and-coming celebrity foodie, namely my ex-fiancé, Jeffery Plank. My distrust of celebrity chefs and food critics aside, there was something else about this town-wide cookie bake-off that had my heart pounding away in my chest like a sledgehammer. Keeping free cookies in stock would require extra baking, and I was already short-handed. How was I going to pull it off and make it into the bake-off?

"This is a lot of extra baking for me. When does this start?"

"Tuesday," Felicity stated. "The winners will be announced Friday evening. Shouldn't be too troubling for you. We at the Tannenbaum Shoppe aren't quaking in our boots. That's because we serve up Christmas cheer all year round." Her condescending grin was just begging for my inner New Yorker to come out and play, but I kept

34

her in check for Betty's sake.

"Just think of all the families flocking to our little lakeside village to partake in this unique and delicious Christmas celebration. Of course, bake your best cookies, my dears, but do be gracious. I have it on good authority that Santa Claus is watching." This Betty punctuated with a cheeky wink.

"I think it'll be fun," I said, getting to my feet. They were still a bit frozen. All I wanted at the moment was to warm up a bowl of my homemade chicken and dumplings, plop down on my leather couch, and snuggle up with Welly as we watched a little TV. I had to be up early. I was getting tired. "You both have obviously put a lot of thought into this festival, and I'm sure it's going to be a great success."

Felicity stood as well and thoughtlessly smoothed her well-fitting dress pants. "I'm just excited," she stated in apology. "While everyone loves Christmas, this is, hands down, our busiest time of year. And Christmas cookies will only make it better."

"Everything is better with cookies," I agreed.

Felicity was at the door. "I need to know the name of your signature cookie by Monday. That's when we're printing up the ballots. Betty, are you coming?"

Betty waved. "You run along. I just remembered that I have to place an order with Lindsey."

Betty waited until Felicity was out of sight before she reached into her purse. "Here, dear," she said, covertly handing me a yellowed, dog-eared, food-smudged recipe card. "You know I'm not much of a baker. And even if I was, where would I find the time? This is my grandma's recipe, bless her soul. It's her famous raspberry linzer cookies. They're the prettiest little things, all covered in powdered sugar with a little window of raspberry jelly. She made them every Christmas. I'd like to order twelve dozen for Tuesday morning."

My gaze shifted from the recipe card to her face. "Betty Vanhoosen, are you asking me to bake your signature cookie? Is that even allowed?"

A mischievous grin played on her lips. "Well, my goodness, they never said it wasn't. The only rule, as far as I know, is that the baker of the winning cookie advances to the live Christmas cookie bake-off competition. And this little linzer cookie is a winner. Felicity is a dear, but my money's on you, kid."

"Betty, you do know that I'll be baking my own signature cookie as well, right? I have to. The throngs of holiday shoppers will demand it," I teased.

"Of course. And I'm confident that it'll be delicious. But the public will be voting, dear, and one can never count on their good taste. The public likes Twinkies, and Ding Dongs, and those nacho cheese chalupas. It's like my dear late husband, Peter, used to say, it never hurts to have two horses in the race."

"Well, as long as we don't get disqualified, I'll have twelve dozen of your grandmother's famous raspberry linzer cookies waiting for you Tuesday morning."

CHAPTER 4

"Guess what?" I said to the voice on the other end of the phone. After a quick supper and a short walk with Wellington, I was finally in my warmest flannel nightgown, snuggled in bed. It was eight thirty p.m., the bedtime hour of the elderly and bakers. My alarm would go off at three thirty in the morning, and if I wanted to function in the kitchen, I needed sleep. But I also needed to hear Rory's voice. Welly, blissfully unaware that one of his very favorite humans was on the other end of the phone, was sleeping soundly in his own bed at the foot of mine.

"You found an assistant baker," he guessed.

"Well, that would be nice too. But no. Felicity Stewart came to the Beacon with Betty this evening to tell me that there's to be a Christmas cookie bake-off in Beacon Harbor."

"Felicity Stewart, the Christmas lady? Bet she's been cooking that one up all year. Poor woman has got to occupy her mind somehow, surrounded by all those weird elves on the shelves, an army of jolly Santas, ornaments galore, and her own herd of plastic reindeer. Did I tell you I made a visit to Tannenbaum last August?"

The thought made me smile. "No. Do tell."

"I was about to go fishing, and I needed live bait. All the tourists had bought out the bait shops, so Bill Morgan tells me that Tannenbaum sold bait as well, the jokester. Dummy me, I believed him. It was a hundred degrees out, and the moment I walk into the shop I was nearly knocked to the floor by a fug of frankincense — at least that's what I think it was. Then," he continued, his deep voice full of animation, "the moment my eyes adjust to the forest of fake firs covered in bright blinking lights, Felicity hands me a cup of hot cocoa covered in sticky marshmallows . . . and with a candy cane poking out. A candy cane! I was sweating buckets, and she hands me hot cocoa? Clearly, she wasn't selling bait."

I was giggling. "You never told me that story."

"Because it's embarrassing." I could hear

the smile in his voice as he spoke.

He brought me up to speed on his ice fishing excursion with the boys, while I told him about the bake-off. "I'm getting up at three to spend some quality time in the kitchen. I have to fill the bakery cases and get a jump on my holiday orders."

"Ouch, that's early. Three in the morning's the witching hour, Linds," he teased, referring to that eerily quiet time between two and four in the morning, when paranormal activity was supposedly at its peak. It was either that or people were just groggy from lack of sleep and believed every odd noise was a banshee. All that aside, Rory knew my lighthouse was haunted, and I didn't appreciate the suggestion. It wasn't that I was afraid of my resident ghost, I just didn't like to be surprised.

"The captain and I have a peaceful coexistence. I don't want to see him, and he doesn't want to see me. I keep to the lighthouse in the wee hours, and he keeps to the tower. We like it that way."

"You might want to tell him that. Isn't he the reason you can't find an assistant baker?"

It was only a half-truth, but Rory was correct. My dad, James Bakewell, had grown up in a bakery in Traverse City and had come to my rescue during the Beacon Bakeshop's second grand opening. Dad and Mom had been invaluable help that first month, but they had their own busy lives to get back to down in Palm Beach, Florida. Before they left, I had hired a promising young man named Fred Nagel. Fred was a thirty-year-old hipster, and supposedly, to use his own words, "loved the vibe the old lighthouse was giving off." Although not a baker by trade, he was like me, a baking enthusiast. I spent a good month teaching him some of my techniques and how to perfect my prized recipes. Then, out of the blue, Fred up and quit at the end of September. Apparently, he ran off to Colorado with his girlfriend, leaving me once again without an assistant baker. Kennedy, my best friend, was miffed about the whole ordeal. She located Fred a month later and told me that he and his lover were in Boulder, Colorado, operating a mobile bakery called Crunchy out of a modified transit van.

Shucking off the slight feeling that I had been used, I next hired an older woman from the next town over, Monica Harlow, thinking that I had finally found a baker I could trust. Monica claimed she could bake, and she could, on the days she decided to show up for work. She also tended to step

41

outside for a smoke when baked goods were in the oven, setting off the fire alarms on more than a few occasions. Burnt bread, scorched pies, and singed cookies were becoming a common occurrence. I knew I was going to have to fire her, but the captain handled the matter for me. The girls and I were getting the café ready to open for the day when we caught a whiff of something burning — just before the fire alarm started to blare. I was about to run into the kitchen when we heard a bloodcurdling scream. Monica burst through the kitchen doors, crashed into the café door, fumbled with the lock, and dashed out of the building. When I finally caught up to her, she was trembling.

"He was there," she said, her face white as a sheet, "the old dead captain, and he was casting me the evil eye!"

Monica quit that morning. Apparently, old Captain Willy Riggs wasn't keen on the thought of his lighthouse burning down. Either that, or he was growing tired of the smell of burnt cookies.

I stifled a yawn, knowing that my days were about to get even longer without an assistant baker. The special holiday orders were already piling up, and now I was committed to baking my own signature cookie as well as Betty's. "Well, there's very little I can do about hiring an assistant baker if no one will answer my ad. I keep posting it and keep hoping for the best. I guess I should add it to my Christmas wish list."

"You have a Christmas wish list?" I could tell by the sound of his voice he was tickled by the thought.

"Of course. Don't you?"

"I have only one wish, and that's spending more time with you."

My heart fluttered to hear him say it. "That was on the top of my list too," I admitted. "But for that to happen, I need an assistant baker I can trust. And you need to be a little closer than a fishing shanty in the middle of nowhere."

"I'll be home Sunday. Don't make any plans. You're having dinner with me. As for that assistant baker, I'll let Santa know. The North Pole is just over yonder."

I gave a sleepy giggle. "You're in the U.P., not the North Pole."

"It's pretty much the same thing. Can't imagine it getting any colder than this."

We said our good nights and I fell asleep, dreaming of sugarplums, Christmas cookies, and Rory Campbell.

CHAPTER 5

It felt like I had just laid my head on the pillow when my alarm went off, jolting me from a dreamless sleep. December nights in Michigan were cold, long, and dark. I knew it wouldn't change much during the months of January and February. Even March was a downer. "Urgh," I growled, and left the warmth of my bed to stumble into the shower. I stood beneath the steamy water until I felt nearly human again. Then I got dressed and left the lighthouse with Wellington to take a short walk along the night-dark beach.

Bundled in a long, puffy coat, mittens, and a thick hat, I followed Welly as he bounded along the icy shoreline, chomping on chunks of ice as he went. His black fur blended so well with the darkness that he was often hard to see. The snow and icy shore of winter, however, made him stand out a bit more. The winds coming off the

44

lake were brutal. Sane people, I mused, didn't suffer such torture. But this was Wellington's happiness — our early morning walks along the lakeshore. I watched as he left the water's edge to trot over the snowy dunes. He stopped, sniffed, then shoved his nose deep into the snow, rooting for some unseen critter. He pawed at the snow, buried his head deeper, and finally gave up, shaking the white flakes off his big, fluffy head. I called him back, and we headed home.

As we rounded the beach between the lake and the light tower, I looked up at the lantern room. It was a habit of mine. I couldn't help it. And every time I did, I wondered if Captain Willy was on duty. Once I had seen the ghostly light up there myself. Rory had explained to me that they were a portent of danger. Unbeknownst to me then, the ghost lights of Beacon Harbor were legendary. Thankfully, all was dark and quiet in the lantern room now. I saluted the tower nonetheless, out of respect for the old keeper. I then put Wellington in the lighthouse with a bowl of his favorite kibble and headed for the bakery kitchen.

There was something comforting about the quiet room with its pristine stainless-steel countertops and wire bakery racks full of bowls and pans waiting to be put to work. Although I longed to have someone assisting me, I found mornings alone in the kitchen to be peaceful and full of possibility. No crowded commute here, no crazy lines at a trendy coffeehouse — I was brewing my own pot at the moment — no hallway of elevators with a press of people waiting for the right one to open. I didn't have a secretary with a list of clients to be handled, or a computer bursting with loads of important spreadsheets and emails. Instead, I had an industrial mixer, a proofing box, a commercial oven, and a book of recipes. It was Saturday morning, our busiest morning of the week. Beginning every morning as I did without an assistant baker, I took out my recipe for sweet roll yeast dough and began the process. We had added scrumptious cinnamon rolls and gooey caramel pecan rolls to the bakery cases, and our customers loved them.

I took out a large saucepan and heated the appropriate amount of milk for the yeast. When the milk was warm, I poured it into the bowl of the mixer, adding melted butter and sugar. After a good stir, I sprinkled the yeast on top, allowing it to sit for one minute. The warm, sugary mixture was the perfect environment for activating yeast, which was the key to light, tender dough. After a short rest, I added most of the flour and started the mixer.

The trick to a perfect cinnamon roll or pecan roll was not to overwork the dough. Overworking dough at this stage would make it tough and chewy. To avoid this, I kept the mixer on low until all the flour had been gently mixed in. The sticky, wet dough was then covered with plastic wrap, and put in a warm place to rise.

While the yeast dough was doubling in size, I turned on the deep fryer and went to work on the two types of dough needed for the donuts we served: cake and yeast. Donuts had become second nature to me. In no time my yeast dough was rising, and I had all the cake donuts made and ready to be frosted by the time my sweet roll dough was ready for part two, adding the last few cups of flour, the baking powder, and salt. I turned my attention from the donuts to finish the sweet roll dough, which was ready for kneading.

The few quiet hours of the morning went on like a well-orchestrated dance. I rolled dough, made fillings, cut donuts, and rolled cinnamon rolls and pecan rolls. I proofed dough, baked dough, and fried dough. When all the donuts and sweet rolls were made, I set to work on three variety of Danish, using premade laminated pastry dough. I had toyed with making my own, but without an assistant baker, who was I kidding? Pastry dough was too time-consuming.

After the Danish went into the oven, I poured another cup of coffee and started on my giant gingerbread muffins. I had worked out a new recipe for a fragrant, warm, moist, spicy muffin that tasted like Christmas morning. This was the morning they were making their holiday debut, giant muffins the size of softballs. As I whipped up the batter, poured them into the greased giant muffin tin, and put them into the oven, the entire kitchen came alive with the heavenly scent of ginger, nutmeg, cinnamon, and cloves.

As the bakery cases were filling up, I was just about to start on our savory options, the mini quiches. Every morning I made a dozen spinach and bacon quiches, a dozen ham and Gruyère, and a dozen tomato, basil, and Swiss. What didn't sell by morning usually sold by lunchtime. As I rolled pie dough for the mini pie tins, Wendy and Alaina came bounding through the door. Dear heavens, was it was six thirty already? I had lost track of time. The bakery would open in half an hour.

"Morning, Lindsey!" the girls chimed. I smiled and gave them a coffee-cup salute.

Wendy inhaled sharply. "It smells like Christmas! You made the giant gingerbread muffins!" Her eyes grew wide with desire as she looked at them.

"I saved one for you two to split." I pointed to a warm muffin that was nearly the size of the plate it sat on. "Grab a cup of coffee and come on over. The Christmas season is upon us. I want to tell you about some of the special things we'll be doing at the Beacon."

As the girls went over to the sink to wash their hands before taking down their personal coffee mugs, I stood up straight and massaged my lower back. I had to admit that my three solid hours of baking had been productive, if not exhausting.

Wendy and Alaina each tied on a bright red Beacon Bakeshop apron. When constructing the bakery café, I had wanted to give it a modern, sophisticated feel while honoring the local lighthouse lore. I went with the original hardwood floors, which were gorgeous, black granite countertops for the bakery counter, and white shiplap walls tastefully decorated with pictures of sailboats, lakeside landscapes, nautical

49

décor, and a smattering of lighthouse history. Red was our accent color, and we splashed it liberally.

"I don't know how you baked all of this," Elaina remarked, looking at the bakery trays bursting with tasty delights.

I grinned. "I found that miracles happen when a proper caffeine buzz collides with extreme time optimization."

"What?" A look of confusion crossed Wendy's face. "I get the caffeine buzz, but still, this is a crazy amount of stuff. Are you sure you're okay?"

I found her look of concern rather sweet. "I'm fine, thanks. But things are likely to get busier. I don't suppose you two have heard the big news."

"The Great Beacon Harbor Christmas Cookie Bake-Off!" Alaina's eyes grew wide with excitement as she sliced off a hunk of the gingerbread muffin. It was still warm, emitting fine wisps of steam into the air that comingled with the steam from her coffee. "O . . . M . . . G!" she mumbled, waving a hand excitedly across her mouth as she savored her first bite. She swallowed and proclaimed, "Amazing!" She indicated for Wendy to take a bite before continuing. "The bake-off is the talk of the town. We're in it, right?"

Wendy nodded approval as she chewed. "I know you've been baking all morning, but you might want to whip up another batch of these. Also" — she cast a cautious look around the kitchen — "don't want to spoil the party, but you did get the special orders I wrote down yesterday?"

My heart thudded. Yes, I had got them, but I hadn't had time to address them. Panic struck as I thought about the Christmas lights still dangling from the awning. I still had a few boxes in the café. I needed to get those into the lighthouse before we opened. Sheesh! There was so much to be done. The morning meeting was going to be quick.

"I'm starting on those now," I assured the girls. "Wendy, I need your help to frost some donuts." Wendy nodded.

"Alaina, since you're our resident artist, can you add our new festive holiday drinks to the menu board? Tom and Elizabeth perfected them last night. We're now serving a gingerbread latte and a peppermint mocha to go along with our regular list of favorites."

"No problem, Lindsey. But I think I'll get the coffee brewing first. Ryan should be here any minute."

Ryan, although always a few minutes late,

was a hard worker. "That reminds me, I'll have to show you both how to make our new coffee drinks. But first I'm going to move some boxes. I had a delivery of Christmas lights last night. As you can see, I'm still working on them."

I turned from the kitchen workstation and headed to the café, thinking about all the work left to do. I needed to finish hanging Christmas lights, I still needed to decorate the café, I needed to bake six specialty coffee cakes, eight fruit pies, two French silk pies, and make fifteen lunch boxes. And all the while I was thinking of what needed to be done, visions of whipping up the winning Christmas cookie began swirling in my head.

As Wendy addressed the unfrosted donuts, getting down a carton of sprinkles and whisking the lush chocolate frosting I had made earlier, Alaina took one more bite of her muffin and followed me out the kitchen door.

"So, about the Christmas cookie bake-off," she began, "you're going to come up with a signature cookie, right?"

"I am," I assured her with a grin. "But with so many delicious Christmas cookies, I'm going to have to give this one some thought."

"Well, don't think too hard. The cookie tasting is just four days away. It starts Tuesday."

As if I needed a reminder. I was already beginning to feel a prickle of panic, but then I made the mistake of glancing out the door. Unlike a normal, lazy Saturday where customers trickled in at a leisurely pace, the crowd waiting outside for the Beacon to open was larger than usual. What in the world was going on?

CHAPTER 6

"Lindsey," Ginger Brooks called, waving me to the side of the bakery counter. Ginger was one of my good friends. She was the owner of Harbor Scoops, the town's famous ice cream shop. One look at Ginger, and I could see she was agitated about something. Ryan was hard at work on the espresso machine. Wendy had just brought out a tray of beautifully frosted donuts. And Alaina and I were filling orders. I finished the transaction and met Ginger at the self-service coffee bar, where she filled her mug with our fresh-brewed Christmas blend.

She lowered her voice. "You've heard about the Christmas cookie bake-off?" I nodded as she nervously stirred cream into her coffee. She threw the stir stick into the trash bin and frowned. "You weren't at the meeting last night. Didn't know how you'd feel about more baking to add on top of your baking." She arched a brow. "I, for one, love the idea of a town-wide event that will bring more holiday shoppers to Beacon Harbor. An ice cream shop, even one as beloved as Scoops, doesn't do so well in the winter, you know."

"Too cold for tourists," I commiserated. "But you do well enough to stay open."

"It's mostly hand-packed take-away pints these days and jars of homemade ice cream toppings." I nodded knowingly. Ginger's ice cream and toppings were the best. I had my own stockpile of Rocky Road and Butter Pecan pints jammed in the freezer waiting for Kennedy's arrival.

"No one wants to order a waffle cone to go," Ginger added, making a face as she pretended to shiver. "I'm excited for the cookie bake-off, but not everyone in town is. Keeping homemade cookies in stock for the week is not only a time commitment, but it can get costly. There were quite a few objections. Not everyone was so keen on the idea. But you should have seen Felicity. She was like a crazed dance mom, pushing her half-baked idea on stage. I get that this is her time of year," she complained, "but the nerve of her springing a celebrity food critic on us like that. There was no backing out. She'd already told him it was a done deal. Chevy Chambers is coming to town, and he's arriving this week to start filming."

"Filming?" I had no idea what she was talking about.

"You know, for his show, *Windy City Eats*? Only it's not just Chicago he covers. Chevy travels all around Lake Michigan, highlighting local restaurants and festivals."

"Betty said he was a food critic. She never mentioned anything about him hosting his own show . . . or that he was filming our Christmas cookie bake-off." The thought made me nervous. It was just like Betty and Felicity to forget to mention this little fact to me. However, it was certain to bring a whole new level of competition to our small-town Christmas festival. I hoped Beacon Harbor could handle it. As far as foodie shows went, I didn't know much about the Chicago food scene, and, quite frankly, I didn't have much time to watch television these days. When I did, it was blissfully mindless viewing.

"That's probably a good thing." Ginger grinned. "Well, it will sure spice up things here for the holidays. What's your signature cookie?" she thought to ask.

I shrugged. "I haven't narrowed it down yet."

"Oh, I know it'll be good. Just so you're aware, I'm making fudgy German chocolate cookies with coconut frosting. They're an ode to German chocolate cake, only in a cookie. They're a childhood favorite."

"Those sound amazing," I told her honestly. I'd never heard of German chocolate Christmas cookies with coconut frosting, but whatever they were, I knew I'd have to step up my game. "Thanks for the heads-up. I guess Felicity is the one to watch as well. Wonder what kind of cookie she's going to bake?"

"Seeing as how she planned this whole cookie bakeoff, she obviously knows what kind and has probably been practicing to perfect it. Think flashy and impractical, like her."

We both giggled. "Glad I won't be baking hers. And speaking of baking, I should get back to work." The line of waiting customers had grown. "Good luck!"

It didn't take long before I realized just how the Great Beacon Harbor Christmas Cookie Bake-Off was going to impact my plans for pulling off the perfect Christmas. I had already agreed to make Betty's signature cookie, as a friend. Betty had sold me the old lighthouse and was the first friend I had made in the town. Baking twelve dozen Christmas cookies for her was the least I could do. However, when I began receiving calls from other frantic shop owners, I realized that Felicity Stewart, Ms. Tannenbaum herself, had sucked the holiday spirit out of the village.

"Who has time to bake extra cookies?" Ali Johnson complained over the phone. Ali and her husband, Jack, had retired to Beacon Harbor with the dream of opening a bookstore. They now owned the Book Nook, a vibrant little bookstore and one of the most charming shops in town. Ali told me that all her grandchildren were coming to spend Christmas with her and Jack. She didn't have the energy to bake extra cookies for the store.

"Don't worry," I told her. "What did you have in mind?"

"Something easy. Jack loves those toffee bars. Do you know the ones I'm talking about?"

"A pan cookie with a buttery shortbread base, topped with melted milk chocolate and a sprinkling of toasted pecans?"

"Yes!" she cried into the phone. "Those are the ones." I breathed a sigh of relief. Pan cookies were far less time consuming than drop cookies, cutouts, or Betty's sophisticated linzer cookies. "Oh, Lindsey, you're a lifesaver!" Ali cried. "I honestly didn't know how we were going to manage.

58

The holidays are always so busy for us, and Jack and I have only enough energy to dote on the kids."

Kids. The thought of having little ones running around my home stopped me in my tracks. In New York, the thought had never crossed my mind. In Beacon Harbor, however, my mind instantly conjured the image of Rory Campbell.

"Lindsey?"

I cleared my throat. "Sorry. How does twelve dozen sound? If you run out, you can always order more."

The moment I hung up with Ali, I got a call from the Beacon Harbor Theater. "Lindsey, this is Zach." Zoe and Zach Bannon were a darling young couple in their late twenties. With only a dream and all their life savings, they had purchased the old, run-down Beacon Harbor Theater. They had renovated it before I moved to town and were working their hardest to turn it into a trendy local playhouse and event center. "I can't bake cookies!" Zach proclaimed. "I mean, I literally can't. Zoe and I don't cook, let alone bake. We have a rice cooker and a microwave oven." I could hear the panic in his voice.

"No problem," I soothed, knowing that baking was not for everyone. Yet just because someone couldn't bake didn't mean that they should be excluded from the festivities. I picked up my pen and asked, "Are you placing an order for a signature cookie?"

"I know it's not in the rules, but we're hosting a holiday craft show and we want foot traffic. We need to be on that cookie list. Any suggestions?"

"I've got a good one for you. How about peanut butter cup cookies? They're small, delicious, and they make a big statement. Nobody can resist them."

I could hear Zach let out his breath on the other end of the phone. "Sounds great. You're amazing, Lindsey. We owe you one."

As the day progressed, I had added pecan crescents to my baking list for Christy Parks of the Bayside Boutique, and a dog-friendly Christmas cookie for Peggy Miller of Peggy's Pet Shop & Pooch Salon. Peggy said she was going to buy store-bought cookies for her human customers, just to turn the tables. I applauded her decision. Coming up with a holiday dog cookie would be fun, not to mention that I had the perfect dog treat connoisseur to help me. Though, to be fair, Wellington would eat dead, bloated fish on the beach if he got the opportunity. But a holiday pup treat was just the thing to add to my baking list. I'd make extra to keep on hand at the Beacon.

After the flurry of phone calls, I glanced at my baking list. A sudden wave of anxiety hit me. In my haste to help everyone, I had overcommitted. Dear heavens, how was I going to fit it all in? I was only one person. I needed a miracle. And I still had the special orders for the day yet to make!

Leaving the café in the hands of my capable employees, I jumped back to the kitchen and set to work on the coffee cakes and pies. Ryan, dark-haired, thick-set, and charmingly witty, thankfully took over the lunch box orders, making delicious sandwiches and packing each in our tidy red boxes along with a cookie and fresh veggies and dip. The order was for a local quilting group that met at St. Michaels Presbyterian Church every Saturday.

Working like a woman possessed, I had just put the pies in the oven with the nearly done coffee cakes when Bill Morgan arrived. "Heard somebody got a big order of Christmas lights yesterday," he said with a smile as he poked his head through the kitchen door. "Something smells good in here."

Bill was a semiretired local who used to own a marina and boat repair shop. His son now ran the shop, giving Bill plenty of time to tinker around on his personal cars and boats. He and his yellow Labrador retriever, Dan, were regulars at the Beacon. "Oh!" I said, remembering that I'd hired him to hang the lights. I was relieved to see him. I left the kitchen and went to unlock the lighthouse door. "I put the boxes in here," I said. The door was barely open when Wellington seized his moment. His large head shoved open the door just before he leapt, catching me off guard. I tripped, hit the floor, and got a slobber-bath on my face as Welly licked me. I'd been so busy I had forgotten to let him out for his lunchtime potty break.

"He needs to go out," I told Bill.

"He can play with Dan while we work on the lights."

"Great idea. After you illuminate the light tower, do you think you and Roger could hang some wreaths in the windows and fix the lights on the awning?"

"You mean those dangling candy lights out there?" Bill grinned knowingly. "Decent effort, Lindsey, but hanging Christmas lights is a tricky business. You should have waited for Rory."

Argh! Why did everyone keep saying that? I got to my feet, brushed off my bum, and looked him straight in the eye. "Rory's not here. He's —"

Bill held up a hand. "I know, ice fishing up north. Smart man. Well, since we're here, we might as well finish the job. By the way" — he gave the café a once-over — "have you thought about putting a splash of Christmas in here?"

"Yes," I said, feeling overwhelmed. The café needed decorating, something I was going to do tomorrow. It was Sunday. The Beacon was closed Sunday and Monday, giving me a little break and time to catch up on my baking schedule. "I plan on handling that tomorrow. First, I have an epic amount of baking to do." The words were no sooner out of my mouth when I smelled something burning.

The coffee cakes!

I waved good-bye to Bill and dashed back to the kitchen. The pies hadn't burned, thank goodness, but the coffee cakes were crispy. I wanted to cry. It wasn't my best work. If I continued to burn things, the captain might chase me out too. Knowing the coffee cakes would be picked up at the end of the day to be enjoyed on Sunday, I threw them into the trash and started again.

I was in the kitchen all day, frantically trying to keep our regular bakery items in stock — cookies, brownies, cupcakes, and pies for the afternoon — while baking special orders. The Beacon was a hub of activity. Wendy and Alaina kept popping into the kitchen with special requests.

"Mrs. Bingham wants to order a chocolate peppermint sheet cake for her Christmas Eve party. Can we do that?" I prayed that I could and told Wendy to write it down.

Alaina popped in next. "Doc Riggles is asking if we can make a boozy mincemeat pie. Do you know what he's talking about?"

"Yes. Nothing you'd be too fond of, I'm sure. Ask him if he's a bourbon or a rum man."

"Gotcha!" She came back a moment later, stating with finality, "Bourbon. Definitely bourbon. He'd like two next Wednesday for the hospital Christmas lunch."

Bill had popped in to tell me I had run out of Christmas lights before they could finish the light tower and that they were going to the hardware store to pick up more. I nodded, marveling at how I could have run out of lights when I had ordered so many.

The wind had picked up. I could hear it rattle the windows and buffet the back door as I baked. A quick check of my weather app told me that a winter storm was on its way. Perfect, I thought as I popped a tray of sugar cookie cutouts into the oven.

Before I knew it, Ryan came into the kitchen. "Whoa," he cried, coming to a halt at the sight of me. "You're still baking? I guess when your name is Bakewell, you just can't —" I held up a flour-covered hand to stop him.

"Yeah, not funny," he apologized with a grimace. "Not now, at any rate. Sorry, Lindsey. I just came to tell you that everything's been cleaned — the coffee machines, the cases, and the countertops have been wiped down, and the café's been swept and scoured. I've turned the sign to closed, but you might want to make sure the doors are locked after we leave."

I nodded and looked at the mess around me. I'd be up all night washing dishes.

It was time to quit baking. After my employees left, I washed my hands and took off my apron. I then walked into the café and opened the lighthouse door, allowing Wellington to join me. I knelt on the floor and gave him a big hug.

"Look at this place," I said to him. His large, sensitive eyes looked at me as if he understood what I was saying, but I knew he didn't have a clue. "I need to decorate the café. I need a Christmas tree. I need to start my holiday baking. I ran out of Christmas lights. Can you believe it?" I was close to tears. "And after so much planning! And I still need to get the lighthouse ready for our guests!" I let out a helpless sob. "Oh . . . Welly," I hiccoughed. "And I need to bake hundreds of dozens of cookies and come up with my own signature cookie by Tuesday. But I'm so tired. I want to have dinner with Rory tomorrow —" At the mention of the name, his silky ears perked up, and he licked my face. "But how can I when I'm ready to collapse under a load of holiday pressure? My sugarplum dreams are killing me. Why do I do this to myself? I don't even have an assistant baker. How am I going to pull it all off?"

The words were barely out of my mouth when the overhead lights dimmed and flickered. Any normal person would have thought it was due to the wind, but I knew better. So did Welly. His tail thumped with anticipation. The sweet smell of pipe smoke confirmed it. Although I couldn't see him, I knew the ghost of Captain Willy Riggs was in the bakeshop.

I looked up at the lights. "If you're listening, Captain, I need a miracle."

I waited for a breath or two. Nothing. And really, what was I expecting? He was a ghost, not an angel. The lights stopped flickering and came back on, making me believe that maybe it was just the wind and my imagination. I felt like a fool for talking to a ghost. I gave a self-effacing laugh, wiped my tears, and got to my feet. That was when Wellington turned to the door.

With a suddenness that sent a wave of tingles down my spine, the bakery door burst open, ushering in a gust of icy wind and an ominous figure cloaked in black.

CHAPTER 7

Spooked would be the word for it if I'd had time to think. But I didn't have time to think. My staff had all gone home, I had forgotten to lock the doors, and I had a pile of dishes yet to wash!

The moment the figure appeared in the doorway, Welly dashed forward, but instead of barking like the guard dog I wanted him to be, his tail swished in the air double-time. He greeted the stranger like an old friend, but I was certain he'd never met this person before.

"Well, hello there," came a woman's voice. A red mitten appeared from the depths of the snowy black cloak, ruffling Welly's head in greeting. The mittens came off, and a moment later the stranger pulled back her hood, revealing a cascade of fluffy white curls, round blue eyes behind dainty glasses, and a chubby face smiling in greeting.

My jaw dangled a bit as my thudding

heart began to settle down. I agreed with Wellington. This woman didn't look like she posed a threat at all. In fact, I found her cheerful, petite presence disarming. "Can I help you?" I ventured.

She peered at the bakery cases. "Are you closed for the day, then? Should I come back tomorrow?"

"Are you here to place an order?" Although I smiled, my heart sank as I asked the question. I could hardly handle another order; yet, on the other hand, I could hardly say no to such a round, smiling face.

"Oh, no, no. I'm not here to place an order."

I breathed a sigh of relief. "You must be hungry. The cases have been wiped down, but I have plenty in back. Would you like a piece of coffee cake, or a sandwich perhaps?" I started for the kitchen until her white curls jiggled around her face.

"Oh, no, no," she said again, quite cheerfully. "Very kind of you, but I'm not hungry."

It dawned on me then. "You're a cookie judge! You must be with that Chambers fellow. Are you here to scope out my bakeshop?"

She squinted her eyes and shook her head again. "I'm not a cookie judge, but I have eaten my share of them." She winked and placed a hand on her ample waistline.

I found her adorable in a grandmotherly way. "Well, I'm stumped. Perhaps I should have asked, how can I help you?"

"Well, and that's just the thing, dear. I think I might be able to help you. I was looking through the paper and saw your ad. Are you still in need of an assistant baker?"

Yes! Yes! Dear heavens, yes! I screamed in my head. Her timing couldn't have been better. However, I didn't want to appear desperate. I didn't wish to chase this woman away. I couldn't explain it, but she had the air of a baker. Sure, I'd been fooled before. But I really was desperate, and Wellington seemed to like her. He was sitting at her feet, his hefty weight pressing on her leg as he tried to lick her hand. One thing was clear, the woman was tolerant.

"Umm," I began, pretending to think. "You know, I believe I am. When can you start?"

She scanned the Beacon with twinkling eyes. "Immediately."

Carol Nichols, or Mrs. Nichols as I kept referring to her for some reason, hailed from up north but was in Beacon Harbor staying with an old friend. She loathed being idle, she told me, and had seen my ad in the paper. She proclaimed it was serendipitous. She had just found out about the Great Beacon Harbor Christmas Cookie Bake-Off and thought she could lend a hand. She had confessed that Christmas cookies were a passion of hers, having collected hundreds of recipes over the years. I loved her enthusiasm, hired her on the spot, and asked her to come in Sunday morning. We weren't open, but it was the perfect time to show her the kitchen and maybe even have her help prep the bakery for the upcoming week. Mrs. Nichols was delighted, and we agreed to meet the following morning.

I felt indulgently lazy, sleeping in until seven and playing with Welly for an hour before heading to the bakery to meet Mrs. Nichols. It was only as I walked to the bakery that I realized my Christmas spirit had returned. Part of it was because Bill and Roger had finished hanging the Christmas lights. Although they had gone a bit crazy — which I appreciated — their efforts had paid off. The light tower was now covered in a swirl of red and white lights, making it look like a giant candy cane when lit. It was the masterpiece of my exterior illumination campaign. The whole lighthouse complex was a vision to behold, from the candy cane–lined walkway to the white lights outlining the lighthouse and bushes, to the family of twinkling white deer on the lawn. Clark Griswold would have been proud, if not a bit envious.

Another cause for joy was that Rory had gotten home late Saturday night and was coming over to take me to a live Christmas tree farm. I had never cut down my own tree. It had been a childhood dream of mine. I wanted a fresh-cut tree for the Beacon to wow our customers and to provide that last important element to their bakery experience — the scent of fresh-cut pine. The bakery would already be suffused with warm gingerbread, citrusy orange, tangy cranberry, heady cinnamon, and spicy cloves. The crisp scent of pine would bring it all home.

My third and final reason to be hopeful was Mrs. Nichols. She had appeared in the nick of time and seemed like she knew how to bake. Once in the kitchen, I could better assess her baking skills. But, oh, who was I kidding? She could possess two left thumbs and I'd still be thrilled. Just having another body working beside me at this point was better than nothing.

I walked into the bakery attempting to whistle "Jingle Bells" and doing a poor job of it. But I didn't care. Rory had returned, and I had just hired an assistant baker the week of the Christmas cookie bake-off. I was itching to get to work. I opened the kitchen door and froze, the discordant tune dying on my lips. "What in the name of —"

CHAPTER 8

It was hard to reconcile the sight that confronted me. I had left the kitchen a mess, too tired to tackle the pile of dirty dishes and pans the night before. And yet they were all gone — washed, dried, and put back on the shelves in their proper places. The kitchen counters sparkled; the stove had been scrubbed to a mirrored sheen. But what really had me flummoxed was that whatever prep work I had set out to do had already been done. How was that possible? And stranger yet? Dozens of freshly baked cookies sat cooling on wire racks. Others had been decorated and placed on bakery trays. I had the surreal feeling of being the proverbial shoemaker visited by busy elves in the night. But there were no elves in sight. The kitchen was empty.

Honestly, I was a bit spooked by the sight confronting me. Had I walked through a time portal? Had I been visited by the Ghost of Christmas Future and was now glimpsing what my kitchen could look like if I wasn't so crabby and tired all the time? Maybe I was still dreaming? Breathing a bit heavily, I kept staring at the cookies. Cookies? They looked too perfect. Who had baked them? I was about to walk out of the empty kitchen, retracing my steps through the lighthouse door to try it again — just to see if I'd get the same results — when a perfectly whistled rendition of "Jingle Bells" stopped me in my tracks. I scanned the kitchen to see where it was coming from, thinking that maybe the captain was playing a trick on me.

"Hello?" I ventured, growing uncomfortable. I had burnt a tray of coffee cakes the day before. Was I being punished?

Just then the door to the walk-in refrigerator creaked open, and the whistling grew louder. I was about to bolt out the door when I heard, "Oh, hello, dear."

Mrs. Nichols appeared, carrying an armload of butter.

Stunned, I stammered, "How . . . how did you get in?"

She smiled. "You gave me a key, remember?"

Had I? I didn't remember. But it was

remarkable. The woman herself was neat as a pin. "Did you bake all this?"

"I keep baker's hours. Always have. Thought I'd pop in and get to work. Hope you don't mind. Try a cookie." Mrs. Nichols set down the butter and picked up a tray of perfectly baked butter cookies. They were a pleasing pale yellow, round, and perfectly piped with crisp edges. Some had bright red cherry jelly in the center; others were dusted in powdered sugar. I selected one that had been dipped in chocolate and rolled in sprinkles.

The cookie was melt-in-your-mouth delicious. "Wonderful!" I exclaimed. "I don't have a butter cookie recipe. Is this yours?"

Her high cheeks had a rosy glow as she nodded. "People love butter cookies, especially around the holidays. These are so easy to make, and so festive. Doesn't hurt to have plenty on hand along with your signature cookie." Her jovial face brightened with excitement as she held up a finger, indicating that I wait as she walked out the kitchen door. A moment later she popped back in, carrying one of our small red bakery boxes. She carefully lined the box with white parchment, then plucked a selection of butter cookies off the trays and arranged them in the box. "All it needs is a pretty bow, and you have a delicious, thoughtful gift."

Who was this woman? I wanted to pinch myself to make sure I wasn't dreaming, but refrained. "Brilliant," I uttered, marveling at the cookies in the box. Why hadn't I thought of it? Probably because I'd been too tired to think at all.

"When customers sample your cookie," she continued, "they'll want to buy dozens of that one too. That's why we should be prepared." Mrs. Nichols leaned in, her face animated by curiosity. "Now, Lindsey Bakewell, what kind of cookie were you thinking of?"

I lost track of time working in the kitchen alongside Mrs. Nichols. For a woman of her age and roundness, I was surprised by her agility. She appeared to glide around the kitchen, from counter, to mixer, to oven, with the ease and grace of a figure skater. The fact that she was neat as a pin only added to her charm. I pulled out my binder of cookie recipes, and we whipped up batch after batch of unique and delicious treats. Mrs. Nichols's vast collection of recipes, I realized, was stored in her head. The woman had a remarkable memory for ingredients and measurements. I had just taken a bite of our latest batch, a lemon-ginger sandwich cookie. The sweet, spicy ginger cookie blended so well with the tangy lemon cream that I started dancing with excitement as I chewed.

"This is it!" I proclaimed. "This is the one! Oooo, it's perfect!" Just then, Rory walked through the kitchen door. He was grinning.

No one could deny that Rory Campbell was a handsome man, standing six-foot-four inches, with hair the color of darkly roasted coffee beans and eyes as bright and blue as the Caribbean Sea. Defined cheekbones graced his face, as well as a strong jawline. But it was his smile that I found most attractive. Rory was ex–Special Forces, and although he had retired to write military thrillers, he still dabbled in matters of national security from time to time. He was also quite an accomplished woodsman and liked to hunt, something this Manhattan girl couldn't relate to but respected. Kennedy lovingly referred to Rory as Sir Hunts-A-Lot. It was a fitting name, but I never called him that to his face.

"Not the greeting I was expecting," he teased, "but I'll take it. Did I just hear you say that I'm perfect?"

"This cookie," I corrected, returning his smile while I held one up for him to inspect. I was a little taken aback at how much I had missed him.

"Oh, well, can't compete with one of your cookies." Still grinning, he turned to Mrs. Nichols. "I'm sorry, but we haven't met."

After introductions, and bringing him up to speed on the bakery, I made Rory sample a lemon-ginger sandwich cookie. The look on his face was reminiscent of the day we had met. He had come to the lighthouse and had sampled one of my donuts. His expression was a mixture of appreciation and bliss. I didn't know why, but I found his look of extreme appreciation sexy.

"Damn," he said. "I've missed you, Lindsey."

"Didn't you ice fishermen do any baking while holed up in that fishing shanty?" I teased.

"Baking, no. But we ate some excellent fish." He patted his trim stomach as he said this. "However, man lives not on fish alone."

"I believe the quote, dear, is 'bread alone'," Mrs. Nichols corrected with a pointed look. "Man needs Christmas cookies too!" She winked, making us all laugh.

After making dozens of scrumptious cookies, and with our signature cookie settled upon, I was going to stay and help my new assistant baker clean the messy kitchen. She'd done enough already. But she insisted

I leave with Rory and Wellington to cut down my Christmas tree at the tree farm. She was shooing me out of my own bakery kitchen! It was very reminiscent of my beloved Grandma Bakewell. And when Grandma Bakewell shooed me out of her kitchen, there was no arguing.

The next few days were picture-perfect, thanks to the help of Mrs. Nichols, Rory, and the Beacon's staff. I finally cut down a fresh Christmas tree — two, in fact, one for the bakeshop and one for my living room. Sure, it wasn't easy. I nearly froze my toes off, and tree trunks, even on seven-foot fir trees, are tough buggers to get a saw through. But we did it. Sticky sap was another problem. Also, it had started snowing . . . a lot. A blizzard struck, but we still managed. Rory had brought a sled, and I brought Welly's harness. With a little ingenuity, gumption, and plenty of doggie treats, we somehow got both Christmas trees through the snow and into the bed of Rory's pickup truck. It was a Norman Rockwell moment. And that moment continued back at the lighthouse as we decorated both trees, drinking peppermint mochas and nibbling on Christmas cookies. We were just about to sit down for a romantic dinner of fresh fish that Rory had prepared when Wellington rushed the front door, barking excitedly.

Mom, Dad, and Kennedy had surprised me by arriving early. They came bearing presents, a mound of luggage, and Mom's two West Highland terriers, Brinkley and Ireland. Mom, a former fashion model and quite famous in the eighties, had named them after her rivals, Christie Brinkley and Kathy Ireland. We simply referred to her pooches as *the models.* Although the two adorable Westies looked nearly identical, they could be told apart by their rhinestone collars, Brinkley with the pink, and Ireland with the emerald green.

Although my family's timing wasn't the best, I was overjoyed to see them. Chaos descended as everyone began talking excitedly at once. Welly, spying his two friends, barked with joy and chased them around the lighthouse. I turned to Rory with an apologetic smile.

"You owe me, Bakewell," he whispered teasingly before slipping out the back door. He was off to his log home to get more fish.

I did owe him, I thought, turning the romantic table for two into a party of five. I then added more lettuce and veggies to the salad bowl, more red potatoes to the pot of boiling water, and threw a par-baked loaf of

French bread into the oven. As Dad carried the luggage up the stairs to the guest rooms, I thanked my lucky stars that the lighthouse looked beautiful bedecked in Christmas lights, and that I had given the place a thorough cleaning.

"Open this," Mom nearly demanded, thrusting a big, beautifully wrapped present with a large, sparkly bow into my hands. We were halfway through dinner, yet I could tell there was something terribly exciting bubbling on the lips of Mom and Kennedy.

"Mom, it's not even Christmas yet," I protested.

"Open it," Dad calmly advised. Taking his cue, I unwrapped the present.

"Oh my!" I exclaimed, spying the pile of thick fleece in black-and-red buffalo plaid. "Cute blanket," I remarked. But when I pulled it out of the box, I realized that it wasn't a blanket at all. It was a long, hooded cape with a giant matching dog coat in Welly's size. It was adorable and totally something Mom would get me. She had a thing for wearing matching outfits with her dogs. I guess during the holidays it was going to be my thing too.

"I love it, Mom," I told her honestly. "Welly and I will definitely turn some heads in our matching coats." Hearing his name,

Welly's giant head popped above the table, looking hopeful. He was so busy staring at my plate that he didn't see the doggie coat in my hands. Before he got wind of what I was about to do, I slipped it over his head. That's when Kennedy chimed in.

"Look at the tag."

It was Welly's lucky day. I took off his coat and looked at the fabric tag, noting the brand name, *Ellie & Company.* "What?" I remarked, casting Mom a curious look.

With wineglass in hand, Kennedy said, "*Surprise!* Your mom is starting a clothing company, and I'm her business partner."

I dropped my fork, the dogs started barking, and Rory burst into laughter.

83

CHAPTER 9

Mom and Kennedy were starting a clothing company! It was a huge surprise, and the more I thought about it, the happier it made me. It was right up Mom's alley — a women's clothing line with matching selections for dogs of all sizes. Dad, no doubt, was handling the finances, and Kennedy, one of the most sought-after influencers in fashion, was her public relations guru. What a Christmas bombshell! It made my measly announcement of entering the Christmas cookie bake-off pale by comparison. But my family had been thrilled with the news.

Once announced, excitement for the Great Beacon Harbor Christmas Cookie Bake-Off had spread like wildfire through the county. Curious shoppers flocked to the town to partake in the cookie sampling and voting. The Beacon Bakeshop had never seen such crowds. It was inspiring — and even more inspiring was Mrs. Nichols.

By Wednesday morning, we knew the routine. The moment our doors were opened, the crowds came, snapping up baked goods, sampling our signature cookie, and buying plenty to take home. Officer Tuck McAllister and Sergeant Stacy Murdock would arrive at eight o'clock for their morning latte. Officer Tuck, in his late twenties, was easy on the eyes, and easy to talk to as well. Sergeant Stacy Murdock, well, about all I could say was that she was warming up to me. I likened my relationship with the sergeant to reading a thousand-page novel. The cover was compelling, the title impressive, and although the beginning had been confusing and slow, there were glimmers of something profound and enjoyable there. Like that epic novel, I was still working on Sergeant Murdock. She admired my baking — point for me! — and had come to sample my signature cookie.

"Not bad, Bakewell. Not bad at all." She gave a reflective nod, sending her wispy blond bangs fluttering.

"So, you're going to vote for me?" I asked hopefully. Her answer was a wink, a click of the tongue, and a finger-gun pointed right at me. Although utterly noncommittal, I took it to be a yes.

Tuck, on the other hand, was a Beacon

Bakeshop devotee. The only thing he loved more than my donuts was filling me in on the local gossip. According to him, Felicity Stewart was the one to beat. As Tuck described her cookie to Kennedy and me, Mrs. Nichols appeared from the kitchen with a tray of warm gingerbread muffins. It was hard to ignore the heavenly scent that filled the café.

"Look, Mommy. It's Mrs. Claus!" A little boy, standing before the bakery case, pointed his finger at her.

The entire crowd looked, causing Mrs. Nichols to blush. Peering through the bakery case, she winked at the boy. With a nod to the officers, she disappeared once again through the kitchen door. Elizabeth and Wendy, filling orders, followed her with their eyes as she left.

"There's no better Christmas cookie baker in the world as Mrs. Claus," Elizabeth told the child. "We're lucky to have her working with us at our bakeshop. Here." She reached across the counter and handed the boy a cookie. He was enchanted. She had him on the hook, and closed with, "Make sure your parents cast their vote for the Beacon Bakeshop!"

Kennedy turned from the counter where she'd been chatting with Officer Cutie Pie, to look at Elizabeth. "Shameless," she said, "and yet brilliant. You should consider a career in marketing."

"Hey!" I chided, as Elizabeth grinned at the compliment. "Don't steal my employees."

Kennedy came to the bakeshop every morning, but not to work. She claimed she was working out a marketing campaign for my signature cookie, but I knew her better than that. It was more the matter of a hot, small-town cop who was infatuated with her. As for her marketing campaign, it consisted of dressing Wellington in an *Ellie & Company Pup-Coat* original and marching him up and down Main Street.

"And here I thought Mrs. Nichols was the Mary Poppins of bakeries," Kennedy continued, "after the way she swooped in with her book of biscuits and saved our Lindsey from a nervous breakdown. But this *Mrs. Claus* angle is even better. Fits the season. Do you suppose she'd make a fuss if we asked her to come to work in a red dress and frilly white bonnet?"

I rolled my eyes while putting the finishing touches on a gingerbread latte for another customer. Tom had premade the spicy gingerbread syrup, blending cinnamon, cloves, ginger, and nutmeg with molasses and simple syrup. The mixture was then blended with hot milk and poured on top of a shot of espresso. The drink was finished off with steamed milk, whipped cream, and shaved white chocolate curls. The last of the curls went on, and I handed the drink to the customer. Only then would I address her.

"We're not going to make her dress in a costume, and we're not using her to win. Our signature cookie stands on its own. We either get in the bake-off due to merit, or not at all."

"Well, you're off to a great start," Kennedy said and pointed toward the door. "You're nearly out of cookies, and you've got a special visitor." She grinned as she shifted her gaze to the bakery door.

I turned to see what had grabbed her attention. Big mistake. My jaw dropped as icy fingers of dread ran up my spine.

CHAPTER 10

I had plenty of experience with celebrity foodies to know that this man was the cookie judge Felicity had spoken about. He looked to be somewhere in his mid-forties, but looks could be deceiving. He was handsome in a prep-school sort of way, and taking a fashion risk, I mused, staring at the newsboy-style cap he wore in bright Stewart plaid. But the real harbinger was the small camera crew that followed him as he pushed his way into the bakeshop, demanding the crowd part to let him through. Irrational fear seized me as he made his way toward the counter.

"Well, I'll leave you to it. I'm needed in the kitchen."

"That man has a camera," Kennedy admonished in a whisper, grasping my arm. "You know my motto."

"Never date a man who thinks he looks cool on a Vespa scooter? I don't see how that's relevant here."

She closed her eyes in annoyance and shook her head. "My other motto. The *never pass up a photo op* motto. That man is publicity gold. Besides, he's infatuated with Welly. We met him yesterday. I told him that if he wanted to taste the winning cookie, he should pop down to the Beacon Bakeshop & Café. Smile." She thrust me to the end of the counter where Chevy Chambers was waiting.

Offering a disarming smile, he introduced himself as the host of *Windy City Eats.* "We're filming backstory for the Christmas cookie bake-off." As he talked, he signaled to his cameraman to pan around the café, shooting the interior and the crowd of people waiting in line. When the camera came back to him again, he said, "If you make it to the bake-off, gorgeous, I could make you a star."

Only because Kennedy was watching, I smiled. "Try a lemon-ginger sandwich cookie," I replied and dropped one in his hand.

Cranking up the charm, he grinned and took a bite. The expression on his face changed. "Damn. That's sensational. I mean, really good. Wherever did a nice girl like you learn to bake?"

The man was a cad. "My grandparents owned a bakery in Traverse City," I told him, trying to keep the interview on a professional level. I gave him a little background on the bakery and my former career as a Wall Street investment banker. Chevy was impressed. However, seeing that I wasn't about to flirt, he turned his focus on Kennedy.

After raking her with his eyes, he remarked, "What a nice piece of real estate."

Kennedy, an exotic English beauty of half-Indian descent, leaned in as well. "Would you be referring to me or this old lighthouse, darling?"

Without flinching, he replied, "Both. Are you available for dinner?"

Kennedy was good. She was pouring on her English charm. "Not tonight, darling. But I'll take your card in case I get bored later in the week."

Chevy asked a few more questions about the bakery and my signature cookie. I kept the interview focused, while Kennedy kept flirting with him to keep his interest. It was wrong on so many levels, and yet it was highly entertaining to watch. There was no doubt that Chevy Chambers knew his way around a kitchen. However, he was also a narcissistic, egotistical food critic with an eye for the ladies. Chicago was a big city and could handle his ego, but in a small, close-knit community like Beacon Harbor, I had to wonder at what mischief he would drum up. One thing was certain, I didn't want him hanging out at the Beacon. Thankfully, I was able to end the interview and get back to work.

I was ringing up customers again when Mrs. Nichols appeared from the kitchen. I didn't know how she did it, but she was bringing out another tray of freshly baked Christmas cookies.

"I just had an interview with Chevy Chambers, the cookie judge for the bake-off. He was impressed with our cookie."

Mrs. Nichols looked across the counter. Chevy and his crew were leaving the bake-shop.

Her round eyes narrowed as she looked at him. "Very naughty, that one. Coal. Coal is all he ought to get in his stocking!"

The way it was spoken, with a motherly look of disapproval, made me chuckle. I never thought to ask why she had said it.

CHAPTER 11

"I love this old place. I had almost forgotten about it."

Dad was thrilled that Rory had suggested we eat at the Moose, although I was doubtful one could ever really forget it. It was one of Beacon Harbor's most popular restaurants, and one that really embraced the whole "Up North" theme. It was a vision in pine paneling and antler décor. And while I wasn't too keen on dining beneath the taxidermied remains of a twelve-point buck, I did have to admit that antlers made great hooks for Christmas lights. In fact, the Christmas decorations in the Moose were awe-inspiring. In the center of the dining room stood a large, illuminated evergreen, swaddled in red-and-black buffalo plaid ribbon, and hung with charming ornaments of woodland animals. The heads on the walls either sported wreaths or twinkling lights, but all were in the same red, black, and hunter green theme. As we took our seats, I had the surreal feeling of being in some magical Christmas forest with the animals peering in at us from the safety of the trees. It was easier to think of them that way rather than the unfortunate wall art that they were.

"I knew it!" Kennedy proclaimed, staring up from her iPhone. "Chevy Chambers is talking up your cookie. Your lemon-ginger sandwich cookie is surging ahead of the competition! You're going to be in the live bake-off."

"Congratulations!" Dad grinned and held out his fist for a fist bump. "Of course, we all knew it. You have a real winner with that cookie."

"Thanks, Dad."

"It's true." Mom leaned in and gave a nod of approval. After a lifetime of dieting and waging war against fatty, sugary carbs, Mom had finally embraced the fact that I was a baker and that she loved what I made. Although still attractive, Mom was allowing herself to age gracefully, which in her case meant not sweating the extra few pounds she was carrying. It was part of the inspiration that drove her to start her own line of clothing — one that was stylish yet forgiving.

We were all celebrating the good news when Karen, our waitress, sauntered up to the table.

"Congrats on the cookie, Lindsey. Saw that you're ahead of the competition. Don't mean to burst your bubble, but that new fella over at the Harbor Hotel Restaurant makes the best shortbread I've ever tasted. Like you, he's a professional." Her remark was meant to remind me that I had an unfair advantage over the others, being a professional baker. All that aside, she was right. I had almost forgotten that the Harbor Hotel Restaurant had entered the bake-off. Their new head chef, Bradley Argyle, was incredibly talented. I had eaten there several times, and everything I had ordered had been top quality. Of course, he'd have an amazing cookie.

"What kind of shortbread did he make?"

She raised her eyebrows at me. "Brown butter shortbread with a chocolate drizzle. Scrumptious. It was a tough choice, mind you. Ginger at Harbor Scoops has a winner with that German chocolate cookie. Then there were those peanut butter cup cookies at the theater. I ate three of those little yumballs. Who doesn't love a good peanut butter cup? Honestly, there are so many good cookies in town it's no wonder folks are clamoring to visit. We've had crowds here all day."

Kennedy set down her phone and locked eyes with the waitress. "And what about Felicity Stewart's cookie?"

Karen met her gaze and shrugged. "Sugar cookies. Pretty little things, and tasty, but nothing special. The usual bottle of wine, Ms. Kapoor?" I was tickled that Karen remembered my friend. Then again, Kennedy had a way of making an impression.

"Why not," Kennedy replied. "And thanks for the info."

"Had to go with the shortbread," Karen added, finishing our drink order. "And here's a little heads-up for you, Lindsey. The Garden Club has their Christmas luncheon at the Harbor Hotel tomorrow. After that group has been wined and dined, my guess is that they're going to cast their votes for Bradley's shortbread. You might be in for some stiff competition."

Kennedy waited just long enough for Karen to leave. "I wouldn't worry about it, Linds. And if you are, just flirt with Chevy." She flashed a challenging smile at Rory. "He was totally into you."

"That's a terrible idea," Rory countered.

"Says the man who fishes over a hole in the ice." Kennedy rolled her eyes.

"Don't listen to her," he advised me. "I'd say she's had too much to drink, but her bottle hasn't arrived yet."

Although Kennedy and Rory genuinely liked one another, they were from two different worlds and seldom saw eye to eye. I knew that Kennedy enjoyed torquing my boyfriend up a bit, just as I knew Rory delighted in challenging her. It was entertaining, but Kennedy was also brand savvy. Flirting was part of her job, but not mine.

"Do put your ego in check, Rory, darling. This isn't about you. It's about Lindsey winning the Christmas cookie bake-off. That little victory will be publicity gold for the Beacon's reputation. After she wins, you can swoop back in and mark your territory like the alpha male you are."

Rory, fuming with pent-up frustration, was about to reply when a bottle of wine was plopped between them, startling everyone.

"Looks like everyone could use a glass of Christmas cheer about now. Shall I pour?"

"Yes. Thank you." I looked up at Karen. "Impeccable timing, as usual."

CHAPTER 12

With a modest lead in the polls and Karen's sage advice about the stiff competition I was facing, Rory, Kennedy, and I decided to have lunch at the Harbor Hotel Restaurant.

Due to an unprecedented number of customers visiting the bakeshop, I was hesitant to leave for lunch. Noting that we were running low on cookies, I told Mrs. Nichols I was going to call Rory and take a raincheck. I had just mixed up another batch and was getting ready to send them into the oven.

"Nonsense," Mrs. Nichols scolded. She knew as well as I did that the other shops in town were experiencing the same rush of customers. Frantic phone calls had been coming in all morning. Cookies were running low all over town, and the shoppers were beginning to complain. "Go. I have everything under control," she insisted. "It's the holidays. Have lunch with that nice young man of yours, dear. He's a keeper."

I didn't need to be told twice.

It was a pleasure to eat lunch at the Harbor Hotel Restaurant with Rory and Kennedy. They were getting along surprisingly well, which was a miracle. To top off the perfect meal of salmon roulades stuffed with wild rice and mushrooms then topped with a zinfandel reduction, and two glasses of wine, Chef Bradley Argyle came to our table with a plate of cookies. Bradley, unlike the other chefs I had known, was humble about his abilities. He looked to be in his late thirties and was on the taller side, with short auburn hair, brown eyes, and a pleasant smile. He had gotten his start in Chicago before moving to the small, touristy town of Beacon Harbor, or so Betty had informed me.

One bite of the brown butter shortbread cookie with a chocolate drizzle and I knew Karen had been right. The cookie was divine.

"So delicious," I told him, still chewing. "Congratulations on an amazing cookie."

Bradley blushed at the compliment. "Actually," he began, "I came out to congratulate you on your signature cookie. Betty Vanhoosen brought some over the other day for me to sample. What a fabulous flavor combination."

It was my turn to blush. After a short conversation, he glanced around the dining room. Then, in a lowered voice, he offered, "Want to see the ballroom? They're getting it ready for the bake-off."

We followed the chef through the kitchen and out a door that opened onto the hotel ballroom. It was a grand room with a vaulted ceiling and exposed wooden beams arching across the top. The room was perfect for large conferences, weddings, and special events, but today it was being transformed into a Christmas wonderland.

A group of workers were standing on ladders, putting the finishing touches on a huge, decorated Christmas tree, the focal point of the room. Wreaths adorned the walls. Large ornaments dangled from the vaulted ceiling on fishing line. Groupings of potted evergreens wrapped in twinkling lights flanked the main entrance and stood in the corners. A stage had been erected along the back wall near the door we had come through. There was a flurry of activity on it as workmen were assembling the four cookie baking stations. Closer to the front of the stage stood four long butcher-block tables, perfect for rolling dough on. Each had a set of mixing bowls, measuring cups, baking trays, and a KitchenAid mixer. Behind the tables and closer to the wall stood two professional double ovens in stainless steel. Not only were they impressive, but each baker would have their own oven to bake in. I had never been in a live bake-off before, but I wanted to now. The Christmas setting was magical, and I could hardly wait until Sunday for the festival to begin.

As I was dreaming up another winning cookie, a shrill voice called me to my senses.

"Why aren't these ovens hooked up yet? There are wires! Stop staring at me with those blank eyes and install these properly!"

Bradley cringed at the sound of the voice. "That'll be Felicity. Quite the taskmaster, but she sure knows her Christmas decorations. I've been bribing the volunteers all week with cookies and cocoa spiked with peppermint schnapps."

"Good man," Rory said, running a cautious eye over the stage.

A moment later Felicity popped up from behind the ovens with a handful of loose wires. I had nearly forgotten that she had taken on the task of decorating for the Christmas Festival.

"Well, I best get back to the kitchen before she spots me," Bradley said. "We're technically not supposed to be in here. Good luck to you, Lindsey. I hope we both make it to that stage."

"Me too," I told him honestly.

Kennedy, fascinated by the woman who owed a year-round Christmas shop, was eager to talk with Felicity Stewart, but I was dreading the encounter. I never realized how competitive she was about Christmas, or how annoying she could be. Besides, I needed to get back to work as well. We had already spent far too long at lunch.

"Come on," I said, and motioned for us to leave. I was about to slip through the door when Kennedy stopped me.

"She's not interested in you," Kennedy said. "Our celebrity judge has arrived."

Sure enough, Chevy Chambers had just walked through the main entrance. Felicity spotted him and waved excitedly.

"Phew. Crisis averted. Come on."

"Has it been?" Kennedy questioned and pointed to the main entrance. Felicity was hugging Chevy Chambers. "Nothing good can come of that. Looks like our celebrity flirt has found a taker after all. Wonder if he promised to make her a television star too?"

"Felicity's married," I informed her. "She's the one who got Chevy Chambers to come here in the first place. They're probably old friends."

"Smart woman. She owns a Christmas store, gets the town to host a Christmas cookie bake-off, and brings in a celebrity food critic to generate interest. All she needs to do is pull off a win for publicity gold. You could learn a thing or two from her, Linds."

I almost laughed. "I don't have to. I have you. And Felicity still has to make it into the live bake-off. Bet she wasn't counting on such stiff competition."

It was a short drive back to the Beacon. I had been gone for two hours, was slightly tipsy, and was beginning to regret it. Spying Felicity with the cookie judge, I had the feeling that Kennedy might be correct. The whole Beacon Harbor Christmas Cookie Bake-Off might have been a setup. I was growing a little miffed, until the sight of flashing lights brought me to my senses. A police car was parked outside the Beacon Bakeshop.

"Oh my God!" I cried, as Rory parked his pickup truck behind it. "Mrs. Nichols! Something terrible has happened!"

CHAPTER 13

I thought my heart would burst with fear as I ran up the walkway through the giant candy cane lights. The *Closed* sign had been hung on the door. Tom, Wendy, and Alaina had all been working with Mrs. Nichols when I left. Now all of them appeared to be gone and the shop empty. What had happened?

"Tuck," I cried, spying Officer McAllister the moment I walked through the door. He was near the coffee bar staring at an empty plate when he saw us.

"Oh, hi, Lindsey, Rory . . . Kennedy." His eyes lingered a bit too long on my friend. Had I not been overcome with worry, I might have remarked on it.

"What's happened?" I asked. "Where's Mrs. Nichols?"

Just then a heart-wrenching sob came from the kitchen.

Rory dashed around the counter and disappeared through the kitchen door. A moment later, he returned with Mrs. Nichols on his arm. Her face was bright red as tears streamed from her eyes. The woman was a blubbering mess.

"I'm . . . so sorry," she hiccupped, wringing her hands. "We've . . . we've been robbed."

"Robbed!?" It had been the furthest thing from my mind. Certainly, it was a terrible violation, but I was relieved to see my assistant baker on her feet. I ran to help her, feeling guilty for having left her and the Beacon for as long as I had.

"Are you hurt? Did they hurt you?"

She sniffled. "Only my pride, dear."

"Where are the others?" I thought to ask.

"I sent them home," she confided with a sniffle. "Af . . . after the robbery, there was no reason for them to stay."

"But they left you alone. They shouldn't have left you alone." I looked at Rory for support. He nodded and helped me get Mrs. Nichols to a chair at a café table.

"Robbed, you say?" Kennedy stood beside Tuck, mimicking his thoughtful expression. If I didn't know better, I'd say she was pretending to be a cop. That thought was confirmed when she crossed her arms and addressed the room . . . as if she knew what she was talking about. "The gangsters!" she theatrically proclaimed. "It was bound to happen. The Beacon grew too big, too fast. I liken it to the proverbial cash cow — a Guernsey with bloated udders just waiting to be milked! How much was taken?"

Mrs. Nichols, like Rory, had momentarily been stunned to silence. Rory furrowed his brows at the same time Mrs. Nichols gasped. "All of it!" she cried, a red wave of anger rising to her cheeks. "The entire plate!"

"Excuse me?" I looked at Mrs. Nichols. "Plate?"

"This one," Tuck said, holding up the plate in question.

"Why are you holding a plate?"

"Apparently, Lindsey, the Beacon Bakeshop has been the scene of the county's first ever reported cookie-napping."

It was hard not to laugh, although doing so would have been cruel to Mrs. Nichols. The poor woman had been scarred by the incident. Apparently, around one o'clock in the afternoon, three nicely dressed, seemingly innocent women had entered the bakeshop. At the time, Tom had been out on a delivery, Aliana was out to lunch, and Wendy was in the back boxing up a couple of cakes for a special order. Mrs. Nichols was at the counter when one of the three women came up to her, asking after gluten-free, sugar-free, and vegan products.

"She was causing a scene," Mrs. Nichols confided. "She was very rude and smug about it too, stating that we should have gluten-free products and things for people who can't eat sugar, butter, eggs — even honey. I've never heard of such a thing!" Tears were brimming in her bloodshot eyes.

At this admission, Kennedy placed a hand over her heart, mouthing to me, *"I adore this woman!"*

"I told her she was in a bakery," Mrs. Nichols continued. "I suppose we could have made macaroons, had we known earlier. But it didn't matter, anyway. She didn't want gluten-free products. She was trying to distract me so her partners-in-crime could steal all of our signature cookies. Every blooming one of them!" To a baker like Mrs. Nichols, the shame of it had sparked another wave of helpless sobs.

I looked at Rory for support, which was a mistake. He was on the verge of bursting into laughter.

Tuck, I realized, was battling laughter, as well, as he picked up the empty plate and pretended to examine it. "It's, ah, empty, alright. How many cookies would you say were on here?"

"Three dozen," Mrs. Nichols replied.

Tuck, doing the mental math, said, "Thirty-six cookies." He was about to write it down in his notepad when Mrs. Nichols corrected him.

"Thirty-nine."

With a great show of patience, he said, "So, not three dozen then," and went to write the new number in his notepad.

"A baker's dozen, dear," Mrs. Nichols corrected with the same look of patience. "Didn't think I needed to specify that. And Wendy had just put them out too. It was all we had left."

The reprimand nearly undid Rory. Tuck pressed his lips together as he looked at his notepad. "Three *baker's* dozen cookies were stolen by three women you can't identify, and you want to report this?"

I shook my head at the same time Mrs. Nichols cried, "Yes!"

"It was a nervy move, to be sure, but do you really think we should report this?"

"I demand justice. They were your signature cookies, Lindsey."

Rory, on the verge of losing it, stared at Tuck. "Any guesses as to why they were taken in the first place, Officer?"

"Uhhh . . . ." Tuck brought a fist against

his lips, pretended to think. On closer inspection, I realized his lips were quivering. He removed his fist long enough to offer, "Laziness?"

Upon hearing the word, Rory hid his face in his hands. I pinched him, thinking that might help, but it didn't.

"You know," Tuck continued, his eyes silently challenging Rory. He pointed a finger at the sign above the empty plate of cookies. "The sign does say *Take One.*"

Kennedy, playing along, arched her perfectly shaped brow. "Are you suggesting these brigands couldn't count, or couldn't read?"

Tuck, barely able to speak, blurted, "Possibly both."

Dear Mrs. Nichols didn't see the humor in any of this. "Take *one*! Not *three dozen*!"

Realizing the recent violation was still painful for her, I pulled Tuck aside for a private word.

A moment later, after regaining his composure, he said, "So, I'll be making a report. And, um, I'll let you know if I find these cookie-nappers."

This seemed to satisfy Mrs. Nichols. "Thank you, Officer McAllister. But I don't think those women were lazy. And I know for a fact they could count. They took the

Christmas cookies because they were trying to sabotage Lindsey."

"What?" I looked at her, realizing for the first time that she might be correct.

"It's a competition," she explained as if we were grade-schoolers. "Lindsey's cookie is at the top of the list. If she doesn't have any more of her signature cookies to offer, shoppers can't taste them, and no one will vote for her. After the women had taken all the cookies, the few customers who came in were disappointed. They were expecting a free cookie to sample, and they had their scorecards with them. Don't you see? No cookies? Angry customers? I had to close the bakeshop early and send the kids home. Somebody doesn't want Lindsey in the Christmas cookie bake-off."

CHAPTER 14

Mrs. Nichols might have been correct to assume that someone was trying to sabotage me. After making a few phone calls, it appeared that the Beacon Bakeshop was the only shop in town that had been hit by the cookie-nappers that afternoon. Another suspicious twist was a recent online barrage of negative reviews targeting the Beacon Bakeshop on the Great Beacon Harbor Christmas Cookie Bake-off voting page. My cookie had been the one to beat, and somebody didn't like the fact that I was doing well in the polls. Kennedy, thankfully, had gotten online and done a little damage control. She was also trying to figure out who was behind the e-sabotage. The names of the reviewers in question were Snap, Crackle, Pop, and Gingy.

"Those definitely aren't Santa's little helpers," she remarked. "Unless he cut a deal with the Rice Krispies elves that we don't know about." She was being funny.

"Cute," I acknowledged. "They could be our cookie-nappers. Then there's Gingy." I read her a line in Gingy's review. *"A plain, underwhelming cookie made by a professional baker who clearly has no idea what Christmas or a Christmas cookie is all about, unlike the Tannenbaum Christmas Shoppe. Their beautifully decorated sugar cookie is as delicious as it looks. Lindsey Bakewell should stick to what she knows best — anything but Christmas cookies!"* I looked up from my iPhone and gave an ironic shake of my head. "Is it just me, or was naming her shop in the review a step too far?"

"Oh, the hubris!" Kennedy playfully exclaimed while placing a hand over her heart. "That's the power of the internet. Presumed anonymity. But like Icarus, she flew too high and couldn't resist naming herself as the best cookie baker in the village."

I gave a little chuckle at this. She was right, it was ridiculous.

Kennedy then teased, "Are you, Lindsey Bakewell, crime-solving?"

Kennedy had been with me last summer when the Beacon Bakeshop had been the scene of a diabolical murder. At one point I had been named as a suspect and felt I had no choice but to go head-to-head with the police and track down the murderer. Kennedy, of course, had been an invaluable help in the ordeal. A cookie-napping, however, was a far cry from outright murder.

I shrugged. "I'm a little miffed somebody stole all our cookies while diverting dear Mrs. Nichols with questions about vegan and sugar-free baked goods. The woman is an old-school baker, like my grandma was. Back in their day, using any substitute for butter, sugar, or flour in a baked good was a sin. Then the bold theft of the cookies right from under her nose! The poor woman was beside herself. I don't want to lose her. The identity of those three women remains a mystery, but I bet Felicity 'Tannenbaum' Stewart knows who they are."

The next morning, the impact of the cookie-napping and the online bashing were apparent. Ginger Brooks had jumped into the lead in the polls with her delicious German chocolate sandwich cookie, closely followed by Bradley Argyle's cookie of brown butter shortbread. Karen's prediction had come true. The entire garden club must have voted for Bradley's cookie. And why not? It was just about the best shortbread cookie I had ever eaten.

My signature cookie had dropped down

to third place. In fact, I was in a tie with Betty Vanhoosen and her raspberry linzer for that honor. It was the first time she'd appeared in the top ten, a fact that made me smile. After all, I had baked her cookie too. What if she made it into the live bake-off and not me? The raspberry linzer was delicate and delicious, but her sudden rise in votes, I believed, had more to do with the fact that she was a very popular woman in the town. If we were still tied by the end of voting, maybe we could enter the live bake-off as a team. That would be hilarious and, very likely, disastrous as well. Betty had many admirable qualities, but baking wasn't one of them.

The next name on the list, however, really got my heart pumping with ire. It was Felicity Stewart and her overdecorated sugar cookie. Felicity's cookie had jumped up five places since the cookie-napping, leaving little doubt as to who was behind it. The moment the Beacon Bakeshop was closed for the day, I was going to pay her a visit.

After the cookie-napping, I had insisted that Mrs. Nichols take the day off. It was the last day of voting, and I knew we were going to be busy. My entire staff had come in, every one of my employees seething with anger at having our cookies stolen. Tom, Wendy, and Aliana, however, were racked with guilt at having been at the Beacon when the incident occurred. Really, as far as burglaries went, it was pretty farcical. Hopefully in a few days everyone could laugh about it, but the damage to our pride was another matter. We were baking to win. How could our winning cookies have been stolen right out from under our noses? Without cookies to offer, we had dropped down to third place. We had all worked too hard for that.

Dad, after hearing of the cookie-napping, had thankfully come in early to help me bake. Once the bakery cases were filled, he informed me that he had promised Mom they'd go shopping. I could see that he wasn't too thrilled with the idea. Kennedy's plan for the day was to dress Welly up again in his plaid coat and hit the streets, promoting our winning cookie.

Our bakery cases were full, and we had plenty of our signature cookies ready to be sampled. I had just refilled the free sample tray when Felicity Stewart burst through the bakeshop door. I was surprised to see her and even more surprised to see that Sergeant Stacy Murdock was with her.

"You!" Felicity cried the moment she

spotted me.

"You!" I said right back, miffed about the mean-spirited review she had posted.

"Me?" She looked affronted and came to a stop before the self-serve coffee bar. "I'm not the cheater here. You are . . . and at Christmastime, no less! What depraved egomaniac cheats to win a Christmas cookie bake-off?"

My jaw dropped as my city-girl anger began to seize me. Had I heard her right? What on earth was she talking about? Aware that there was a line at the counter and that all the café tables were full, I kept my inner New Yorker in check. New York Lindsey wanted to wring the Christmas Lady's neck. Beacon Harbor Lindsey knew she'd spook the locals if she tried it. I motioned the sergeant and Felicity to a quiet corner where we could talk, civilly I hoped.

After flashing Felicity a look of warning, Murdock explained, "Felicity phoned the station this morning. Said there was some illegal shenanigans going on with the Christmas cookie bake-off. You know how I feel about shenanigans, Bakewell, illegal or otherwise." Murdock, doing her best not to break a smile, stared at me from under her wispy blond bangs and crossed her arms. Apparently, the entire police force thought

116

shenanigans at Christmastime were not funny.

"What illegal shenanigans have I been up to?" I asked the sergeant.

"How about the fact that you're baking cookies for half the shops in town," Felicity blurted.

My stomach clenched painfully at the accusation as thoughts of my perfect Christmas began slipping from my grasp. It was true. There was no denying that fact. But before I could confess, Wendy stopped me. She had come over to see what all the fuss was about.

"Lindsey is a baker," she told the ladies. "We sell baked goods here and take special orders. If we've been asked to bake Christmas cookies for others, it's not our place to ask what they're doing with them. The real question is" — Wendy, anger rising to her fair cheeks, turned to Sergeant Murdock — "why would *she* hire three women to steal our signature cookies? That's right. We think it was her."

Murdock looked thoughtfully at Wendy. "Well, now, that's a very interesting theory." She turned her deep-set brown gaze on Felicity.

"What?" Anger rose to Felicity's cheeks as she glared at the three of us. "I've done no such thing! I'm not the cheater here." She pointed a Christmas-red fingernail at me and cried, "She is!"

Sergeant Murdock, realizing that she was in the middle of a lady-squabble and not a Christmastime shenanigan, looked troubled. I got the feeling she'd rather be kicking down doors and tackling baddies in the gutter instead of listening to our complaints.

"Beacon Harbor was blindsided by the Christmas cookie bake-off," I calmly explained. "It was short notice. Every business in town wants to offer cookies to entice shoppers, but not everyone has the time to bake them. It's the holidays."

"Fair point." Murdock nodded.

"But they have to bake their own cookies, like I do," Felicity cried. "That's the whole point of this bake-off. Hiring a professional baker is cheating!" She waved her hand dramatically, declaring, "You should all be disqualified."

As Felicity listed her complaints, Murdock plucked a free cookie off the *Take One* tray and took a bite. Noting that Felicity had stopped talking, she finished her cookie. "Well, that doesn't sound like a crime to me, Felicity. Sounds like Lindsey and her hardworking staff are only trying to run a business here and win a cookie bake-off."

"Exactly," I concurred. "And we're not stealing the signature cookies of other shops to do it either!"

Felicity was seething. "What does that mean? You can't blame me for that!"

"No, but it is interesting that since the cookie-napping and the barrage of bad online reviews from a person named *Gingy,* I've dropped in the polls and you've jumped up."

"You can't prove anything you read on the internet," she said with a flair of hauteur. "And people love my Christmas sugar cookies!"

"*Gingy* probably shouldn't have compared her cookie to mine," I warned.

"I don't know what you're talking about, and I don't need to. I own a year-round Christmas shop. I'm the queen of Yuletide splendor! I know what a Christmas cookie is supposed to look and taste like. You're just mad because you're not on top anymore!"

Murdock, apparently realizing this little squabble had gone on too long, held up a hand. "I think you all know how I feel about these cookie shenanigans. Offering free Christmas cookies is risky, not to mention what it does to the waistline." Although a handsome woman in her mid-forties, Murdock wasn't what one would call trim. However, since the Christmas cookie bake-off began, it did appear that her uniform had shrunk a little. "Also, if Felicity-slash-Gingy did post a negative review online, that's not a crime. It's the internet, the wild, wild west of words. Most importantly, however, there is no proof linking Felicity to the cookie-nappers."

"Of course, there isn't. Because I didn't do it!" Felicity's face had turned as red as her hair. "The Tannenbaum is experiencing unprecedented crowds! I've been working, and decorating, and baking cookies!"

"And writing negative reviews about the Beacon Bakeshop," Wendy added, narrowing her eyes at Felicity.

"Again, not a crime," Murdock reiterated.

"She's right. Besides, when in the world would I have time to steal *your* stupid cookies?"

"Ladies, ladies!" Murdock, reaching the end of her patience, jumped in. "Both of you, calm down. Clearly this Christmas cookie bake-off has gotten to everyone."

"Lindsey has admitted to baking signature cookies for others. I want a list! I want her and everyone she's baked for disqualified."

I looked helplessly at the sergeant. "Surely you can't arrest me for baking cookies? It's my job!"

Murdock surprised me by chuckling. "Whoa. I'm not here to arrest anyone. I'm simply here to inform you on behalf of Mayor Jeffers that Felicity has filed a move with the Christmas Festival Committee to have you disqualified from the bake-off."

I was reeling from this news. Wendy looked angry enough to snap. That was when I felt a gentle touch on my arm.

"What's all this about?" I was shocked to see Mrs. Nichols standing beside me. She wasn't supposed to be here. I had no idea she'd come into the bakeshop. With a softly questioning look, she turned to Sergeant Murdock.

Felicity, glaring at my baker, said, "This bakeshop is being disqualified from the bake-off!"

A thoughtful look crossed the older woman's face. "You own that little Christmas shop at the other end of town, am I correct?" Felicity nodded. "Then you of all people should know that Santa doesn't abide grinches. Your job is to spread Christmas cheer, not dump coal in everyone's stocking. You are attacking Christmas cookies, those little sugary delights that embody the spirit of Christmas. Why would you want to ruin that for everyone? Shame on you," she admonished, and headed for the kitchen.

CHAPTER 15

"Whoo-hoo, Lindsey?" Betty Vanhoosen called, walking into the lighthouse. Welly and the models ran to greet her.

It was after dinner. Taking a page from Bradley Argyle's book, I had made everyone a hot cocoa and peppermint schnapps topped with mounds of sweet whipped cream and a drizzle of chocolate. It had been a ridiculous day. Betty, catching wind of Felicity's move to have me disqualified, had called an emergency meeting of the Christmas Festival Committee. Mom, Dad, Kennedy, Rory, and I were sipping spiked cocoa by the fire anxiously awaiting the news.

"You're in the live bake-off!" she proclaimed, throwing her arms in the air.

Dad let out a hoot. Kennedy smiled and gave a proper royal soft-clap. Mom cried with joy. Rory set down his cocoa and gave me a hug, whispering congratulations in my ear.

"That's wonderful news," I told Betty, handing her a mug of spiked cocoa as well. "How did you pull that off?"

"It was unanimous. Everyone you've baked cookies for this week agreed to bow out of the competition in order to keep you in it. It was a fun idea, this Christmas cookie bake-off, but none of us really wanted to be in the live competition. Felicity fought hard to have you removed. That's because she wants to win this darn thing so badly. But she had no ground to stand on. I actually felt sorry for her, thinking she might not have enough votes to be in the live bake-off. But once the votes were tallied, she made it. She's going to be on that stage with you."

"Who else made it?" I thought to ask.

Betty smiled. "The bakers in the live Christmas cookie bake-off will be you, of course, Ginger Brooks, Bradley Argyle, and Felicity Stewart. It's going to be quite the competition!"

All four of us had only one day to prepare for the two challenges required in the live bake-off. The first was a Christmas cookie to be baked on-site. For this, Dad had given me one of Grandma Bakewell's special recipes. It was for a frosted southern pecan cookie. I had never seen this recipe before or even heard of such a cookie when he handed me the recipe card. But I was touched and honored to know that it was one of my grandma's favorite cookies of all time.

Dad and I whipped up a sample batch, including the tricky penuche-style frosting that had to be cooked over a stove. Dad had given me a little tip on how best to spread it on the cookies before it hardened, which was always the problem when using such a frosting. It was best to make the frosting in small batches. I then lined eight of the buttery pecan cookies close together on a cooling rack at a time and poured a tablespoon of warm frosting over each of them. While the frosting was still warm, a pecan half was pressed in the center of each one. I continued the process until all the cookies had been frosted. Then it was time for the real test. I handed one to Rory and watched his face as he took his first bite. Yep, it was a winner. His double groan of knee-weakening pleasure sealed the deal.

The second challenge was a gingerbread house showstopper. This required a little more prep work than the cookie. To save time, the gingerbread panels were to be designed and baked beforehand then brought to the bakeoff, where they'd be assembled and decorated. Not only did the gingerbread house have to look good, but it needed to taste good as well. Instead of a traditional house, Rory helped me design a gingerbread replica of the Beacon Bakeshop complete with light tower. It was a real team effort. Everyone had piled into the kitchen to help. I put Mom and Kennedy on the candies I'd use for decoration. Dad helped me mix up batch after batch of a tasty yet stout gingerbread batter. The batter was then put into the molds Rory and I had made, and baked. It was tricky business. A few of the gingerbread panels cracked or broke as they were being removed from the mold, making this challenge the favorite of Welly, Brinkley, and Ireland. By the end of the day, the three dogs were gingerbread aficionados, having developed a real taste for the spicy cookie.

"Ready for this?" Rory asked. It was the morning of the bake-off, and I had just turned into the crowded parking lot of the Harbor Hotel. I parked my Jeep, turned off the ignition, and flashed him a confident smile.

"Ready as I'll ever be." What I didn't tell him was that butterflies were terrorizing my stomach. Although I had baked nearly every day for the past eight months, the thought of this bake-off made me nervous. I was prepared. I believed I had thought of everything. The back of my Jeep was testament to the fact that I had packed up nearly my entire kitchen, with the exception of the kitchen sink. And yet there was something bothering me. Apparently, Rory was more perceptive than I gave him credit for. His handsome face was pinched with concern, prompting me to add, "Even if I don't win, it will still be fun."

"I hope," he added, with a pensive gaze out the window.

"What does that mean?" The others had pulled up behind us in Dad's rental luxury SUV. They were about to get out, but something was troubling Rory.

"Were you up in the light tower last night?" His untimely mention of the old light tower tripped off another wave of terrorizing butterflies. The Beacon Harbor light tower was rumored to be haunted, and I had good reason to believe the rumor. Although I loved hanging out in the lantern room in the warmer months, it was bitter cold in the winter. Besides, I had been too busy to even think of going up there, and he knew it.

"What did you see?"

He answered cautiously. "Maybe the lights."

Urgh! The mere mention of the lights sent my heart tripping away with the same physical annoyance as the butterflies in my stomach. This wasn't good. The lights he was referring to were the ghost lights of Beacon Harbor, a quite famous phenomenon that was thought to be a portent of danger. "The whole light tower is wrapped in Christmas lights," I reasoned. "What you probably saw was a reflection of them."

"Yeah." He nodded. "Could have been that. But just in case, stay sharp up on that stage today."

With arms loaded with supplies, we entered the ballroom where the bake-off was being held and where the Beacon Harbor Christmas Festival was soon to begin. All thoughts of impending doom faded as the sights and smells of Christmas enveloped me. I knew the room was going to be decorated, but I hadn't realized that it would be transformed into a remarkable winter wonderland complete with a German-style Christmas market. I was enchanted with the little wooden stalls, bedecked in Christmas lights, that had been erected in the main hall and around the perimeter of the ballroom.

Mom and Kennedy, the fashionistas of our group, were wearing matching *Ellie & Co* Christmas sweaters. I could tell they were enchanted by the prospect of shopping while I baked, and I really couldn't blame them. Each stall sold little delights, like handmade ornaments, wooden puzzles, toys, sugared nuts, hand-dipped candles, knit hats, scarfs, mittens, and far more. It was a charming touch and one sure to bring smiles to all the visitors.

Moving to the stage, we spied Mrs. Nichols looking festive in a timeless red dress with white fur trim, white hose, and black buckle shoes. She was standing in a group with the rest of the gang from the Beacon Bakeshop. I had to laugh when I noticed that all my young employees had donned their craziest Christmas sweaters and hats for the occasion.

"Let me help you with those," Tom said, taking a bag from me. We had stopped to chat with the group for a moment, but I was getting nervous. All the other bakers were already at their baking stations on stage, setting up for the Christmas cookie challenge.

"Thank you," I said, as Ryan took the other bag. The young men bounded up the steps and headed for the empty baking station.

"Relax. You've got this, Lindsey," Rory said, handing me the box of carefully packed gingerbread panels he'd been carrying. "Looks like your Christmas cookie nemesis is going to be too busy wooing the cameras and Chevy to bake."

I looked to where he indicated on the stage and spied Felicity Stewart. She was wearing a frilly red apron over a green Christmas sweater. She was also standing so close to Chevy Chambers that she was nearly on top of him.

"Wow, she's not even trying to hide the fact that she's flirting with the judge," I remarked. "And look at her over-the-top baking station!"

"That's got to be a little distracting," Rory remarked with a shake of his head. Felicity had covered her entire station in mini white lights. She had a mini Christmas tree set up beside her mixer (that was going to be awkward!) with a little miniature train running beneath it. Her hand-painted white mixer sported festive holly leaves and red berries. All her mixing bowls were red and green, and even her antique rolling pin reflected the season. It had wooden handles and a decorative ceramic roller embellished with little gingerbread men. I had to admit that it was kind of adorable. I had been so concerned with gathering all the things I was going to need for my two challenges that any extra thought of decorations had gone out the window. If we were being judged on our stations, Felicity would surely have that title in the bag.

Tom and Ryan bounded down the steps and gave me the thumbs-up. I thanked them, thanked Rory, and went to finish setting up my baking station. That's when the ballroom doors opened to the public. The Christmas Festival had begun!

Chevy, spying me, broke away from Felicity and his camera crew. "Lindsey," he said, taking hold of my arm while accompanying me to my baking station. "Naughty girl," he whispered close to my ear. "I heard you've been baking cookies for nearly every shop in town."

Conscious that people were watching us, I gently pulled away and forced a smile. "Not every shop. Only the ones who asked me. I do run a bakery, you know."

He stood a little too close for my taste and smiled brightly. "Well, the ones I tasted were delicious . . . except for the dog biscuit at that pet groomer's. Nasty."

Conscious that I was running behind, I

frantically began unloading my bags. I set down my container of flour and looked at him. "You ate that?"

"The woman behind the counter handed it to me, even though I didn't have a dog."

Peggy, I silently mused, *bless you.* To Chevy, I said, "Excuse me, but I need to get my baking counter set up."

Chevy didn't take the hint. Instead, he leaned close. "How about after you win this thing you have dinner with me? With that body and those high cheekbones, you'd look great on camera. If you play your cards right, I could see you hosting your own baking show. I can make that happen."

Dumbfounded, I stared at him. What the heck was happening? Did he just tell me he was going to let me win? I was about to set him straight when Felicity appeared.

"Chevy! I have something else to show you. You're going to want your camera crew to see this." With a flirtatious smile, she placed a hand on his arm. Grabbing his attention, she glared at me. "I hope Lindsey's not trying to bribe you. And look, how typical. She's given no thought to decorating."

"Hold on a minute," Ginger said, stepping between Felicity and Chevy. Her baking station was all set up and looking great. "He's been at your station for fifteen minutes," she complained, looking at Felicity. "I've been promised some camera time as well, and a nice blurb about Harbor Scoops. I want to remind people that we're still open and have fabulous hand-packed ice cream take-away pints in all our flavors, as well as jars of our homemade ice cream toppings."

"Good luck, Lindsey." Chevy tossed me a wink and left arm in arm with Ginger. Felicity stormed off in a huff. Bradley, in the manner of a true chef, ignored us all and focused instead on the pound of butter he was unwrapping.

We were all ready for the bake-off to begin when Betty Vanhoosen walked onto the stage. She looked adorable in her own bright, cotton candy–pink version of what Mrs. Claus should look like. Wearing a short white wig and glasses for effect, she waved at us before picking up the microphone. Betty, unbeknownst to me, was the other cookie judge and host of the Great Beacon Harbor Christmas Cookie Bake-Off. After welcoming the crowd, and after giving a few short community announcements, she proclaimed that the bake-off had begun.

The butterflies in my stomach were long gone as I mixed up dough for my frosted southern pecan cookie. I was just about to scoop the delicious buttery batter onto a parchment-covered baking sheet when Mrs. Nichols hailed me from the foot of the stage. I had half a mind to ignore her, but the look in her wide blue eyes went straight to my heart. She was troubled about something. I set down my scoop and walked around my station to see what was troubling her.

"One of the cookie-nappers is here!" she exclaimed in a loud whisper.

It wasn't exactly the best timing. I needed to get my cookies into the oven. "Are you sure?"

"Yes. She's over there . . . the platinum blonde in the tight pink sweater."

I looked at the woman in question but couldn't see her clearly. The crowd watching the bake-off had grown, and the woman was swiftly moving away, weaving through people as she left. All I could see was her back and the fall of her thick white-blond hair. I didn't know what to do. Thankfully, Rory and Kennedy had seen me.

"Lindsey, what's wrong?" Rory's eyes flashed concern as he came to the edge of the stage.

I shrugged. "It's probably nothing. Mrs. Nichols thinks she's spotted one of the cookie-nappers. Can you two check it out for her?"

"We've got it," Kennedy assured me. "You just keep baking!"

I turned away as Mrs. Nichols began describing the woman to them. The cookie-napping was hardly relevant now that I was in the bake-off, but Mrs. Nichols was highly agitated. With Rory and Kennedy handling the matter, I was able to return to my cookies. I had no sooner put them into the oven when I noticed that something else seemed very strange. Chevy Chambers was nowhere to be seen.

CHAPTER 16

Where had the cookie judge gone to? The thought that he had left the stage made me nervous, especially since Rory had planted the seed that something bad might happen. Why did Rory have to mention the ghost lights? Then there was the fact that Rory and Kennedy were still gone, too, which made me nervous. However, I didn't have time to dwell on it. I lined up the cookies and quickly poured the hot, glossy penuche frosting on them before it hardened, just like I had practiced. With my cookies done and sitting on a decorative Christmas plate, I was about to go look for Chevy. The moment I got to the end of the stage, I saw him walk through the back door of the hotel kitchen. It was the same door Kennedy, Rory, and I had walked through when Bradley had shown us the ballroom.

Chevy must have taken a bathroom break, I thought, watching him return to the stage.

He had come back to judge the first round of cookies and was looking a little flustered. His face was red, and he wasn't smiling as he went to meet Betty Vanhoosen at the judges' table. But like a true professional, he plastered on a smile and began entertaining the crowd with witty comments as he sampled Ginger's Oreo truffle cookie.

I was third to be judged. I had just set my plate on the judges' table when I noticed Rory and Kennedy standing at the foot of the stage motioning to me. The moment Chevy and Betty had finished sampling my frosted southern pecan cookie, and after answering all their questions for the crowd, I quietly slipped away to talk with my friends.

"Did you find her?"

"We did," Kennedy announced, "but only from a distance. She was talking with that man over there." She pointed to Chevy.

"With Chevy?"

"Didn't look like they were strangers either," Rory added. "I think she was flirting with him. However, the moment she spotted us, she took off, slipping out a side door. Chevy took off, too, but we caught up with him. He looked flustered but swore he didn't know her. Said she was a fan. I'm not sure I believe him."

"Interesting. So, Chevy might have a connection to one of our cookie-nappers," I remarked.

Rory shrugged. "I don't know, but I do think we need to keep an eye on Mr. Chambers."

It wasn't long before the winner of the Christmas cookie challenge was announced. I half-expected to win because of what Chevy had insinuated to me before the bake-off began, but he surprised me. Although I had baked an excellent cookie, Bradley and his beautiful turtle-topped shortbread had taken first place, while my frosted southern pecan cookie came in second. Ginger took third with her Oreo truffles, and Felicity came in last with her old-fashioned figgy bars with hard-sauce glaze. Really, what was she thinking? Clearly put out that her gelatinous bar-cookie hadn't won, she flashed Chevy a look that could have killed before storming back to her baking station. There was something about her anger that made me think that Chevy might have promised her a victory as well.

I was satisfied with second place. It meant that Chevy wasn't on the take. Bradley's cookie was a work of art. He was also an excellent baker. Had I come in first place after my little conversation with Chevy, I might have been suspicious. Sure, I wanted to win the bake-off, but not that way.

After a short break, the final challenge was announced. Although all four of us bakers had known the two challenges we were to face, the festivalgoers had remained ignorant. Therefore, when the second and final challenge was announced, the gingerbread house showstopper, the crowd erupted in applause.

Ginger, grabbing an array of food coloring for her icing, had come over for a word. "These gingerbread panels were the worst," she confided. "Didn't realize we'd be made to construct a gingerbread house from scratch when this town-wide Christmas cookie extravaganza began. I usually just buy a kit for Kate. We have a blast making it, but last night I wasn't having a blast baking large pans of gingerbread."

I smiled in agreement. "It was a pain, but I had the whole gang helping out. Needless to say, we broke a few panels. Welly was happy about that." As I talked, I gently eased a gingerbread panel out of the shirt box I had transported it in.

"I'll bet he was. Hey" — she leaned in and lowered her voice — "did Chevy offer to come over to the lighthouse and help you bake?"

Stunned, I looked at her. "No, he didn't. Did he come over to your house last night?"

"When he learned that I was a single mother, he offered. Of course, I didn't take him up on it." She made a face, indicating that the whole notion was ridiculous. She then walked back to her station.

I glared at Chevy as I turned on my mixer to whip up the thick royal icing that would act as the glue to my gingerbread. What a creep.

I was in the thick of constructing my festive, edible lighthouse when I heard a familiar voice hailing me from the edge of the stage. I looked to where the voice had come from and saw Mrs. Nichols. Her normally jovial face was pinched with anger once again. It was like bad déjà vu.

Noting that Chevy and the cameras were busy with Felicity and her over-the-top Christmas cheer, I set down my bag of icing and went to the edge of the stage.

"Sorry to be a bother, dear, but I've spotted another one of the cookie-nappers." I could have guessed as much, I thought, but I put a concerned look on my face nonetheless. "She came right up to the stage," Mrs. Nichols continued, "right over there!" She pointed her finger, aiming at a large gentleman standing beside her. "Oops, not him," she demurred. "But four spaces down there."

"Stay right here," I told her. "I'm putting Rory and Kennedy on it." Although they should have been next to Mrs. Nichols, watching me decorate my gingerbread lighthouse, even I knew how boring spectating a bake-off could be — especially for two non-bakers. They had meandered off to browse around the little Christmas booths with Mom and Dad and the rest of the Beacon's staff. Walking back to my baking station, I pulled out my phone and sent Rory a text. A moment later he appeared with Kennedy beside him. They found Mrs. Nichols and were taking note of her description of this new cookie-napper.

All my candy bags were open, and I was decorating! I had crushed a bag of Oreo cookies and pressed the crumbs on a layer of icing to create the distinctive black dome of the light tower. I was using white Chiclets gum for the base of the tower to mimic the brick construction. For the roof of the main house, I had layered chocolate nonpareil discs to look like a snow-covered roof. I was currently placing thin pretzel sticks on the lighthouse to look like windowpanes. I had just finished my second window when Betty picked up the microphone and made the announcement that Santa had arrived.

The crowd cheered. I looked up from my work just in time to see one of the jolliest, best-looking Santas I had ever seen walking through the ballroom doors with a giant sack of presents slung on his back. When I realized that Santa was really Dr. Bob Riggles, the town medical examiner and Betty's current heartthrob, I laughed. It was a great surprise. I started clapping too!

"Linds! Over here!"

The familiar voice startled me. Pulling my attention from Santa, I saw that this time it was Kennedy who was hailing me from the edge of the stage. Noting that everyone else was distracted, too, I went over to join her. "Santa's just arrived. This better be good."

She cast me a cheeky grin. "It is, darling. Rory and I found our woman in question. And guess what? She and Mr. Chambers were having a private conversation as well. Cookie-napper number two isn't quite the looker number one is, but she sure had his attention."

"But how can that be? Chevy's been here the whole time," I explained, gesturing to the stage. I realized that Kennedy was correct. Chevy was nowhere to be seen.

"You've been busy decorating, Linds, which is a good thing. Your gingerbread lighthouse is looking grand." She gave a slight nod of her head toward my half-decorated lighthouse. Then she was back to the matter at hand. "Chevy comes and goes as he pleases," she explained. "I honestly don't know what's going on here, but these cookie-napping women are shifty. The moment number two spied us coming, she gave us the slip. I went after her while Rory questioned Chevy."

"That's right." Rory, weaving through the crowd, suddenly appeared beside Kennedy. He was breathing a bit heavily, I noted, as he pointed down the stage to the steps. Chevy had returned. Once again, he looked flustered. "I take it you didn't catch her?" he asked Kennedy. She shook her head in dismay.

"What did Chevy say?"

Rory, disappointed, shrugged his broad shoulders. "Absolutely nothing. The smug bastard just smiled and said she was a fan as well. Claims it happens all the time."

"Oooo!" I cried in frustration. "Clearly, he's lying! I mean, if they hadn't stolen my cookies, I might give him a pass on this one, but clearly something is going on."

We were all in agreement but couldn't

figure out the point of it. What were Chevy and the cookie-nappers up to?

"Look, I have a lighthouse to decorate. Will you two keep an eye on Mrs. Nichols and let me know if cookie-napper number three shows up?"

"Will do, boss," Rory teased, but then his smile faded. "If we can find her."

I looked out over the crowd. For the first time since the bake-off began, Mrs. Nichols was nowhere to be seen.

CHAPTER 17

There were some real Christmas shenanigans going on in the ballroom, but it appeared that only my friends and I were aware of them. Chevy was as slippery as a watermelon seed, I thought, watching him bound around the stage, going from Felicity, to Bradley, to Ginger, then to me, before disappearing to parts unknown. Chevy was a big boy. I wasn't concerned about him, but I was concerned for Mrs. Nichols. At first, we thought that she might have joined the crowd over at the North Pole where Santa was entertaining the kids. Mrs. Nichols was clearly a fan of the big guy, but Rory didn't find her there.

I kept decorating as my friends kept searching. Finally, Kennedy appeared with Mrs. Nichols on her arm. She was escorting her back to her spot near the stage. *"She was in the ladies' room,"* Kennedy mouthed to me. I breathed a sigh of relief. Of course!

How stupid of us. She was an elderly woman and had been standing on her feet for quite some time. She had also made several trips to the cookie and punch table. With a little wave in greeting, I picked up my icing bag and set to work finishing my gingerbread showstopper. I didn't know why, but I felt that the cookie-nappers might pose a threat to dear Mrs. Nichols.

As we continued to decorate our gingerbread structures, Betty and Chevy visited each station with the camera crew, offering a little commentary and color on each of our showstoppers.

"This is the yummiest lighthouse I have ever seen," Betty remarked, watching me decorate. "If I was a captain of a ship, I'd drive it onto the rocks just to take a nibble." She made a face that caused the audience to break out in laughter. "How remarkable. It looks so much like the Beacon Bakeshop!"

Chevy agreed and congratulated me on my unique design, and my clever use of pretzels for windows and white Chiclets gum for painted bricks.

The duo next went to visit Felicity. She was overly cheerful as she explained her design to the judges. Like me, Felicity had chosen to make a mini replica of her business. I had to admit that her Bavarian-style

Christmas shop was adorable. She had used a lot of fondant to cover her gingerbread, red on the roof and white fondant to simulate the stucco walls of the building. The windows had been meticulously piped on, as had the door. She had used Kit Kats for the dark wood beams and molded chocolate for the shutters and window caps. She had even made window boxes out of the molded chocolate but had piped on the brightly colored flowers that hung over the sides. Most of the candy had been used on landscaping or for decorating her cookie-cutout Christmas trees. I was impressed, but Chevy, unfortunately, was not.

"Fondant goes on cakes, not on gingerbread houses. I thought you of all people would know that!" He crossed his arms and cast her a look of displeasure. "That just looks lazy."

I sucked in my breath when I heard that. Felicity, the smile wiped from her face, blew a gasket. As Betty tried to soften the blow with compliments, Felicity turned on Chevy. She slapped him with her icing bag while uttering a profanity that should never be uttered at a Christmas festival. Chevy laughed, which infuriated Felicity to new heights. She picked up a sheet of fondant and threw it at him. Chevy was still laughing as he pulled it away. He ducked but wasn't quick enough to evade her flailing fist. Yet before Felicity could land another punch on the laughing food critic, she was lifted by a man and carried off the stage.

At first, I thought he was from Security. But then I realized that the man was Stanley Stewart, Felicity's embarrassed husband. Apparently, he was used to dealing with such tantrums and was attempting to calm her down. Who knew that baking cookies could cause so much drama?

Musing over cookies and drama, I had just put the last gumdrop on my showstopper lighthouse when Mrs. Nichols hailed me for the third time. One look at her and I knew she had spotted cookie-napper number three. Dear heavens, had they all come to the Christmas Festival?

I announced to Betty that I was done with my gingerbread lighthouse and set down my icing bag. Looking around, I realized that I was the only one left on stage. Betty consoled me by telling me that the others had finished early and that the judging wouldn't begin for another fifteen minutes.

"Over there." Mrs. Nichols pointed at a woman who was less than twenty feet away. "That's the woman who wanted vegan baked goods. She just walked up a minute ago."

The woman in question had a pretty face with well-balanced features, a little upturned nose, and soft brown eyes rimmed with thick black eyelashes. I put her to be somewhere in her early fifties. Her shoulder-length brown hair had been layered with highlights. She was slender, well-dressed, and her makeup had been expertly applied. Like the other two ladies whom Mrs. Nichols had pointed out to us, this woman didn't look like she needed to steal Christmas cookies. She looked affluent and well cared for. In short, she looked like a woman who could buy as many Christmas cookies as she wanted. So, what was she doing in my bakery stealing mine? What was her connection to Chevy, or Felicity? Maybe she was connected to them both? I didn't know what her deal was, but I knew that I was going to find out.

It only took a few seconds to size her up, but in that short time, cookie-napper number three had locked eyes with me. Realizing Mrs. Nichols had spied her, and that I was on to her, too, she spun around and began weaving through crowd of festivalgoers.

"I got her!" I said to Mrs. Nichols and jumped off the stage. I called back over my shoulder, "Tell Rory and Kennedy when you see them."

I wove though the crowd in pursuit of the woman, never taking my eyes off her. She was a slippery one, I thought as I followed her. She dashed around the refreshment table, then turned and skirted the giant Christmas tree in the center of the ballroom. I ran around it, too, and thought I had lost her. Stumped, I walked halfway around it again. That's when I spied her highlighted hair bobbing through a sea of crazy Christmas hats and light-up headbands. I ran after her and watched as she disappeared in the small gap between two of the little German-style Christmas booths.

"Nice try," I growled under my breath, and followed her.

The booths she had chosen looked to be the most popular ones in the Christmas market, one selling warm spiced nuts and the other slabs of Mackinac Island fudge. Although I'd been baking cookies all morning and working with gingerbread, the scent of the warm, sugared almonds and mouthwatering fudge was intoxicating. With the mantra, "Excuse me. Excuse me!" I elbowed my way to the front of the crowd and tried to follow cookie-napper number three, squeezing my body between the narrow gap between the booths. A sign on the side post read *Do Not Enter,* and yet I did, all in the name of cookies.

Once through, I thought the woman had shaken me. The three-foot gap between the back of the booths and the wall was void of people. But then I spied a door and knew she had used it to evade me. I ran past three more booths and opened the lone door, stepping into a large, nearly empty hallway in the hotel. The woman I was chasing was at the far end of the hallway. Hearing me, she dashed to the right and disappeared once again down another hallway. The woman was fast, sneaky, and didn't want to be caught. My stolen cookies aside, the thought intrigued me. What was this woman hiding?

"Stop," I cried, running after her. "I just want to ask you some questions."

Obviously, she didn't want to speak to me. She ran to the end of the hallway and threw open a door with an *Exit* sign above it. Yet instead of leaving the hotel through another door, she ran down a set of stairs. I was catching up to her fast and she knew it.

I followed her to the hotel basement, where again she disappeared through another door.

I realized her mistake immediately. She

had gone into a storage room of some type, and I doubted that there was another way out. Steeling myself for a confrontation, I opened the door.

The lights had been turned on, but all that confronted me were tall rows of boxes. A quick look told me that the boxes contained extra linens, dishware, silverware, chafing dishes for the buffet, and other dry goods for the kitchen.

I proceeded with caution. "Look, I know you're in here," I said, walking farther into the room. "I don't mean to cause you any harm." I looked behind a row of boxes. Finding it empty, I added, "I just want to talk with you."

"Too bad," a voice behind me said. Yet before I could spin around, an entire stack of boxes came crashing down on my head. The weight of them knocked me to the ground. Then the lights went off, and the door clicked shut. Trapped under the boxes, I let out a cry of frustration. She was gone, and I had been left in the dark.

CHAPTER 18

The boxes on top of me were heavy, but I was angry enough to wiggle my way free. Once on my feet, I pulled out my iPhone and flipped on the flashlight app. I had never been comfortable in utter darkness and was instantly grateful for the amazing technology at my fingertips. I gingerly made my way to the door, but when I turned the knob, I found that it had been locked.

"What?" I cried, growing infuriated. "No way!" The nerve of the woman. Leading me on a wild goose chase, only to be locked in a storage closet. My inner New Yorker was fit to be tied. Who was she? Stupidly, I began pounding on the door, hoping someone would hear me. But even I knew that the hotel basement was empty. Then, regaining my composure, I called Rory.

"Where are you?" he said through the crackling connection. The cell service wasn't the best, but at least it was working. "I've been looking for you."

"I'm locked in a storage closet somewhere in the basement of the hotel. You're going to need a key. And please hurry. The judges will be announcing the bake-off winner any minute."

It took Rory a while to find Chad, the hotel kitchen manager, and a few minutes longer to locate the correct storage room I'd been locked in.

"Damn," I heard Chad utter as yet another key was forced into the lock. "Wrong key again."

"Try that one," Rory's impatient voice suggested.

"How many keys do you have with you?" I asked through the door.

"I have them all," Chad replied. "It's the master key ring from the front desk. The problem is, we have a lot of storage rooms in the hotel, and most of the keys aren't marked."

"Not a great system," I called back, trying to be as patient as I could. A good minute later, however, the right key had been found, and I was freed.

The first thing I saw was a look of relief on Rory's face right before he wrapped me up in a hug. I needed that hug and didn't mind hugging him back just as tightly. "You okay?" he asked.

"I am now," I assured him. "I'm a little sore, and there might be a box or two of broken dishes. The woman I was chasing pushed a whole stack of them on me before locking me in there."

Neither man liked the sound of that. Chad, frowning, peered into the room. "I'm a little unclear. What where you doing in the storage closet in the first place?"

I had met Chad shortly after moving to Beacon Harbor. As the manager of one of the best restaurants in town, he knew most of the locals. Forty, unmarried, and with a distinguished air about him, Chad also had a reputation as a bit of a playboy, charming the bored wives of wealthy guests staying at the Harbor Hotel. His exploits were often the town's favorite topic of gossip. It was usually harmless stuff, but for reasons of her own, Betty loved sticking her nose in Chad's business. I thought, given his reputation and his eye for the ladies, that maybe he'd be able to identify our mysterious cookie-nappers if I described them. Still a bit shaken, I explained to both men what had happened.

Chad, listening thoughtfully, finally shook his head. "I'd love to help you, Lindsey, but unfortunately your description is rather generic. As you know, it costs a few shekels to stay at the hotel. You've just described a good chunk of our clientele. Handsome, fit, well-dressed women who might even be bored enough to steal Christmas cookies. I'll keep a lookout and check with Ludlow at the reservation desk." He jingled his key ring and stuffed it into the pocket of his Christmas plaid pants. He turned to leave but stopped short. "It just dawned on me. You said that you followed a woman into this storage room. It might have been left open. That does happen from time to time, but she would have needed a key to lock you in."

Rory cast Chad a penetrating look. "Are you saying that this woman planned on locking Lindsey in this closet?"

Chad shrugged. "I'm saying that she would have needed a key. But she doesn't sound like anyone I know who works here. Very strange. Would there have been a purpose in luring you down here and locking you away?" His light hazel eyes held on to mine as he asked this.

"The bake-off!" I blurted, looking at Rory for support. "I wasn't at the Beacon Bakeshop when the women stole our cookies, but Mrs. Nichols was. She was the only one who could identify them. Throughout the course of the live bake-off, all three women came near enough to Mrs. Nichols for her to recognize them. Rory, you and Kennedy chased after the first two, but maybe they were trying to lure *me* off the stage."

Rory considered this. "In the middle of a bake-off?" he questioned. "That doesn't sound right. And anyhow, you had finished both your challenges when the last woman showed up."

"True. So, why would they want me off the stage? Could it be that somebody didn't want me up there when they announced the winner? Honestly, I don't see what difference that would make. And anyhow, I've already missed it." I could feel my mood plummeting at the thought.

Chad offered a look of sympathy. "Sorry about that. If I find out anything, I'll let you know."

As Chad headed back toward the stairwell, Rory decided to take another way back to the ballroom.

"I've chased two women through this hotel today. I'm getting to know this place like the back of my hand," he explained with a grin. "I found a little something I wanted to show you."

"What did you find?" I asked, filling with curiosity.

"If I tell you, it'll spoil the surprise." The playful grin was still on his face as he took my hand.

Honestly, I wasn't in any hurry to get back to the Christmas Festival. Thanks to the crazy woman who had locked me in the closet, I had missed the bake-off judging. By now I knew I hadn't won. Kennedy or Mom would have called me immediately, congratulating me and wondering why I wasn't on stage to accept my award. No call meant no award. I hated to admit it, but being locked in the storage closet wasn't nearly as depressing as the thought of losing the Christmas cookie bake-off. The way my luck was running, I was convinced Felicity Stewart had taken the prize.

"You okay?"

"Yeah," I replied glumly.

"You're going to have to do better than that," he teased as we walked up a set of stairs. We had traveled an empty corridor and were now on the opposite end of the large hotel. "Do you realize that this is the first time we've been truly alone since this Christmas cookie bake-off began?"

The thought had barely occurred to me. I looked into his bright blue eyes. "You might be right."

"Trust me. I am."

"We're in the middle of a Christmas festival," I reminded him, thinking perhaps he had found another private closet for us to get lost in.

"I'm well aware."

Leaving the stairwell, I saw that we were in a short hallway that ended in what looked to be another glittering Christmas paradise. The back of a puffy leather couch faced a wall of windows. On either side of the couch was an equally puffy leather chair. From past experience I knew there was a built-in bookcase along one of the walls. This was a little library for hotel guests, tucked away in a secluded corner of the building. In the summer it led to a secluded patio surrounded by a lush, fragrant garden. Guests could walk through the garden on a path that wound down to the lake. The view was still breathtaking, but this time of year the patio and the landscape beyond had been covered by a thick layer of pristine snow. Potted poinsettias and a decorated Christmas tree now filled the room. And then I spied it, dangling from the ceiling on a long ribbon before the windows. My heart stilled as all thoughts of the bake-off fizzled away. This was the reason Rory had brought me here.

"Rory Campbell, and here I didn't think

you had a romantic bone in your body."

"I had a feeling you wouldn't mind being pulled under the mistletoe for a kiss."

"You don't need to find a sprig of mistletoe to kiss me."

"It's not just the mistletoe," he confided in all seriousness. "It's a quiet room."

I took his meaning. We were utterly alone. Smiling, feeling giddy, we practically ran to get under the mistletoe, excited for that long-awaited kiss that had escaped us ever since the Great Beacon Harbor Christmas Cookie Bake-Off had begun. Spending more time with Rory had been that one Christmas wish that had escaped me. The bake-off was over. The mistletoe was in sight. There was still time. Fighting to get there, we nearly tripped over the couch. But once around that obstacle, we came to a screeching halt.

Crumpled on the floor beneath the mistletoe was a body. The gruesome sight of it shoved all thoughts of a romantic kiss out the window.

CHAPTER 19

"It's . . . it's Chevy Chambers!" I cried, sputtering the obvious. I was in total freak-out mode. Seeing the body there had been a shock, but even more unnerving was the blood pooling around his head, matting his thick brown hair and staining the blue, patterned carpet. He also appeared to be sprinkled with crumbs — as if sneezing while eating a crumbly baked good. "Is he . . . ?" Looking at Rory, I ventured the question. The moment the body had been spotted, Rory went into action, feeling for a pulse. He removed his fingers from the prone man's neck and shook his head.

"He's dead?" I squawked. "Are you sure?"

"Do *you* want to check?" he offered sarcastically, already knowing the answer to that. He pulled out his cell phone and called the police.

People often thought that by living in New York City for as long as I had, I would be used to the sight of dead bodies — like the streets were littered with them or something. Seriously? Sure, crime happened in the Big Apple, but I had never seen a dead body on the ground. Last summer in Beacon Harbor, however, I had seen two and hadn't liked the experience one bit. I was sorry to say that one of them had even induced me to toss my cookies. I was in danger of that now, and Rory likely knew it.

"I'll take your word for it," I replied, taking a step back. I was sorry I had even questioned him. I was even more sorry that we had to stay with the body until the police arrived. I hadn't particularly liked Chevy when he was alive, but even I knew that we couldn't abandon him in death. The mere fact that he was lying on the floor in a quiet corner of the hotel, bleeding on the carpet, was a good indication in my book that somebody had done this to him. I couldn't help myself from asking the obvious question.

"What . . . what do you think happened?" I pointed at Chevy's head. "Do you think it was someone from the bake-off? Do you think someone got mad that they didn't win and killed him?"

Rory, careful to avoid the pooling blood as he stood, shrugged his broad shoulders.

162

"It's hard to know what to think besides the obvious. He's split his head open."

"He could have slipped," I offered. But as soon as I said it, I regretted it.

Rory frowned. "Even if he had come in here to be alone with his thoughts and accidentally fell, there's little in this room, besides the corner of that coffee table way over there, that would cause such a spectacular gash to his head. My best guess is that someone hit him on the back of the head with something hard."

The thought was ghastly. Covering my mouth with one hand, I used the other to point to the body. I lifted the hand over my mouth just enough to venture, "Are those cookie crumbs?"

He raised a brow in question. Rory had been so busy checking the body for a pulse he must have ignored them. He knelt again to get a better look at the crumbs. "Lindsey, remind me again the name of the Christmas cookie you baked?"

"Frosted southern pecan with penuche frosting. Why?" My heart began to pound even louder in my chest as I asked the question.

"Was anyone else using penuche frosting?"

"I can definitely say no to that. It's a tricky frosting to get right," I told him, watching as he gingerly plucked a golden crumb off of Chevy's Christmas blazer, careful to avoid contaminating the crime scene.

"I've eaten this cookie," he said, examining the crumb. "It's the only reason I know what penuche frosting looks like. Lindsey, these crumbs are from your cookie."

"What? Nooo," I balked, in utter denial. "I mean, how can that be? Why would he be eating one of my cookies when he was . . . you know, bumped off? Are you sure it's not Felicity's figgy bar?"

"Don't know what that one looks like," he admitted, then handed me the crumb.

I didn't want to touch it, but he left me with no choice. Apparently, Rory had no such qualms. And why would he when he was used to hunting animals and field dressing them on-site? My stomach heaved as I glanced at it. "Yep. It's mine," I affirmed, then quickly tossed it back. Unfortunately, it landed in Chevy's matted hair.

"Seriously?" he chided, narrowing his eyes at me.

My response was a cringing shrug of shame. "Sorry. But why was he eating one of my cookies?" Somehow, that thought disturbed me nearly as much as the blood.

"Good question." Apparently, like me, Rory had no answer.

"I have another question," I ventured. I was now nervously wringing my hands. "Why do you suppose his left hand is balled in a fist?"

It was the first time I had noticed it and thought that maybe Chevy was still holding on to the cookie he'd been eating when he was killed. Rory, with dark brows furrowed, stared at the hand in question. He gave a quick look around the room to see if we were still alone and reached for it.

"No!" I cried, startling him. "Don't touch it." I was on edge. Opening the hand could possibly be interpreted as tampering with a crime scene, and I had already been accused of that once before by scary Sergeant Murdock. She didn't have a sense of humor about such things. Another reason? I didn't think I could handle seeing my beautiful Christmas cookie in the cold, stiff hand of a dead man. "I have a better idea," I told him, pulling out my iPhone. "I'm calling Santa."

"Lindsey!" Tuck had been the first officer to arrive in the secluded corner of the hotel. We hadn't waited long. With so much traffic around the Christmas festival, I had a feeling he had been keeping an eye on things. The moment he spied me, he noted Rory and the body. Walking toward us, he spoke into his walkie-talkie, reporting the location, as he termed it, of the crime scene and calling for backup.

"Is that . . . Chevy Chambers?" Tuck's face darkened with recognition. "The food critic? What happened?"

"We're not sure," Rory told him honestly. "Appears that someone hit him on the head. We found him like this."

Tuck's guileless blue eyes shot to mine. "What are you two doing here — in this quiet corner of the hotel? I thought you were in the bake-off, Lindsey?"

"I am in the bake-off," I said a little defensively. Rory and I then proceeded to tell him about Mrs. Nichols spying the cookie-nappers at the festival and how we had both followed them. When he heard that I had gotten locked in a storage closet in the hotel basement, he shook his head in admonishment.

"Why didn't you call me?"

Voices filled the adjoining hallway. More first responders were coming to the crime scene. Shifting my attention back to the young officer, I said, "Honestly, it was just cookies."

"Well, it's not just cookies anymore, is it?" After holding me in a troubled grimace, Tuck stood and faced the hallway, ready to debrief the new arrivals.

The first man to appear was jolly old Saint Nick, or, more correctly, Dr. Bob Riggles, the county medical examiner. I had to admit, he was a fine-looking Santa as he strolled into the room with rosy cheeks glowing above his fake white beard. Betty, dressed in her Mrs. Claus outfit, trotted right beside him, obviously hearing the news. Tuck stared at the man with a quizzical look on his face. "Doc Riggles?"

"Ho-ho, yes." The doctor, recalling himself, stopped and shook his head. "Sorry, Tuck. Been saying that all afternoon. It's become my mantra. So many happy children. Had a hard time getting away. Damn." Doc Riggles's face clouded as he stared at the body on the floor. "Is that —"

"Chevy Chambers!" Betty confirmed, answering his question. Her face blanched, and she crossed herself.

"Betty." Tuck placed a gentle hand on her shoulder. "This is a crime scene. I'm going to ask you to stay behind those chairs."

Betty ignored him. "We've been looking all over for Chevy. He was supposed to announce the bake-off winner twenty minutes ago."

"He never announced the winner?" Rory and I exchanged a look. This was interesting news. I had been locked in the storage room for at least fifteen minutes before Rory and Chad came to my rescue. I was certain I had missed the big announcement.

Betty shook her head. "No. He disappeared . . . like the rest of you."

"What do you mean, like the rest of us?" I asked, guiding her behind the chairs Tuck had indicated. I had stared at the body long enough and was grateful to leave such matters to the professionals.

Betty's red lips pulled into a frown. "Well, one minute you were all frantically decorating your gingerbread houses, and the next thing I knew, the stage was empty." Her eyes locked onto mine, willing me to explain myself.

"I think you know that I was the last contestant to finish," I reminded her, remembering her telling me how the others had finished before me. I then filled her in on what had happened to me since leaving the bake-off stage.

"That's frightening," she offered, casting a covert glance at the men kneeling beside the body. "But how did you and Rory come to be in the hotel library in the first place?"

I pointed to the mistletoe hanging from the celling in answer to her question. "A romantic gesture gone awry."

Betty sighed as she gave a sympathetic shake of her head. She placed a hand over her heart as she looked at the man in question. "Leave it to Rory to be romantic. I mean, what are the odds of you two finding a dead body? I hope this moment doesn't linger — you know, scar either one of you for life? That would be a pity."

Pity? More like a private hell. Why did she have to say that?

Before I could banish the thought, Rory came walking over to us. He looked troubled. "Doc Riggles has just uncovered something. You were right about Chevy's hand. There was something clenched in his fist."

"Don't tell me it was my cookie?"

"No." He shook his head. "It was a note. It said, and I quote, *Meet me under the mistletoe.* Someone lured Chevy here, and I think they might have been using your cookie as bait."

My mouth dangled open in shock and revulsion. "What are you saying?"

"I'm saying that Doc Riggles found a note and confirmed that Chevy was indeed eating a cookie right before he was murdered. Your cookie!" He lowered his voice. "Lindsey, I think Chevy thought he was sneaking away to this private little corner of the hotel

169

to meet you."

For the second time since discovering the body, I wanted to gag.

CHAPTER 20

The moment Sergeant Murdock arrived on the scene the investigation began in earnest. Chevy, having been declared dead by Santa, aka Doc Riggles, had been removed to the county morgue. The suspected cause of death had been a blunt-force blow to the back of the head. In other words, Chevy likely never saw it coming. Doc Riggles, still in costume, left shortly after the body. He would follow it to the morgue to conduct a more thorough autopsy. The perimeter of the hotel was then secured, and the Christmas Festival was officially cancelled. All parents with children had been allowed to leave, while the rest of the people in attendance were asked to give a quick statement to the police. What had started out as a day of fun and festivities had swiftly degraded into a tragic and tedious affair. The silver lining to the long line of festival-goers trying to get out the door as fast as they could was that plenty of gingerbread and punch were on hand. There would be no winner of the Great Beacon Harbor Christmas Cookie Bake-Off this year, not without our celebrity judge.

"I'm told that you and Mr. Campbell found the body," Murdock stated, looking all business in her crisp, yet slightly too tight sergeant's uniform. She was holding a pen and a notepad. "I'd like to know what time that was. I'm also curious about why you both came to this remote hotel library during the festival?"

"I brought Lindsey here," Rory told her.

"Any particular reason why?"

Although he didn't flinch, color rose to his cheeks. "The mistletoe," he informed her, pointing to the ball of festive greenery dangling from the ceiling on a red ribbon.

The sergeant looked to where he pointed, acknowledged the Christmas decoration, and nodded. "And how exactly did you know it was in here?"

"I found it by accident," he explained. "I was tracking one of the cookie-nappers who passed through here."

Murdock stared at him with her probing brown gaze. "Are you referring to the cookie-nappers reported by the Beacon Bakeshop?"

Rory nodded. We then told the sergeant all about the three mysterious women who had shown up during the Christmas cookie bake-off. Kennedy, whom I had been texting with since the police had arrived, was brought into the room for questioning as well. She and my parents had been so busy shopping at the little Christmas stalls that they hadn't noticed I was missing. They'd been waiting for the announcement of the bake-off winner, but it never came. When I called them, they were shocked to learn about Chevy.

"It's times like these I actually wish I had a child," Kennedy confessed, envious of the parents who had gotten to leave the stuffy hotel.

"You don't really mean that?" I teased. "That would require you to make a commitment, first to a man, then to motherhood."

"It was a joke," she snapped and rolled her eyes.

Murdock listened intently as each of us regaled her with our cookie-napper encounter. When I told her that I'd been locked into a basement storage closet, she stopped.

"Are you sure these were the same women who stole your signature cookies?" Her deep-set eyes had the look of a hungry bear, both curious and intimidating at once. Reflexively I shook my head.

"I guess the answer would be no, since we never saw these women before. We were simply going off what Mrs. Nichols was telling us."

"Interesting." Murdock made a note. Looking up once again, she queried, "If they had never seen you before" — she shook her pen at the three of us — "then why do you suppose they ran?"

"Guilt?" I ventured.

Rory raised a finger. "I second what Lindsey said. They were running because they were hiding something. Also, I wouldn't assume that they didn't know who Lindsey was. She was in the bake-off and owns the bakeshop they robbed."

Kennedy, with a straight face, offered, "I'm suggesting fear. Rory bears a remarkable resemblance to your fabled Paul Bunyan. That can scare a woman, especially those in middle age."

Murdock nearly cracked a smile but buried it deeper as she turned to Rory and me. "I'm not going to disagree with you. The matter of these three mysterious women is curious, but there's nothing yet to link them to the murder of Chevy Chambers."

"Rory and I saw two of the women in a heated discussion with Chevy," Kennedy offered.

"Well, now, that is something. Can you describe the two you saw?" Murdock asked.

"The first woman we went after was a platinum blonde," Rory told her. "She's the tallest of the three and the skinniest, with plumped-up lips and pumped-up breasts. She obviously has the best plastic surgeon. What?" he implored with a manufactured look of innocence. "You asked me to describe her."

"Cookie-napper number two," Kennedy butted in, casting a gimlet eye at Rory, "is shorter, bigger-boned, and has rather ordinary brown hair spruced with red highlights. She wore the same trendy black leggings as her leggy friend, and a similar pair of riding boots, but number two clearly wasn't wearing Spanx."

Still writing, Murdock lifted her eyes from the notepad to look at her. "Any other distinguishing features besides clothing, Ms. Kapoor?"

"Slight middle-age spread with visible cellulite."

Murdock, sucking in her stomach, set down her pen. "That's rather common in women over forty. I mean, distinguishing,

175

like a mole or a crooked nose."

"She did have glasses and looked a bit like Elton John, you know, with a wee gap between her two front teeth?"

Murdock smiled. "Excellent." She scribbled another line and shut her notepad. "I have to let you three know that you are not to leave town until given the okay. Also, if you remember anything else that might be important, call me. We'll get to the bottom of this murder, don't you worry. And, Bakewell, don't go sticking your nose into this one either. Just because you found the body doesn't make you a detective. Got that? The same goes for you two. This is a police matter."

Like a trio of mindless robots, we all nodded. Although I couldn't speak for Rory or Kennedy, I was fairly certain that I was lying.

CHAPTER 21

While Mrs. Nichols was being questioned, the three of us headed back to the ballroom to find Mom and Dad. Mom was in a state. Her face was pinched with worry, and she was wringing her hands as she leaned on Dad for support. Dad, used to the volatile nature of money and the making and losing of fortunes, was better at schooling his emotions. However, being sequestered in a crowded room had set his fingers drumming away on his jeans.

"I can't believe you two found the body," Mom uttered, looking ill. "What a terrible thing for you to see. The police don't think you had anything to do with this, did they?"

"He was sprinkled with cookie crumbs from one of my cookies," I explained. "And there was a note asking him to meet under the mistletoe. I didn't know there was mistletoe in that room until Rory brought me there."

"That's what you were doing?" I didn't like the look Dad was giving Rory. "In the middle of a Christmas cookie bake-off?"

"Dad," I admonished. Why did I feel like a sneaky teen plotting my first romantic interlude? I was a grown woman! I ran my own business! Flustered, I uttered in my defense, "Well, we obviously didn't do anything. Chevy's dead body kind of ruined the mood. By the way, Rory and I are still on the suspect list."

"But you didn't know about the mistletoe," Mom reminded us.

"Rory did, I didn't. However, I can't really prove that either. They're just going to have to take my word for it. Sergeant Murdock is starting to warm to me, but she's a by-the-book kind of gal. Nope, the surest way off the list is to —"

"Find the killer," Kennedy finished for me. I noticed that her attention was on the stage. The bake-off was over, but I saw that my fellow bakers were still up there, sitting glumly by their baking stations. The woman who held Kennedy's interest was none other than Felicity Stewart.

"Linds, we've given our statements. Don't you think we should pack up your baking supplies and go home?"

"Good idea."

Mom and Dad waited by the giant tree as we went to get my things. I waved to my fellow bakers as I climbed the steps.

"Heard you found the body." Bradley shook his head, relaying how sorry he was, and got off his stool. "Is it true? Is it really Chevy Chambers?"

I nodded.

"Lindsey, what happened?" Ginger asked with heartfelt concern.

As I gave them all the edited version of what had happened, omitting blood, cookie crumbs, the note, and the fact that I'd been locked in a closet, I noticed that Felicity was strangely quiet. Her eyes flashed my way as she nervously picked hardened royal icing off her countertop. She would have deconstructed her entire gingerbread house, I mused, if Betty hadn't removed them. All the showstoppers were gone. Once the police had arrived, they'd been offered up as beautiful, candy-coated fodder for the festivalgoers stuck in the ballroom. I didn't mind. Although it had taken me a long time to construct, it was being put to good use.

"He was murdered?" Bradley looked astonished. "How? When?"

I shrugged. "You know as much as I do."

"Do you find it a little ironic that he was murdered before the winner was announced?" Ginger looked more miffed than saddened by Chevy's untimely death as she asked this. "Is it just me, or does anyone else think that's crappy? We've been baking our hearts out all day up here, and what do we have to show for it?"

Felicity piped up. "We'll never know who the winner is now. However, I feel that I must speak up here. I have it on good authority that I was to be the winner."

"What?" Ginger flushed with anger. "That's outrageous! How can you say that? I have it on equally good authority that I was going to win. You all saw my showstopper. Chevy loved it. It was a gingerbread version of Harbor Scoops. I even had little candy ice cream cones on it!"

"Lindsey, were you supposed to win too?" Bradley's brown eyes narrowed in question. "I'm not blind, you know. I saw the way Chevy was flirting with all of you ladies. I'm the only dude up here, and I can honestly say that I wasn't told I was going to win."

"Well, I was. He loved my figgy bars with hard-sauce glaze. Figgy pudding is a well-loved holiday tradition —"

"Not in this country or century, sister," Ginger cut in with a bite of pure attitude.

Felicity huffed. "I don't expect you to

know anything about holiday traditions. Stick to ice cream toppings. Chevy was a real professional. He had to rank my figgy bars fourth just to make it seem like a fair competition."

Although Ginger and I nearly gagged, Bradley didn't. Instead, he stared at her with rapt curiosity. "How so?" he asked.

"Because he knew that my gingerbread chalet was going to be the best showstopper. How could it not when I'm the best at Christmas cheer and holiday bedazzlement?"

Ginger held up her hand as her face pinched with disgust. "I just threw up in the back of my throat! You make me gag. Literally!"

Rory stepped forward. "Everyone, calm down. The competition is over. Did you ever think that all of you are the winners? You four are the best bakers in this village. End of story. I think it's time for everyone to clean up and go home."

Felicity, visibly unsettled by the thought, shook her head and walked back to her bake station. She was about to start packing up when I noticed that something on her busy countertop was missing.

"Felicity, where's your cute rolling pin — the one with the gingerbread men on it?"

"It's here," she affirmed with miffed certainty and began looking around. But after a moment of searching, she couldn't find it. "I must have misplaced it . . . unless you took it, Lindsey. I saw the way you were eyeing it."

I raised my marble rolling pin. "I have my own, thank you."

"No. Seriously, it's gone." Panic seized her. "It was an antique. That rolling pin was my grandmother's. This isn't funny. Did one of you take it?"

We all looked at one another. Ginger was shaking her head. "Why would someone want to steal your ugly rolling pin?" she challenged. "You must have misplaced it."

It was an antique, " Felicity cried, horror-struck. A helpless look crossed her face. "It's one of a kind."

I looked at Rory to see if he had any thoughts on the matter. It was then that we both noticed Kennedy. She was standing near the edge of the stage texting on her phone.

"What are you doing?" I asked, coming up beside her. Rory stood on her other side.

"Putting two and two together. Missing rolling pin and a murder victim with a bashed-in head?" She waved her hand, then continued texting. "Unless we are mistaken, the murder weapon was missing from the crime scene. I'm asking Tuck if the missing rolling pin could be our smoking gun." She sent the message. A moment later, her phone beeped signaling it was answered.

"What? What did he say?" I was a little disturbed she had Tuck's number readily on hand.

She glanced at her phone then looked at us. "It can't be confirmed yet, but he thinks it's a strong possibility. He's passing it by Doc Riggles just in case. Also, Mrs. Nichols is with Sergeant Murdock. She's been asked to identify the cookie-nappers in the line of people waiting to give statements. She hasn't seen them yet."

"They could still be here." Rory came alive at the thought and turned his sights on the long line of festivalgoers waiting to leave the building. Thinking again, he shook his head. "If one of them is our murderer, she wouldn't wait in that line."

"Tuck wants to know if we've spotted them." Kennedy, knowing the answer to this, thought to ask us just in case. "Aside from Mrs. N, we now have the dubious distinction of being able to identify them as well." With a sarcastic smile, she said, "Ooo, lucky us."

"We might know what they look like," I

offered, "but we still don't know who they are. What I'd like to know is, why are they targeting me for their dirty work? First, they steal cookies from the Beacon. Then I have reason to believe that one of them might have used my bake-off cookie to lure Chevy Chambers under the mistletoe. Those women are really getting under my skin."

"You're not the only one, Lindsey dear. Tuck believes they've slipped out of the hotel. There's no sign of them anywhere." Her large dark eyes held to mine as she shook her head. "Missing rolling pin, missing cookie-nappers, and a dead celebrity food critic? This isn't the ordinary holiday I'd been expecting. But I like it."

184

CHAPTER 22

Thoughts of the day's events swirled in my mind as I drove back to the lighthouse with Rory sitting shotgun beside me. It was late in the day. Mom, Dad, and Kennedy had a ten-minute start on us, but I didn't care. I needed time to think.

There was so much to consider, including the way the Christmas cookie bake-off had just ended without a clear winner. Was Chevy murdered because of the bake-off? He was, after all, an integral part of it. The celebrity food critic had traveled from Chicago to our small village to help drum up interest in the town-wide Christmas cookie bake-off and then the climactic live bake-off at the Christmas festival. Everyone had been so excited, especially Felicity. She had wanted to win. Heck, we all had wanted to win. So, why had Chevy been killed before the winner was announced? That made no sense.

If Chevy had announced the winner before he was murdered, then there might have been a motive for his death. I hated to admit it, but tensions had been running high since the bake-off had been announced. It had inspired healthy competition, and at times some not-so-healthy competition. But even now I couldn't imagine that one of us would actually do the deed.

I thought about our village and about the three other bakers who had competed beside me. Ginger Brooks came to mind first. She was not only my friend, but she also owned a successful business in town. Her ice cream shop was a town staple, a go-to for tourists and residents alike. It was true that during the winter months she struggled. Ginger was also a single parent of a twelve-year-old daughter. Would she risk everything to kill the food critic before the winner of the bake-off was announced? Again, not very likely.

Then there was Felicity Stewart. I'd known her for a while now, and we normally got on just fine, except during the holidays, as I had painfully learned. Owning a year-round Christmas shop, her biggest season was in the fall, topping out at the day after Thanksgiving until Christmas Eve. I couldn't really blame her for wanting a little extra attention by luring more Christmas shoppers to town with a Christmas cookie bake-off. It had been her brainchild, after all. Of course, she wanted to win the whole thing, but would she kill Chevy Chambers — the man she'd been flirting with all week — right before the winner of the bake-off was announced? I couldn't see it. Felicity wanted the glory of a win and bragging rights.

Then there was Bradley Argyle. He was the only man, and the person I knew the least about. What I did know was that he appeared to be a stand-up guy, and his cooking was sublime. He was a successful chef working at the hottest hotel restaurant around. Why would he jeopardize a brilliant career by murdering a narcissistic food critic — before the winner of the bake-off was announced? That would be bonkers, and Bradley didn't appear bonkers.

Then there was another oddity to consider. Chevy had made every woman in the bake-off believe she was going to win. Felicity thought she had the competition in the bag. So did Ginger, apparently. Heck, I did too. Bradley was the only one not promised a win because Chevy wasn't schmoozing him. However, Bradley's Christmas cookie had won the first round of the bake-off. That suggested Chevy Chambers knew how to do his job. When push came to shove — regardless of his flirting and false promises — he had picked arguably the best cookie of the bunch. Bradley was winning. I didn't think that was a motive for murder. Puzzled by the thought, I shook my head.

"Thinking about Chevy?" Rory asked, noticing that I was unusually quiet.

I nodded and turned my attention back to the road.

"Me too," he said. "I'm also struggling with the very pressing fact that I'm starving. Hear that?" He placed a hand over his growling belly. "No more cookies. I need food. I never expected to be at the hotel for so long."

"I'm sorry." I took a hand from the steering wheel and placed it over his. "Here's the good news. I can solve your hunger problem. I have a giant lasagna in the fridge ready to go into the oven, and a salad waiting to be tossed. Dad is making his famous garlic bread, and Mom has prepared a beautiful charcuterie board for us to nibble on while we're waiting."

He exhaled loudly, as if a pressing weight had been lifted from his shoulders. "You're the best. Also, I can't believe that my romantic efforts were thwarted again by Chevy Chambers. The moment he came to town, all anyone could think about was this crazy Christmas cookie bake-off. It's occupied your every thought since it began. The guy has some nerve getting killed under my mistletoe."

He was joking, of course, but there was some truth to his frustration. "Well, you did succeed in surprising me. Gave me the shock of my life," I admitted, pulling the Jeep into the boathouse that was now my garage. Dad's rental car already occupied the other bay. I turned off the engine and unbuckled my seat belt. "There's no mistletoe in here, but I'm willing if you are?"

Rory offered his heart-melting grin and leaned across the center console. I leaned in too, inching my lips ever closer to his. They were about to touch when his stomach rumbled.

"We should go inside," I offered.

"Not yet," he said with a determined set to his jaw. He cupped my face in his hands and slowly brought his lips to mine, both of us fighting to ignore his rumbling belly. I silently wished that I could turn off my ears. That wish became void the moment the Jeep gave a violent shudder.

"What the . . . ?" Rory looked at me.

The Jeep rocked again.

"Not me. Wellington!"

Dad must have let him out when he saw my Jeep in the boathouse. Welly, prone to serious bouts of separation anxiety, was standing on his hind legs, peering at me through the driver's side window. His doleful brown eyes were imploring me to get out and feed him. To illustrate just how much he missed me, he began to whine as he licked the frosty window, streaking it with drool.

"That's going to be fun to scrape off once it freezes."

"Welly, down!" I commanded and heaved a sigh of relief when my dog obeyed. I cast Rory a look of apology. Once again, our quiet, romantic moment had been thwarted, this time by a ravenous Newfie.

"I better get you both some food," I told him, reaching for the door handle. "You are about to pass out from hunger, and Welly's about to lick the paint off the Jeep."

Dad, bless him, had already put the lasagna in the oven, and Kennedy was working on the drinks when we walked in. She handed us each a mug of mulled wine and slipped Welly a treat. She then shooed us to the living room. "You've been baking all day," she remarked. "James has got this."

Dad, hearing his name, looked up from the mixer and nodded. He was whipping up his special garlic herbed butter to lather on the crusty Italian loaf.

"I would say that I was helping, but this is the extent of my domestic abilities." She lifted a mug of mulled wine.

Rory grinned and took a sip. "Aren't you going to make someone a good mommy." Before Kennedy could reply, I pulled him into the living room.

Rory and Welly spotted the charcuterie board on the coffee table at the same time. Rory plopped down on the couch and began helping himself, while Welly, using a tried-and-true canine strategy, sat at his feet with imploring eyes. It was certain to land him a piece of cheese, and quite possibly some fancy sausage meat as well.

Mom, looking as tired as I felt, smiled the moment we came into the room. She was sitting by the fire, cocooned in the puffy armchair with both little dogs in her lap. Brinkley and Ireland lifted their heads in greeting, then plopped back down, lulled back to sleep by the gentle touch of Mom's hand. I sat down beside her.

"I'm sorry things got so out of hand today," she said, mindlessly stroking each little dog. Their white fur matched her angora sweater. "You worked so hard. I was sorry to see your beautiful gingerbread lighthouse broken into pieces before anyone could properly admire it."

Mustering a gallant smile, I offered, "True. But what is gingerbread for if not to be eaten? Although, I do have to admit it would have made a pretty awesome centerpiece for my Christmas Eve dinner. We'd, of course, have eaten most of it by the end of Christmas Day."

She smiled at this. "Your father would have said the same thing." She stopped petting Ireland, who was closest to the end table, and reached for her phone. "Here, I took a picture of your showstopper before they destroyed it." She found the picture and handed me the phone. I had to admit, it was some of my best work. Seeing it on the table made me wonder what would have happened if Chevy hadn't been killed. Would I have won? Would it have been Ginger or Felicity? There were a hundred what-ifs.

"What a marvelous job you did, Lindsey. I can't believe it was all made out of cookies and candy. I wish you could have seen the children's faces when they brought it out. All the gingerbread houses were truly impressive, but one little boy declared yours the best he'd ever seen."

I looked up from my mulled wine, thinking of all the planning and hard work. "Thank you for telling me that."

Mom placed her hand over mine. "There's a murderer running loose in this town, Lindsey. What brazen person would strike in the middle of a Christmas festival? It rings of desperation. I'm sorry that you and Rory discovered the body, but I think you should let the police handle it from here."

I could see how troubled Mom was by the thought of murder in the small village of Beacon Harbor. Murder happened all the time in New York City, and there were probably a few in Palm Springs, Florida, as well. But Beacon Harbor was a small, close-knit community, and the thought had her on edge. The real reason was that it had struck too close to home. What I didn't have the heart to tell Mom was that Chevy had been eating one of my cookies when he was killed. And what about that note? Who did he think he was meeting under the mistletoe? I looked at Mom and nodded.

"That's wise advice, and I'll do my best to heed it. I promise I won't let this ruin our perfect Christmas."

"I'm not worried about Christmas, dear. I'm worried about your safety."

CHAPTER 23

Mom had a good point. I should just forget about the terrible murder of Chevy Chambers and leave it to the police to solve. They were the professionals. They should be able to figure it out . . . eventually. However, there was one giant problem with Mom's advice. I couldn't follow it. It would be like asking me to unsee Chevy sprawled on the floor beneath the mistletoe sprinkled with cookie crumbs. It had been burned into my memory — at Christmastime, no less. The only way I could get the horrible vision out of my head was to try to make sense of it. And in order to do that, I was going to have to think about Chevy and why someone would feel compelled to end his life in such a manner. Another fact that was urging me on was that someone at the Christmas Festival had done the deed. Who? Why? I had no idea. It was a mystery. It had piqued my curiosity, and I could no sooner turn that off than I could turn off the moon.

Therefore, the moment everyone had retired to their respective bedrooms, I got into my flannel pajamas, climbed beneath a pile of warm blankets, and invited Welly on the bed to join me. Although I had left him all day in the company of the models and had given him a scrumptious dinner of kibble and roasted chicken breast, he was longing for some cuddle time. It was our nightly ritual. He would snuggle with me for a while before retiring to his own bed at the foot of mine.

"I'm just going to see if Rory's awake," I told him, opening my laptop. At the mention of the name, Welly picked his head up and looked at me with his soft, bear-like eyes, as if to ask, *Where? Where's Rory?* I ruffled his head and began to type a message to his second-favorite human.

Captain Rory Campbell, I typed, using his military rank to grab his attention. Although he seldom used it, I was proud of the fact that he was a captain. *Are you still awake, dear captain?*

Of course. I've been waiting for you. And, like you, I'm thinking about Chevy.

I smiled at his words. He knew me so well. *Couldn't talk about it tonight, not with Mom and Dad adamant we leave it to the authori-*

195

ties, I typed. *But I can't stop thinking about him, lying on the floor like that. Care to make any guesses as to who would do such a thing?*

There was a pause on his end, and then he typed the name I had been thinking about all day. *Felicity Stewart.*

Her name keeps popping into my mind as well. Do you think she was the one who lured him beneath the mistletoe?

His words flitted across the screen. *She'll deny it through her teeth, but I think the cookie-nappers were working for her. Mrs. Nichols kept spying them, which means they were watching the bake-off. I never thought to look, but Felicity could have been sending them hand signals or messages while she was baking. Her baking station was closest to the stage steps.*

She could have been, I typed back. *We were all so busy baking it would have been easy to miss.*

Also, those three women knew who we were. Every time they caught sight of me or Kennedy, they did their best to avoid us.

True, I replied, then added another thought. *We did think Felicity was behind the cookie-napping. She wanted to be part of the live bake-off come hell or high water. After our cookies were stolen, we dropped in the polls just enough for her to be in the bake-off.*

She couldn't very well steal them herself — too obvious — but she did try to have you disqualified as well, he reminded me.

She was also flirting shamelessly with Chevy the whole week, especially during the bake-off. I didn't tell you this, but at one point, when Felicity slapped Chevy, her husband had to remove her from the stage.

There was a pause. I could only imagine his shocked expression. Then he answered, *What? Why didn't you tell me this earlier?*

I forgot. You were off chasing a cookie-napper. It all started when Chevy called her use of fondant on her gingerbread house lazy. She flipped out and slapped him with her icing bag. She also threw a sheet of fondant at him.

Damn. Wish I had seen that.

It wasn't pretty. She was causing a scene, but the odd thing was, I typed, recalling the whole ordeal, *Chevy appeared to be amused by her anger. It was like he was pushing her buttons because he knew she would blow up at him.*

Very interesting. I can't imagine that sitting too well with her. Ms. Christmas Cheer gets yanked off the stage by her embarrassed husband. There's also the fact that her rolling pin went missing, which is a little suspicious

197

given the fact that Chevy was bludgeoned on the back of the head by an unknown object that fit that description.

Felicity appeared puzzled that it went missing, I reminded him.

Could be an act.

I thought a moment, stroking Welly's soft head. *Or,* I typed, *what if the cookie-nappers were trying to frame Felicity?*

Interesting. One of them could have written the note insinuating it was from her — especially if they had seen the blow-up.

Would Chevy be vain enough to believe Felicity would do anything to win, including a little romp under the mistletoe to change his mind about her gingerbread house?

Possibly. Or . . . and bear with me here, he typed, *but the blowup could have been an act — a little lovers' public foreplay?*

Eww, I pecked the keys, trying to push the mental image from my head. *But why kill Chevy and frame Felicity? If that's the case, one of the cookie-nappers would need to have issue with both Felicity and Chevy.*

True. But why was Chevy eating one of your cookies before he was murdered? Rory queried.

I stared at the screen and shook my head. I had no good answer for that. I took a stab with, *Because he liked them?*

Could be as simple as that, or something far more sinister. I say we sleep on it and go pay Felicity a little visit in the morning.

Sounds like a plan. But what am I going to tell my parents?

Lindsey, you're an adult. Besides, what harm can there be in going to the Tannenbaum Shoppe during the week leading up to Christmas? Before I could protest, he added, *Pick you up at nine.*

I couldn't say no, and I didn't have a good excuse. Rory knew the bakery wasn't open on Mondays.

As we said our good nights and signed off, I silently wished that Rory wasn't on the other end of my laptop, but rather in bed beside me. However, it was the holidays, and I didn't want to deal with all the curious looks and sly questions from Mom, Dad, and Kennedy. Also, we had decided to take it slowly. Having dated a lot of losers and realizing that I wasn't the best judge of character where men were concerned, I was still trying to figure Rory Campbell out. He liked his independence and could be a bit secretive regarding his freelance work with the DEA and the Coast Guard. I respected that. But still, there were times I wished we hadn't taken it quite so slowly. I sighed and gave Welly a big hug. Then I shooed him to his own bed and snuggled deeper into mine.

As my head hit the pillow and my eyes closed, I was relieved to find that the terrible image of Chevy Chambers was fading. Yet, just when I was about to fall asleep, another face popped into my head, elbowing all thoughts of sleep aside. I sat up and stared into the murky darkness as the sweet, faint smell of pipe smoke tickled my nose.

I sucked in my breath. "Captain?" I ventured. I rubbed my eyes and gasped when I opened them again. My heart leapt in my throat as I realized the giant face staring at me from the end of the bed was a dog's.

"Welly," I breathed with relief. The dog, hearing his name, took that as an invitation to join me on the bed. Maybe I had been dreaming. Maybe I hadn't really smelled the pipe smoke. After all, the captain and I had an understanding. My bedroom was off-limits. But even as I snuggled next to Wellington, allowing my pup to stay on the bed, the face that had pulled me from my sleep had bubbled to the surface again. It was unmistakable. So was the expression that flitted between anger and embarrassment. It was Stanley Stewart, Felicity's husband.

"Alright," I said to the empty space in my bedroom, half certain that the name had been conjured by a ghost. "Good point. I'll look into it, Captain. But please don't do that to me again."

CHAPTER 24

I was cleaning up the breakfast dishes when
I saw Rory's truck pull into the lighthouse
drive. Mom was scrolling through Facebook
on her iPad while Dad was reading the
news. Both had a dog on their lap, and both
were enjoying their third cup of coffee. Kennedy had gone upstairs to her room to do
some work. With everyone thus occupied, I
went to the closet and quietly grabbed my
coat. "Welly and I are going to run to the
grocery store," I said nonchalantly. "We're
almost out of coffee. Need anything?"

Four pair of eyes shot to me with interest;
two were human and two were canine.
Mom smiled and shook her head. Dad narrowed his eyes. "You're going now?"

"Best get there early, you know, before all
the good coffee is sold out."

Dad wasn't convinced, yet he said nothing as he patted Ireland and took another
sip from his mug.

Welly, feeling a bit superior, wagged his tail proudly as he slipped out the door with me. Once in the cold air, we dashed for Rory's truck. After settling my big dog in the back, I climbed into the passenger seat and winked conspiratorially at the driver.

"Gave them the slip, did you?" he teased with a grin. "Playing detective becomes you."

"Why, thank you, sir." I gave his hand a little squeeze.

We were just about to pull out of the driveway when the door behind me suddenly opened, letting in a burst of cold air and Kennedy.

"Seriously? You were just going to sneak out and leave me with them?"

I craned my neck to look at her. "I thought you were working?"

"I was dabbling, throwing my influence behind a new line of clothing called *Ellie and Company.*" She waved her hand as if I should have known. "Posted a pic of Wellington in his buffalo plaid coat. Irresistible. Planting a little last-minute gift idea for the dog who has everything." She ruffled Welly's head. "You're blowing up on the internet, my dear." Welly, not caring about such human things, gave her a shifty glance, then brought his eyes back to the man driving the truck.

"Also," she continued, "I overheard your parents making a lunch date with Betty Van-hoosen and Doc Riggles. It's a couples out-ing. It's either third-wheeling it with you two or fifth-wheeling it with them, and I'm not a sadist, darlings. Besides, I have a feel-ing you two are about to do some snooping around. Am I correct?"

Ignoring her comment on snooping, I asked, "My parents are having lunch with Betty and Doc?" I looked at Rory. "Does that sound right to you?"

Rory shrugged. "It doesn't sound weird, if that's what you're asking. They're all of a *certain age.* Do you want me to stop the truck so you can join them?" he teased.

"Step on the gas, Captain Campbell!" I mock-ordered. "I don't want to be involved in that lunch date. It's just that —"

"Betty's a gossip and Doc has examined the murder victim?" A sly, knowing look animated Kennedy's face as she spoke. "If I had to guess, I might be inclined to think that Ellie and James are snooping around too. And what better place to start than with the town gossip and the county medical examiner? By the way, where are we headed?"

Rory's eyes shot to the rearview mirror.

"The Tannenbaum *Shoppe.*" Instead of pronouncing the old spelling of the word as *shop,* Rory had chosen to pronounce it *shop-a.*

Kennedy nodded her approval. "Fabulous. Going for the jugular, I see."

The Tannenbaum Shoppe, residing in a charming Bavarian-style building, was awash in Christmas cheer. Outside on the snow-covered lawn, parents accompanied their children as they ran to pet live reindeer in a pen, or to climb on a replica of Santa's sleigh. Employees dressed like elves handed out hot cocoa with marshmallow goo dripping down the sides of the Styrofoam cups and a candy cane poking out the top. It was a happy, sticky mess. Wellington, who was on a short leash, wanted nothing more than to come nose-to-nose with a reindeer. Unfortunately, the reindeer didn't share his curiosity and sprang for the opposite side of the fence. The annoyed high school–age elf working the line yelled at me for the intrusion.

Kennedy, in a very New York city girl manner, held up her hand to him, stopping his tirade. "This dog is a celebrity," she told him. That was overstating the truth just a wee bit. To prove her point, she drew her phone and showed the kid an Instagram account featuring my dog. Maybe I'd been too busy, but even I hadn't known the account existed.

"Unlike fickle reindeer, children adore him," she told the elf. "He also smells better. Now, if you'll kindly take us to Ms. Stewart. She's expecting us."

I had to admit, Kennedy was good on her feet. Oozing confidence while spinning a pack of untruths, she had gotten the kid to leave his station and escort us through the main doors of the Christmas shop. He then ushered us to the front of the line at the very busy sales counter. Both registers were ringing up shoppers double-time. The team of gift-wrapping elves were doing their best to keep pace with the cashiers. We were getting dirty looks as our elf picked up the phone at the first register and dialed his boss.

"Ms. Stewart, there's a celebrity here to meet with you. I have him at register one." He then hung up the phone and took out his cell. Looking at Rory, he asked, "Can you take a picture of me with him?"

Rory, tickled by the request, gave a military nod. The elf knelt beside Wellington, put his arm around my dog's thick neck, and smiled. It was an utterly adorable moment. Kennedy, never one to miss a photo op, stood next to Rory and snapped a picture as well.

Taking his phone back, the elf checked out his picture, smiled, and thanked us as he headed for the door.

"This is going straight to Instagram." Kennedy raised a slender brow and set to work pecking the tiny keyboard with her thumbs. A few seconds later, she showed me the caption before launching Welly and the elf into the ether of the internet. *Santa's little helpers working overtime at the North Pole.* I had to admit, it made me smile.

A moment later, Felicity appeared. She saw us, stared at Wellington, and frowned. "I was told a celebrity was waiting for me."

I smiled a little too brightly. "Just us, I'm afraid. We'd like a word."

Noting the large crowd waiting at the registers, she nodded and indicated that we follow her.

"I've already spoken with the police," she informed us, sitting behind her red-painted desk. The edges were trimmed in white and had been painted with holly leaves. I had never been in her office before; it was anything but dull. Her crowded seasonal store was an overload for the senses, but her office was an oasis, offering subtle touches of Christmas that made you feel welcome and not claustrophobic. Although the walls had been painted white, red was her accent color. Judging by the wall behind her desk, she apparently had a thing for cardinals. Replicas of the bird were perched on a shelf, while above them hung a tasteful grouping of pictures depicting them in snowy winter landscapes, accentuating their stunning color. On the wall to her right was a gathering of pictures depicting snowmen and quaint villages covered in white.

The wall to her left was different. That wall was dedicated to her personal photos, each one depicting a happy family of four in idyllic outdoor activities — planting a family garden, playing on a beach under the summer sun, riding bikes on a country lane flanked by autumn colors, building a snowman on the edge of a barren forest in the winter. Felicity and Stanley were easy to recognize, even as they aged from their early thirties to the late forties. What I didn't realize was that Felicity had a son and a daughter. They were a handsome family, both children sporting the same rich shade of red hair as their mother. From the progression of the pictures, I assumed her children were in their late teens or early twenties. I mused at how the happy woman in the photos seemed so at odds with the desperate Christmas diva of the cookie bake-off. Trying to process it all, I cleared my throat, knowing that I had come here to ask questions.

"You have a lovely office." I thought it best to start with a compliment.

"I do," she agreed with hooded eyes. "And I don't appreciate you bringing that hairy beast in here with you."

"I told you to wait outside," Kennedy said to Rory.

"I meant the dog, you pack of imbeciles!" Felicity barked before Rory had time to react to Kennedy.

Teetering on the verge of giggles, I took the high road and feigned ignorance instead.

"Is it because of his size?" I asked while leaning forward. Although Welly was on his best behavior, he wasn't exactly the type of animal one put in their shopping cart and wheeled into the store, ignoring the *No Pets Allowed* sign. Unfortunately for Felicity, there wasn't any such sign posted at the entrance of the Tannenbaum Shoppe. That wasn't unusual. Beacon Harbor was a very pet-friendly town. I gave Welly a pat on the head for being so patient with us humans.

"He's a drooling Newfie," she stated, pointing out the obvious.

Seeing that Kennedy was looking at Rory

again, I jumped in with the offer, "I could shoo him out the office door, but I can't promise he won't lick a few ornaments while he waits."

She narrowed her eyes as she slowly shook her head, reinforcing our imbecile status. "You're missing the point!" she huffed. "Let's just get on with it, shall we? I assume you've come to ask me if I murdered Chevy." It was a blunt opening. Kudos to her.

"Did you?" Rory, getting the jump on Kennedy, used his most intimidating look on the woman. Unfortunately, Felicity was made of stronger stuff and refused to cave under his direct gaze.

"I'll tell you what I told Sergeant Murdock. No, I did not kill that man. Why would I? He was my friend. If you ask me, you two are the guilty party." She turned the tables on Rory and me with a look that was more darkly amused then probing. "After all, you two found the body. And, if rumor is to be believed, the poor man had crumbs from your bake-off cookie on him."

"How did you learn about that?" I asked.

"I just told you, the rumor mill. It works fast around here. By your reaction, I assume it's true."

"Well, by now everyone obviously knows

that we found the body, but we are not murderers. What motive do Rory or I possibly have to kill Chevy?"

Her response was a grin of pure smugness. I was sorry to think that New York Lindsey wanted to wipe it off with the back of her hand. Dangit! Why did this woman infuriate me so? I didn't come to pick a fight, I reminded myself. I came for answers, and I was going to get them.

Felicity tilted her perfectly coiffed head. "My guess is that you wanted to win the bake-off, like the rest of us, but you took it a step further. And you brought your henchman." She narrowed her eyes at Rory. "When you put pressure on Chevy and realized that he wasn't going to pick you, one of you killed him. My guess is that you did the deed, Mr. Campbell."

Rory, clearly not amused, told her, "I'm not even going to respond to that, Mrs. Stewart."

While the three of us argued our cases, each of us swearing innocence, Kennedy, I noticed, stood to the side in quiet observation. Waiting for the right moment, she finally pounced. "But you, Felicity, *were* having an affair with the man." It was spoken in the tone of common knowledge.

If Felicity's face had been flushed while

arguing her innocence, the mention of the affair opened the floodgates, turning her fine porcelain skin the color of Santa's hat. "What? That's . . . the most ridiculous thing I've heard yet. I'm a happily married woman!"

"Well, the flirting was obvious," Kennedy stated. "You were either lovers, or you were promising services you had no intention of delivering on. Either way, it sends a man a message."

"We were not having an affair," she affirmed.

"But you were close," I said, picking up on Kennedy's lead. "You were the one who brought Chevy Chambers to Beacon Harbor in the first place. How did you meet him?"

Felicity was quiet a moment. Then she exhaled and leaned back in her chair. "If you must know, we met in Chicago. I often accompany my husband there on business. It's the perfect getaway. Stanley meets with his clients, while I go shopping. At night we go out to dinner with clients or friends. The night we met Chevy Chambers we were dining with old friends. They were taking us to a new restaurant that had just opened. They told us that Chevy Chambers, the famous restaurant critic, was joining us for dinner. He was an acquaintance of theirs and would often invite them along when dining at a new place. Stanley and I were so excited when we heard the news. We met Chevy and realized that when dining with a famous restaurant critic, you get service and cuisine that is above and beyond the normal dining experience."

Felicity looked pointedly at me as she added, "You wouldn't know anything about this, Lindsey, being a mere baker, but dining with a celebrity foodie is quite a heady experience."

Although Kennedy smiled at her ignorant presumption about me, I took silent offense. The reason I owned a lighthouse in Michigan was because of a celebrity foodie, namely my ex-fiancé, Jeffery Plank. Felicity was correct. Professionals knew the ins and outs of a restaurant because it was their domain. They enjoyed food and knew the right dishes to order and the right questions to ask when visiting a new establishment. As fun as it had been for me, I was quite happy discovering my own path in Beacon Harbor.

"He was testing the menu and the service for his column," Felicity continued. "If he liked the place, he'd film an episode of his show, *Windy City Eats,* there. Chevy, as you well know, was a charming man. We instantly hit it off."

"Did he flirt with you — in front of your husband?" I asked.

She grinned like a mischievous child. "He flirted with everyone, Lindsey. But you might say that he had a soft spot for me."

Kennedy, in a lowered voice, whispered to me, "I'll bet he did."

"How many years ago are we talking?" Rory asked.

She shrugged. "Two years."

"And you kept in touch with him?" Kennedy cast her a suspicious look.

"I always knew that one day I could entice him to come to Beacon Harbor."

"Easier to carry on an affair that way, I'm sure." Kennedy, bless her, was being ruthless.

Felicity took the bait. She slammed her fist on her desk, causing Welly to flinch. His soft brown eyes shot to her and hardened a measure, as if sizing up a wily cat to be chased.

"How many times do I have to tell you? I was not having an affair with that man, nor did I kill him! I was a fan of his work."

Sensing that Kennedy was ready to go for the kill, I placed a hand on her arm, signaling for her to relax. "Very well. We didn't mean to rile you up. As you can imagine, his death during the Christmas festival has affected us all. I have another question for you. Did you have anything to do with the three women who came to the Beacon Bakeshop and stole my signature cookies?"

Felicity glared at me, then threw up her hands. "Are we back to this again? I didn't have anything to do with stealing your cookies, Lindsey, just as I didn't have anything to do with Chevy's murder."

"But your rolling pin is missing," I reminded her.

"That has nothing to do with this! My rolling pin was a valuable antique. Somebody obviously stole it. For the record, I've reported it missing. The police are looking for it."

Of course they were, I thought. It was the obvious murder weapon. But to Felicity I merely nodded. "Well, that's all we've come to ask you. I don't like the idea of a murderer running loose in our town right before Christmas any more than you do, I'll wager. Thanks for talking with us."

As we stood to go, Rory remarked, "Nice-looking family. Do your kids help with the store?"

Felicity turned to the wall of pictures. When she looked back at us, her face was a pale porcelain once again. "They used to.

This year they've decided to spend the holidays in warmer climates. Kara, my daughter, attends Arizona State University and will be spending Christmas with her boyfriend's family there. Kevin, my son, is in computers, like his dad. Yet instead of working with Stanley after he graduated, he took a job in Hawaii. He won't be coming home either."

The thought was obviously painful for her. Personally, I couldn't imagine spending Christmas without my family. "I'm sorry," I said and truly meant it. "That must be hard for you."

She gave a little nod. "The irony is that I started Tannenbaum because of them," she offered with a watery smile. "I'm going to guess that none of you have children yet, but let me tell you, Christmas is a wonderful time for a parent. There is nothing on earth to compare with the way a child's face lights up when reading books about Santa Claus, or the magic of presents under the tree on Christmas morning. Kara and Kevin used to love to help me decorate the house in anticipation of Christmas. Each year they made a special ornament for the tree. It was just one of our traditions. Cookies were another. My children loved helping me in the kitchen, making our favorite cookies for our family and our friends. Every year we threw a big party."

She paused a moment, her eyes misting over from the memories. "Everything was perfect. There was nothing to match the joy on their faces when carrying on our family traditions, silly as they might be. When I told Stanley that I was going to open a year-round Christmas shop, he laughed at me. But the kids loved the idea. They were still in grade school at the time. When they were teens, they used to work in the store dressed up as elves. But somewhere along the way, Christmas lost its appeal for them. They've rebelled against the holidays, and it breaks my heart. But what can I do? I still believe in the magic of the season." It was the first true thing I believed she'd said since speaking with us, and my heart ached for her.

"I do too," I confessed, then left her in the privacy of her office.

CHAPTER 25

In desperate need of a sugar buzz, we parked ourselves on a bench outside Felicity's shop with a cup of complimentary hot cocoa. Welly sat on the packed snow at my feet, staring at me as I took a cautious sip. I removed my glove, plucked a sticky marshmallow off the top, and offered it up as a treat for being a good boy. I took another sip and said, "She's definitely lying."

My dog was working Rory over as well, but he was made of stronger stuff. Giving him a pat on the head instead of a marshmallow, he asked, "You think Felicity murdered Chevy?"

Kennedy turned to him and rolled her eyes. "No, silly. About the affair. Possibly about the murder, and most definitely about having children." This last remark earned her a hardened stare.

"Don't get your knickers all in a bunch, Rory dear. I'm joking. Although I did find

218

it sad that *Mommy Cheeriest* drove her little holiday helpers away at her favorite time of year."

"I do too," I agreed, recalling Felicity's face as she talked of her children. The fact that both had ditched her at the holidays was sad, if not telling. "You know what I think? In a weird way, I think this could be about Felicity's children. She knew they weren't coming home for Christmas. Think about it. What if she was trying to prove to them that they *should* have come home? Maybe that's why she felt the need to have a Christmas cookie bake-off a week before Christmas. According to Felicity, Kevin and Kara loved baking Christmas cookies. What better way to make them take notice of their home, Beacon Harbor, than having their mom head up a town-wide Christmas Cookie bake-off that was to be judged by celebrity foodie, Chevy Chambers? Of course, Felicity would have to win to prove her point to her children — the point that she really is the queen of Yuletide splendor."

"You think *Mommy Cheeriest* was trying to make them jealous — trying to make them believe that her Christmas was going to be better than theirs?"

I nodded. "Yeah. Something like that. Remember, the cookie bake-off was her idea in the first place. Sure, it really could have been about boosting foot traffic in the town during the run-up to Christmas, as she had told the Chamber of Commerce and the festival committee. But maybe it was also about shining the spotlight on her at Christmastime. This is Felicity's holiday, after all. Anyone who owns a year-round Christmas shop must walk the walk, you know?"

"Not going to argue that," Rory agreed.

"Imagine being one of her biological little holiday helpers," Kennedy said. "Imagine the horror of growing up in a home where Christmas music is played all year, living with candy cane décor, and where Santa and his elves are always watching."

Although she was just speculating, I cringed just thinking about it.

"And being forced to drink hot cocoa with candy canes and marshmallows in the summer instead of Kool-Aid, or water," Rory added with a disparaging shake of his head.

"Look, we can all imagine that she's not an easy woman to live with. But it really is December. Christmas is just around the corner, and her children aren't coming home. To Felicity, a self-proclaimed Christmas aficionado, not having her family with her at Christmas has got to be the biggest blow to her heart and ego."

Rory gave a subtle nod. "Might explain how strangely desperate she's been acting."

"And we all know that desperate people do desperate things." Punctuating this sentiment, Kennedy crumpled her empty cocoa cup and threw it in the trash can closest to the bench. She peered back at us with eyebrows raised. She was trying to be sly, but her marshmallow mustache ruined the effect. Knowing that Rory would let her walk around like that all day, I handed her my little napkin square.

"Thanks." She mean-smiled at Rory before picking up the thread of our theory. "When her plans went awry, and she knew she wasn't going to win the bake-off, she might have taken matters into her own hands. Imagine sleeping with that wanker, Chevy Chambers, just to win a Christmas cookie bake-off?"

"I've known people who've done more for less," Rory added nonchalantly.

"I'm sure you do, darling. After all, whatever happens at deer camp stays at deer camp, isn't that the motto?"

"Hey," I said, forcing Kennedy's attention back to the matter at hand. "Remember, Felicity has emphatically denied having an affair with Chevy. She claims she's happily married. But whenever she was around

Chevy, she didn't act like she was."

Kennedy nodded. "Here's another thought. What celebrity foodie would travel all the way to this little frozen dot on the map to judge a cookie contest if he wasn't getting a little nookie on the side?"

Rory drained his cup. "She's got a point."

"There is one person who might be able to weigh in on this discussion with a bit more clarity. Last night, just before I fell asleep, his name popped into my head."

"You better not say Santa," Kennedy warned.

"No," I chided. "Stanley Stewart, her husband. Yesterday, when Felicity was going after Chevy at the bake-off and you two were chasing cookie-nappers, Stanley stormed onto the stage and carried her off to save her from further embarrassment. I say we pay Mr. Stewart a visit."

All I knew about Stanley Stewart was that he was married to Felicity and had a software company somewhere in Traverse City. I didn't know where his company was or what it was called, but I did have a pretty reliable source to help nudge us in the right direction. With the heat blasting in the pickup truck and Bing Crosby singing "White Christmas" on the stereo, Rory drove in the direction of Traverse City while I dialed Betty's number. The phone had barely rung before she was on the other end.

"Lindsey!" Her voice was over-bubbly. "What a surprise."

The clanking of glasses and dishware in the background told me she was at a restaurant. The unmistakable sound of my mother's laughter was telling as well. "Have I caught you at a bad time?" I asked.

"Oh, no. I was just . . . I was just . . ." The woman was stumped. She was obviously having lunch with Mom and Dad but didn't want to admit it to me. I caught my dad repeating my name as my mother laughed again. Betty, bless her, tried to muffle the phone. Her voice echoed loudly as she finally settled on, "I was just wrapping a few presents."

Really? Wrapping presents at a restaurant? Betty was a terrible liar. And why was she lying to me in the first place? What were they hiding? I had a suspicion that they were snooping into Chevy's murder behind my back — and after Mom had told me to leave it be. The nerve!

I could have rattled her, stating that I knew she was with my parents, but I decided to let her continue with her little charade. "Cool," I replied. "Go sparingly on the tape.

Nobody likes a lot of tape on their presents. Hey, I have a question. Stanley Stewart. Where does he work?"

"He owns a company called Tartan Solutions —" She wasn't finished talking, but I had all I needed. I shot a "thank you" in before ending the call.

"That was awkward," I remarked, pulling up the website for Tartan Solutions on my phone. I loaded the directions into Google Maps and placed it in Rory's cell phone holder. "We'll be there in twenty minutes."

I hadn't realized it from the website, but Tartan Solutions was an impressive business. The investment banker in me knew that tech companies were hot commodities, but they came and went on the fickle tide of the economy. Tartan Solutions, from all appearances, had weathered that tide. Set a few miles outside of the downtown business district on a rolling five acres of land, Tartan Solutions operated out of a modern, four-story glass and steel building, one that I believed had been specially built for Tartan Solutions. Stanley Stewart wasn't some lone-wolf programmer, as I had imagined him to be, but he was the CEO of an impressive tech company. All kinds of questions popped into my head as Rory parked the truck.

Kennedy stepped out, zipped up her coat, and sniffed the icy air. "Ooo, I smell money."

"You can smell that from here?" Rory looked amused.

"It's more of a sixth sense, darling," she admitted. "Most women are born with it." She slowly raked him with her dark eyes. "Maybe not Lindsey."

"I can smell it," I said. "But I prefer to make my own." I cast Rory a wink.

Welly was going to need to stay in the truck for this one, but he was already sprawled across the back seat, assuming his nap-time position.

"Not sure what to expect here, but I hope Stanley will give us more insight into his wife's relationship with the food critic. There's something about Felicity and Chevy's relationship that doesn't sit right with me."

"Probably because it ended in murder," Kennedy remarked, heading toward the stylish building.

CHAPTER 26

Stanley Stewart's office was on the fourth floor. Having gotten through security, and after Stanley agreed to meet with us, we were greeted by a young woman as we stepped off the elevator. I might have thought she was his daughter had I known better. The girl looked to be in her mid-twenties, with a slight frame and mid-length dark hair tinted bright red. She had multiple piercings in her ears and a small diamond stud popping out of her right nostril. Her nails were painted black, perhaps to match her short black sweater, black tights, and ankle-length black boots. Her skirt, however, or what little there was of it, was a bright Stewart plaid.

Her blue eyes, aggressively rimmed in black, took in the measure of us. "Hey-ya. I'm Alyssa." I was surprised to note she had a Scottish accent. Or maybe it wasn't so surprising for a company named after a multicolored Scottish fabric. "He's busy, so yer lucky he'll meet with ya today. This way."

We marched down a long hallway behind the girl, around a corner, past a wall of windows, to a large area that was reminiscent of a trendy loft apartment. Along the far wall was a modern kitchen sporting a large refrigerator, cement counters, sink, microwave, and what looked to be a specialty beer on tap. A long island counter separated the kitchen from the rest of the room. There were leather chairs and couches, tables, and two arcade video games. On the other side of this impressive room sat a very messy desk with two large monitors.

"Your desk?" I asked our moody guide.

She glared at me. "Not fer yer eyes, lady!" she snapped, and turned one of the monitors just enough so I couldn't see it. I took that to be a yes. Apparently, Alyssa, although privy to one hell of a private kitchen-lounge area, preferred Red Bull, black coffee, and Sour Patch Kids candy to real food.

"I wasn't . . ." I was about to say "looking," but it didn't matter. She walked past the desk to another door. She gave a knock before opening it.

"Hey, that baker's here," she announced with a lack of enthusiasm, then stood aside to let us in.

"Impressive setup you have here," Rory said, extending his hand to Stanley. "We haven't met. I'm Rory Campbell, the baker's friend. This is Kennedy Kapoor, her other friend."

Stanley stood and took Rory's hand. "Sorry about that. Alyssa can be a little curt, but she's a whiz at computers."

"I picked up on that," Kennedy remarked with a hint of sarcasm. "It was the whole *Girl with the Dragon Tattoo* vibe she puts off. Edgy, smart, and with a truckload of daddy issues."

"She's joking, of course," I told Stanley, noting that he couldn't puzzle out if she was or not. "Thanks for seeing us on such short notice. Nice place you have here."

The perplexed look on his face melted away. "Lindsey, nice to see you again. Please, all of you, take a seat."

We removed our coats and sat in the proffered chairs. I silently marveled how our host, well into his late forties, had the perpetually youthful appearance of a gangly teenage boy who'd recently filled out. He was tall, slender, with light brown hair gelled to perfection and hazel eyes that sparkled with intelligence behind wire-framed glasses. To break the ice, I asked the question, "What exactly does Tartan Solutions do?"

"Mostly software," he replied.

Rory, no stranger to technology, sat back in his chair and crossed his legs. "What's your niche?"

Stanley, momentarily taken aback by the question, raised an eyebrow. "Agriculture in general, but our niche, as you put it, is small batch, locally sourced alcoholic beverage production. Microbreweries, wineries, and producers of popular spirits, like whiskey, vodka, and gin, have become a booming business, not only in Michigan but elsewhere. Our name Tartan, like the woven fabric of intertwining colors, represents the many intertwining stages of beverage production, from the farms that grow the hops, grains, and malted barley, all the way to bottling and distribution, be it beer, whiskey, or wine. Beverage makers are artisans, but most are at a loss when trying to manage a business. Our software is designed to harvest data and streamline payroll and expenditures while optimizing profits. We also provide web services and web hosting in house. Then there's —"

"Whoa, fella!" Kennedy, smiling coyly, held up her hand. "You had me at 'wine.'" She honed her smile in like a laser. "I don't suppose you have any on hand for sampling, do you, Stanley? A nice full-bodied spicy red with notes of Christmas?"

To our amazement, Stanley leaned forward. His lips twitched into a grin as he said, "But, of course. Alyssa would be happy to pull such a bottle from our collection."

I didn't know how she did it, but Kennedy had him in the palm of her hand. As Stanley made the call, I cast my friend a look that screamed, *Really?* Her reply was a look that suggested, *Why not?* The conversation had gone off the rails. I cleared my throat and addressed Felicity's husband.

"None for me, thanks." Rory refused the wine as well, stating that he was driving. "While you and Kennedy wait for your wine, I'd like to ask you a question about your wife." Stanley raised a brow in question. "I don't know how to put this, so I'll be blunt. Was Felicity having an affair with Chevy Chambers?"

My question landed like a painful slap in the face. For one tentative moment, I thought he might throw us all out of his office. But then he did something even more surprising. He threw back his head and laughed. I assumed he thought the notion ridiculous, until he reined himself in and said, "Of course she was. She didn't bother to hide it."

Shocked, I asked, "And you know this for a fact?"

"Are you asking if I caught them doing the deed?"

"It's just that, well, Felicity has emphatically denied having an affair."

"Blagh!" he spat. "She was lying to you. She lied to me. But Chevy wasn't lying when he bragged to me how he was banging my wife. The smug bastard. Can't tell you how many times I paid for his dinner in Chicago, and this is how he repays me?" For the first time since we arrived, Stanley looked truly upset.

Rory and I exchanged a look, prompting me to ask, "When did he tell you this?"

"At the Christmas Festival." Stanley grew quiet a moment, his brows furrowed in thought. "I've been so busy with work lately. Felicity runs the Christmas store. It's her baby. She's good at it. I honestly never thought there'd be a problem. But then Kara, our daughter, called at the beginning of December saying that she was spending Christmas in Arizona. Felicity pleaded with her, but Kara wouldn't budge. Shortly after that, Kevin, our son, backed out of Christmas as well. He's working in Hawaii. Told him I'd fly him home, but once he heard that Kara wasn't coming, he didn't want to either."

Kennedy crossed her long legs, stared at him, and tilted her head. "Any guesses as to why?"

A bubble of derisive mirth escaped his lips. "Yeah. The drama. Christmas at our house isn't" — he looked at us and drove his point home with — "normal. We have seven huge, fully decorated Christmas trees in our house, each one with a different theme. Seven! Who does that? When the kids were little, they honestly didn't know which tree Santa would place the presents under. We have special holiday music for every day of the week leading up to Christmas — can't play them out of order or you'll get in trouble. Then there's the fifty thousand Christmas lights, the Christmas cards, the barrage of specialty holiday foods, the weird cookies, and the matching Christmas sweaters that we're required to wear. It's always an over-the-top production put on by Felicity, for Felicity. The rest of us are miserable. But we grin and push through it." He plastered on a grin for effect and swung a determined fist across his body. His grin faded to a grimace. "This year, however, the kids bailed on me."

Rory shook his head in silent solidarity.

"Man, that's rough."

Stanley appreciated the gesture. He leaned forward and lowered his voice. "True confession? I've been hiding out here. And Alyssa isn't my assistant. Jane is, but she's taken the week off because of Felicity. Knows how crazy the woman gets. Alyssa doesn't know any better. She's a new hire, a programmer who specializes in imported Scotch. That edgy child out there has imbibed more of the stuff in her twenty-five years in Scotland than most middle-aged men. I can't tell if she's sober or not, but I'll tell you one thing. She isn't intimidated by Felicity."

Kennedy nodded her approval. "Stanley Stewart, I underestimated you. You've put a whiskey-swilling hound at your door. But let us back up a moment. Are you saying that your wife had an affair with Chevy Chambers so that she could win the bake-off?"

It was an uncomfortable conversation, but Stanley was willing to talk and we were willing to listen. He looked at Kennedy and nodded. "It sounds crazy, but I believe the thought of spending the holidays without the kids really got to her. I didn't know how much until I observed my wife shamelessly flirting with that little scumbag in front of everybody at the bake-off. But I never guessed that she was actually sleeping with him. That's not like Felicity. She can be a little crazy at the holidays, but I love her. She's crushed me, you know?"

"But I thought you said that she denied having an affair?" I reminded him.

He shook his head. "Of course, for the sake of our marriage, she has to deny it. But Chevy wasn't shy about admitting to the affair. Can't tell you how angry I was when I confronted him."

I looked at him. "Was that before or after you pulled Felicity from the bake-off stage?" I thought this an important question to ask. Chevy had disappeared after inspecting everyone's gingerbread showstopper and had never returned.

"After," he replied glumly. "Felicity and I have been married for thirty years, and to my knowledge she had always been faithful. But watching her up there making a fool of herself really made me wonder. Then, when she slapped Chevy, I knew that I had to do something. I pulled her off the stage to calm her down but realized how distraught she was. That's when I went to find Chevy. I wanted a private word with him."

I honestly thought Stanley was on the cusp of admitting to the murder of Chevy

Chambers. I had it on good authority, namely Kennedy, that Murdock and McAllister hadn't pulled him in for an interview yet. He had given his statement yesterday, like the rest of us, but he must have left his private conversation with Chevy out of it. Now he was with us, laying his soul bare. Rory held the man in his calm, collective gaze while Kennedy squeezed my hand.

Stanley continued. "I found him at the end of a long hallway standing in a private sitting room . . . a library, I think it was."

I shot Rory a covert glance, knowing that he was thinking what I was thinking. Stanley was describing the room where we had found Chevy's body.

"He was shocked to see me."

"I'll bet he was." Kennedy, hanging on his every word, cast him a knowing look.

"But he knew why I was there," Stanley added. "Probably thought I wouldn't have the nerve to confront him. I'm a techie, not a fighter." He held up his hands as if to illustrate that fact. "However, it was my wife he was messing with. When I asked if he was sleeping with her, he didn't deny it. In fact, he did the opposite. He grinned. I wanted to wipe that condescending look of pity right off his face. He then told me that my wife's desire to win the bake-off was greater than her respect for our marriage." He looked at us, mustering all the rage he had felt. "He then had the nerve to tell me — the nerve to admit — that he couldn't pass up such an opportunity."

"What a class A creeper!" I exclaimed. "It might be hard to hear this, but we all had a feeling that Felicity was on the take."

Stanley, his face flooded with the memory of his anger, held up his hand. "No. I mean, she obviously thought that she was, she was that desperate. But Chevy did something far more despicable. He admitted to me that he was only using her, knowing that she would sell herself for the win. But he had no intention of picking an inferior baker over an expert just because she slept with him. If she earned it, so be it. But if not, he wouldn't ruin his reputation because some hussy thought he could be bought."

Terrible as the revelation was, it was all beginning to make sense. "So, that was what the fight was about? Felicity hit Chevy with the frosting bag because she realized that he had no intention of letting her win?"

Stanley, looking ill at the mere memory, nodded. Then his eyes flashed to the door. Alyssa had arrived with two glasses of wine.

Stanley waved her over and took one. Without waiting for Kennedy to join him, he pressed the glass to his lips and drank it down in four large gulps. Kennedy, bug-eyed, gave him a wineglass salute.

Rory and I were still trying to process what Stanley was telling us. Rory, with a distasteful grimace, needed to be sure of what he had just heard. He leaned in and asked, "Are you suggesting that Chevy coerced Felicity into sleeping with him to win the bake-off but never had any intention of letting her actually win it?"

Stanley set down his glass. "That's exactly what I'm telling you. That man deserved what he got."

In a calm, level voice, I offered, "So, you knocked him on the head with your wife's rolling pin to teach him a lesson." It all fit together so well — a slighted husband, a cheating wife, and a ruthless cookie judge . . .

"What? No!" Behind the wire-rimmed glasses, his eyes looked like ginger cookies, they were so large. "Oh my God! You think I killed him? Is that why you're here?" Unbelievably, it had just dawned on him. "I thought this was just small talk. You know, being relatable with a prospective client? I thought you were interested in our software for the bakery."

Kennedy, dumbfounded, lowered the

wineglass from her lips and looked up at him with her large dark eyes. "Sorry, Stanley, boy, she's not. Didn't you kill him?"

Stanley shoved his chair back from his desk with shocking abruptness and stood. We all watched in silence as he strode to the window, glanced out at the snowy landscape, then turned to us. "I think you all need to leave."

We got to our feet, but none of us was ready to leave. "Look, Stanley," I began, "we're not the police. We're just trying to figure out what happened to Chevy Chambers."

"I didn't kill him," he stated again, his face flushing with anger. He took a deep breath and added, "I might have wanted to, but I didn't."

Rory, holding him in a scrutinizing gaze, asked, "What stopped you?"

Stanley shrugged. "Cowardice. That and the fact that there was obviously another person he was waiting for."

Shocked, I asked, "Did you see this person?"

Stanley nodded.

Kennedy set down her wineglass. "Was it Felicity?" She was ready to be scandalized.

But Stanley shook his head, knocking the hopeful look off my friend's face. However, what he said next shocked us all.

"It was an older woman who had come for him. I could tell the sight of her frightened him, and I didn't know why. She looked harmless enough to me. What business did Chevy have to be afraid of a short, portly woman dressed like Mrs. Claus and carrying a cookie?"

CHAPTER 27

We couldn't get out of Stanley Stewart's office fast enough. The poor man might not have seen any harm in a short, portly woman dressed like Mrs. Claus visiting the cookie critic, but we sure could, especially since Stanley had described Mrs. Nichols to a tee.

"Are we sure he didn't mean Betty?" Rory voiced the question we were all mulling over in our heads. We were driving down Grandview Parkway in Traverse City, heading to Wags Dog Park, a place I had been wanting to take Wellington. It was thirty degrees with a light snowfall, the perfect weather for my dog to romp around in while we tried to clear our heads. "She was playing Mrs. Claus to Doc Riggles's Santa," Rory continued. "Betty's old and portly."

"Stanley Stewart has lived in Beacon Harbor a long time," I reminded him. "He'd know Betty Vanhoosen. She practically runs the town. And she's not old and portly, Rory. Betty's middle-aged and pleasantly plump."

Rory shrugged. "Same difference. But there have to be other older ladies who fit that description."

Kennedy, with a glass of red wine coursing through her veins, leaned her head over the front seat between us. "Doubtful Betty knows how to use a rolling pin. Mrs. N, on the other hand —"

"Okay, let's just stop thinking about this for a moment." I couldn't hide the anxiety in my voice. Truthfully, I didn't even want to entertain the thought that Mrs. Nichols might be involved.

Rory took his eyes off the road long enough to cast me a questioning glance. "Lindsey?"

"I've had enough snooping for one day, and I think Mom was right. I don't think we should pursue this. Chevy was murdered. This is a matter for the police."

"I know what this is all about." Kennedy, still resting her crossed arms over the front seat, looked at me as only a friend could do. "This sudden call-off-the-dogs about-face has nothing to do with murder. You're Lindsey Bakewell. You like being snoopy. You like poking your nose into other people's business. It's essentially what an investment banker does," she added breezily, as if she knew. Apparently, that's all she had picked up from our many conversations on the subject. "This sudden change of heart is about losing the best assistant baker you've ever had."

Leave it to her to hit the nail on the head. I knew it wasn't right to just drop the subject, but I suddenly lost my appetite for cookie bake-off justice.

"It's the holidays," I protested, feeling a panic attack coming on. "I'm swamped at the bakery. Cut me a break! That woman — although mysteriously appearing on my doorstep — is a godsend."

"And possibly a sly murderer." With another pointed look, Kennedy sat back, settling in her own seat next to Welly.

"Look, it was all fun and games while we were investigating Felicity. Then Stanley had to ruin it by dropping that little brain bomb on us. If he is to be believed, Mrs. Nichols approached Chevy Chambers in the very sitting room he was murdered in — carrying a cookie, no less!"

"He could be wrong," Rory added, although his tone lacked conviction. "Look, Mrs. Nichols was standing at the foot of the stage the whole time."

"That's mostly correct," I told him, feeling a wave of dread wash over me. "When Chevy went missing, Mrs. Nichols did too. The whole day while I was baking, she was spotting cookie-nappers, sending you two all over the hotel to find them. I even went after one of them myself and got locked in a storage closet. But before that, there was a point during the bake-off when I noticed that she had disappeared for a while. I grew nervous thinking that one of the cookie-nappers had gotten to her."

"I remember," Kennedy chimed in. "You sent me to look for her. I found her standing near the ladies' room. Whatever else she had gotten up to before then is anyone's guess."

What Kennedy had said got me thinking. The truth was, I had no idea what Mrs. Nichols could have gotten up to the moment I left the bake-off stage to chase after the woman she had pointed out to me. I'd been gone awhile that time, having been locked in a closet. I wasn't sure how much time had passed from that moment until we found the body in the library. The unknown was too daunting to consider, and thankfully I didn't have to consider it for very long. Wellington's anxious whining had reached a hypercritical level. The reason he was making so much noise was because we had pulled into the parking lot of the dog park and he could see the other dogs playing in the fenced-in yard.

"Look," I said, as Rory parked the truck. "We've peered under the lid on the proverbial Pandora's box that is the Chevy Chambers murder investigation. Let's give it a rest a moment before we throw it open and release Christmas chaos on my bakery and possibly the entire town of Beacon Harbor as well."

Rory turned to me and grinned. "I know you, Lindsey. Your curiosity is going to get the best of you."

With a grimace of my own, I relented. "Alright. But we're going to need to think this through. And Kennedy, don't you dare text Tuck with this latest development until we give you the okay."

"What?" She looked offended. "I wouldn't dream of it." Although she sounded convincing, I didn't know if I could trust her anymore where Officer Cutie Pie was concerned.

"This is our lead," I reminded her. "Mrs. Nichols is an elderly woman and my employee. She deserves the benefit of the doubt. Also, James and Ellie are to be kept in the dark about all of this as well. We don't want to create any more Christmas drama than necessary."

"Gotcha." Rory gave a heart-melting smile of approval. "I guess that means we'll be meeting tonight in the usual place?"

I nodded. "Dress warm. It can be a bit chilly this time of year."

At dinner I realized that Kennedy and I weren't the only ones keeping a secret. I had made a hearty dish of creamy Tuscan chicken over penne pasta. It was one of my favorite go-to meals. It looked beautiful, tasted amazing, and wasn't too hard to throw together in a pinch. My version called for plump, pan-fried chicken breasts in a garlic cream sauce flavored with dried tomatoes, spinach, and my special addition of mushrooms. When served over pasta, it was hard to resist. Although my parents loved Tuscan chicken and enjoyed the meal, they managed to evade the question of how they had spent their afternoon.

"We were sightseeing," Dad had said when I asked him. "Traveling down memory lane. I had forgotten how beautiful this part of Michigan can be."

Mom had smiled and patted his hand. "Your dad even admitted to me that he missed Michigan winters. Can you imagine?"

I really couldn't, although I had to agree that Michigan was beautiful in all seasons.

Any mention of lunch with Betty and Doc was strategically left out, and it made me wonder what they were up to. Sure, I could have pried, but I thought it best to let it go. When they asked how we had spent our afternoon, I told them, "We took Welly to a new dog park in Traverse City. We had lunch there too. It was loads of fun." And that was the end of that.

Rory had graciously bowed out of another family dinner, claiming that he needed to get some work done. I also suspected that he was doing a little poking around on the internet before tonight's meeting.

After dinner, we played a round of euchre over hot cocoa and cookies. My parents were on a roll and soundly beat Kennedy and me. The dogs were taken out for their nighttime romp in the snow, after which Mom and Dad retired to their room on the second floor, with the models trotting happily behind them up the stairs.

Once they had settled down, I made another thermos of hot cocoa and grabbed three mugs. Kennedy, being the savvy diva that she was, laced it with peppermint schnapps before the lid went on, then plucked a can of whipped cream from the fridge. I placated Wellington with a cookie before putting on my coat. Then, with fortification in hand, we headed for the light tower stairs.

"I've been waiting for a good excuse to climb up here," Kennedy said, reaching the lantern room. "Ooo, I like what you've done to this place."

In the summer months, the lantern room was my favorite place to hang out. Sitting high above the lighthouse, and with a three-hundred-and-sixty-degree view of Beacon Harbor and Lake Michigan, the views were amazing and the sunsets spectacular. It was the scene of many romantic dinners, as well as a place to talk, to reflect, or to be alone with my thoughts. In keeping with the season, I had brought up a space heater to take out the chill. I had also hung some holiday greenery and placed flameless pillar candles around the edge of the circular glass window. My four white wicker chairs now sported red-and-white plaid cushions, each with an accent pillow depicting either Santa or one of his reindeer. I kept blankets in a wicker basket on the floor next to the wall where the old blackout panel had been. In the old days, the blackout panel had protected the lighthouse from the bright revolving light. But the great Fresnel lens had been decommissioned long ago. It now resided in the boathouse, along with the recently removed blackout panel. Beyond the glass, a full moon illuminated the ice-covered shoreline and the cold, midnight-blue lake beyond. It was a stark, dramatic sight. However, a quarter turn from the frozen lake and a stone's throw inland, the view was something quite different. Bright, colorful Christmas lights shimmered on a blanket of snow, transforming the village of Beacon Harbor into a winter wonderland. The sight was breathtaking. Kennedy, filled with awe, heartily approved of both the view and my sparse, yet cozy Christmas décor.

"I call Santa," she announced, removing said pillow and plopping in the chair. We had no sooner poured two mugs of spiked cocoa topped with a swirl of whipped cream when we heard Rory climbing up the wrought-iron steps.

"Ladies." He tipped a pretend hat to us the moment he appeared in the lantern room. When his eyes landed on the mugs of cocoa in our hands, and the empty mug reserved for him, he smiled. "Hope there's something a little stronger than hot cocoa in there. I have a feeling it's going to be a long night."

"Let's start by writing down the facts as we know them."

We had all settled into our respective chairs as I opened a leather-bound notebook. It had been a gift from my old boss, specially made to look like an authentic lighthouse logbook. I kept it in the lantern room for inspiration, never thinking it would be used to sort out suspects in a murder investigation. I flipped it open and gave it a dramatic title: *Murder of Christmas cookie critic, Chevy Chambers.*

After writing down the details of Chevy's death — the remote library where we found the body, the note in his hand, the suspected cause of death, and the fact that he had crumbs from my cookie on him — we began adding our own information.

"Felicity was having an affair with him," Kennedy noted.

"Suspected affair," Rory corrected as I added her to the list. "Suspected because she's denied it. The fact that Chevy bragged about it to Stanley might suggest it was an act of revenge for something else we don't know about. Why else would he throw it in Stanley's face like that, angering him? What did he have to gain?"

For the first time, I thought about the possibility. "It does seem odd."

"They knew each other, remember?" Rory paused to take a sip of his cocoa. "Stanley remarked about having bought him dinner on several occasions. We know from Felicity that they met Chevy in Chicago through mutual friends. Maybe there is a business connection we don't know about."

I wrote Stanley's name in our suspect book. Twirling the pen between my fingers, I added, "Chevy obviously knew how desperate Felicity was to win the live bake-off and possibly took advantage of her. But you're right. Why would he promise her a win and not follow through with it? That seems unusually cruel."

"Hard to believe anyone would be that much of a wanker." Kennedy, having plucked a blanket out of the basket, wrapped it around her legs. "Recall, if you will, Stanley Stewart's bread and butter. His 'niche,' as you called it, is micro brewed spirits. What if there was a kerfuffle over a bad review of one of Stanley's clients? Stanley retaliates in some way, and Chevy counters by manipulating Stanley's wife? He wouldn't have to sleep with her to do it either. He already knew Felicity was a nutter about Christmas. All he'd have to do was encourage her a bit, and *boom!* Bob's your uncle! Everyone thinks she was having an affair with him, including her husband."

We all agreed it was a possibility. I made a note of it, adding my thought about the three cookie-nappers. If Chevy was trying to embarrass Felicity, he would need her to be in the live bake-off. He could have hired the women to steal my cookies, which had effectively taken the Beacon Bakeshop out of the competition for one day. That had been enough to let Felicity and the Tannenbaum Shoppe rise in the polls. But Chevy was dead, and the identity of the three women remained a mystery.

However, there was another name we needed to add to our list, a name we'd all been tiptoeing around. Rory, rising to the challenge, was the first to address the troubling matter.

"If Stanley Stewart murdered Chevy Chambers, why did he tell us about the woman Chevy was waiting for, the one who fits the bill for Mrs. Nichols?"

I shook my head; Kennedy picked up the thermos. "I'm going to need more zippy cocoa to wrap my head around this little mystery, darlings."

Rory and I watched as she emptied the last of the spiked cocoa into her mug. It only filled half of her cup, a fact that was swiftly hidden by an equal measure of whipped cream.

"What?" she challenged. "Are you going to remark on my abuse of canned whipped cream as well?"

"Wouldn't dream of it." Rory plucked the can from her grasp. "Just hoping you didn't hog it all." He then proceeded to shoot a stream of it straight into his mouth.

"Like that's not disgusting." Kennedy laid on the attitude.

Rory, with a conspiratorial grin, handed me the can. A shot of whipped cream was just what I needed. "When in Rome," I said, and pulled the trigger, so to speak. After my whipped cream shot, I handed the can back to Kennedy.

"Why not?" she proclaimed and joined us.

After emptying the entire can of whipped cream, we were finally ready to face the name that bothered me most, namely that of Mrs. Nichols. I scribbled her name in the logbook, then added her background information, namely her sudden and timely appearance at the Beacon Bakeshop. She was a skilled baker, knew every Christmas cookie recipe by heart, and had a knack for filling the bakery cases. She told me she had come from "up north," but she had never stated the town. She said she was staying with a friend, but she'd never told me her friend's name. Shame on me for not prying. Sure, there was her instant dislike of Chevy Chambers and her subtle but telling remark that he was a very naughty man and ought to get nothing but coal in his stocking. But, really, I chalked that up to a killer intuition. On second thought, maybe "killer" wasn't the right word to use.

I lifted the pen from the page and looked at Rory. "You have to admit that she's so wonderful and jolly."

He placed his warm, comforting hand on my shoulder. "I know this is hard for you, Lindsey, but according to Stanley, Chevy was either shocked or frightened to see her."

"That's rather telling, given that her appearance is so harmless." Kennedy's expression softened. "You have to agree that her behavior is a wee bit odd, and that we don't know much about her."

"She's an older woman," I reasoned. "There's something charmingly nostalgic about the way she speaks and the way she dresses. Older people don't like change. Maybe Chevy's shock at seeing her was because he mistook her for the real Mrs. Claus. Chevy was definitely on the 'naughty list,' if you know what I mean." Although I was joking, I could see that both Kennedy

253

and Rory gave me an extra-hard stare. Rory gave my shoulder another gentle squeeze and took hold of my hand instead.

"It's important to remember that Mrs. Nichols answered your ad after the bake-off was announced, not before it. She would have known that Chevy Chambers was coming to town. Another odd fact is that it seems as if Mrs. Nichols is the only person who saw the three cookie-nappers, therefore she's the only one who can identify them."

Kennedy gave a nod of approval, adding, "This seems to be the case. As you might be aware, I talk with Officer McAllister on occasion. What? Don't look at me like that," she admonished as the corners of her mouth lifted coyly. "I'm sure I'm not the only one who likes a little candy at the holidays."

Rory bristled and raised our entwined hands. "This isn't candy. We're in a committed relationship."

She rolled her eyes. "I'm staying in the lighthouse. I know how much *candy* you two crazy kids are pinching. Boresville."

I was about to defend our relationship and the fact that fate had not been kind to our romance when she held up a hand to stop me. "Let me finish. According to Tuck, Mrs. N is the only one who can identify those women. Tuck believes they're not from around here, and neither is Mrs. N."

"What are you suggesting?"

Apparently, Rory was quicker to pick up on this little nugget than I was. With a look of gentle pity, he said, "What Kennedy is trying to say is that maybe the cookie-nappers were working for her the whole time."

CHAPTER 28

I didn't want to believe it, but it had to be considered. Mrs. Nichols had been the only one working at the Beacon Bakeshop when the three women came in and stole our cookies. If she had anything to do with them, why would she willingly sabotage our bakery? The day it had happened, she'd been distraught. Had it been an act? Then, at the live bake-off, she had spied each of the three cookie-nappers on separate occasions. Rory and Kennedy had chased after two of them, realizing that both women had confronted Chevy. It was Rory's opinion that these little run-ins hadn't been pleasant. I couldn't really say if the cookie-napper I chased had a run-in with Chevy as well. I'd been locked in a storage closet.

"If they were working for Mrs. N, they might have been delivering a message, one meant to poke away at Chevy's puffed-up confidence." Kennedy gave the air a half-hearted punch. "Getting in a few jabs before the knockout blow, so to speak."

It was an unpleasant thought. I stood up from my chair and looked out over the night-black lake. The vastness was what I thought floating in deep space might be like, only without a spectacular earthrise to focus on. Although secure in the lighthouse, I found the blackness daunting. "It doesn't make sense. Every time Mrs. Nichols spotted a cookie-napper, she grew agitated. I really don't think it was an act." I turned from the window, hoping for reassurance. Yet the questions that surrounded Mrs. Nichols were too great.

"It all comes down to the fact that we really don't know much about her," Rory said. "I even tried delving into her background on the internet while I was at home."

The look of uncertainty on his face did nothing for my queasy stomach. "Please don't tell me she has a rap sheet."

I was hoping he'd smile, allaying my fears, but his lips remained firm. "Honestly, Lindsey, I'm not sure. As you can imagine, there are a lot of Carol Nichols out there, but none that fit the description of *our* Carol Nichols. Granted, I didn't have much to go by. I suspect it might not even be her real name. But I did find something of interest." Rory bent down to pick up his laptop. He opened it, turned it on, and brought up the page in question.

"What are we looking at?" Kennedy stroked her chin as she focused on the screen.

"A possible link between Chevy Chambers and a woman I think might be Mrs. Nichols."

After a couple of hours of searching the internet for clues to the identity of Mrs. Nichols, Rory had come up with more questions than answers. He then changed course and began looking into Chevy Chambers. The man had a huge online presence. However, after sifting through the online articles, videos, and social media posts, he decided to go back even further and focus on the newspaper columns Chevy had written before becoming a famous food critic. That's when Rory stumbled on an old review written about a well-loved bakery in a small town in Michigan's Upper Peninsula. Chevy's scathing critique of the local landmark was hard to read. It was derisive, smug, and self-serving. Having firsthand experience owning a bakery, the mean-spirited review boiled my blood. Yet as bad as his review had been, it was his personal attack on the owner that I couldn't stomach.

"What a jerk!" I flopped back in my chair, feeling as if I had been kicked in the shin with a steel-toed boot. "How did he get that published?"

Kennedy was just as dumbfounded as I was. "Us Brits generally like a clever turn of sarcasm and snark in a review, which is all in good fun. But this here is a bloodbath." She looked at Rory. "You think this bakery has something to do with Mrs. N? I must point out that this article clearly states the owner's name as Patrick Wagner."

Rory nodded. "That's the issue. There's no mention of a Carol Nichols. I only point it out because it fits with her story. As far as I can tell, this bakery was the only one Chevy Chambers critiqued in the Upper Peninsula. Patrick Wagner could be her relative, or even her husband."

"Years have passed, and she's changed her name." I thought about it a moment. "You could be right. If she, in fact, had an issue with Chevy Chambers, I provided her with the perfect opportunity to get close to him again. Maybe the Mrs. Claus getup is a disguise, one meant to throw him off. Also, she helped me come up with my signature cookie, knowing it would be good enough to get me in the live bake-off."

A dark thought crossed Rory's face. "If she did have her sights on teaching him a lesson, we all could have been her puppets. Think of it. She swoops into the bakery and helps Lindsey get into the live bake-off. She fakes a cookie robbery, possibly to get Felicity into the bake-off as well, but also to draw attention to the fact we were robbed. Getting Felicity there is important. If Chevy's mode of operation is talking women into sleeping with him for the win, then Mrs. Nichols would know Felicity was being used. Look, the woman stated, and rather cryptically mind you, that Chevy Chambers was a bad man. Felicity might be her foil. Didn't we all jump to the conclusion that Felicity is the obvious choice for wanting to kill Chevy? Even the fact that her rolling pin went missing is suspicious."

"Hold up a second, Tex." Kennedy, embracing her phony American accent, wiggled her finger at him. "Are you suggesting that our sweet Mrs. N is a clever, diabolical murderess?"

"I'm just pointing out that, unlikely as it seems, it's not out of the realm of possibilities."

A self-deprecating huff escaped me. "I knew her sudden, timely appearance seemed too good to be true. I guess tomorrow at the bakeshop I'll have to confront her."

"What? No." Rory closed his laptop and gave me the full heat of his vibrant blue stare. "She could be dangerous, Lindsey. Don't let on that you suspect her."

"Dangerous? She's an old woman."

"One who knows how to use a rolling pin." Kennedy pointedly raised a brow before draining the hot cocoa from her mug. "Also, do try to get her address."

"What, so you can give it to Tuck?"

"Goodness, no." She feigned innocence. "This is our lead . . . well, it will be once you get it."

"Alright. I'll try," I said, although the mere thought of prying into Mrs. Nichols's private affairs gave me an unsettling feeling. As if reading my thoughts, all the flameless candles around the window flickered and went black.

Kennedy gasped. "What just happened? How could they all just go out at the same time?" She fumbled for the flashlight app on her phone. "This isn't funny!"

"Probably just my subpar batteries," I said, hoping to console her. However, Rory and I knew that the sudden blackout had nothing to do with batteries. A subtle scent of pipe smoke indicated that we were not alone.

"Did you just pull out a pipe?" She turned to Rory. "What's wrong with you?"

"I don't smoke," he told her, packing up his laptop bag.

The candles flickered back on. Kennedy spun around, her large eyes wildly inspecting the candles. "What the heck?"

"Time to leave," I said, casting Rory a covert glance. "It's late, and I have to get up in a few hours. Those donuts don't make themselves."

It was either something we said, or we had overstayed our welcome. Either way, Captain Willy Riggs had arrived to stand the graveyard watch.

CHAPTER 29

What was Mrs. Nichols doing meeting Chevy Chambers in that remote hotel library? It was this question that robbed me of sleep. The gingerbread showstoppers had been about to be judged, arguably a hard job. Everyone, including Felicity, had created an amazing and delicious work of art out of cookie dough, frosting, spun sugar, and candy. Adrenaline had been running high, the baking competitive. And Chevy had been flitting about, flirting with the contestants, and disappearing to parts unknown. So much had been going on around me during the Christmas cookie bake-off that it was hard for me to make sense of it all.

I was trying to quiet my careening thoughts, but it was proving hard to do. I was worried about Mrs. Nichols and the fact that I'd been so trusting of her. For instance, every other employee that I had hired had been required to fill out the proper paperwork, the W-4s and the I-9s, including a full name, address, and date of birth. There was a process to running a business, and it had all gone out the window when Mrs. Nichols appeared. She had started right in, taking over my kitchen like a tidy tornado. I knew she lived with a friend but had never bothered to ask after her friend's name, or an address. We had never discussed salary. Friday morning, when my entire staff had their checks electronically deposited, I counted out cash and gave it to Mrs. Nichols in an envelope. Dear God! I had paid her under the table! What the devil was wrong with me? I tossed and turned under the blankets, cursing my sugarplum visions. They had taken control and had clouded my judgment to the point of negligence. I would have to make it right.

After a night of restless sleep, I woke up realizing that I had overslept. I rushed through my morning activities, trying to make up the time. I was doing a good job of it, too, until the moment I let Wellington out of the lighthouse. Knowing that I was in a hurry, he took matters into his own paws and disappeared behind a large snow-bank, chasing after some unseen creature. I threw on a coat and chased after him, calling his name in a loud whisper. Ten minutes later, I found him waiting before the door of the bakery kitchen, his tail wagging with delight.

"Thanks for coming when you're called," I admonished sarcastically, knowing my snappy wit was lost on his fluffy, puppy-dog brain. I stroked his cold black fur. As if not to be bothered by my petty complaint, he tossed me a glance, then focused all his canine energy on the back door.

Wellington and I seldom used this entrance. It was mostly used for deliveries and employees. I didn't have the key on me but figured Mrs. Nichols had arrived and hadn't locked it. I was given to understand that people from *up north* weren't in the habit of locking their doors. Generally, Beacon Harbor was a safe place to live, but there was a murderer on the loose.

I made a quick survey of the dark driveway and parking lot, noting that there wasn't a car in sight. I blamed myself for not knowing how the woman got to work. I shook my head and opened the door.

The lights were on. It was a cold morning, but the kitchen was warm, indicating that the ovens had been on as well. And the most telling sign of all was the smell of fresh baked cinnamon rolls that hit me as we came through the door. That comforting yeasty, sweet bread smell was something I would never grow tired of. I called out her name as I entered the kitchen, but pulled up short when I realized that she was nowhere in sight.

I relaxed and told myself it wasn't the first time. I then marveled at the woman's productivity. Mrs. Nichols had already baked the gingerbread muffins and all the cinnamon rolls and pecan rolls. There were two trays of her scrumptious Christmas butter cookies, and on the back counter sat five round layer cakes, each one decorated like a glorious Christmas present.

"You've outdone yourself, Mrs. Nichols," I said to the room at large. Wellington, knowing that the kitchen was off-limits, had pushed through the kitchen door. I followed him out and spied the treat she had left for him on his mat behind the bakery counter. It was a gingerbread dog cookie. Lucky dog, indeed. As Welly gobbled up his cookie, I mentally berated myself for ever thinking that this generous and thoughtful woman could be involved in murder.

"Mrs. Nichols," I called out again, thinking it odd she hadn't replied, or at the very least, hummed her favorite holiday tune. Seized with a sudden, irrational fear, I threw open the door to the walk-in refrigerator.

I let out the breath I'd been holding. The refrigerator, aside from a vast number of dairy products, eggs, and produce, was empty. I tuned back to the counter. It was then I spied a note tucked under one of the beautiful cakes.

Sorry to have to leave so abruptly, but I have a matter to attend to. The donuts are in the proofing oven. Carol

The note was vague, perhaps by design, and I wondered if I'd ever see the old woman again. From my short time with her, she had always been punctual and professional. Leaving such a note seemed odd, and yet it really didn't. My entire experience with the woman seemed, well . . . odd. I half-wondered if she'd caught wind that we knew she was seen talking with Chevy right before he was murdered. But then why had she come back to the Beacon Bakeshop this morning? Duty, perhaps? Maybe the cakes and muffins were her way of saying good-bye. Either way, I found the whole affair a bit sad, especially since I didn't have a way to reach her — no address, no phone number, and maybe not even her real name. A derisive huff escaped me as I thought it was probably better this way. If she was somehow involved in Chevy's murder, my ignorance where she was concerned would save me the embarrassment of being the one to rat her out.

I cringed at the thought. No one who baked like she did could be evil. It made no sense. Yet I had little time to dwell over the note or Mrs. Nichols's sudden disappearance. I had a bakery to run.

"She what?" Kennedy blurted.

It was past eleven o'clock in the morning — well after my short staff meeting where I assured everyone that I was not a murder suspect this time, and after the morning rush, where gossip and wild theories about Chevy's murder had abounded. Kennedy, leisurely strolling in for her complimentary gingerbread latte and muffin (she was my houseguest, after all), had just heard the news about Mrs. Nichols.

I put my finger to my lips to keep her from bursting out again. Elizabeth, Wendy, and Tom were working with me. They were all very fond of the older woman. I didn't want them to worry.

As it was, Tom cast me a questioning look at her outburst before handing Kennedy her latte. She waved it off with a look indicating that I was the crazy one and shoved a fifty-dollar bill in the tip jar.

I lifted a brow at her. "Generous of you. Why don't you pick up your latte and muffin and come back to the kitchen with me?" She didn't need to be asked twice.

"What are you talking about — she just left a note?" Kennedy looked troubled by the news. "How are we supposed to find her now? And isn't it illegal in this county to employ someone without documentation?"

"She was in her *trial phase*," I said, knowing it wasn't a viable excuse, and handed her the note.

Kennedy ran her curious gaze over the words. "Well, we know she's not a psychopath. Her handwriting is so round and neat. I hear that's clearly a sign that one is not crazy."

I took the note from her. "You read that off the internet," I chided. "There's a lot of garbage floating around online. You're not being helpful. If Rory, with all his professional training, couldn't find any information on her, how are we supposed to?"

Kennedy took a sip of her latte and shrugged. "I'm sure somebody knows something about her." She took another sip and, as if a light bulb went off in her head, slowly set down her cup. "Oh my God!" she exclaimed. "I think I know." As if being stuck with a hot poker, she popped off her stool and headed for the door. "I'm going to need to pinch a couple of donuts," she warned, then ran back and grabbed her latte, leaving her muffin on the countertop untouched. "Be a dear and save that for me."

An hour later, Kennedy came strolling back into the bakeshop, looking like a cat that had lapped up all the cream before going for the dog's food as well. I couldn't say the look suited her.

"And here, I always thought you were the clever one," she said, handing me a folded piece of paper.

"Should I be impressed?"

"With my tactics, no. But my result speaks for itself. Go ahead. Open it."

To my utter surprise, an address of sorts had been scribbled on the paper. I say "of sorts" because all it said was *Candy Cane Cottage, Tall Pine Way.* The shocking part of it was that the note had apparently come from the desk of Sergeant Stacy Murdock. I looked at my friend. "I don't mean to pry, but did you really bribe the noble Sergeant Stacy with donuts?"

Kennedy blinked. "Of course not. The woman scares me." She then made a theatrical motion with her hand. "Follow me if you will. I remembered that everyone who

270

was at the Christmas festival had to give a statement to the police. A statement naturally contains contact information. I then remembered seeing Tuck talking with Mrs. Nichols. I put two and two together and went to see if he couldn't be moved to scribble an address down for me."

"Oh. So, you bribed *him* with donuts."

"The donuts, Lindsey dear, were not a bribe. They were for a much-needed energy boost. Don't ask any more questions. Just rejoice that I have an address for that cookie vixen, Mrs. Nichols."

CHAPTER 30

Rory studied the address in his hand and grunted. "This sounds totally made up. It's the type of nonsense somebody gives when they don't want to be found. There's no address, just a name, Candy Cane Cottage. It doesn't appear on Google Maps or any other GPS system. This is garbage." His eyes shot to the rearview mirror, where they met the equally dreamy blue gaze of Tucker McAllister. Rory's look, however, was gently rebuking. He then crumpled the note and tossed it in the back seat at the man who wrote it.

As Rory drove his truck down the highway, looking for Tall Pine Way, Tuck leaned his boyishly handsome head over the seat. He wasn't smiling. "You think taking statements at the Christmas Festival was a walk in the park? It was crowded, hot, and let me tell you that when murder happens around a room full of kids, parents aren't in a chatty mood. They want to get the hell out of there. Also, I think I have a good read on people. I can tell when someone is lying to me. I'll bet my badge that Mrs. Nichols wasn't lying. She held me in a look that reminded me of my grandma and said . . ." Tuck did his best granny impersonation, launching in with, *"I'm staying with a friend at Candy Cane Cottage. Do you know it? It's just off Tall Pine Way, dear."* He cleared his throat. "She said it like I should have known it. And I kinda do. I mean, I know Tall Pine Way, so it has to be here."

"I love your confidence, Tucker darling. But there's no need to bet your badge. Rory's just a bit chafed his technology has failed him. Technology is his sword and shield. Without it, he feels naked."

Rory, bless him, showed an impressive amount of self-control and didn't take the bait. Besides, Tuck wasn't even wearing his badge. It was late afternoon, and he was in street clothes, wearing jeans, a down jacket, and a skull-fitting knit hat. After giving Kennedy the address, Tuck had made her promise not to investigate without him. She hadn't revealed that little nugget to me until later — when Tuck showed up at the bakeshop. For him, it was a strictly off-duty outing since Sergeant Murdock wouldn't have approved. She was a by-the-book kind of cop, he explained, a fact I was well aware of. The sergeant was methodically going through statements and interviewing suspects, Felicity and Stanley Stewart being at the top of her list. I found that very interesting. However, the fact that I still hadn't heard a word from Mrs. Nichols had put my nerves on edge.

Tuck directed Rory to Tall Pine Way, an unpaved road a few miles out of town that wound through a thickly wooded area. It was a typical access road for vacation homes and secluded cabins. Each property had a cute little sign indicating the name of the cabin or the family who owned it. However, most properties had addresses as well. We drove up and down the road once, failing to spot a driveway leading to the Candy Cane Cottage. Tuck, sweating a bit in the back seat, asked Rory to make one more go at it. Rory agreed, and that's when I saw a little white sign partially obscured by a huge, snow-covered pine tree. The lettering had faded, but the candy canes, crossed like swords at the top, were, I felt, a pretty good indication we had found the right cottage.

"Well, I'll be damned," Rory uttered, and turned his big truck down the partially hidden, snow-packed driveway.

"I never knew this place existed," I said, catching my first glimpse of the dwelling.

"Neither did I," Tuck marveled, sitting easy now that he could keep his badge.

At the end of the long, winding driveway sat a tidy, turn-of-the-century cottage with plenty of curbside appeal. It was a small, two-story dwelling with a steeply pitched roof, a quaint second-story balcony, and gingerbread work at the eaves. The cottage had been painted white with green shutters, red trim, and a red front door. Flanking the door were two identical seven-foot red-and-white-striped candy canes, the arch of each one curving away from the door. They had been constructed out of plywood, yet the effect was charming and whimsical. Another pretty touch was that under every window was a flower box overflowing with poinsettias. Fresh greenery and wreaths added to the Christmas charm. In a funny way, it was exactly the kind of house I had pictured Mrs. Nichols living in.

Rory parked the truck, and the four of us walked up the wide steps to the front door.

I had no sooner knocked than the door opened, revealing my assistant baker. If she thought it odd that we had come to pay her a visit, she didn't show it. Instead, she smiled and ushered us inside as if she had been expecting us.

"I'm so glad you found the place," she said, whisking us toward the kitchen. "I just put the kettle on for a pot of tea." She pulled up a bit and turned around. "Or perhaps you would like coffee? I can make that too."

We assured her that tea would be fine. As we walked to the small kitchen in the back, I marveled at all the little touches of Christmas that held the eye, adding to the coziness of this cottage in the woods. My eyes lingered on the long, built-in bookcase that sat beneath a row of windows in the living room. The shelf on top provided space for a miniature Christmas village, a grouping of reindeer, Christmas candles, and a collection of Santas. There was a love seat and two plump chairs near the fireplace that reminded me of chintz-covered clouds. The curtains were white lace, and the fresh tree by the window had been wrapped in gold ribbon, hung with old-fashioned ornaments, and lit by tiny white lights. The room was like a nostalgic snapshot in time, and I found that I loved everything about it. I knew that Kennedy admired it too. The look on her face said it all.

"I never thought it possible, but this place reminds me of my gran's cottage in the

Cotswolds, only without the moldering thatch roof."

The moment we were seated around the little kitchen table, I felt like a traitor. And the feeling didn't lessen any as I watched our kindly hostess pour freshly steeped tea into fancy teacups. The tea smelled like Christmas, I thought as I took a sip from my own dainty cup. It was a delicious blend of dark tea leaves, orange rind, cinnamon, cardamom, and cloves, with just a hint of honey.

Because she was a baker, I knew she couldn't resist the impulse to set out a plate of cookies for us to go with our tea. This she did without hesitation, and they were delightful in their variety — iced sugar cookies, snickerdoodles, chocolate crinkles, Swedish sandwich cookies with currant jelly, lace cookies, orange-cardamom crisps, shortbread, Mexican wedding cakes, macaroons, peanut butter drops with chocolate kisses, Mississippi mud bars, lemon bars, and my personal favorite, seven layer bars. With her baking schedule at the Beacon, I silently marveled at how she had managed it.

"You've come about this morning. I'm sorry I had to leave so abruptly, but I knew you would find my note." She peered at me over her round glasses.

"I did, and I was concerned. By the way, your cookies look divine." Unable to resist, I plucked a Swedish sandwich cookie from the tray. It looked like a linzer but with a dusting of crystal sugar instead of powdered sugar. I took a bite, savoring the hint of ground almonds and the tang of currant jelly.

"I usually don't abandon my duty," she apologized. "But my friend quite suddenly decided to spend Christmas with her son and his family after all. I was hoping she would. Anyhow, once she made up her mind she asked if I could drive her to the airport this morning. How could I refuse a friend?"

"Very kind of you." Rory had been watching her closely. He gave a small nod before asking after her friend's name. Good move, I thought, and relayed my silent approval.

"She's letting me use her car," Mrs. Nichols added, pouring her own cup of tea. She sat down and joined us.

"The soul of generosity," Kennedy agreed. "And does your friend have a name?"

"Yes. Forgive me, Mabel Bennett. Her friends call her Bell." She paused to take a sip of her tea. "It's really quite sad when families are torn apart by silly, senseless squabbles. I told her to swallow her pride and visit her grandchildren. It's worth it in the end. Spoiling children at Christmastime is one of the great pleasures in life."

Rory, with a thoughtful look on his face, said, "I imagine so."

The sincerity in his voice sent my heart tripping away like the wings of a hummingbird. What was wrong with me?

"Someday you'll have children of your own, dear, and you will know what I mean." She spoke as if it was a certainty, before casting him a wink. Reflexively, or perhaps by design, his eyes shot to mine. The intensity behind them made my heart beat even faster, which I didn't think was possible. Kennedy, noting my dumb stare, rolled her eyes at me.

"Mrs. Nichols," she began, not caring a hoot about children and only mildly about Christmas, "I don't mean to be a bore, but we have it on good authority that you were seen with Chevy Chambers before he was murdered. Could this be true?"

Mrs. Nichols pursed her thin lips as she gave my friend an owlish stare. "It is."

Her frank admission sent my extremities tingling unpleasantly — as if I were standing on the edge of a cliff looking down. "You . . . followed Chevy Chambers to the library at the other end of the hotel?" My worst fears were coming true. Alarm bells sounded off in my head. They grew even louder with her next reply.

"Yes."

We'd been expecting a bit more of an explanation than that. Tuck's eyes narrowed in speculation as he leaned on his elbows. Obviously deciding to match her word for word he asked, "Why?"

"Because everyone else was."

He shook his neatly trimmed blond head — as if to dispel a tangle of pernicious cobwebs. "Mrs. Nichols, when you gave me your statement on Sunday, you never mentioned that you had a conversation with the deceased."

"I didn't think it was relevant."

"Not relevant!?" Tuck blurted. Kennedy slapped a hand on his shoulder, reminding him to use his indoor voice.

"Excuse me, but can you back up a moment?" Although Tuck had a legitimate complaint — and really, who thought the woman would omit such important information? — I was still stuck on that one kernel of information she'd dropped. Rory, obviously stuck on it, too, urged me on with his eyes. "You just said that everyone else was meeting with Chevy. I want to know, who else met with him during the bake-off?"

The round blue eyes behind the glasses homed in on me. "Chevy Chambers was a very naughty man." Her words were a little cryptic, I thought. Not quite what I was expecting. She then leaned forward, as if telling us a great secret. "He wrote mean-spirited reviews for perfectly good restaurants. He took pleasure in destroying the reputations of talented bakers and chefs. He had no right to judge your cookies."

Aha! I thought. This *is* about revenge. And who could blame her for hating the nasty food critic? I then reminded myself that she was my assistant baker. I couldn't bear the thought of losing her too. I swallowed hard and tried to make sense of what she was telling us. "So, you met with him in that private sitting room to give him a piece of your mind. We know about that. Stanley Stewart told us that he saw you coming to meet with Chevy."

"I'm sure he did. But don't believe everything Felicity's husband tells you. Chevy was taking bribes. He liked playing with people. A very naughty man."

"I have to agree," Rory told her. "Mrs. Nichols, you seem to indicate a familiarity with Mr. Chambers. Did you write him a letter asking him to meet with you?"

"No." She stood firm on her response.

He then asked, "How did you know where to meet him?"

She cast Rory a sly grin, then picked her teacup up by the handle with her pinkie finger extended, like Kennedy had a habit of doing. She took a languid sip before setting it back down on the saucer. "Felicity's angry husband," she said. "He was fit to be tied. I watched him slip away and decided to follow him . . . at a prudent distance, of course."

Tuck McAllister was sitting at the table sipping tea and taking it all in. However, the fact that Mrs. Nichols had followed Stanley Stewart — one of the prime suspects — made him slam his cup down with force. The poor man was having a bad day. "You followed Stanley Stewart to the library?" His face turned red with frustration. Mrs. Nichols politely nodded. "Well, did you hear their conversation, at least?"

"Oh no. It's not polite to eavesdrop, dear. Stanley was angry. I couldn't hear Chevy's voice at all. I waited until I thought they were done."

"So, Stanley Stewart didn't kill him?" It was a revelation for Tuck. I was certain he'd tell the sergeant this little tidbit of information.

"Not at that point," our hostess said.

"They both saw me coming. Chevy wasn't pleased."

I'm sure he wasn't, I thought. In fact, if Stanley was to be believed (and I was beginning to believe the poor fella), Chevy Chambers had appeared frightened at the sight of the older woman. It sounded laughable, until one thought that maybe there was a history there. Whatever Stanley's original motive might have been, the appearance of Mrs. Nichols had chased him away. But her story did coincide with what he had told us. I looked into her round, guileless face and asked, "Why did you confront him?"

"I was recalling him to his duty." Her answer was as straightforward as her expression.

"And how did he take that?" Tuck asked.

"Not well. Like most black-hearted people, he didn't like being revealed."

My hand flew over my mouth. I lifted it slightly to ask, "Did he threaten you?"

"Oh no," she assured me with motherly comfort, which, truth be told, wasn't very comforting at all.

By confronting the food critic in the very room where Rory and I had discovered his dead body, Mrs. Nichols had put herself in a precarious position. And as far as we knew, she was the last person to have seen him alive. What I still couldn't understand was why she had met him there in the first place. She said she was "reminding him of his duty." What on earth did that mean? Either she was as innocent as she appeared and just wanted a word with him, or she was an utterly diabolical murderess. This last thought was not sitting too well with me. I could feel a raging case of anxiety coming on.

But the hard question had to be asked. Looking around the table at my partners-in-crime-solving, I got the distinct feeling it was up to me. Since there was no liquor to provide a much-needed dose of Dutch courage, I went with the next best thing. I shoved a whole seven-layer bar in my mouth, chewed it for all I was worth, and washed it down with an unladylike gulp of tea. Then, propelled by a string of poor choices, I blurted, "Did you murder Chevy Chambers?"

The thought, apparently, had been the furthest thing from her mind. Her sage, crinkled eyes shot so wide that all the wrinkles vanished. "My goodness, no."

"No?"

"No?"

"No?" We all said it, looking at one another for confirmation. Yep, we had heard her correctly.

Rory, staring at the older woman, nervously raked a hand through his wavy hair. "Then what on earth were you doing in that remote wing of the hotel with him? And please, for God's sake, do not tell us that you were trying to bribe him with carnal favors like the others."

If Mrs. Nichols was offended, she didn't show it. Instead she let out a little melodious giggle, one that had the cadence of jingling bells. "Oh, Mr. Campbell! I'm a married woman. I told you that I was reminding him of his duty. Chevy was supposed to judge cookies honestly and fairly. That's why I gave him one of Lindsey's cookies."

"What?" It was my turn to choke on my tongue. "Dear heavens, why?"

She looked at me with all the concern of a beloved grandmother. "Because you, Lindsey, bake with joy in your heart, and it shows. Your frosted southern pecan cookie was inspired, truly it was. Chevy knew it too. I made him taste it again. I made him admit it to me. You deserved to win, but I knew you never would. One of the bakers had gotten to him."

This made Rory angry. Kennedy, also

miffed, flipped her long black hair with force to her other shoulder as her face darkened. Tuck, maintaining his composure, merely looked confused. "The bake-off was fixed?"

A deprecatory huff escaped my lips. "It was hardly a secret that Chevy was a player. He even tried to get me to take the bait." Noting that Rory was not amused by this, I felt compelled to add, "But, you know, I can't be bought."

"I must apologize to all of you for not speaking of this earlier," Mrs. Nichols said. "Chevy was a naughty man and not worth your time. But I will tell you something that just occurred to me. As I left the library, heading for the ladies' room, I did spy one of the cookie-nappers marching down the hallway. She didn't see me."

"Was she meeting Chevy?" Tuck asked.

"I couldn't say. I was in a hurry."

"Could they have been working for him?" Kennedy offered.

Tuck shrugged. "They could have been, but we really don't know anything about them other than they are somehow involved in this case. Without names, photos, or proper identification, we might never find them."

The thought was unsettling. We were just about to leave when Rory asked Mrs. Nichols a seemingly random question. "Do you know a man named Patrick Wagner?" It was the name of the man who had owned the bakery in the Upper Peninsula.

Mrs. Nichols shook her head.

"Did you ever own a bakery in the U.P.?"

This, apparently, made her chuckle. "Oh no!" she exclaimed. "I've been a home baker since the dawn of time."

CHAPTER 31

"Now what?" I looked at Kennedy, expecting her to have something witty to say about our meandering murder investigation.

She looked up from her phone and shrugged like a distracted teen. "Don't think our Mrs. N is a murderess, but I do think she's hiding something."

After leaving the Candy Cane Cottage, we decided to head out to Hoot's Diner to discuss our visit with Mrs. Nichols. Hoot's was one of my favorite places to eat, mostly because breakfast was served all day. It was a family-friendly restaurant with a huge menu, reasonably priced meals, bottomless coffee, and a slightly kitschy Up North theme — made even kitschier in December with the trappings of Christmas. It was also a few miles out of town and close to the interstate, giving it the feel of being a little more private, which really wasn't the case. It was a favorite of the locals and the area's summer residents.

Kennedy, slouching in the green leather booth, was checking her Twitter feed. She was sandwiched between Tuck and a pile of our hastily discarded winter coats. I marveled at how, even in the bitter cold, her long black hair remained silky smooth. My ash-blond hair became the texture of straw in the cold, making a long ponytail my seasonal choice.

Tuck was drumming his fingers on the menu. "Did you catch the name of her friend? Bell Bennett. Sounds made up to me."

Rory lowered his menu enough to peer over the top of it. "Right. Because you know everyone who lives in Beacon Harbor."

Tuck blushed. "I'll run it tomorrow. Anyhow, I'm still mad she didn't mention the fact that she spoke with Chambers when I was taking her statement. She also omitted following Stanley Stewart and handing the victim one of your cookies, Lindsey. At the time, she had seemed so honest and believable."

"She didn't lie," I pointed out, which was technically true. But even as I said this, I knew it sounded a little fishy.

Tuck shrugged nonchalantly. "Well, now we know why your cookie crumbs were found on the victim. We have Mrs. Nichols to thank for that."

Kennedy looked up and set down her phone. "Do you believe her? I mean, she corroborated Stanley Stewart's story. She just told us that Stanley left when she arrived, which places her alone with Chevy Chambers in that room."

"Not necessarily," I chimed in, thinking. "What if Stanley meant to kill Chevy but realized that he wasn't alone? He could have waited in one of the hallways, then doubled back once she had left. Remember, Stanley was very angry with him. He had motive — Chevy was having an affair with his wife. He had means — confronting Chevy in a private room. And his wife owned the rolling pin slash murder weapon. We know that Mrs. Nichols had means, being in that same remote room. But what motive did she have to want Chevy dead?"

Rory set down his menu and turned his attention to me. "You want to believe Stanley is the murderer for Mrs. Nichols's sake. We all want to believe it, but we must stick with the facts. Unfortunately, Stanley Stewart can vouch for the fact that your assistant baker was the last person seen with Chevy."

"But she wasn't," I countered. "Mrs.

Nichols told us that one of the cookie-nappers was on the way to meet with him when she left."

Tuck threw his hands in the air. "That's hearsay. Now we're back to the mysterious cookie-nappers again! May I point out that Mrs. Nichols is the only one who saw this person? They targeted your bakeshop, Lindsey, yet she's the only witness. Then she sends you two" — he wiggled an accusing finger between Kennedy and Rory — "chasing after them. We don't have names; we have vague descriptions."

I raised a cautious finger. "I chased after one, as well, and got locked in a storage closet. Hey, wait." A jumble of thoughts collided in my head all at the same time. I was sorry to think that I was struggling to make sense of them. So many people had issues with the food critic that it was hard trying to keep all the facts straight. But one thought kept popping to the surface. Why was I locked in a storage closet by a woman I had never met? Since Tuck was a professional, I addressed my question to him.

"The first two cookie-nappers were seen talking to Chevy. If I remember correctly, the man returned to the bake-off stage looking flustered. Cookie-napper number three shows up and I chase after her, but I never saw where she went." I glanced at Rory. "How long was I locked in that closet?"

"At least fifteen minutes. Maybe twenty before Chad and I got there."

"Right, and immediately after being let out, we decided not to go back to the ballroom. Do you remember why?"

Although his dark brows were pinched with troubling thoughts, a smile played on his lips. "A small romantic gesture." He placed his warm hand over mine before addressing the two people sitting across from us. "There was a ball of mistletoe hanging in the room Chevy had been murdered in. I saw it earlier when chasing after one of the cookie-nappers."

"Chevy had a note in his hand, remember?"

Tuck perked up. "Of course. Definitely written by a woman, in my opinion. It said, *Meet me under the mistletoe.* Was that the only room in the hotel with mistletoe?" His questioning eyes flicked back and forth between Rory and me.

"As far as I know."

"At least one of the cookie-nappers would have known about the mistletoe as well. My bet is that all three of them did. I think the woman I was chasing locked me in that closet to buy more time. With me out of the way and everyone else occupied by the festival and the bake-off, she had plenty of time to do the deed."

Tuck didn't like this at all. With his elbows resting on the table, he dropped his adorable head onto his awaiting hands. "Great. An unknown woman murders Chambers for an unknown reason with an unknown blunt object suspected to be a rolling pin. I say 'suspected' because Felicity's antique rolling pin mysteriously vanished around the time of the murder. This day just keeps getting better."

Indeed, I thought. For at that very moment my parents came strolling through the door of Hoot's Diner, and with them, Betty Vanhoosen.

CHAPTER 32

"I'll have what he's having," Mom teased, scooching on the bench next to the deflated Officer Tuck. Betty sat next to Rory, and Dad pulled up a chair.

"We were just discussing Christmas," Kennedy blithely lied. "Tucker forgot to get a gift for his mother. And here, I thought devoted sons were supposed to be thoughtful."

Tucker, as she called him, picked up his head and cast her a pained look.

"I wouldn't know," Mom replied equally as blithely. "I have a daughter. She's not only thoughtful, but so very honest. She can't keep a secret from me. Isn't that right, Linds?"

"If you're referring to Hoot's Diner — the best-kept secret in town — then guilty as charged. You found me out, Mom."

Dad grinned, appreciating my effort to deflect. Having lived with his wife and daughter for quite some time, he was used to our snappy banter. "Betty spotted your truck in the parking lot," he said to Rory. "In a town overrun with pickup trucks, I thought she was working on a hunch."

"James," Betty gently admonished, "not all pickups are the same, just like not all sedans are the same. There are subtle nuances, like brands, and colors, and things like doors and dangles. And even if I didn't know that Rory drove a black Chevy Silverado, which he does, and even if I didn't know that he and Lindsey like to dine at Hoot's Diner, which they do, a hunch is a hunch. It's the secret of my success. I live on hunches, gut instinct, and intuition." Her bright pink lips pulled into a smile.

Tuck stared at her like a deer in the headlights. "Good thing you're a Realtor, Betty. In my line of work, instinct might save your hide, but it doesn't hold up in a court of law."

Betty held him with a conspiratorial twinkle in her eyes. "True confession? When Ellie got that text from Lindsey, stating that she was having dinner with her friends and all, and that they should dine on their own, I had a hunch you'd be here."

"No kidding." Kennedy sighed, eyeing the Realtor with manufactured hero worship.

Her real hero worship, as I well knew, was reserved (this week at least) for Officer Cutie Pie.

"But that's not all. I also had a hunch that you four have been putting your heads together over the troubling matter of Mr. Chambers's death. Am I right?" She looked so hopeful. To her credit, she had hit the nail on the head. Tuck, however, looked nervous. One understood why when they remembered that his boss was the unbending Sergeant Stacy Murdock.

Tuck took a hasty gulp of his complimentary ice water. "Betty, once again, your amazing *hunching* powers are correct. As a police officer of this town working under the sergeant, it's my duty to look into the matter. However, you're wrong about them."

"Are we?" Mom used her own superpowers on him. I wished to God she had better instincts or hunches, like Betty had. But Ellie Montague Bakewell's superpower was her steely-eyed, nose-in-the-air runway smirk. Rory, catching a glimpse, shivered beside me as if poked with dry ice.

Noting that Tuck was shrinking in his seat, I jumped to his rescue. "We were just helping him make sense of everything. There was so much going on at the Christmas

Festival and the live bake-off when Chevy was murdered. Tuck wasn't there. He was on traffic duty. We were just supplying him with additional information. Isn't that right?"

He nodded, unable to hide the shades of guilt coloring his fair cheeks.

Mom's face thankfully returned to normal. "Well, then," she said brightly, this time using her cover girl smile. "You're going to love to hear what we have to tell you."

Damn Betty and her unholy instincts, Rory typed.

After another whirlwind day with the Bakewells and friends, Rory had retreated to his log home sanctuary, defeated but not broken, thank goodness. Defeated because he had tried yet another romantic gesture, this time in the privacy of the quiet passageway between the lighthouse and the light tower. I commended his choice. The inconspicuous door was conveniently located between my front door and the staircase. It was normally dark, quiet, and overlooked. But not, apparently, in the middle of a rip-roaring game of charades.

She said she thought it was the front hall closet. Although I typed the words, I cringed at the memory of the bubbly platinum blonde who threw open the door and then screamed bloody murder at the sight of us kissing. Thanks to my offer of dessert and coffee at the lighthouse, and Mom's enthusiasm for charades, our moment of romance had been thwarted the moment my lips touched Rory's. It had gone downhill from there.

I've survived midnight raids on foreign soil . . . been shot at by crazed terrorists, but nothing prepared me for the likes of Betty Vanhoosen . . . or charades with your parents.

Betty was her own disaster. Mom's curse had been getting the movie title, *Yes Virginia, There Is a Santa Claus.* Acting out "yes" had been no problem. "Virginia," however, had really tested her acting skills. Dad, doing his best, kept guessing incorrectly, "Yes, sex?" with a puzzled look on his face. We were doing Christmas charades, for all love. Not a proud moment.

Giving my fingers a little massage as I tried to expunge the memory, I typed, *You did fine. You held your ground.* I thought it best to point out that he'd been the stoic one. I, on the other hand, had screamed when Betty had screamed, which caused everyone to rush the door, hoping, no doubt, to catch a glimpse of the famed lighthouse ghost. But there was no ghost,

298

just Rory and me looking incredibly guilty for thinking we could sneak away from the group for a moment.

I appreciate that, he replied. *But what an evening. I'm still wrapping my head around what Betty and your parents got up to.*

Quite frankly, I was too.

Although Mom had strongly suggested that I not get involved in Chevy's murder, it appeared there was a bit of a double standard where she and Dad were concerned. I knew they'd been up to something, just as she knew that I wasn't about to listen to her either. So, while I had been investigating with Rory and Kennedy, Mom and Dad had coerced Betty into working with them. Betty was a natural busybody. To be fair, she was a good choice. Betty was dating the medical examiner, and she knew virtually everyone who lived in Beacon Harbor. Thanks to Kennedy, we had Tuck on our side, although he wasn't all that comfortable with what we were doing either. But I really didn't think Mom, Dad, and Betty had the nerve or the skills to actually pull off what they had pulled off.

It was like watching a bad mash-up of Nancy Drew and the Hardy Boys live, Rory had typed.

I chuckled the moment I read it. It wasn't

too far off the mark. There had been a wholesome quality about the hip senior trio as they told us whom they had talked to and the gossip they had gleaned from various shop owners about Chevy and his salacious dealings.

In this scenario, who is Nancy Drew? Mom or Betty? I just had to ask.

Ellie, of course. She's a natural. Betty is the Shaun Cassidy to James's Parker Stevenson.

Wrong as it was, I was impressed he'd given it so much thought. And I was even more impressed that my parents and Betty had gone around town hunting for clues. Much of what they told us, we already knew. It seemed almost general knowledge by now that Felicity Stewart was thought to be having an affair with the cookie judge. However, Jack Johnson from the Book Nook had told them he'd overheard Stanley Stewart threatening to kill Chevy. According to Jack, it had happened in the men's room. Jack had been insistent the threat was made before the cookies had been judged. It was a revelation for us and Tuck. It meant that Stanley Stewart had had at least two confrontations with Chevy, one in the men's room and the other in the library, where we had discovered Chevy's body.

Another interesting tidbit was that Peggy

Miller, whom I had baked the dog cookies for, had seen Felicity arguing with Chevy near the refreshment table. It was after Felicity had been removed from the stage by her husband. I must have been decorating my gingerbread lighthouse at the time.

One thing I hadn't counted on was that somebody had seen Ginger Brooks arguing with Chevy as well. According to Betty's source, Ginger was flaming mad at the cookie judge. I didn't like the sound of that. I also didn't like the fact that the argument had taken place in the hallway near the restrooms. Although no one could be certain of the time, I assumed it was before the final judging of the showstopper. I recalled that I had been the last contestant to finish decorating.

There were other things Betty and my parents had told us as well. Chevy had been seen talking with three unidentified women. No surprises there. Betty and my parents had then marched down to the police station, asking to speak with Sergeant Murdock. This had surprised Tuck. When he asked them why, Betty turned to him with an expression that was spot-on Angela Lansbury's nosy Jessica Fletcher. With her well-padded chin confidently thrust in the air and her round eyes locked on him, she stated, "The cameramen. We wanted to know if they had been questioned. And what of all the footage taken during the bake-off? We figured they must have captured something of interest, like who stole Felicity's rolling pin, and the identity of the cookie-nappers."

Tuck, keeping his professional air, had offered, "I'm sure the sergeant told you that the two men had already been interviewed. Also, if they did happen to film the cookie-nappers, how were we to know? Only Mrs. Nichols can properly identify them."

He was made aware that Rory, Kennedy, and I had seen them, too, and that we'd be willing to go through the footage. But it was agreed that Mrs. Nichols had the most experience spotting them. I volunteered to approach her with the request. She always had the option to refuse, but I was nearly certain she'd be happy to help if she could.

If anything, this little exchange had given Tuck hope. If the women had been filmed and properly identified, then recognition software might be used to get names and addresses. It was a long shot, but it was a move in the right direction.

However, as busy as they had been, the most amazing item of interest was on Mom's phone. Rory, as if reading my mind, typed, *Still, I can't believe they actually took a picture of that note.*

Rory and I, after noting Chevy's tightly closed fist, had figured he'd been holding something when he was murdered. It was later that Doc Riggles confirmed it had been a note. However, even if we had pried Chevy's fist open and read the note, it was doubtful that either one of us would have had the gumption to pull out our phones and start snapping pictures.

I bet Doc Riggles doesn't even know they did that, I typed back. *Devious Betty diverted his attention, and Mom snapped the picture. You have to admit, it's kind of badass.*

I'm just amazed they want to join forces. But that note is important. Someone had lured Chevy to that room with the promise of romance under the mistletoe. It could be anyone. But the writing, I'm willing to bet, is that of a woman's. We find a match for the handwriting, and we find our murderer.

He was undoubtedly correct, but I knew it was easier said than done. However, my tired brain was hatching a plan. I typed my good night wishes, with the addition of some tantalizing future promises. I then closed my laptop and gave Welly a big hug for being so patient. He wasn't complaining. He'd already had his night-night treats.

With Wellington tucked into his bed at the foot of mine, I settled down for a quick five-hour sleep. Damn my sugarplum visions! The lighthouse had been perfectly illuminated to look like a giant candy cane, and the Beacon Bakeshop buzzed with Christmas cheer. Wellington was in his glory, having furry friends to chase around the house, and my family and friends were enjoying my hospitality. I had even baked my heart out in the live Christmas cookie bake-off. During any normal year, it would be enough. My perfect Christmas was upon me — it was happening! And yet I knew that this year, those elusive sugarplums had been hijacked once again, only this time by a brazen killer. There was nothing else for it. I was going to need to up my game.

CHAPTER 33

"Have a holly jolly Christmas, it's the best time of the year . . ." I was belting out the song along with Burl Ives as I danced around the bakery kitchen, adding ingredients to the industrial mixer. It was one of the best parts about early morning baking. Aside from Wellington, who was watching me from the doorway between the kitchen and the bakery, I was utterly alone. For once, I was up before my alarm had gone off. I wasn't even that tired — because I was on a mission. I was baking up a plan that might get us closer to discovering the killer.

Still singing along with Burl, I twirled before adding the wet ingredients — eggs, oil, buttermilk, vanilla, some white vinegar, and a shocking amount of red food coloring. It hit with a splash. I flipped on the mixer and twirled again.

Wellington sat up and barked with joy. He

wanted to dance too — I could see it in his eyes. I walked over to him and patted my chest. In a moment, he was on his hind legs, landing his giant paws on my shoulders. I laughed as his tail swished to the music. "Somebody waits for you, kiss him once for me," I sang and kissed Welly on the nose. I then set him back on all fours. But the music was infectious. He wanted to keep going.

"I have to add the dry ingredients," I told him, dancing back to the mixer. I continued singing as I measured out the flour, sugar, baking soda, salt, and cocoa powder. It was all blending together nicely.

The next song on my playlist was "O Holy Night." It wasn't as lively as "A Holly Jolly Christmas," but that didn't stop me from attempting it. I was getting my pans ready, brushing them with melted butter followed by a dusting of flour, as I sang the verse, " *'Til He appears and the soul felt its worth . . .*" That's when I caught a whiff of pipe smoke.

When the Captain arrives, it happens quickly. Wellington was on his feet, looking at me from the doorway, his great busy tail thumping with anticipation. The lights dimmed, then flickered, prompting me to stare at the ceiling. What else was I to say but "Merry Christmas, Captain?"

Would he respond? Would he finally show himself to me? It wasn't as if we were strangers. My answer came in the form of a chilling prickle that ran up the back of my neck. I knew with a certainty something was directly behind me.

"Merry Christmas!"

I screamed and spun around. "Holy mother!" I cried and dropped a pan. "Where . . . when did you arrive?"

Mrs. Nichols looked neither frightened nor alarmed as she scooped up the pan and handed it back to me. "Did I startle you? So sorry, dear. No wonder with all the singing . . . but it was lovely," she assured me with what I perceived was forced enthusiasm. "What are you making?" She shrugged off her coat and placed it on the hook beside the door.

"Uhh . . ." Pausing until I had mastery over my raging nerves, I finally said, "Red velvet Bundt cakes. Gift-sized." Why did I feel the needed to clarify that?

She glided over to the mixer. "Looks sinful. Special order?"

I shook my head. "Special delivery. They're gifts I'm giving to the bake-off contestants, and a few select others."

That got her attention. No doubt Mrs. Nichols had her secrets, but there was something about her that demanded my trust. She might have meddled on my behalf at the bake-off, but she wasn't a killer. And I was pretty darn certain she hadn't written the note found in Chevy's hand either. In order to be sure, we had checked it last night, placing the note she had written to me against the one on Mom's phone. It wasn't a match, and I suspected the sage woman had an inkling of what I was up to.

"Would these gifts have anything to do with your investigation into the murder of Chevy Chambers?"

"They do," I admitted. "I'm using them to narrow the field of suspects."

I put the cakes in the oven, then turned my energies to making the Beacon's staple items. Mrs. Nichols, without missing a beat, deftly worked beside me. As we mixed up the dough for the donuts, muffins, sweet rolls, and Danish, I confided to her my plan. I didn't tell her that the inspiration had come from the simple note she had written to me. All I told her was that we had an image of the note found in Chevy's hand, and if we could find a match to the handwriting, we'd know who had lured him to that remote room for a romp beneath the mistletoe.

"You're using red velvet Bundt cakes?"

Her powdered nose wrinkled with question.

I had just mixed up the decadent cream cheese frosting to be piped on each cake when I turned to her. "I couldn't very well go up to everyone and demand they write me a note. They'll know what I'm up to. I thought it would be nicer if they received a beautifully decorated, delicious Christmas cake from an anonymous source — which is me." I grinned.

"But you'll be putting them in your signature red boxes. Everyone will know they're from the Beacon Bakeshop, dear."

"True. But it's not unusual that we get special orders all the time. We don't need to tell anyone who ordered the cakes . . . although it was me." Again, I grinned.

She deftly pulled a tray of gingerbread muffins out of the oven and placed them on a rack to cool. "Very kind of you, indeed. Yet I don't understand how giving them one of your beautiful cakes will help you find the killer."

"Well, that part I'm leaving up to Ryan."

My staff at the Beacon knew I was meddling in the murder of Chevy Chambers. I cared for them deeply and really didn't want them involved in my dealings. However, during our brief morning meeting, I felt it

309

was important to make them aware that I had talked with a few of the bake-off contestants. I also briefed them on my plan for helping the police (unbeknownst to them) by narrowing down the suspect list with my *anonymous* Christmas cakes.

"That's diabolical," Tom had remarked with a fleeting grin. He then sobered and asked, "Rory's helping you with this, right? I mean, comparing the handwriting. It's not like you're an expert at that sort of thing." It was no secret Tom had a man-crush on Rory, but I really could have done without his *Rory fandom* leaking into *my* plan.

"Ah . . . he's working his own angle," I told him. It wasn't a lie. But the cakes were my own little baby. I would only tell Rory and Kennedy about them if my plan worked.

"Well, I, for one, think it's brilliant." I could count on Wendy to have my back. "And you don't need to be an expert at analyzing handwriting to tell if one person's scrawl matches the other. The police will handle that."

"Yeah, Tom." Elizabeth hit him with her dishcloth. Tom pretended to look offended, but the two were grinning at one another. "Since Rory's busy, maybe you'd like to help and deliver a couple of the cakes?"

"Good idea," I said, looking at him.

"But that's Ryan's job." Alaina, using her expressive eyes, let them know how she felt about that. I got the feeling she might not be defending my original plan as much as the young man chosen to execute it. "He has a gift for getting people to do things they might not normally want to do."

"Like getting you to prep the sandwich counter for him or clean the panini maker?" Elizabeth rolled her eyes at her.

"We're friends." Alaina turned her attention to me and asked, "Can I tell him when he gets here? He's not only going to love delivering the Christmas cakes, he's going to love convincing people to sign for them too. I doubt Tom has the charm to pull that off."

"Hey?" Tom's hands were in midair as he looked at her. "I have plenty of charm." To make his point, he graced us with his dazzling smile. One thing was certain. He had a great dentist.

But Tom's white-toothed smile hadn't moved Alaina the way it used to. Apparently, she was now immune to it. Smart girl, I silently applauded. But when did that happen? I'd been too busy to notice before, but on closer inspection, Tom and Elizabeth seemed very comfortable together. In fact, they had grown exceptionally close over the holidays. Was there a romance budding between the two? And what about Alaina and Ryan?

But I didn't have time to dwell on the possible budding romances happening around me. I had a bakery to run.

We opened our doors to the usual rush of caffeine seekers, Danish lovers, and donut dunkers. The comforting melody of friendly gossip drowned out the soft Christmas music playing in the background. Wendy and Alaina were cheerfully working the counter as Tom and Elizabeth whipped up an astonishing array of our specialty holiday drinks. Ryan wasn't due to come in until after the morning rush.

"How ya holding up, Bakewell?" Sergeant Murdock was standing in line for her peppermint mocha when she addressed me. I had just come out of the kitchen with a tray of warm, gooey cinnamon rolls. Did she know I'd been meddling in her murder investigation? I prayed not, but I could feel the blood drain from my face as I tossed her a wan smile in response.

"I'll have one of those." Tuck, coming to my rescue, stood beside his boss. He looked a bit tired, and I could only venture a guess as to why. "They look delicious, Lindsey.

Hey, Sergeant Murdock and I were just talking about some footage we acquired from the bake-off. I suggested to her that Mrs. Nichols might be willing to take a look at it. Is she still here?"

Judging by the looks of it, Tuck had spilled the beans before Murdock was ready to broach the subject. But the question had been asked, and the sergeant decided to run with it. Plucking two complimentary cinnamon rolls from the tray, I put them on plates and led Sergeant Murdock and Officer Cutie Pie to a private table where we could talk. Unfortunately, the entire town was still reeling from the murder of the Christmas cookie critic, and more than a few curious eyes followed us.

"Look," Murdock began, attempting a conversational tone. "You know how I feel about citizen crime solvers. I don't like 'em. I don't much like anything that will put a citizen of this town in danger. That being said, I'm also aware that we can't solve a crime without the help of witnesses. It's a thin line, Bakewell. A witness is not an investigator." She felt the need to emphasize this by raising a brow at me.

"I understand." In theory, I really did, but I also knew that sometimes snooping couldn't be helped. It brought to mind my

313

innocent-looking red velvet cakes cooling on the kitchen counter.

Murdock cut her cinnamon roll with a fork and took a bite. There was nothing to soothe the savage beast, I thought, like a mouthful of warm bread slathered in butter and sugar. "It's a matter of these cookie-nappers." She pointed her fork at me while still chewing. "We think they might have more to do with this case than we originally thought."

"I see."

"And Mrs. Nichols is the only one who can identify all three," Tuck added helpfully, pretending we hadn't already discussed this in private.

Murdock took another bite and nodded, her wispy blond bangs fluttering as she did so. "Do you think she'd mind coming down to the station with us?"

A short while later, Mrs. Nichols left the kitchen to accompany Sergeant Murdock to the police station. I thanked her for her help and told her to take the rest of the day off. The moment they were out the door, I sent Kennedy a text. No doubt she was still in bed somewhere.

Officer Cutie Pie just left with Mrs. Nichols to look at the bake-off footage. Work your magic on him. I'd like to know if any of those women were caught on camera.

She replied with a lazy, *K.*

A few hours later, Ryan arrived. As Wendy and I boxed up the festively frosted Christmas cakes, Alaina told him my plan.

Ryan held me with his charmer's smile. "Why, this is most devious of you, boss. But I love it. You've put the right man on the job. For the record, I'm placing my money on that whack-job, Mrs. Stewart."

Me too, I thought, then sent him on his way.

CHAPTER 34

As the hours dragged on and Ryan still hadn't returned, I was beginning to wonder if my plan had backfired. He'd had four cakes to deliver in exchange for signatures. There was no guarantee my crazy plan was going to work. Just as there was no guarantee that the crazy killer wouldn't catch on to what Ryan was doing and call his bluff. That would be bad. This last thought prompted me to pull out my iPhone. I was about to call Ryan when Bradley Argyle walked through the bakeshop doors.

"Lindsey," he said with a wave. He marched up to the counter with a big grin on his face. I suspected I knew what had caused such a grin. I had sent him a cake, and now guilt was threatening to knock me on the head.

"Bradley, so nice to see you." I smiled back at him, pretending I didn't know why he had come to the Beacon. "Have you recovered from that disastrous bake-off? What a fiasco that turned out to be."

He gave a slight huff in response. "What I'd like to know is what idiot invited that clown to Beacon Harbor in the first place?"

I'm sure my eyes were as wide as saucers. "You didn't know?"

This time Bradley grinned. "Of course, I know. Felicity Stewart. Wish I'd had the forethought to protest her silly bake-off before it all started, but hindsight's the devil to live with. I hear she's the prime suspect in his murder." A pitying look crossed his face as he shook his head. "And here I was even beginning to like the guy after he awarded my turtle-topped brown butter shortbread cookie first place."

"It was well-deserved."

I thought he'd be happy with my compliment, but his face darkened. "I'm not so sure," he said, looking troubled. "It's a good cookie, but all of us — with the exception of Felicity — had great entries. No. I got the feeling he was placating me."

"Really? Why?" I found it curious he should think so.

Again, he shrugged. "I don't know. Maybe because he was so obviously flirting with all of you women? He was trying to stir the pot between all of us, trying to create animosity."

"Or more drama," I offered. "Remember, the cameras were rolling."

"He didn't flirt with me, thank God, but he was taking subtle jabs at the fact that I worked at a hotel restaurant in a small, touristy town."

Mrs. Nichols's voice popped into my head. *"Chevy is a very naughty man."* He certainly was, but why go after Bradley? It prompted me to ask, "Did you know him?"

He stared at me a moment, as if not hearing what I had asked. But then he shook his head. "I knew of him. But no. I didn't know him."

"Thank goodness for that," I declared and offered to make him a coffee drink. "We're almost closed for the day, but why don't we sit at a table? I'd like to hear what Chevy told you. Maybe you saw or heard something important to this case?"

Bradley politely declined my offer. "Thanks, but I just got off work. I didn't come to complain about a dead man, and I really don't want to talk about him either. I came to thank you for the cake."

I knew it! My stupid plan! The subtle deceit of it caused a wave of butterflies fluttering uncomfortably in my stomach. I instantly regretted sending a cake to this man. The writing on the note had been that of a woman's, but I'd thought it was important to leave no stone unturned. I looked at the chef and forced a smile. "Glad you liked it."

"It's beautiful. I'm sure it'll taste as good as it looks. You know, I've been so busy at the restaurant, and with that ridiculous bake-off stuff thrown into the mix, I haven't had time to make anything for Christmas. By the way, I'd like to know who sent it?"

It was hard to stare into the eyes of another and offer a bald-faced lie. As a former investment banker, I couldn't do it to a client, so why did I consider doing it now? I decided to take the middle ground and play up the mystery angle.

"I'm not at liberty to say." The words were no sooner out of my mouth when I began to look around for one of my employees to come to my rescue. But Ryan was still out, Tom had gone home, and the girls were in the back cleaning up for the day.

"Come on," he prodded, pulling my attention back to him. "Was it a woman?" He looked so hopeful.

"Ahh . . . yes," I conceded. "But that's all I'm going to tell you."

"Was she pretty?"

"I couldn't say."

"Was she older or younger?"

"Older." Why did I say that?

"God, it wasn't my mother, was it?" I didn't know his mother, but the thought clearly was freaking us both out.

"Betty Vanhoosen!" I blurted, the name popping into my head at the very worst moment. But it was out, and there was no taking it back. "There you have it. Such a sweetheart. But please don't tell her that I told you."

The name appeared to satisfy him. "Betty," he softly mused. "Not quite what I was hoping for, but it makes sense. Thanks, Lindsey. See you around."

As he turned to go, I happened to look out the window. Ryan was coming up the front walkway. I breathed a sigh of relief, knowing that my fears had gotten the best of me. The thick-set young man with the kind face and jaunty smile came through the door just as Bradley was heading out. The younger man raised a hand in greeting. The other hand, I saw, was holding the four signed receipts.

Bradley followed Ryan with his eyes as he headed for the counter. Then, however, he caught sight of me. My heart sank. This time his expression wasn't open and friendly but fraught with question.

CHAPTER 35

Baking calmed my nerves, but the kitchen had been cleaned for the day and I wasn't about to muck it up again. Instead, I turned to the espresso machine and began making three gingerbread lattes as I waited for Rory and Kennedy to arrive. Ryan, that industrious young man, had come through like a champ. Not only had he gotten each recipient to sign the receipt, but he had also gotten them to add a Christmas word, his own holiday challenge. The kid was a genius.

Before Ryan had left on his sneaky errand, we had discussed the objective, which was to get a sample of each person's handwriting. The four Christmas cakes I made were to be delivered to my fellow contestants plus one: Stanley Stewart. Since we felt the note had been written by a woman, Bradley Argyle was a long shot, but I felt that I had to include him for consistency. I didn't know what his handwriting looked like. He could have written the note (who was I to judge the gender of handwriting?), although I really couldn't see him having any clear motive to harm Chevy. But I wasn't crossing anyone off my suspect list yet.

Stanley, on the other hand, had motive and opportunity to do the deed. His wife also owned the murder weapon . . . or the suspected murder weapon, at any rate. He could easily have taken it when he walked onto the stage to remove his wife. But why would he use his wife's antique rolling pin? Maybe it was all that was at hand? Or maybe he was trying to frame her for Chevy's murder — a sinister form of punishment for having an affair with the celebrity food critic and causing his public humiliation? In my opinion, anything was possible where Stanley Stewart was concerned — even hiring three unknown women to steal my cookies and harass Chevy Chambers.

And speaking of hiring women, it wasn't a stretch to imagine that he might have even been sly enough to get his young secretary to write the note that had lured Chevy to that quiet corner of the hotel for him. True, I had never seen Alyssa before our visit to Tartan Solutions, but that didn't mean she hadn't been present at the Beacon Harbor

Christmas Festival.

"Signatures are very personal and sloppy," Ryan had told me upon his return with the receipts. "That's when I decided to challenge them to write a Christmas word next to their name — in honor of the season. I used the word *mistletoe* as an example."

"What a clever young man you are," I had told him.

The compliment had made him blush. His head dropped with embarrassment as he shoved his hands into his pockets. He looked up again and brushed a rogue lock of brown hair out of his eyes. "I found it interesting that only one person didn't write *mistletoe* next to their name. Not everyone is swayed by the power of suggestion." I got the feeling he knew more than he was letting on.

It wasn't until Ryan left that I looked at the four receipts. The moment I did, the annoying children's song kept playing in my head on a broken loop. "One of these things is not like the others, one of these things just doesn't belong. . . ." I blamed *Sesame Street* and the word *Rudolph* that jumped off the receipt in round, lovely strokes. Why couldn't the writer have just written *mistletoe* like everyone else had? I looked again and understood. Guilt. The last time the word had been written in such a manner, a man had died. The name next to it, written in equally lovely strokes, caused my heart to pound out an uncomfortable rhythm that was at odds with the song. *Calm down,* I told myself, *calm down.* But instead of heeding my own thoughts, I took a sip of my gingerbread latte. There were just some things you had to face head-on, with a fresh dose of caffeine pumping through your veins.

I had run around the lighthouse grounds with Wellington and the models four times before I spied Kennedy driving up the lighthouse driveway in my Jeep. Running through snow was exhausting, but they needed the exercise, and I needed to calm down. We ran over to the boathouse, where Kennedy was in the process of parking my vehicle. I knocked on the window, startling her.

"What are you doing?" She looked confused and, if truth be told, a little guilty as well. I didn't care that she had taken the Jeep to have a romantic Christmas lunch with Officer Cutie Pie, if that was what she'd been doing. I was on edge. Running with the dogs had done all of us some good, but I needed a second pair of eyes on those receipts.

"I made you a latte. Rory should be over soon. I need you to look at something."

"My dear friend, how many times have I told you that I am not a doctor?"

"This isn't about a suspicious, misshapen mole."

"Thank God. In that case, I shall venture a friendly observation. Lay off the caffeine. It's affecting your brain. Point in fact, it's freezing out here, and you're not wearing a coat."

"I'm exercising the dogs," I explained, turning back toward the Beacon. "I need you in the bakeshop."

"You have been a busy little bee today, haven't you?" Kennedy looked genuinely impressed when I told her what I had done. In spite of her own advice, she took a sip of her latte. "You've managed to get handwriting samples from all our current suspects. And here, I thought we were meeting to plan a daring raid on private journals and grocery lists."

"Not quite. Making and delivering cakes was easier."

"I don't think that's true," she remarked and took out her phone.

After some convincing, Kennedy had gotten the image of the note from Mom. She opened it up and began studying the four receipts. I hadn't told her what I had discovered. I wanted to see if she came to the same conclusion.

Just as Kennedy set to work, Rory came into the café. After a tail-wagging greeting from three happy dogs, he took a seat beside me. Brinkley and Ireland settled under the table, while Welly wedged himself between Rory and me. I was bringing him up to speed on what we were doing when Kennedy exclaimed, "We have a match!"

"What? Really?" Apparently, Rory didn't think Operation Christmas Cake would actually work.

"Look here." She passed us her phone and the receipt in question. "Granted, it's not much to go by, but it's remarkably close."

Rory, after a skeptical lift of his brow, studied the photo of the note and the signature on the receipt. He then took the other receipts from Kennedy and studied those as well. As he did, I silently prayed that I had missed something important. When Rory finally looked up and held me in his singular gaze, I knew that my prayer had gone unanswered.

"Lindsey . . ." The tone of his voice was warning enough.

"I know," I said. "I looked at all the

receipts the moment Ryan had left. I just wanted to make sure we were all on the same page." I then explained how Ryan had asked each cake recipient to write a Christmas word next to their name, and the fact that he had used *mistletoe* as a suggestion.

Rory, thoughtfully stroking his firm, square chin, offered, "It's either a sign of laziness, a lack of creativity, or an admission of guilt."

"And she seemed relatively normal," Kennedy offered. "Shall I call Tuck?"

I shook my head. "Not yet. Let me speak with Ginger first. If she really did write that damaging note, there must be a reason."

Kennedy's face filled with concern. "I thought the reason was obvious. Murder!"

CHAPTER 36

Ginger Brooks lived in a little bungalow a block and a half from her ice cream shop. It was slightly farther for me, but I insisted on walking to her quiet neighborhood as I always did, arguing that it would be less suspicious that way. Rory had wanted to go with me, referring to Ginger's home as the "Devil's Den" (men were so ridiculous!). Although I wanted him to come, I had argued against it on the grounds that it might inhibit her from being candid with me. Regarding Kennedy, my argument was much the same. Ginger might be suspicious if both of us showed up on her doorstep uninvited. Also, and what I didn't add for the sake of my friendship with Kennedy, was that her newfound desire to impress the village's youngest and hottest cop might induce her to do something crazy. With Kennedy, conversations were always in danger of going off the rails. But the fact that she had been the one to confirm the handwriting for me had gone to her head. I didn't need her going rogue and bursting through Ginger's door with a *gotcha* moment. Nope, Kennedy was just fine doing what she was doing, which was communicating via text with Tuck. According to Kennedy, Mrs. Nichols was still at the police station going through footage with Sergeant Murdock. So far, there had been no sightings of the three mysterious women referred to as the cookie-nappers. A troubling thought had occurred to me. Could they have been working for Ginger? I hoped not. But honestly, I didn't know what to think anymore.

The sun had already set, and the air had grown colder by the time Wellington and I set out for Ginger's house. Welly, dressed in his *Ellie & Co Pup Original* coat, was the obvious choice. Everyone in town knew my dog, and his presence would neither be suspicious nor threatening. Besides, he was a good listener, or at least he pretended to be whenever I shared my own concerns with him.

Walking through a neighborhood at night was so much better at Christmastime. True, it was cold, and the sidewalks were never really cleared of snow for long. But the lights and decorations made up for the inconvenience. They were a feast for the eyes and set a joyous, hopeful mood. However, the moment we turned down Beach Street, the feeling changed. Ginger's house, dark and quiet, stood out from the rest. Although the wide front porch had been wrapped in lights, they hadn't been plugged in. My heart sank, thinking she might not be home. If I couldn't get ahold of her, I'd have to pass my information along to Tuck and let him handle it. But the thought rankled me. Probably because I had put a lot of time and effort into getting the damning piece of information in the first place.

I stood on Ginger's dark porch with my nerve fading as fast as a winter sunset. Welly, however, knew where we were. To him, Ginger's house meant a yummy treat, usually in the form of a broken waffle cone. Not to be deterred, he sat at her front door and whined. I was about to pull him away when I caught a shimmer of light seeping through a small opening in her heavy curtains. I went to the window and peered through the crack. The lights were most definitely on, and someone was inside. It was all the impetus I needed to knock on her door.

Whoever was inside was ignoring me. I

knew they had heard me. I looked at Welly. My dog ramped up his whining to pitiful levels as I gave the door another thumping with my gloved fist. A moment later, the front light turned on, and the door opened a crack.

"Oh, hi." The door opened a little wider. Although Ginger smiled, I could tell it was born of politeness and not feeling. "I, um . . . meant to thank you for the cake. It looks delicious."

"I'm glad you like it. It's partially why I'm here."

"Oh God, you haven't come to tell me who my secret admirer is?" Her face paled as she took a step back from the door. She still hadn't invited us in, a fact that Wellington was about to remedy by sheer brute force. "I'd rather give you back the cake."

I tightened my grip on Welly's leash, holding him back. Ginger was clearly worried about something. Although I had carefully prepared for what I was going to say to her, all that went out the window as guilt and opportunity seized me. "I'm the one who sent you the cake. Can we talk?"

Refusing anything to eat or drink, I sat on her couch, relieved to learn that her daughter, Kate, was having dinner with her grandparents. I really didn't want the poor child to hear what was going to be a tough conversation between her mother and me. Wellington, on the other hand, had searched the house for his friend until finally being lured back to the family room by the promise of a treat. After devouring a pile of waffle cone pieces, he had stretched out on the carpet and was now sleeping peacefully.

"I guess I'm missing something here. I don't understand why you would send me that cake and claim it was from somebody else?" She looked hurt by the notion. I suddenly felt very guilty.

I looked down at my thick wool socks and wiggled my toes. "I'm sorry to have misled you. I did it because I'm looking into the murder of Chevy Chambers."

Her voice was fraught with emotion as she said, "That bake-off was a disaster! And Chevy was a creep! That still doesn't explain why you sent me a cake."

I mustered the courage to look her in the face. "Remember that Rory and I found his body? We were the first ones there. We know that Chevy had a note crumpled in his hand."

A micro expression flashed across her face and vanished. I couldn't tell whether it was from surprise or guilt. "He was holding a note?"

"He was. Not a long note. It said, *Meet me under the mistletoe.* Ironically or perhaps, tragically, Chevy's body was found beneath the only sprig of mistletoe in the entire hotel. The police believe he was lured there under the guise of a romantic interlude."

Ginger closed her eyes as if pained, then took a deep breath. When she had opened them again, she said, "I've already talked to the police. I told them everything." She wrung her hands, then suddenly stood up from her chair. She took a few steps toward the fireplace, stopped short of my dog, then turned back to look at me.

"Lindsey, I consider you one of my good friends, and as my friend, I'm going to ask you not to put your nose where it doesn't belong."

I looked up from my folded hands. "It's too late for that. I know you wrote that note."

She stopped pacing and glared at me. For a brief second, I thought she might run. She changed her strategy, however, and doubled down. "Not funny, Lindsey! How dare you accuse me of such a thing? We're allies, friends! We're both single women who own thriving shops in Beacon Harbor! Don't be silly. If anyone wrote that note, it was

Felicity Stewart. She . . . she was having the affair with Chevy. Everyone knew it."

"Maybe," I agreed. "But you were the one who wrote that note."

"What makes you think I would do that?"

"I honestly didn't think you were the one. But I have proof."

"Proof? Ha! I don't believe you! I think all this snooping around and sticking your nose where it doesn't belong has gone to your head. You, my friend, are delusional. How could you possibly think . . ." She stopped in the middle of her tirade as a horrifying thought seized her. "The cake! Oh my God, you sent me that cake to get my signature!"

Guilty as charged. Like most of my grand visions, my anonymous Christmas cake delivery scheme had looked great on paper. It had also worked like a charm. What I hadn't counted on, however, was the welling of guilt at having betrayed a friend. It wasn't sitting well. I silently cursed the obnoxious cookie critic whose death had forced me into it. I turned to my friend and tried to explain.

"When I sent that cake, I never thought . . . look, I never meant to hurt you. I wanted to shift the blame on Felicity or her husband, Stanley, for Chevy's death. I never expected —"

"You think that I killed him?" she finished the thought for me. I watched as her resolve slowly crumbled. She reached for her hair and nervously twirled a brown lock between her fingers. She clearly didn't know what to do. "Okay, look. You caught me. I did write that note. But I didn't kill him."

"Ginger, I'm one step ahead of the police. But you know that they're going to figure this out eventually. Why don't you tell me why you wrote that note? I know you. If you did it, you obviously had a good reason."

Casting a wary sideways glance at me, she uttered, "I wouldn't be too sure about that."

We sat at her kitchen table with a bottle of red wine between us. The first glass had gone down swiftly over a light dusting of nervous small talk. Ginger bristled with inner turmoil as she poured herself a second glass. Deciding to get on with it, she finally blurted, "Okay, don't judge me, but Chevy and I were having an affair."

I was in mid-sip when she said this, and I was sorry to think that the sudden spewing of red wine from my lips would be interpreted as judging. I choked, sputtered, and reached for a napkin, hoping to breeze by my little faux pas unnoticed. "Y' don't say?"

"Don't try to pretend it's not revolting. It is. It was. Just thinking about it makes me want to gag too."

Gently dabbing at the mess I'd made on her table, I asked, "Then why did you do it?"

She shrugged. "Greed, stupidity, loneliness, and maybe a little jealousy too. Damn Felicity and her stupid Christmas cookie bake-off!" The mere thought of the frantic week leading up to the Christmas Festival had caused a welling of anger and frustration to play out on her face. I could empathize with her. I had felt it too. Although it had started out as a friendly competition, the pressure of the holidays, the extra baking, and the manipulating by the cookie judge had taken its toll.

"I blame Felicity," Ginger continued. "She was a friend of Chevy's and thought she had victory in the bag. But then Chevy started stirring the pot, so to speak. He started flirting with me and making promises. I knew he was flirting with you as well." She gave a disparaging shake of her head. "I didn't know if you'd take him up on his offer, but my competitive spirit got the best of me. I went out to dinner with him. Unfortunately, Felicity caught us kissing and flipped out. Chevy was her link to being the end-all and be-all of Christmas."

"Wait! Are you suggesting that Felicity

337

wasn't having an affair with Chevy Chambers?"

Ginger shook her head. "We all knew that Felicity was desperate to win the bake-off. Chevy knew it, too, and he fueled that flame with false promises." She shook her head. "That man was a special kind of devil. He promised the world, or as much of it as he could give, in exchange for a roll in the sheets. Felicity, the silly idiot, already has a successful Christmas shop, and a husband. I'm a single mother. I love my daughter and want to give her the world, but there's only so much I can do. Harbor Scoops doesn't exactly thrive during the winter months. They're lean and quiet. It makes the holidays particularly stressful for me, not to mention lonely. Then in walks charming Chevy Chambers flaunting his celebrity and his sway over the Christmas cookie bake-off."

"He propositioned you." By now, I knew how the man worked. He had come into the Beacon Bakeshop with the same strategy, hitting on both Kennedy and me. But I had the love of Rory Campbell and was, thankfully, financially sound. However, what if I had been a single mother struggling to make ends meet? Would I have been sucked in by Chevy and his promises too?

Ginger drained her wineglass and shook her head. "I took the easy way out, Lindsey." Her face darkened as she added, "He promised to be discreet. He promised he'd make sure that I won. He even dangled the promise of a regular segment on his television show. I played his little game, but that creep had no intention of keeping any of his promises."

"When did you write him that note?"

"At the Christmas Festival. It was after our first bake, when he judged our cookies. He was still flirting with Felicity. The two were nauseating. I had slept with him!" The shame of it was written all over her face as she relived the memory. "I sold out, and he didn't seem to have any qualms about shoving it in my face! In fact, he seemed to thrive on his broken promises. He gave the win to Bradley!"

There was no denying that Chevy was despicable. But I had to point out that Bradley's cookie truly was sublime.

"Yes, it was. But that's not the point. Chevy was on the take, and I took, so to speak. But my currency wasn't doing it for him anymore. I wrote him the note so that we could speak in private. You read it. I wanted him to think that I was willing to ignite his passions again for what I knew to be false promises. I knew he'd bite, but this time I wouldn't. I was going to give him a piece of my mind."

The fact that Ginger's note had worked was troubling. Chevy had, indeed, been found beneath the mistletoe — the same mistletoe she had directed him to meet her under. She admitted to being angry and desperate. She also had easy access to a rolling pin. Although she had denied killing Chevy, what I couldn't deny was that she had motive, opportunity, and possibly the murder weapon as well. With a sinking feeling in the pit of my stomach, I poured another glass of wine. I tried to smile, but fell short of the mark as I asked, "Did you hand him the note?" She nodded. "When was this?"

"During the gingerbread showstopper. He came to look at my gingerbread rendition of Harbor Scoops. I felt like a spy, passing it to him discreetly under the all-seeing eye of Betty Vanhoosen. Betty was talking so much and adding so many snappy comments that she didn't notice."

I hadn't noticed, either, being obsessed with my showstopper lighthouse. It wasn't until I had finished that I realized everyone else had left the stage. It prompted me to ask if she had met with him.

She crossed her arms and sat back in the chair. "I had every intention of doing so," she said. "But then I caught him flirting with another woman."

"Who?" I sat up and stared at her.

She shrugged at the memory. "I don't know, just some woman."

"Can you describe her?"

"Older, but still quite attractive."

Alarm bells sounded off in my head as she said this. Ginger must have seen Chevy talking with one of the mysterious cookie-nappers. I asked, "Did you recognize her?"

"No, I didn't. I did see that she had brown hair with highlights and a trim figure. That's about all I noticed."

From her brief description, she might have been describing the mysterious woman I'd been chasing. The fact that Ginger had never seen the woman before was testament to the fact that they weren't working for her. The three middle-aged women remained a total mystery. The only thing that I knew for certain was that they were somehow connected to Chevy. They were either working for him or trying to cause him harm. "Where did you see him talking with her?"

She gave a little huff of exasperation. "Under the mistletoe, of course."

CHAPTER 37

"You're still alive!" Kennedy's cheerfully sarcastic greeting hit me the moment Welly and I walked through the lighthouse door. It was Mom's night to make dinner, and she didn't disappoint, judging from the astounding array of Chinese take-out cartons crowding the countertops. I hadn't ordered Chinese takeout in months, and the savory smell of spicy beef, chicken almondine, stir-fried vegetables, sweet and sour pork, fried rice, spring rolls, and other delights I could only guess at made me instantly ravenous. It was making Welly ravenous too. After our brisk walk in the cold night air, I couldn't blame him.

The models rushed to greet us with their little yips of excitement and a flurry of fluffy white tail wags. I gave each dog a pat as they took a moment to sniff each other in the manner dogs do. Then, with curiosity satisfied, all three trotted off to the kitchen, where Mom was transferring a carton of beef and broccoli into a serving bowl. Welly, I noticed, had induced her to "drop" a piece of tender beef on his awaiting tongue.

Rory had been helping Dad set the table. He was holding a pile of napkins, clearly debating whether to just plop them down in the middle, as instinct dictated, or neatly fold each one and place it next to a plate — a waste of time and effort to the calculating bachelor mind. The sight of me tipped the scales. He dropped the napkins in favor of helping me with my coat. Apparently, chivalry was not dead.

"What happened?" he asked. Although he turned to hang my coat in the front hall closet, I could tell the suspense was killing him. "Did Ginger write that note?"

Everyone had stopped talking. Mom, about to pop a crab Rangoon into her mouth, stilled with the fried wonton delight poised before her lips. All eyes were on me, everyone anxiously awaiting the news.

"She did. But I don't think she killed him."

As we sat at the table enjoying our Chinese feast, I told them about my visit to Ginger's house.

Kennedy, hanging on my every word, picked up a piece of broccoli with her chopsticks. "So, Ginger wrote the note, and Chevy took the bait, leaving the bake-off stage for a remote wing of the hotel. How simple men are." Her eyes flashed to Rory as she bit the head off her broccoli spear.

"I don't blame Ginger for being angry," Mom said. "He pitted Felicity and Ginger against one another, and angered Felicity's husband as well. What did he expect would happen?"

Dad looked at me from across the table. "Do you believe her? I mean, she lied to you about writing the note. She could be lying about the rest."

"They could all be lying." Rory stood up and crossed to the kitchen. He grabbed the carton of kung pao chicken off the counter and brought it back to the table. "Think about it. Everyone we've talked to was seen in a private conversation with the victim at some point during the bake-off. Felicity cornered him in a hallway. Stanley let him have it in the men's room and again in the room where he died. Ginger is the one who lured him to the library in the first place, but she claims she was too angry to confront him. Heck, even Kennedy and I saw those two cookie-nappers cornering him. Lindsey and Bradley were the only two people who didn't corner him. I don't know what's going on, but I do think we really need to find those cookie-nappers."

Kennedy set down her fork and stared at him. "Of course we do, but we can't! They weren't on any of the footage Mrs. N looked at, and the police have nothing to go on. If we had the murder weapon, we'd at least get some fingerprints. But we don't even have that!"

"Then we keep searching," Rory said with a determined set to his jaw. "Three middle-aged women don't just disappear into thin air."

We had no sooner cleared the table when Betty and Doc arrived. Betty came bearing a dessert in the form of a beautiful English trifle. Kennedy's eyes nearly popped out at the sight of it.

"Betty, you angel! You've brought a Christmas trifle! I could kiss you! My gran used to make one every year for us. So much better than fruitcake." She took the glass bowl from our guest's hands and whisked it away to the kitchen. The trifle looked delicious. I followed her and began making coffee and tea.

The lighthouse was a flurry of activity as drinks were poured and the table was made ready for English trifle and a game of dominoes. I had just poured a pot of fresh coffee into a carafe and was ready to take it to the table when Betty popped up behind me.

"Don't say anything to Bob, but did you find out who wrote that note?" She cast a glance at Doc Riggles, who was laughing at something Dad said.

I didn't know whether to tell her or not, due to her reputation for spilling secrets. But since Betty had supplied Mom with the opportunity to snap the picture of said note, I decided to be honest. "I did. Ginger Brooks wrote it." Before Betty could scream, I swiftly added, "But she didn't kill him."

"The jury's still out on that one." Kennedy, passing by with a tray of dessert plates, had paused long enough to add her two cents. She tossed Betty a wink before heading to the table.

"We don't know who did it," I told her. "All we know is that Chevy made a lot of enemies in this town in the short time he was here. I'm passing all my information along to the police."

"Are you giving up on this case?" She looked more troubled than relieved.

Her confidence made me chuckle. "Betty, I'm a baker. I run a bakery. I was never really on the case. We were just trying to help."

"Well, I'll keep my eyes and ears open all the same." She picked up the teapot and the decorative basket holding my collection of teas. "One more thing. Bradley Argyle called to thank me for sending him a cake. You wouldn't happen to know anything about that, would you?"

"No," I lied. "I wonder where he got that idea?"

CHAPTER 38

The murder of Chevy Chambers had stumped the best of us, but I wasn't about to give up just yet, and neither were Rory and Kennedy. I had a bakery to run, but the two of them had time on their hands. Therefore, it was decided that while I worked at the Beacon, they would set aside their petty differences and put their heads together, scouring the internet for any clue as to the identity of the mysterious cookie-nappers.

I was eager to speak with Mrs. Nichols the moment I arrived in the bakery kitchen. The poor woman had spent an afternoon at the police station watching confiscated footage. Although she hadn't been able to spot the three women in question, she might have picked up on something of value.

As she mixed up a giant batch of her now-famous butter cookies, she thought about my question. "He was a camera hog," she announced. "I enjoyed watching each of you bake. But Chevy was a vain man and liked to be seen. What was also evident was that he was a shameless flirt. You didn't bite. You bake with confidence and didn't need the flattery." I blushed at the compliment. "But Ginger and Felicity did . . ." Her voice trailed off.

While Mrs. Nichols was talking, I had been working on cupcakes. A tray of rich chocolate was just about done baking in the oven while another tray, this one containing carrot cake batter, was ready to go in. Wendy had talked me into making holiday-themed cupcakes. Since she wanted to practice her decorating skills, I had encouraged her to be creative. The cupcakes had been her palette, and she hadn't disappointed me. Her whimsical designs out of frosting and candy had created cupcakes that looked like reindeer, snowmen, snow-flakes, Christmas trees, and even ones that looked like Santa. Not only were they adorable and delicious, but we sold out of them every day. Since Christmas was only a few days away, I was confident we could move a few dozen more.

"What is it?" The flow of her narrative had stopped. I opened the oven and swapped out the trays before turning to look at her.

She pursed her lips. "It's just that he seemed so confident with you ladies, but I forgot about Bradley."

"What about him?"

"Chevy left him alone."

I laughed. "Only because he was a man."

"Well, there is that. And maybe that's all it was. But Chevy was more cautious of him than he was of you ladies. I might even suggest he was respectful."

That got me. I shook my head, bristling slightly at my colliding thoughts. "That would suggest he was a chauvinist as well as a pig. I should have figured as much. I'm afraid our victim was riddled with unsavory vices."

Mrs. Nichols agreed, and the conversation ended. Her only regret had been leaving the police station without identifying a single cookie-napper.

With the bakery cases full and the customers lining up for their morning coffee and treats, I waved good-bye to Mrs. Nichols. She had worked her usual magic and needed to run some errands. I told her to enjoy the rest of her day.

When Sergeant Murdock and Tuck came in, I left the bakery counter and waved them over to the coffee bar. Since they were both slightly addicted to our holiday drinks, I brought each a peppermint mocha. It was my way of buttering them up before I handed over the signed receipts I had gathered through my Christmas cake deception. Being cops, they were going to find out about the anonymous Christmas cakes eventually.

Although Tuck had been party to some of our meddling, he hadn't been aware of all of it. I knew I had shocked him, just as I knew I had angered the sergeant, losing any points I had thus made with her. But the so-called burden of proof had been too much for me. I briefly explained what I had done with a few choice edits, then handed them over.

Sergeant Stacy Murdock, being a clever person, was still stuck on the one detail I wasn't willing to give them.

"One thing I still don't understand, Bakewell, is why you bothered in the first place. I specifically told you not to meddle in this case."

"And I was honestly trying not to." Her look of aggressive skepticism was so chilling it almost made me confess everything. But I wasn't just protecting myself on this one. It was for the sake of Mom and Betty that I couldn't reveal the real reason I had gone through so much trouble to get four signatures.

"What good were these signatures to you?"

"Ah . . . well, if you must know, I saw the note."

"What note?" Now she was playing me.

"The one found in Chevy's hand. It said *Meet me under the mistletoe.* I thought that maybe I could match the handwriting and find the killer."

"Without the note?"

"Umm . . . yep. I have a good memory for letters."

"I thought it was numbers," she pointedly remarked, before sipping her mocha.

At this point in the conversation, Tuck was staring at me in a most uncomfortable way. With the exception of his crush on Kennedy, he was a very astute man. His look suggested he knew we had somehow gotten a copy of that letter.

Ignoring him, I turned to the sergeant and shrugged. "That's why I'm handing them over to you. I thought you might have better luck matching the handwriting."

When Tuck and Murdock left, I sent Ginger a quick text alerting her to expect a visit from Murdock. She was my friend, and I had believed her when she told me that she hadn't killed Chevy. But the twisting, turning events leading to the cookie critic's death was proving nearly impossible to unravel. Without knowing the identity of the cookie-nappers, the murder of Chevy Chambers just might remain unsolved. That would throw a shadow over my perfect Christmas for sure.

There was one other person I needed to talk with to clear the air, so to speak. After the lunch rush, I took off my apron and left the Beacon in the capable hands of Elizabeth and Wendy. I then put on my coat, hat, and gloves and headed across town to the Tannenbaum Shoppe.

I couldn't help but smile as I came upon the busy shop that pushed Christmas cheer all year round. There was no denying that there was something quite special about a person who displayed so much passion for the season. It struck me for the first time as I walked past the crowded parking lot, just how lucky the town of Beacon Harbor was to have such a store. Thanks to a woman with a vision, the place was the embodiment of Christmas. Children were still lining up to meet Santa and pet his reindeer at this late date. It was the place for last-minute Christmas wishes, gifts, ornaments, and hot cocoa with sticky marshmallows. I walked through the front door, found an elf, and asked to speak with the owner.

The young lady with pointy ears and a floppy hat walked over to the wrapping station and picked up a phone. A few minutes later, she apologized and told me that Felicity was somewhere on the floor.

Not a big problem. I thanked the elf and set out to explore the crowded store. I walked down aisle after aisle, fighting the crowds while looking for Felicity. I finally spotted her near a nine-foot fully decorated tree in the Christmas tree forest, set apart in a separate room. I could see that she was talking with someone — a customer, I presumed. I made my way toward her and called out her name.

Felicity turned, revealing the person she'd been talking with. It was Mrs. Nichols.

I was shocked to see my assistant baker there. To be fair, Mrs. Nichols looked just as surprised to see me as well. Before I could say hi, she waved and disappeared behind the tree. Felicity straightened her green velvet Christmas skirt and walked over to meet me.

"You were talking with Mrs. Nichols." The words tumbled out of my mouth as both a statement and a question. I peered around the woman, who was blocking my view.

Felicity seemed unaware.

"I talk to a lot of people. But seeing you here *is* a surprise. Don't you have a bakery to run?"

I tried to peer around her other side, but she blocked me. "Like you, I have helpers. Was that Mrs. Nichols?"

"A lovely woman. We were just talking." She took hold of my arm and gently guided me in the opposite direction. "Why are you here?"

I stopped and looked at her. "I came to apologize. Can we talk?"

I sat in Felicity's office, attempting to explain why I had come. "I was so certain that you were having an affair with Chevy, but now I know that you weren't."

She looked at me with all the trust a mouse regards a viper with and scratched her chin. "I don't understand. How is that an apology?"

I blushed. "Because I thought you were the one responsible for Chevy's murder."

That pushed some buttons. Felicity bristled with indignation. "Really! I told you I didn't kill him, just as I told you that I wasn't having an affair with him either. I can't believe you were smart enough to work on Wall Street." She flipped her red hair and tilted her head as she stared at me.

"There are many different brands of clever," I told her. "Only a select few of them relate to financial success. I freely admit that I screwed up on this one."

"Good. That's a start." I was happy to see her anger morph into thoughtful reflection. "By the way, you might be the only one in this town who believes me."

"I take it your husband doesn't?"

At the mention of Stanley Stewart, her bravado crumbled. "I made a fool of myself," she whimpered as her chin began to tremble. "I put winning that damn bake-off ahead of my marriage and now I'm paying the price. You might be right about different brands of clever. I'm not clever at all. I can't see a way out of this one."

My heart went out to her. There were some people who spent a lifetime playing it safe, venturing small risks to gather small gains. It was a comfort for them to know that the ground would always rise up to meet their feet.

And then there were those like Felicity. Her passion for Christmas was so great that in a moment of greed, fueled by visions of grandeur, she had risked it all. I, of all people, knew there was a lot to admire in that. Felicity and I weren't so different after all. But I never risked more than I was willing to lose. I also relied on the numbers, because, unlike the vagaries of human nature, numbers could be trusted. Putting one's trust in an emotional saboteur like Chevy Chambers was a recipe for disaster. Yet perhaps I could help her out of this one.

"The reason I'm here is because I know who was having an affair with Chevy."

Her eyes shot to me like two pointy darts. "You?" I didn't think I deserved quite all of the accusation and venom in her glance.

I deflected it with my well-practiced *gag me* face. "It was Ginger."

The thought was so salacious that a hand flew over her mouth. "No! That little liar."

"Honestly, can you blame her for lying?" I knew that poor Ginger had been embarrassed enough by her foolish mistake. It was now time to put that behind us. I doubled down and told her, "My point is, Ginger can help you. She can tell Stanley the truth."

She thought about that. "She would do that for me?"

"I know she will. We are the shop owners of Beacon Harbor. Your silly Christmas cookie bake-off nearly tore us apart. But we can't let that happen to us, Felicity. I'd like to think that our love for this beautiful village and all who live here is stronger than our need to bake the best cookie. They're

Christmas cookies, for heaven's sake! Anyone who bakes a Christmas cookie is a winner. Our mistake was letting Chevy Chambers convince us otherwise."

"You're right," she said, nervously wringing her hands. "And I'm partially to blame. I let Chevy sweet-talk me into believing that I might have my own Christmas-themed baking show. I fell in love with the idea. All I needed to do in return was . . ." She seemed embarrassed to continue.

"I know," I said and held up a hand. I didn't need to hear any more. "I'm beginning to understand how that man worked. He was torquing each one of us up by flirting and making false promises. I think he felt all the drama would be good for ratings."

Her face flushed with anger. "The horrible truth of it was, I actually entertained the idea. But I could never take that final leap."

"Thank goodness," I said and smiled at the woman across from me. "It's now time to put that behind you. Heaven knows, I'm trying to as well. Christmas is only a few days away, Felicity. We can't let the ghost of Chevy Chambers ruin it for us."

CHAPTER 39

As I walked down the snowy sidewalk back to the lighthouse, I felt better. I had made peace with Felicity and had handed the receipts over to the police. I was trying to let go of the tragedy at the Christmas Festival, and in doing so, it felt like a weight had been lifted from me. Death was always sad, I thought. And murder, quite frankly, terrified me. There was also the element of anger — that someone had cornered Chevy Chambers and had murdered him at the village Christmas Festival during the live bake-off! The shock of finding his body was something I wasn't soon to forget, and in a selfish way, it made me mad. The Christmas Festival was supposed to be a safe event for families. It was supposed to be fun and filled with good cheer. Chevy and his need to stir the pot had ruined it for us. He had pushed someone too far and had paid the price. I silently cursed him and his giant ego. But I wouldn't let him ruin Christmas.

The moment I caught sight of my home, my heart beat a little faster. The old Beacon Point Lighthouse never failed to capture my imagination, standing tall over a freshwater sea. Covered in Christmas lights, it looked even better, reminding me of my task. There were still plenty of cars in the parking lot and plenty of baking left to do.

I walked through the front door, greeted Wendy and Elizabeth, then headed back to the kitchen. There, I looked at my baking list, gathered my ingredients, and set to work on the special orders for the next morning.

"Hey, Lindsey." I looked up from the cake I was decorating and saw Elizabeth. I waved her in. She came through the door carrying a red mug that was topped with a heavy dose of whipped cream. "While you were out, I mixed up this. Care to try it?"

It smelled good, and vaguely familiar. "Of course. What am I drinking?"

"Taste it and try to guess." I liked her confidence, and the challenge issued behind her smile. I always encouraged the Beacon's employees to be adventurous. We had our set menu of crowd pleasers, and a rotating list of daily specials. But I loved it when someone other than me came up with an idea. Wendy had embraced cupcakes and was becoming a big help in the kitchen. Ryan liked to throw a twist on our sandwich menu. Alaina was still a bit shy when it came to expressing new ideas for our edible offerings, but she was our resident chalk artist. I had given her free reign over our menu board and had never regretted it. Then there was Elizabeth and Tom. They both loved coffee and weren't afraid to try new things. This little drink was one of them.

I looked at the spice sprinkled on the whipped cream and sniffed. I sniffed again and ventured, "Nutmeg?" She nodded. I then took a sip. The strong espresso had been blended with thick, creamy eggnog and steamed milk. It was so silky, rich, and flavorful, it tasted like Christmas Eve.

"Elizabeth, this is amazing! I love it. It's so perfectly blended. I know that I don't have eggnog here. Did you buy it?"

"We made it last night. It's my mom's recipe and one of our holiday traditions. She makes a batch with alcohol and one without for the kids. I asked if I could take a pint of the nonalcoholic batch and brought it to work today. I wanted to see if we could make a good eggnog latte."

I took another sip and toasted her. "Mission accomplished! This tastes so good. If I bought the ingredients, would you be able to make the eggnog here? I know there's only a few days left until Christmas, but I want this to be our Christmas Eve special. What do you think?"

Elizabeth beamed with delight. "Really? I would love that! Wow. Thanks, Lindsey."

I made a note to have Alaina add it to the menu tomorrow. Everything was falling into place, I thought. The Beacon was returning to normal.

But my thoughts had spoken too soon. The moment we closed for the day, Rory and Kennedy came bursting through the lighthouse door. The intensity on their faces and the air of urgency that swirled around them stopped me in my tracks. One look at them and the weight that had lifted began to settle around me again. It didn't help that all three dogs raced into the café, too, feeding off the excitement. I had a biscuit and a pet for each, which calmed them back down. I silently wished that the same offering would work on the hyped-up human duo, but I knew it wasn't going to be that simple.

"Lindsey!" Kennedy cried, heading for the nearest café table. "You are never going to believe this. Rory is a genius!"

For some reason, the way the words tumbled from her lips made me smile. "I already know he's a genius." Although the man in question was carrying a laptop, I wrapped my arm through his and led him to the table. "I've been telling you that for months."

Kennedy, caught in her compliment, ran a scrutinizing eye over my boyfriend. "Don't blame me for not believing you. The whole Paul Bunyan vibe" — she wiggled her hand at him as she spoke — "and the freezer full of wild meat confuses the senses. In general, the jury's still out, but Rory dear has a knack for sniffing out information."

After staring at her for a beat or two, he looked at me, shook his head, and opened his laptop. "What she's trying to tell you is that we found something of interest. All day long we've been reading through a cache of articles written about or by Chevy Chambers. Then we stumbled across this." Pulling up the article in question, Rory turned the laptop to me.

"What is this?" I asked, taking a seat.

"It's an old article from the *Chicago Tribune*. We have a connection to Chevy Chambers."

I took a deep breath. Kennedy added, "It's a review Chevy wrote for a new restaurant on the Chicago food scene called Tall Ships."

I cast her a questioning look. "Interesting . . . And why is this important?"

"Where's the fun in telling you? Read it for yourself."

I did, and the instant I began reading the article I regretted it. The review was mean-spirited and brutal; from the name of the restaurant down to the choice in cocktail straws, nothing was spared. Then, however, Chevy admonished the chef. I could feel the blood draining from my face as my eyes landed on the name. My head rang with dread as my hand flew to my mouth. Rory, taking that as a cue, reached across and placed his finger on the mousepad. There was little need to read the rest of the article. I had gotten the gist of it. But then he scrolled down the page for me and landed on the photograph.

What a proud day, I thought, looking at the young man who stood so confidently before the doors of his restaurant. As all great ventures do, it had started with a dream and a willingness to take a risk, one calculated against talent. Not a bad risk, I mused. But opening a restaurant was always a risky business. There were so many factors involved — soliciting investors, gathering capital, finding the right spot, signing loans and leases, planning the menu, finding a good manager, hiring an accountant, and then beginning the costly buildout. I knew from experience it was a labor of love. And that love was clear as day in the smile of a younger Bradley Argyle. Although his hair was thicker, his face slimmer, and his smile brighter, it didn't take much to recognize him. At the time the picture was taken, he'd had no idea what the article would say, only that he and his restaurant had made it into the *Chicago Tribune*.

"There's our connection. But it still doesn't make sense. Bradley always seemed so composed around Chevy, and he never left the stage at the bake-off."

"Maybe he didn't need to." Kennedy leaned over my shoulder and placed her finger on the screen. "There. Look at that woman standing off to the side. She barely made it into the photo. Her face is slightly turned, and it's a little blurry, but . . . I don't know, she just struck me as familiar."

I looked at the image, then inhaled sharply. "I don't suppose it's any coincidence that she looks like the woman who locked me in the storage closet."

CHAPTER 40

The discovery of the connection between Bradley Argyle and Chevy Chambers was the link we'd been searching for. They had a past, and I had a pretty good idea — due to the fact that Bradley was working at a hotel restaurant in Beacon Harbor, Michigan — that the damage done by that review had been devastating. That, however, was mere speculation. It was the image of the mysterious woman in the photo that I couldn't stop thinking about. Although it had been taken many years ago, and the woman in question was slightly out of focus, there was a striking resemblance between her and the woman I'd chased at the Christmas Festival. It was so close that I needed a second opinion to be certain. That's why a visit to the Candy Cane Cottage was in order.

Mrs. Nichols pushed her glasses higher on the bridge of her nose as she stared at the picture in her hand. Rory, not wanting to drag his computer all over town, had printed the article. "Oh my," she exclaimed, taking a closer look. "That's her! That's the one who was being so rude in the bakeshop, asking if we had gluten-free products." She shook her head, as if the thought of such products was still preposterous. Her owlish eyes then held to Rory's. "But this little missy didn't want gluten-free anything. She wanted to steal our cookies!"

"Are you sure it's her?"

The spritely old baker nodded. "I only wish her name had been printed below the photo. Then we'd know who she was."

"I do too," I said, taking back the paper. "At least this time we have a man who might be able to help us with that."

A troubled look crossed her face as she stood up from the kitchen table. "Do be careful, you three. And be sure to take a cookie for the road."

A short while later, we were back in my Jeep, heading for the Harbor Hotel. Looking at the crowded parking lot, I realized it might not be the best time to pull the head chef aside for a quick chat. My fears were confirmed the moment we walked into the restaurant, where we were met by the hum of pleasant conversation, the soft clank of dishware, and the whiff of untold savory smells.

"Maybe we should come back," I ventured, noting there wasn't an empty table in sight.

"No time like the present," Kennedy said, rooting through her purse. Her hand landed on something, and she smiled.

"Do you have a reservation?" Our attention was pulled away by a young woman standing behind the hostess station. She was looking at us, awaiting our answer. Before Rory or I could shake our heads, Kennedy, wearing black fashionista sunglasses — even though it was dark outside — pushed between us and marched up to the young woman.

In her most intimidating accent, Kennedy snapped, "No. We are not here to dine." With a dramatic flourish, she removed her glasses and stared at the girl, who couldn't have been more than eighteen. "My name is Lillian Finch. Perhaps you've heard of me? No?" Kennedy flipped her long black hair, leaned an elbow on the lectern, and smiled. "How about now?" The poor girl didn't know what to make of her.

"Ah . . . no, ma'am."

"No? Seriously? It's just as well. I'm an investigative reporter here to follow up on a lead regarding the troubling matter of poultry smuggling."

The girl's jaw dropped, and so did mine.

Kennedy had pulled out her favorite alter ego, Lillian Finch — a name and a persona I had always found hilarious. But was she really going with poultry smuggling? Rory grabbed me by the arm to keep me from laughing. He was grabbing me, I realized, to keep him from laughing too.

The hostess backed away. "Ah . . . come again?"

"Poultry. You know — chickens, ducks, turkeys, Cornish hens, and the occasional gray goose? Sound familiar?"

I was nearly certain that last one was a nod to her favorite vodka brand.

"I . . . I know what poultry is, ma'am. Is this some kind of joke?"

"Are you asking if the health and safety of poultry is a joke?" The girl shook her head. "Good. That's a start. Now, tell me, where are you hiding them?"

"I'm . . . I'm not hiding anything."

"I can smell them," Kennedy added, pointing to the dining room. "Chicken Marsala, Chicken cordon bleu, Cornish game hen, grilled chicken breast over a bed of greens. That's how it starts. Everybody wants to serve free-range chickens. They think it's humane, but, tell me, what is humane about plucking those little darlings from the range and smuggling them into your kitchen?"

"I . . . think we get ours from a delivery truck," the hostess informed her.

"Can you check?"

The girl stared at Kennedy, uncertain how to go about doing that. At last she said, "I could call the manager."

"No. I think it's best if you phoned the chef directly. Clever chefs can smuggle a live turkey right under a manager's nose. Ring the kitchen. Tell Chef Argyle that I'll meet him in the back hallway between the kitchen and the ballroom."

"Um . . . yeah. Okay." The girl picked up the phone and made the call.

"Poultry smuggling?" We were just out of earshot of the hostess when Rory looked at her as if she was crazy. "Did that just pop into your head, or is this something you've been cooking up for an episode of *Kennedy's Crusades*?"

"Already covered it, darling. It is a thing, but not so much in this country. All fingers point to China on this one, I'm afraid. China ships poultry, live or frozen, to developing nations for a fraction of the price of producing it in-country. The practice not only hurts the local poultry farmers, but it can often transmit diseases to healthy poultry populations and humans alike. It was part of the reason the Asian avian influenza spread throughout the world in the late nineties and early two thousands. You really should be tuning in to my podcast."

He tossed her a sideways glance. "I hardly need to now. Do you really think Chef Argyle is going to bite?"

"Shh!" I pressed a finger to my lips and pointed to the door in question. "Let's wait and see."

A short while later, Bradley Argyle, dressed in his chef's coat and hat, came bursting out of the kitchen door. He saw us, looked down both hallways, then looked at us again.

"I don't understand? I was told to come out here regarding a matter of poultry juggling. I'm a little busy for games. Lindsey, Rory, and . . ." He looked at my friend, forgetting her name.

"Kennedy," she supplied for him.

"Ah, yes. Kennedy. Now, what's this all about?"

Rory handed him the printout of the *Chicago Tribune* article. Bradley, looking uncertain, took it. The moment he realized what was in his hand, his ruddy face turned the color of parchment.

"What's this?"

"You never told us you had a connection to Chevy Chambers." Rory held him in a probing gaze.

The name of the food critic caused a slight tremor to seize Bradley's chin. He then took a calming breath and nodded. "This," he said, shaking the paper, "was a long time ago. As you can imagine, this review did some damage. But I've put all that behind me."

"Until Chevy Chambers came to Beacon Harbor," I offered.

As if caught with his hand in the cookie jar, a guilty look crossed his face. "You can only imagine how I felt when I learned of it. I would have talked Felicity out of it had I known what she was thinking. Obviously, I didn't learn of it until after the Christmas cookie bake-off had been announced."

"You lied to the police," I accused, knowing that he must have.

Bradley nodded. "The truth is, I didn't think I had a choice. When Chevy was murdered, I grew afraid. I mean, how would that look? I didn't like the man one bit. Yet there was something in me that wanted to compete in the cookie bake-off. I guess I wanted to show him that regardless of his scathing review of my restaurant, I had survived. No, I have flourished here. He might have been correct when he wrote that I wasn't cut out for the big city scene. I can now admit that I had bitten off more than I could chew with that restaurant, and he called me out on it. I wasn't happy. In fact, I was furious. But you need to realize that a lot has happened in both our careers. Chevy stayed in Chicago and made a name for himself on television. I moved to Beacon Harbor. I'm head of this kitchen, and I couldn't be happier." He shrugged, then offered a wan smile. "So, no poultry juggling?"

"They take to the air because they can," Kennedy told him. "I bet you wish you were a bird right about now?"

"Are you accusing me of something?" He gave her a hard stare.

"Bradley," Rory began, "you know how this looks. You have both motive and opportunity. Do you expect us to believe you didn't murder Chevy Chambers?"

Bradley laughed. "The trouble is, I think we all wanted to kill him. But no. This time was different. Beacon Harbor is my town, not his. I decided not to care, and it worked.

The poor bastard actually liked my cookies."

"Because you baked a winning cookie," I told him. I could tell the compliment pleased him. While his back was down, I gently continued. "I'm very sorry about your restaurant. Chevy's review was mean, but this is a great picture of you at any rate. By the way, who is this woman?" I pointed to the woman in question.

Without much thought, he answered, "That's my mother."

My stomach lurched at the thought. It was a revelation! His mother had stolen my cookies! Dear heavens, what had compelled her to do that? Fighting to remain calm, I asked, "And, um, what's her name?"

It must have been the tone of my voice. His head jerked up, and he shot me a look that chilled me to the core. "It's none of your concern. And here's a little advice for all of you. Stay out of this."

He was turning to go when I blurted, "I would, but your mother and two of her friends stole all of the Beacon's signature cookies."

"What?" It must have been the first time he'd heard of it. His face fell as embarrassment struck him. "Oh, God. I'm sorry. I didn't know. Look, my mother is a . . . a kleptomaniac. She's a lovely person, but she can't help herself. As you can imagine, it's a huge embarrassment for me. How much did she take, Lindsey? I'd be happy to pay for whatever loss you incurred."

"No, no. I don't want your money. I just thought maybe you'd tell me her name?"

Pain flashed across his face. He tried to fight it, but it was a powerful emotion. "Please," he said, "leave my mother out of this." He hung his head and walked back to his kitchen.

Chapter 41

We were barely buckled into our seats when Kennedy remarked, "It just goes to prove the old adage, you can choose your friends, but you can't choose your family."

"He clearly has mommy issues," I agreed.

"Did you see the look on his face when you mentioned the cookie-napping? Like a kid caught with his hand in the biscuit tin. I bet he knew but was too embarrassed to admit it."

I gave this a thought as I drove out of the parking lot heading for the lighthouse. "I feel sorry for him," I admitted. "First Chevy Chambers, a prickly ghost from his past, comes to town, and then his mother steals our cookies. Who knows what else she's taken since she's been here?"

"You think she's here in this town?" Rory, riding shotgun, looked at me. He'd been rubbing the bridge of his nose between thumb and forefinger, something he did when deep in thought or troubled. His hand came away. "Is she visiting? Do you think she's at his house?"

"I don't know what to think," I told him honestly.

"Look, I consider myself to be a good judge of character."

Kennedy leaned forward. "Wish we could say the same about our Lindsey."

Ignoring her, Rory continued. "There's something about that guy that sends up all kinds of warning bells. Think about it. He works at the hotel. Bradley would know all the ins and outs, all the hallways and sitting areas."

I turned my head to look at him. "Go on."

"Another point, the woman we now know to be his mother locked you in a basement storage closet. She stole your signature cookies. Big deal. It's hardly the crime of the century. So, why lure you down there and get you out of the way?"

"I never thought of it like that. Do you think she was planning to lock me in the closet?"

Kennedy leaned forward, this time with a serious thought. "Doubtful she was planning it, but Rory's correct — don't gloat, darling — she was familiar with the hotel, so clearly it was an option."

"Those are locked storage closets," Rory pointed out. "She would have to have had a key to open the door. The closet you were locked in, Lindsey, contained kitchen supplies. It's not a huge leap of the imagination to think that the head chef would have had the key. Most likely a master key. Chad, unfortunately, didn't have one. He had a key ring instead. If there is a master key, maybe it had been stolen."

"She could have lifted it without him knowing," Kennedy offered. "She's a klepto, remember? Hardly a challenge to those with Sticky Finger Syndrome."

I smiled at her made-up disease. "I agree. But what's her real motive? Why steal my cookies? Why lock me in a closet? I don't know her." I paused to park the Jeep in the boathouse, turned off the ignition, and looked at Kennedy in the rearview mirror.

"Maybe she thought you were trying to steal her son?" She flashed a devilish smile. "Tit for tat. Mommy Sticky Fingers wants you out of the picture."

Hardly, I thought. I barely knew Bradley. But I did know that Kennedy delighted in making wild guesses. I patted Rory's hand, and told him, "I have all I need right here." The approval in his bright blue gaze inspired me. On impulse, I yanked him closer for a kiss. Our lips were about to touch when Kennedy thrust her hand between us, blocking lip-to-lip contact.

"What?" I cried. Rory, kissing the fleshy side of her hand, made a sound packed with all the revulsion of a man being tickled with a dead, sand-covered fish.

"Save it for the mistletoe, you two. We're in the middle of an investigation. Now, tell me, do we think Bradley Argyle or Mommy Sticky Fingers is our killer?"

The way Kennedy had clarified it, making it a choice between Bradley and his mother set the wheels in my head in motion. While it was true that every contestant in the live bake-off had a motive to cause harm to Chevy Chambers, Bradley Argyle and his failed restaurant seemed to stand above the rest. His mom had been there. She'd been in the photograph. And Bradley would not give us her name. Although he had claimed that he'd moved past all ill will toward Chevy, it could have been a lie. Certainly, his mother's behavior had been very odd, even suspicious. I couldn't quite put it all together, but I thought Kennedy had hit the nail on the head.

"What if it was both of them?" I offered. "Think about it. Here is what we know. Bradley's mom and her friends, our cookie-nappers, were in the audience during the bake-off, and each one was seen talking with Chevy. Bradley, as far as I know, never left the stage until he was done with his gingerbread showstopper. That was around the time his mom was pointed out to me by Mrs. Nichols. I chased after her and ended up being locked in a storage closet. How long was I in there?"

Rory shrugged. "Fifteen minutes, maybe? But you're right, Lindsey. There was about fifteen or twenty minutes between the time you called me from that closet until the time we entered the library, where we found Chevy's body. We know that he was seen talking to Felicity, Stanley, and even our Mrs. Nichols in that room. But no one ever saw him talking with Bradley or his mom. They would have had plenty of time to corner him in the library and hit him over the head."

"With what, though?" Kennedy, resting her head on her crossed arms, looked at him.

"Bradley had a rolling pin," I offered.

"But his wasn't missing. Only Felicity's went missing. But wouldn't it be just like Mommy Sticky Fingers to take it in order to shift the blame onto Mommy Cheeriest? After all, she had been flirting shamelessly with Chevy."

"Good point, Kennedy. Don't let that go to your head." Rory tossed her a wink. "If we're lucky, she might still have it. I suggest we try to locate Bradley's mother."

While Kennedy and Rory shared our latest discovery regarding the death of Chevy Chambers with Mom and Dad, I jumped into the kitchen and started dinner. All the delicious smells from the hotel restaurant had made me hungry. Welly and the models, staring at me with hope in their eyes, were ravenous as well. Dogs were always hungry, I mused, and began the preparations for both human and canine dinners.

The dogs were satisfied with their favorite kibble doctored with a little roasted chicken. For the humans, I was making pasta Bolognese. I knew it was one of Rory's favorite dishes, containing three different types of meat blended in a red sauce. I took out a pound of thick bacon, cut it into inch-sized pieces, and threw it into a skillet. I let the bacon cook for a few minutes, then drained off the fat and added a pound of lean ground beef and a pound of Italian sausage.

Mom walked into the kitchen to get drinks. "That smells both fattening and delicious."

"Everything delicious is fattening," I told her with a grin. "Remember my lighthouse Christmas rule? No talking about diets until January second. Now, put down that fattening bottle of wine and help me crush this garlic and chop this basil." I smiled as I handed her a garlic press and a knife.

As Mom set to work, she said, "So, Bradley's mother is one of the cookie-nappers." I could see that the thought both troubled and intrigued her. "And he wouldn't give you her name or address? That sounds very much like he's hiding something."

"That's what I thought," said Dad, coming in to pluck a piece of bacon out of my pan. The scent of its sizzling had lured him into the kitchen. Sheer male boldness made him believe that he could put his fingers into my hot pan of meat. I slapped his hand away with my spatula and scooped out a piece for him.

"Honestly, you're as bad as Wellington," I chided, watching him gobble it up. "Thank goodness Welly doesn't have opposable thumbs."

"I'm starving, and it smells so good in here. Can I help?" I kissed him on the cheek and relinquished the meats to him.

As Dad drained the fat out of the pan, he asked, "Regarding Bradley's mom, can't

Rory Google that or something? I mean, if he found that article with her picture in it, I'd think a man of his talents would be able to find out her name."

"And what talents are those, James?" Kennedy swooped into the kitchen to grab the bottle of wine Mom had abandoned. Rory, finding himself alone, had come in behind her. My lighthouse kitchen, although recently gutted and remodeled with white upper cabinets, blue lower cabinets, and white granite countertops, wasn't very large. But that didn't stop everyone from wanting to be in there.

Dad turned from the sink to look at Kennedy. "Special Forces. They know how to do things we mere mortals don't. Isn't that right, Rory?"

My boyfriend blushed. Captain Rory Campbell, ex–Navy SEAL, was being modest, and I found it utterly adorable. "James. I wish it were that easy. But personal information like that is usually protected."

Dad winked. "For normal people."

Rory cleared his throat uncomfortably. "Right, well, there's also the problem of matching a face with a name. We'd need facial recognition software for that, as well as a government-protected database."

"Hello, everyone. I'm shagging a cop.

Mightn't we give this to him to solve?" Kennedy waved the scathing review in the air.

"No!" we all cried, although Mom was giggling.

"I mean, of course, we should," I said, gently removing the review from her hand. "Just not yet. We might be wrong about all this, and then how would that look? Murdock would come down on us for snooping. And Tuck, well, no one likes mixing business with pleasure. Let's give Rory a crack at this first."

Kennedy was outnumbered on this one.

I finished the sauce by adding two cans of crushed tomatoes, the four cloves of crushed garlic from Mom, and the fresh basil. I also added a teaspoon of dried oregano, a teaspoon of salt, and a teaspoon of sugar to cut the acidity of the tomatoes. After adding half a cup of heavy cream, I stirred it all together. I covered the pan and turned the heat to low to let it simmer. While the sauce was finishing up, I cooked the spaghetti. Needless to say, dinner was a hit.

After dinner, we all bundled up and hiked along the snowy pathway to Rory's log home with only the moon and the lights from my candy cane light tower to guide us. Sure, the dogs knew the way, and we all had flashlights on our cell phones. My hands were full, however, carrying the apple pie I had made earlier. Mom was toting a carafe of coffee. Over dinner we had cajoled Rory into contacting one of his buddies currently working at the Pentagon. We were having dessert at his house while he worked on the puzzle of matching the face in the newspaper photo to a name. If that failed, our backup plan was to pay a visit to Bradley's house in the morning.

After we had finished the pie, we gathered around Rory's Christmas tree drinking coffee. His tree was a beautiful ten-foot Douglas fir wrapped in white lights. There were no ornaments on it, just lights. But it looked lovely, placed before the tall wall of windows that overlooked his snowy deck and the frozen lake beyond. Wellington was lying at my feet. Brinkley and Ireland were snuggled in the laps of Mom and Dad respectively. Kennedy was sipping coffee while flipping through her Instagram feed. A moment later, Rory, who had been in his office on the second floor, appeared in the loft.

"We got it," he said, looking down on us. "Sophia Argyle-Huffman. I have her most recent address. She lives outside of Petoskey, in the village of Bay Harbor."

"Bay Harbor!" Mom sat up and looked at us girls. "I was just there. That's a wealthy little neighborhood right on the lake, and full of shops, restaurants, and trendy clothing boutiques. In short, that's my territory."

Dad, recognizing her euphoric expression, ventured a tentative, "Ellie, what are you saying?"

"I'm saying that I know how to get into the house of Sophia Argyle-Huffman, no cops needed. No offense, dear." This, she directed to Kennedy with a sympathetic pout. "I'm cooking up a plan as we speak. Ladies, are you in?"

Mom was a model, not a cop; her plans were usually half-baked and wacky. Nonetheless, my curiosity got the best of me. "Yes," I cried. "I'm in."

Kennedy clearly thought I was crazy, yet she set down her phone and addressed my mom. "Right. Me, too, Ellie."

CHAPTER 42

I opened the bakeshop as usual but only worked until eleven. That's when Dad tied on his apron and came behind the bakery counter to relieve me. He was taking over while I helped Mom spring a trap for Sophia Argyle-Huffman. Mom, a fan of drama, had kept her plan to herself, building it up in our heads as a home run. "Ladies, you have to learn to trust me," she told Kennedy and me. "I've got this." Her confidence was not only impressive, but convincing. We knew she had put a lot of thought behind this, but when she handed us our garment bags, I was assailed by doubt.

"Umm . . . this is your plan?" Why had I thought it was going to be a little more complex than putting on an *Ellie & Co* original? I had been expecting something clever and daring, something that would require me to carry a Taser. Clearly, Mom was going with what she knew, and that was being a model. Kennedy and I were parading as models as well. My *disguise,* as Mom put it, was a soft, thick-striped black and white turtleneck tucked into a pair of flowing black palazzo pants. I had to admit, my outfit was as comfortable as pajamas, but looked, well, elegant. As for accessories, I was given a pair of beautiful, dangly silver earrings, a bright red cape, and a black leather crossbody purse with a silver buckle. I looked inside, hoping to find a Taser buried in the tissue. Again, I was disappointed. Another disappointment came when I was given a wide, floppy black hat that I was to wear *rakishly* over half my face. Kennedy didn't have to wear a hat.

"We need to hide your identity," Mom explained, positioning the hat and arranging my loose, bouncy curls around my face. "We don't want Sophia to recognize you."

Good point. My one rebellion against Mom's plan was tossing the high heels aside for my trusty black Dansko shoes.

When Mom strutted into the living room, I began regaining my confidence. The celebrity eighties fashion model was back, only better. Her beauty and poise had always been there, but now they seemed somehow more real to me than that old

Vogue cover of her that popped up on my phone whenever she called. Her face was a little rounder and made far more interesting by the laugh lines around her mouth and the spidery beginnings of crow's feet around her eyes. She looked gorgeous and natural in the ankle-length, flowing skirt that was the color of an evergreen tree. On top, she wore a snowy-white mohair sweater, the perfect choice for the holidays. Her one accessory, besides a full-length fake fur coat, was a spectacular, dangling emerald and diamond necklace.

Kennedy, always a fashionista, looked stunning in the strapless dress with a fitted bodice that Mom had picked out for her. The deep gold of the material wasn't only festive, it suited her skin color and black hair to perfection. The skirt fell around her like a liquid bell, fluttering as she walked. To add a touch of panache to the ball gown look, Kennedy had been given a crimson bolero jacket with tails. And, of course, impractically high heels.

Bay Harbor was roughly an hour north of Beacon Harbor, situated on Little Traverse Bay. It was a playground for the wealthy, a modern resort community devoted to yachting, golfing, equestrian pursuits, and fine dining. I had never been to the town but had heard a lot about it. Rory had been there for one of his *business trips,* and he was driving us there in the high-end crossover vehicle Mom and Dad had rented.

Rory pressed Mom for her game plan. "You really think this is going to work, Ellie?" He took his eyes off the road to look at Mom.

"If you'll remember, Mrs. Nichols described the women who stole the cookies as looking like they didn't need to steal them at all. She said they were well-dressed, attractive, and middle-aged. From all your descriptions, they appeared to like fine clothing."

"Mom, honestly, I don't know where you're going with this. Are we supposed to be the pied pipers of fashionistas — summoning the clotheshorses and power-shoppers with the clopping of our high heels as we march down Main Street in our designer clothing? It's twenty degrees outside with a windchill of zero. Everyone in their right mind will be inside, hovering around a crackling fire."

"Or last-minute shopping in the village clothing boutiques. I told you that I've been here before, earlier this week with your dad. We had lunch but didn't have time to shop. However, while I was here, I wanted to scout out some of the boutiques and see if they'd be interested in carrying our clothing line."

"Brilliant idea," Kennedy quipped. After all, she had a stake in the brand. She leaned forward. "Is that what we're doing?"

Mom nodded. "It's our cover story. It works because it's real. Bay Harbor is a small, lovely, very wealthy town. If Sophia Argyle-Huffman frequents any one of the boutiques there, the owner will know her. Shop owners always know their best clients." Mom looked at Kennedy and me in the back seat and winked. She was winding up for her big reveal, the essence of her brilliant plan. Her voice filled with drama as she added, "And once we find the boutique where Sophia shops, we shall convince the owner to contact Sophia and tell her she's won a pop-up Christmas fashion show, by me, in the privacy of her own home. That's how we're getting in."

Rory nearly drove off the road, he was laughing so hard. He swerved back, sobered, and cleared his throat. "Wow! This is a joke, right?"

Mom grew incensed. "Why would you think this is a joke?"

"No offense, Ellie, but this is the real world, not an episode of the *Kardashian*s.

People don't just let three strange, albeit beautiful, women into their home because they're wearing nice clothes."

"Rory Campbell, do you know anything about women's clothing or women's fashion?"

"Nooo, ma'am. I shop at Cabela's and stick to the woods."

"Well, that's a good thing. You, dear boy, are way out of your league on this one. Now, mark my words, we will get into that house."

"I don't mean to be a bucket-dipper, but the only way we're getting into that house, ladies, is if I kick down the door."

In general, I'd have said Rory was correct. But Mom was a celebrity, one recognized in very unique circles. After strutting into three different boutiques in the luxurious village of Bay Harbor, modeling our outfits, and soliciting orders for *Ellie & Co*'s new spring line, Mom struck gold.

"Sophia's one of our best clients!" the woman in the chic leather pants gushed. Mom explained her private pop-up Christmas fashion show idea, stating that Sophia and her friends would be the perfect audience. As Mom spoke, the woman snuck out her phone, angled it at her, and snapped a picture before shoving it back in the drawer under the register. Kennedy and I saw the whole thing.

"She was just in this morning," the woman continued, "with Cynthia Goddard and Barbie Blankenship. They were looking at our new shipment of organic, sustainably sourced, hand-dyed, handmade scarves. She'll be so surprised. We have her phone number on file. I'll give her a ring."

"Did she buy one?" Kennedy asked the woman holding the phone.

"One what?"

"A scarf."

The woman shook her head, and uttered, "She bought a cute little tam off the sales rack today, but she'll be back for our Christmas Eve sale. Hello, is this Sophia?"

Twenty minutes later, we were standing before the door of a lovely home one block from the town center. Rory, dumbfounded that Mom's plan had gotten us this far, parked at the end of the road, where he could keep an eye on things.

"Lindsey, lower your hat," Mom reminded in a whisper. "Alright, ladies. Time to put on your cover girl smiles and sparkle." Mom, flashing hers, gave a loud knock on the door.

CHAPTER 43

"Ellie Montague! It really is you!" Sophia Argyle-Huffman answered the door in a holiday sweater gussied up with a loosely draped scarf around her neck and a black tam on her head. It didn't escape my notice or Kennedy's that the scarf looked suspiciously like the ones in the boutique. Mommy Sticky Fingers had struck again, I mused.

As Sophia ushered us inside her home, beaming from ear to ear, she continued to extol her good fortune. "What an unexpected surprise! We were just finishing lunch when Piper called. Are we really the first women to see your new clothing line? Such an honor. Such an honor. I had no idea you lived in Michigan."

"My husband grew up in Traverse City," Mom informed her, taking off her gloves one finger at a time. This wasn't a lie. She added, "We're here visiting relatives. I've always loved Michigan. For me, there was no better place to launch Ellie and Company."

As I walked inside the house with my head down and my face partially covered, I was struck by how normal Bradley's mother appeared. Last time I had seen her, she had run from me and lured me into a storage closet. Now she was schmoozing my mother in the name of fashion. As we entered the spacious living room, her two friends were seated on a floral couch. Kennedy suddenly grabbed my hand. "Those are the women Rory and I chased after in the hotel," she whispered. She squeezed my hand again. "Don't be obvious, but look at the coffee table."

Sophia's friends, dressed in the same uniform of designer holiday sweaters, black yoga pants, and knee-high boots, were holding chunky white coffee mugs in their hands while listening to Mom's spiel about Ellie & Company. I shifted my gaze to the coffee table and inhaled sharply, a faux pas I quickly covered with a loud cough. I had drawn attention to myself, but nothing could have prepared me for the cold slap-in-the-face of seeing my beautiful signature cookies displayed on a Cookies for Santa plate. Did the woman have no shame?

Although I was ready to crack, Mom was still in character. "I'd like to introduce you to my two models, handpicked by me to showcase our holiday collection." As Kennedy smiled and curtseyed, I stood as still as a statue.

"Although some of our fabrics are imported," Mom continued, "all our clothes are made right here in the United States. Ms. Kapoor is wearing our holiday evening gown with a playful bolero jacket coverup . . ."

Kennedy, hearing her cue, mustered attitude and marched up to the coffee table. There she took off the little jacket, threw it over her shoulder, looked left, looked right, and spun around. It became apparent that she had practiced this. As the women clapped and commented on the beautiful dress, I swallowed painfully. Although Mom had been a model, I was never comfortable parading my clothes in front of people. I suddenly wished I had been a more astute daughter.

On my cue, I chose to focus on my stolen cookies. I had no problem mustering my Lindsey-tude and marched right up to the coffee table. However, instead of a graceful swirl, I bent down and plucked one of my lemon-ginger sandwich cookies off the

Santa plate. The platinum blonde with the good plastic surgeon remarked, "Oh my, I thought models aren't supposed to eat cookies." She then had the nerve to giggle.

"Some of us are lucky," I said, flashing a pointed look. "Where did you get these cookies?"

"I baked them," Sophia glibly lied.

I tilted my head and stared at her with my one exposed eye. "Really? These look familiar. What's your recipe?"

"I'd have to look. Might have thrown it away. It wasn't very good, but you can take them all after the show if you like."

As hard as I tried to keep my Lindsey-tude in check, I lost the battle. "Am I in crazy town?" I shouted, then flung off my hat. "Not very good!? These are my signature cookies! You women stole them from my bakeshop!"

The chubby woman with the reddish hair and tooth gap looked at her friends and stammered, "I . . . I don't know what's going on right now. I . . . I thought we were having a fashion show?"

"The fashion show's over, ladies," Mom informed them, stepping up beside me.

"But . . . but you are fashion models." The woman with the reddish hair was clearly not the ringleader.

"She's a model," I said, gesturing to Mom. "I'm Lindsey Bakewell. I own the Beacon Bakeshop in Beacon Harbor."

Sophia shot out of her chair. "I'm going to have to ask you all to leave!"

"You stole my cookies and locked me in a storage closet at the bake-off. You're Bradley Argyle's mother. I've been looking for you all week. I'm not leaving your house until I get some answers!"

The platinum blonde stood up as well. Her face was contorted with self-righteous indignation. "How dare you come into this house and accuse us of stealing your cookies. You can't prove it! They're cookies!" To illustrate her point, she plucked a cookie from the plate and tried to eat the evidence by shoving it into her mouth. Her chubbier friend, catching on, began eating cookies, as well, until I grabbed the plate.

"Ladies, let's be civil," Mom called out as I fought three desperate women for control of the Santa plate.

"Lindsey, look what I found."

I turned to look at Kennedy, who was standing in the kitchen. I loosened my grip on the plate, but it was worth it. While I was scuffling over cookies, Kennedy had set to work, snooping around the kitchen. She was holding a paper towel that was protecting the antique ceramic rolling pin she had in her hand. The rolling pin was covered with little gingerbread men.

"That's Felicity Stewart's missing rolling pin!" I exclaimed, recognizing it. "Call the police!"

"What?" Sophia was in my face. "I bought that." She backed away as a sudden flash of horror crossed her face. "I am not a murderer!"

Chaos erupted. Sophia turned and chased after Kennedy as Mom and I were assailed with a barrage of lemon-ginger sandwich cookies. "Hold them off," I told Mom and ran after Sophia.

Kennedy could walk like a pro on stiletto heels, but they weren't designed for much else. She had trotted through the kitchen and was stumbling on the tile floor of the foyer, tripping on the hem of her long ball gown while holding the heavy rolling pin in the air. She saw me and tossed it over Sophia's head.

I caught it with both hands, letting the flimsy paper towel fall to the floor. I then raced for the door.

"After her!" Sophia cried to her minions.

I knew that Rory was sitting in a car at the end of the road. All I had to do was get the rolling pin to safety. It was the murder weapon. Sophia had confirmed that fact the moment she saw it and protested that she wasn't a murderer. How would she have known it was the murder weapon if she hadn't used it on Chevy Chambers?

As I struggled with the doorknob, Sophia grabbed me from behind and reached for the rolling pin. She had almost pulled it from my grasp when Kennedy wrangled her off me. Adjusting the rolling pin, I turned the knob again. This time the door burst open with a gust of icy wind. Still wearing my red cape, I ran for the icy street. Unfortunately, every woman in the house ran after me.

Models didn't make the best runners. Models on ice were even worse. Mom was clip-clopping and slipping her heart out on the frozen pavement. I turned and saw her whack Sophia in the back with her handbag. Bradley's mother wasn't wearing heels. Although she slipped a little, she regained her balance and continued the chase. Kennedy, on the other hand, had kicked off her heels, hiked up her gown, and was braving the snow in her bare feet. Unfortunately, she was being outrun by the chubby fifty-year-old with the reddish hair.

Spotting Mom's rental car, I called out to Rory. I waved a hand to get his attention, but the car door remained shut. I silently cursed YouTube and all their addictive video content. Rory had been beyond bored and was probably reclining in the front seat watching football highlights.

The woman with the platinum-blond hair was in shape and had nearly reached me when I lunged for the car. I shifted the rolling pin in my other arm and tried to open the door. I yanked harder on the handle and cursed. It was locked. Rory wasn't inside. The blonde was relentless. Panic took hold the moment she yanked the rolling pin out of my hand and shoved me to the pavement.

"That outfit makes you look fat!" She flung the insult with mean-girl glee. She then turned and started running for the harbor.

Although the shoreline was covered in ice, and some of the harbor had frozen over, there was still open water a few yards out. If she threw the rolling pin into the bay, it might never be found. This thought plagued me as I scrambled to my feet and ran after her. We had only made it halfway down the block when she suddenly screamed. Rory, emerging from behind a snowbank on the side of the road, had grabbed her from behind and wrestled the rolling pin out of her hand.

"Where were you?" I cried, doubled over and breathing heavily.

"In the bushes at the back of the house watching a pop-up fashion show." He flashed a private grin as he handed me the rolling pin. He then secured the woman's hands behind her back with a zip tie. "Keep an eye on this one," he said, motioning to the woman fuming with anger beside me. Then with a straight face, Rory added, "I was hoping for a little more twirl out of you." Before I could reply, he was off again, heading this time for the frantic woman who was racing hell-for-leather back to her house.

I had never realized how fast Rory could run. Sophia was down in the snow before she knew what hit her.

Chapter 44

Sophia Argyle-Huffman was arrested for the murder of Chevy Chambers. Her two friends were brought down to the station, as well, but were released after questioning. A pair of bored, wealthy women, they admitted to the cookie-napping. Apparently, as a professional baker, Sophia had targeted me because I posed a threat to her son's chances of winning the live bake-off. She had convinced her friends that by taking my cookies, I wouldn't have any to offer shoppers and no one would vote for me. They thought they were helping a friend. They had also admitted to speaking with Chevy Chambers at the bakeoff, purely to sway his vote in favor of their friend's son, Bradley Argyle. The only crime the two women seemed guilty of was being a loyal friend to a kleptomaniac murderess.

After our harrowing visit to Bay Harbor, and after explaining to Sergeant Murdock how we had found the cookie-nappers and the murder weapon, we had driven back to the Beacon Harbor Police Station to give a new set of statements. Murdock, true to form, was furious with me. But I could tell she was also a little relieved. Police had to operate by certain rules of law in order to catch a criminal. Things like pop-up Christmas fashion shows were beyond the scope of what was normal or accepted. Thanks to Mom and her utter confidence in the wacky plan, it had worked for us. No one wanted a murderer at large during Christmas.

While we were giving our statements, Officer Tuck McAllister, aka Officer Cutie Pie, walked in with Bradley Argyle. Bradley, having learned that his mother had been found with the murder weapon in Bay Harbor, was visibly upset. Last night at the restaurant, he had tried to protect her by withholding her name and address, but he'd admitted that she was a kleptomaniac. It occurred to me that he might have known she had stolen Felicity's rolling pin. The antique rolling pin would connect Sophia to the crime scene, and for reasons that must be very painful, Bradley could never make that mental leap.

When young, attractive, and totally smitten Officer Tuck McAllister came out of the interrogation room, he waved Kennedy and the rest of us into another private room to tell us what they had learned. Sophia Argyle-Huffman had sung like a canary.

"It's all rather sad," Tuck began, and shook his blond head before revealing Sophia's motive for murder.

As we had discovered, Bradley Argyle had opened his first restaurant in Chicago eight years ago. Sophia, wanting her only child's restaurant to be a smashing success, had done what Ginger Brooks (and nearly Felicity) had done during the run-up to our own Christmas cookie bake-off. Sophia had agreed to an affair with the food critic in exchange for a glowing review of her son's restaurant. Bradley, of course, was blissfully unaware of the bargain struck between his mother and Chevy. We had read the scathing review of the Tall Ships restaurant ourselves and knew that Chevy had never honored the bargain.

"Chevy Chambers was notorious for that type of bad behavior," Tuck reminded us. "He was trying his hardest to create havoc in our own town, and we all know the result of that. I really wish you guys had come to me with that newspaper article the moment you found it." He looked truly hurt by the way we had kept from him our most important find.

"Tuck, darling," Kennedy soothed. "We were only trying to scope out the territory for you. You would have had to work with the sheriff in Bay Harbor." Tuck knew all we had done to get Sophia's name and address.

He nodded and continued to tell us how Bradley had lost everything after his restaurant tanked. He went bankrupt and started drinking. Those were dark times, according to Sophia.

"I can only imagine," Rory interjected.

"Tuck, why did she wait all these years to kill him?" I asked.

"That's the thing. She said she had no intention of killing him. Bradley had landed on his feet in Beacon Harbor and was making a name for himself at the Harbor Hotel Restaurant. Sophia, having divorced Bradley's father when Bradley was ten, moved to Michigan shortly after her son did. She remarried a wealthy businessman by the name of Douglas Huffman. Douglas was older than Sophia and died two years ago of a heart attack. Her story checks out," he added.

"So, if she hadn't meant to kill Chevy, what happened? Sophia stole our cookies and locked me in a storage closet during the bake-off."

"Right. Once she heard that Chevy Chambers was coming to Beacon Harbor, the town her son lives in, to judge the Christmas cookie bake-off, she hatched her plan. She wanted Bradley in the live bake-off. She wanted Chevy to know how talented her son really was. She stole your cookies, Lindsey, because you were his only real competition. She was trying to knock you out of the live bake-off, but it didn't work. That forced her to spring a new plan. She had her two friends confront Chevy at the bake-off. Since it was no secret that Chevy was soliciting bribes, she had Cynthia Goddard and Barbie Blankenship work him over on behalf of Bradley Argyle. At that point, Chevy didn't know that Sophia was in Beacon Harbor. She was a blast from his past. Anyhow, Sophia caught wind of that note passed to Chevy by Ginger Brooks. Sophia's girlfriends relayed the information that Chevy was to meet someone under the mistletoe in the library."

I shook my head. "And here, I thought everyone was too busy baking cookies and frosting gingerbread houses for shenanigans of that nature."

Tuck shrugged. "Sophia believed that Felicity Stewart was having an affair with

Chevy. She imagined that Ginger Brooks found out and was trying to bribe him as well. That, for some reason, made her angry."

"She probably believed Felicity would win," Mom added.

"It was after you chased her, Lindsey, that she decided to make sure Bradley would win. He had won the cookie round, but she was going to corner Chevy and make sure Bradley had a clear victory when the gingerbread houses were being judged. When she realized that you, Lindsey, had recognized her as the woman who stole your cookies, she panicked. She had taken Bradley's master keys before the event, planning to lure Chevy in a closet for their private chat, but she didn't need to do that, thanks to Ginger. Once she locked you in the closet to get you out of the way, she then doubled back, snuck onto the stage and took Felicity's rolling pin. Then she went to meet Chevy under the mistletoe."

I looked at Rory. The timeline fit. "But why did she steal Felicity's rolling pin if she didn't mean to kill him?" I thought to ask.

"Two reasons. She wanted it, being a kleptomaniac, and she wanted to teach Felicity Stewart a lesson, thinking she was the one having the affair with Chevy. Are you guys following all this?"

Rory grimaced. "Unfortunately, yes."

"Anyhow," Tuck continued, "Sophia said that Chevy was shocked to see her there. Remember, he thought he was meeting Ginger. Sophia thought he was meeting Felicity and called him out on it by showing him that she'd stolen her rolling pin. Sophia knew Chevy was on the take and threatened to expose him if he didn't make amends for what he had done to her son. She reminded him of their bargain all those years ago and how he had failed to keep it. But instead of apologizing, Chevy, true to form, mocked her for being a fool. He also threatened to tell Bradley — who, he admitted, was a talented chef — how his mother had sold herself for a positive review of his restaurant. That shameful incident was a secret Sophia wanted to protect. She never wanted her son to know what she had done. Knowing Chevy Chambers was an evil-spirited man, she believed he would actually tell Bradley about their affair. She grew angry and clubbed Chevy on the head with the rolling pin. The moment she realized that she had killed him, she called her friends and they swiftly left the hotel. Neither Barbie nor Cynthia ever knew what she had done. They simply thought their plan was in motion.

How messed up is that?" He shook his head.

"How sad," I said, my heart going out to poor Bradley Argyle. "She really should have had more faith in her son's abilities."

We left the police station with heavy hearts and drove straight to the Beacon Bakeshop. Although the bakeshop was closed for the day, Dad and Mrs. Nichols were still there waiting for us and our news. So, too, were the dogs. The moment we entered and were greeted by our three excited furry friends, the horrible events of the day seemed to dissipate in the festive atmosphere. Bing Crosby was singing "White Christmas" over the speakers as the scent of pine, cinnamon, cloves, and nutmeg tickled our noses. The Christmas tree was lit, shedding its festive glow on the two bakers who were dearest to me, Dad and Mrs. Nichols. They were sitting at a table wearing floppy red Santa hats while sipping eggnog lattes. A plate of beautiful Christmas cookies sat on the table between them. I suddenly wanted one very much. There was nothing like a Christmas cookie to lift the spirits.

As Rory, Mom, and Kennedy pulled up chairs to join them, I went to the kitchen and brewed a pot of coffee. While the coffee was being made, I took out another plate and filled it with more cookies and thin slices of a rum-soaked fruitcake I had made before the Christmas cookie bake-off had been announced. Fruitcakes were always better the longer they sat. With coffee, mugs, and a new plate of goodies, I went to join them.

"Oh my!" Mrs. Nichols exclaimed, after hearing our story. "I never imagined so twisted a tale at Christmas. All mothers love their children," she said, directing her kindly blue gaze at Mom. "But to go to such lengths to see one's child succeed is dangerous for both mother and child."

"I agree," I said, thankful that my parents were supportive without being overbearing. I valued their guidance as much as my independence. "The whole village is reeling from this. Chevy and his deceitful ways have ruined everything; his death has overshadowed our Christmas festival. I do think the Christmas cookie bakeoff was a good idea, but it spun out of control the moment we put the judging into that man's hands. The worst part is, now we'll never know who actually baked the best cookie!"

Mrs. Nichols held me with a thoughtful look. "Why, dear, Christmas cookies are baked with tradition and love, and because they are, every person who bakes a Christmas cookie is a winner. You are all winners."

"I agree," Dad said with a grin. "I always thought it was folly to think that one Christmas cookie could be better than another, when my favorite is clearly all of them."

Kennedy laughed at his remark and held up a piece of fruitcake. "My mum makes a dry fruitcake cookie without the booze, so maybe not all of them?"

Rory laughed. "Lindsey and Mrs. Nichols have baked so many cookies these last few weeks, and I've had the pleasure of tasting them all. I agree with James. Variety is what makes them so special. Sometimes a lemon-ginger sandwich cookie is the way to go, while at other times, it must be chocolate chip. By the way, are there a lot of cookies left?"

"Tons of them," Mrs. Nichols and I replied at the same time.

That got me thinking about all our Christmas cookies and what to do with them. A moment later, I blurted, "We need to have another Christmas festival!"

"But tomorrow is Christmas Eve, dear," Mom reminded with a frown. "Isn't it too late?"

"No. It's not!" Rory's face came alive with the possibility. "The ballroom at the hotel is still decorated. Doc Riggles hasn't returned his Santa suit. And I know that Felicity Stewart has a stash of that sticky hot cocoa somewhere. Let's do this again, and this time let's do it right."

I nodded. "No judges. Just cookies, hot cocoa, Santa, and lots of holiday cheer." I looked at Mom. "Will you call Betty? She'll get the ball rolling. She can tell Doc to put on the Santa suit and get ready for visit number two. Kennedy, can you ring Tuck and let him know what we're doing? I want him to be a part of this."

"On it!" She looked up from her phone. "Tuck can help me get the contact information of all the shops and the residents and come up with a media blast. Say the word, and I'll spread the news."

"Great. I'll call Felicity and Ginger. Between the three of us, we should have enough cookies to feed the entire county."

CHAPTER 45

I was filled with new purpose. We were throwing the town another Christmas festival, and this time I had my family and friends to help me. I had stayed up late into the night, talking with Felicity and Ginger. We had all been so swept up in the Christmas cookie bake-off that we had forgotten the most important part — that we were neighbors and friends. I told them about Sophia Argyle-Huffman, a story of a woman they could both relate to. Although death was always tragic, somehow the woman who had wielded the rolling pin seemed less of a monster than the victim. Felicity, having caused serious damage to her marriage due to her foolishness, was grateful to know that her rolling pin had been found intact. Ginger, on the other hand, hadn't lost much but her self-esteem. Both women were working to put the bake-off behind them and make amends. The new Beacon Harbor

Christmas Eve Festival was a good place to start. Felicity offered to supply all the cocoa. Ginger offered to bring more cookies and a few gallons of her surplus ice cream.

Christmas Eve morning, I was bursting with excitement. I awoke early, played with Wellington, then joined Mrs. Nichols in the bakery kitchen. We had a lighter baking schedule due to the fact we were closing at noon. There were still a few special Christmas orders to be made and picked up, as well as our usual assortment of donuts, sweet rolls, coffee cakes, mini quiches, and muffins. And while it was true that we had plenty of cookies for the Christmas festival, it was Christmas Eve, after all, and Mrs. Nichols and I just couldn't help ourselves. We baked even more cookies.

When Wendy, Elizabeth, and Tom arrived to open the bakeshop, I brought them up to speed regarding Sophia Argyle-Huffman and her confession to the murder of Chevy Chambers. I then told them about the new Christmas festival that would begin at two in the afternoon.

"Will you please call Alaina and Ryan and fill them in?" I asked. "Tell them to spread the word to all your families as well as to our customers. Free cookies, ice cream, and cocoa at the Christmas festival! Also, I hear

Santa will be making one last appearance."

With my Jeep packed with platters and platters of cookies, I left the Beacon early to help set up the ballroom at the hotel. On the drive over, I gave Rory a quick call.

"Are you on your way to the hotel?" he asked.

"I am. I'm meeting Ginger there shortly. We're going to start setting up the refreshment tables. Betty is picking up Kennedy and Mrs. Nichols. They'll come a bit later. Also, Felicity will be over as soon as she closes the Tannenbaum Shoppe for the day. They're running a big Christmas Eve special. Did I tell you how happy she was to hear that her antique rolling pin has been found intact? She couldn't believe it."

Rory was silent a moment. "It was intact, wasn't it?" he remarked. "There wasn't a scratch on it. Mrs. Nichols made a similar remark, I think."

His remarks about the rolling pin sent a wave of chills up my spine. My mind began to race through the sequence of events that had taken place since the live bakeoff. Finally, I ventured, "Are you thinking what I'm thinking?"

"I hope not. I mean, I am thinking it. I'm not a forensic scientist, Lindsey, but that was an old rolling pin. A killing blow would, at the very least, have cracked it."

"Maybe not. Like my dad always says, back then they built things to last."

"Dear God," Rory uttered, his voice fading like the wind from a luffing sail. I didn't like the sound of it one bit. "How tall would you say Sophia is?"

"I don't know . . . Five-foot-six, maybe. She's shorter than I am. Why?"

"She told Tuck that she was facing Chevy when she hit him with the rolling pin. I don't think she was. I think she was behind him. We saw the body. Chevy was clearly struck from behind."

My heart was beginning to quicken. "What are you saying?"

"I'm saying that I think there were more than two people in that room, Lindsey, and possibly a different rolling pin. Chevy was talking with someone else when Sophia hit him. Who is meeting you at the ballroom?"

"Betty and Kennedy. Oh, and Ginger."

"Ginger wrote the note. Lindsey, hang on. I'll be there as soon as I can."

My conversation with Rory had set me on edge. Ginger had admitted to having an affair with Chevy, just as she'd admitted to writing the note that had lured the cookie judge into the room with the mistletoe. She said she had chickened out and never went to meet him. But maybe she had. She might have even known Sophia Argyle-Huffman. Although it was probably nothing, I knew that my mind would spiral out of control if I let it. I had promised to remain vigilant, and I would. But I wouldn't let my imagination get the best of me. I still needed to set up for the Christmas festival that I had talked the entire village of Beacon Harbor into having.

I entered the hotel carrying two platters loaded with Christmas cookies and walked to the doors of the ballroom. I opened one and looked inside before I entered. Aside from the giant Christmas tree in the center of the room, the place was empty. I was the first to arrive. If Ginger got there before Betty and Kennedy, I'd see her and give her a wide berth.

Only two tables had been set up, and these were sitting against the far wall. I walked across the empty room and set my cookie trays down on one of the tables. I then looked around, thinking of where the best place would be to set up the refreshment tables.

I was scanning the room when a noise from behind the Christmas tree startled me. I turned and saw the form of a man. A moment later, Bradley Argyle, dressed in his chef's coat, walked out of the tree's shadow carrying a tray of cookies.

"I brought you these," he said with a smile. He came toward me, but for some reason, I suddenly didn't want to be in the room alone with him.

"By the way," he said, and paused to set the tray down on the table next to mine. "I don't appreciate the fact that you found my mother. I specifically told you to leave her alone."

"I had every intention of doing just that," I lied as I slowly backed away. "But, um, we found her. And then she admitted to killing Chevy Chambers."

For some reason, he laughed. "That's the problem. She would admit to it. She'd admit to anything if she thought it would help me."

Warning bells sounded off in my ears, causing a deafening *whoosh*. My instincts knew what my brain was trying to figure out; I was standing in the room with the killer. I took a deep breath and realized I should keep him talking. "Your mother must be very devoted to you. You should count yourself lucky to have her."

"Ha!" he cried. "Lucky? She has never believed in me. Ever since I was a child, she never let me do anything on my own. In school, she always had to write my papers, fill in my math worksheets, and make my dioramas. Heck, even when I tried to get into college, she had to hire someone to take the SAT for me. She's a helicopter parent on steroids who never believed in her son's abilities." Pained by the memories, he shook his head. Obviously, Bradley had snapped. Fascinated and horrified, I took a step backward as he talked.

"That's why I went to culinary school," he continued. "She couldn't figure out how to cheat to get me in, and she didn't need to. I was good at cooking. Cooking gave me confidence. When I got my first job as a cook and she tasted a meal that I had prepared, she was actually surprised. She was proud of me, Lindsey. Genuinely proud of me. She encouraged me to open my first restaurant. She helped me find the perfect location and set the menu. We were working together. *I thought she trusted me.*" The hurt behind his eyes as he spoke was visceral. "And then what does she do? She goes behind my back, solicits a food critic, and sleeps with him to ensure I'd get a good review. Again, she thought she was doing me a favor, but again, it backfired. The food critic she picked was a sociopath!" He looked disgusted.

"Your mother killed Chevy Chambers because she slept with him and he lied to her. It was revenge, wasn't it?"

"Oh, Lindsey. Simple Lindsey. She wasn't trying to kill Chevy Chambers. She was trying to bribe him again. She roped her friends into stealing your cookies because she had convinced them that I needed a leg up in the competition. I got mad at her and told her not to come to the live bake-off. But she didn't listen. When I saw her and her friends in the crowd, I knew they were up to something. Fortunately for me, it seemed that everyone was up to something. You remember. I baked a damn good cookie. It won the first round, and yet she still had the gall to push that reprobate under the only sprig of mistletoe in this place and make out with him. I followed her there. I saw the whole thing. It was disgusting. She was selling herself all over again to a man who had less scruples than an alley cat. Chevy was encouraging her and laughing at her the whole time. What choice did I have? *She is my mother!* And she was making a fool of herself without even caring about the consequences." He shook his head in disgust.

"Well, I cared," he hissed, frightening me.

421

"You guessed it, didn't you? You know that I snuck up behind him and put a stop to it."

"I . . . umm, didn't know until just now." Why did I say that? How stupid of me! Clearly, confronting a murderer had freaked me out. Then, to my horror, Bradley flung open his chef's coat and drew out a marble rolling pin. With his face contorted with rage, he brandished the heavy implement like a sword, then waved it wildly about his head.

The moment I saw it, I knew it was the murder weapon.

The rolling pin stilled in his hand. "When she saw what I had done, and that Chevy was dead, she ran back and stole Felicity's rolling pin off her baking station." He rolled his eyes at this — as if she was the crazy one. Unfortunately, Mommy Sticky Fingers wasn't the only brand of crazy in the family. "Even then, she was trying to put the blame on someone other than me. Felicity was an easy target. But I killed him! And now she wants the world to believe that she did it. Don't you see? She won't even let me claim credit for that!"

He spat on the carpet in anger. "You know what? She deserves to be in prison. She can't try to help me from there. I only wish

I had thought of this sooner."

Bradley was unhinged. It wouldn't take him long to realize that he'd just confessed everything to me. He might have been crazy, but he wasn't stupid.

"You're right," I said. My plan this time was to throw him off guard. "It's undoubtedly better. Your secret is safe with me." I smiled, then bolted for the door.

I'd made it two steps before I was grabbed by the hand and flung backward, crashing into the empty table. The rolling pin was in his hand. He raised it over his head. He brought it down with crushing force, but not before I rolled out of the way. The solid marble landed next to me, cracking the table. I kicked him, then got to my feet, but I was instantly shoved to the ground. As I scrambled toward the doors, I screamed at the top of my lungs. *Help! Help!*

He grabbed me by the leg and tried to haul me back. I fought against him, but his grip was strong. I felt like a frantic rabbit caught by the leg while the hunter tried to club me to death. His first attempt had gone wide. Yet I knew that eventually the hunter would win.

The moment I thought about the hunter, the ballroom doors burst open, and Rory ran inside. I knew how fast he could run.

Like that poor hare, unaware that it had been caught in the hunter's sights, Bradley Argyle never knew what hit him.

CHAPTER 46

With the murder of Chevy Chambers finally solved, the town had a lot to celebrate. For me, however, the horrible incident with Bradley Argyle and his deadly rolling pin was still fresh in my mind. But with each excited child and happy adult who entered the ballroom, my spirits began to lift. Rory, of course, had begun the process by immobilizing Bradley first, then hugging me until I stopped shaking. Betty, Kennedy, and Mrs. Nichols had arrived shortly after Rory, pulling me into their warm circle of comfort as the police arrived to whisk the murderer off to jail. The ballroom had been the scene of chaos. Police and hotel staff filled the room, giving statements and removing the broken table. The only person not entirely happy that Bradley had been apprehended was Chad, the restaurant manager.

"I'm sorry he almost killed you, Lindsey, but he was really talented in the kitchen. I wish this could have waited until after our New Year's Eve party. It's sold out, and now I don't have a chef." Chad, standing with arms crossed, couldn't hide the worry on his face.

Kennedy glared at him. "You ridiculous man! No one wants to eat on New Year's Eve. Stock up on liquor and put out loads of charcuterie boards and hors d'oeuvres. I'll text you some ideas. Now shoo." She waved him off like a pesky fly, then she gave me another hug. "Pay no mind to him, Linds. You're the hero of the day. You caught the baddie, and now you're saving Christmas too."

I wasn't sure it was true, but I loved her confidence. There was a reason Kennedy was my best friend. Besides the fact that I loved her, she always had my back.

With the tables filled with refreshments, and villagers pouring through the ballroom doors, Mrs. Nichols came up beside me.

"I find that there is something extra special about a village gathering on Christmas Eve to celebrate this sacred night when our Savior was born. It's the season of warmth, made more special by the spirit of giving."

"And Christmas cookies," I added, making her smile. "You know, I've always tried to pull off the perfect Christmas. This," I said, gesturing to the crowded room, "might not have been my sugarplum vision, but I think it's loads better. A celebration before the celebration. And you, Mrs. Nichols, are now part of our family. You will come to my Christmas Eve dinner at the lighthouse tonight, won't you? Afterward we're all trudging through the snow to St. Michael's Presbyterian Church for the midnight service. Betty says it's not to be missed."

Mrs. Nichols gave me a hug. "Christmas happens as it will. There is no right way to celebrate. It's about joy. And I am so happy to be considered part of your family. I must run home, but I will be there for dinner."

Shortly after Mrs. Nichols left the hotel, Felicity came through the ballroom doors with her husband and two handsome young adults. One look and I knew that her son and daughter had made it home for Christmas.

"Lindsey!" Felicity waved as she pulled the young adults over to meet me. "You will never believe what happened. My Christmas wish came true! Can you believe it?" Her large eyes misted over with tears of joy as she spoke. "This is Kara and Kevin, my children. They decided at the last minute that they didn't want to celebrate Christmas

427

alone. We're celebrating as a family! I promised them that this year is going to be different, very low-key," she assured everyone within hearing. "They get to decide on the traditions they want to celebrate and the food they want to eat, even if it is chicken Parmesan." This she said with a smile, looking at her husband. "I've put Stanley in charge of the Christmas music. I don't even care if 'Grandma Got Run Over by a Reindeer' plays over and over. Whatever he thinks is best."

That made me smile. I knew how hard it must be for Felicity to let go of her ideal Christmas, but I was happy she did. She was realizing that Christmas was not about her and her rigid ideas, but about the importance of family. I was truly happy for her. After I'd greeted Kara, Kevin, and Stanley, Felicity shooed them off to the refreshment table. "It's really remarkable. I know this may sound odd, but I think your Mrs. Nichols had something to do with it. She came to my store that day I saw you. She saw that I was . . . well, unhappy. Then she asked me, if I could have one Christmas wish, what would it be? Of course, I told her that all I wanted was for my children to come home. She asked a little bit about them and then told me" — she lowered her voice — "she told me she'd let Santa know."

I started to laugh. "She does that. It's so cute. Kennedy once told me that Mrs. Nichols was rocking a look. What she meant was that Mrs. Nichols is a kindly old woman who looks like Mrs. Claus, so she's embracing the spirit of the season and acting the part for us. Believing with all your heart, she once told me, is a powerful gift. Maybe it was Stanley who convinced them to come home. But I'll let Mrs. Nichols know that your Christmas wish came true."

It was so good to see Ali and Jack Johnson and all their grandchildren. The kids, all five of them, were making a beeline for Santa. I thought Doc Riggles was playing Santa until he strode up beside me with Betty.

"If you're here, who's over there?" I asked, pointing to the festival's version of the North Pole, designed and donated by Felicity Stewart, who really was the queen of holiday décor.

"Bill Morgan," he said with a grin. "I've had my time in the Santa chair. I felt it was time to share the privilege. Bill's grandkids are going to love this."

Betty and Doc then proceeded to the refreshment table. While Betty put some cookies on her plate, Doc went straight to the ice cream. Ginger gave him a generous scoop of fudge ripple. It was at that moment her daughter, Kate, ran over to her. Ginger abandoned her scoop and took her daughter by the hand. The two ran to the dance floor and began wiggling and shaking to "Rockin' Around the Christmas Tree." Rory had taken charge of music with his holiday playlist. He was hitting it out of the park.

Wendy, who had come with her entire family, was also dancing. She was with her two younger sisters; all three girls were holding hands dancing in a circle. Wendy's younger brother and his friends were making a game of trying to get into the middle. Everyone was having a good time.

Just off the dance floor stood Zack and Zoe Bannon. They were chatting with Tom and Elizabeth, who in many ways resembled a younger version of the trendy couple. Those two, I mused, were standing awfully close to each other. However, when I saw Alaina and Ryan enter, I took it back. They were definitely holding hands. The thought of young romance at the Beacon made me smile. It was in the air. Maybe it had even struck Kennedy, I mused, watching her laughing at something Tuck had said. I would never have believed it if I hadn't seen it with my own eyes, but she looked incredibly happy.

"Bakewell." I turned to look at the speaker. It was Sergeant Stacy Murdock, only she wasn't wearing her uniform but a lovely green and white blouse over a long black skirt. She wasn't wearing her usual ponytail, either, but had left her dyed blond hair loose to drape over her shoulders. I nearly choked on my cocoa. She looked . . . well, feminine.

"I'd like you to meet the kids," she said matter-of-factly, embracing the Sergeant Murdock I knew best. "They already know you."

"From my cookies," I suggested with a grin.

She held me in her unflinching gaze. "Yeah, we'll go with that."

I met Stacy Murdock's three lovely children and the tall, thick-set man who was with her. She introduced him as Brian Brigalow, the man she'd been seeing for two years. That shocked me. Some women were really good at keeping their private lives a secret.

"Merry Christmas," I told them all. "Take all the cookies you'd like."

I was just refreshing the cookie trays when Betty and Doc came over and stood beside

431

me. With them were Mom and Dad. The two couples were laughing and carrying on so, that I began to question whether they were really drinking just cocoa.

Betty looked at Doc for guidance. He nodded. Bubbling with some tasty news, she leaned close to me. "Lindsey, your parents have something to tell you."

Dear heavens, I wasn't sure I wanted to hear what it was. Aside from nearly being clubbed on the head by a rolling pin, my evening was going rather well.

"We were going to surprise you with our news tomorrow morning," Mom said, looking at Dad. "But Betty and Bob convinced us that now would be the perfect time."

Betty, with eyes wide, gave a vigorous nod.

I looked at Dad. He had a good poker face when he wanted to, but he wasn't using it now. Like Mom, Betty, and Doc Bob Riggles, he was excited about something.

"Wait. Let me get Rory. You four are scaring me." I waved Rory over. A moment later I said to him, "My parents have some big surprise to tell me. I thought you should be here in case I pass out."

Rory laughed, then caught himself, realizing that my day had been quite stressful. "I'm here for you. Go ahead, Ellie."

Mom clapped her hands together. "We put

an offer on a house in Beacon Harbor and it just got accepted!"

"Wha . . . what?" I stumbled backward. Rory caught me. Dad also reached out and took my hand in his.

"Beacon Harbor has always been special to me," Dad said with a misty smile. "My parents loved bringing me here when I was a boy. It's now even more special to me because you are here. You are our amazing daughter. Nothing is more important than family. Your mom and I realized some time ago that we wanted to be closer to you and share in your life. Besides, I'm not ready to retire yet, Lindsey dear. Although I'm not looking for anything fulltime, I want to help out at the Beacon Bakeshop."

Tears were clouding my vision. I could see that Mom was tearing up too. "Isn't it marvelous? We're moving to Beacon Harbor! And one more thing. Kennedy and I have talked about launching Ellie and Company in a real brick-and-mortar store. I finally found the perfect place to start our flagship clothing boutique. I'm renting the building on the other side of the Book Nook."

"You're telling her our big surprise?" Kennedy and Tuck came up beside us. "I thought we were waiting until tomorrow!"

Her momentary displeasure melted away under her bright smile. "The surprise is, I might be spending more time here too. I'm going to help Ellie run the flagship store."

"Dear heavens, you are all moving here?" I really felt that I might pass out.

Rory was helping me in the kitchen, whipping up enough mashed potatoes to go along with the giant platter of Swedish meatballs and lingonberries that made up our traditional Christmas Eve feast. It was nearly ready to go on the table when I realized that Mrs. Nichols was still in the bakery kitchen.

"She's whipping up a special dessert. I can't wait to see it. Come with me, and we'll get her together." I smiled at him, turned off the mixer, and took him by the hand.

All my guests were in the living room, enjoying the beautiful charcuterie board Kennedy had made, with cheeses, imported meats, crackers, grapes, gourmet olives, and smoked nuts. Betty and Doc had joined us. Tuck McAllister was there, as well, of course. If Kennedy spent more time in Beacon Harbor, it was safe to assume that he'd be around more often. Wellington, who'd been near the coffee table begging shamelessly with the models for a taste of prosciutto, must have sensed that we were on a mission. He gave up his prime begging spot and came to join us as we walked through the doorway to the bakery.

"This is the best Christmas ever," I told Rory. "I can't believe Mom and Dad will be moving here."

"Most of the year, anyhow," he reminded me. "They're not crazy enough to stay for the entire winter."

"Oh my," I said and walked to the bakery counter. Wellington began to whine.

"What is that?" Rory asked, gazing at the beautiful Christmas cake, surrounded by fresh greens and frosted cranberries. "It looks like a birch log."

"This is a *Buche de Noel,* cake," I told him, staring in awe at the masterfully decorated delicacy. "It's the traditional Christmas cake of France. It represents the Yule log, an ancient tradition where one special log was chosen to be lit, bringing light and warmth to the house on Christmas. Where is she?" I asked, noting that the kitchen was dark, and that Mrs. Nichols wasn't in the bakery. My heart sank when I saw the note beside the cake. With my hands shaking a little, I picked it up and read it.

So sorry, dear, but I had to pop back up north, where I belong. Thank you for allowing me to be a part of your lighthouse bakeshop. It is a very special place, indeed. Merry Christmas to you all, and to the Captain. Tell Wellington that I haven't forgotten. Oh, and please look up.

"What the . . . ?" Still holding the note, I looked up. Above us hung a large ball of mistletoe tied with a red bow and a sprig of white berries. "I didn't hang that there . . ."

Rory, staring at the mistletoe in awe, shook his head. "I swear that wasn't there a second ago. I would have seen it when we came in."

"It was dark. Maybe we missed it," I offered, then shook my head. "She's gone. Just like that. The best assistant baker I've ever had just goes away . . . like Mary Poppins?"

"Or . . . not Mary Poppins, but Mrs. Saint Nicholas?" Rory was hardly a man to grasp onto children's tales, but I had to give him credit for thinking outside the box. He shook his head. "We all thought she was from the U.P., but maybe she was really from the North Pole?"

"Listen to yourself. You are getting as batty as I am. You, Rory Campbell, are the glue that holds my crazy life together. Oh my, Wellington has a bone!"

We both looked at Wellington on the floor by our feet. My dog was gnawing on the

436

largest rawhide bone I'd ever seen. "Did you buy him that? That seems like something you would do."

Rory grinned and pulled me into his arms. "Not me," he whispered near my ear. "But I'd take credit for a bone that big."

The way he said it made me giggle. *Men,* I thought, but then all thoughts melted away as I reveled in my surroundings. My bakeshop truly was a sight to behold. The fresh-cut Christmas tree Rory had helped me get still resonated with the essence of the pine forest it had grown in, only now it was the focal point of the bakery, adorned with beautiful ornaments and hung with soft, colorful lights. Outside the window, the scene was as perfect as anything I could have imagined. The pristine blanket of snow looked magical, broken only by the walkway leading to the bakery steps, now lined with cheerful candy cane lights. They had been a struggle to put in, mostly due to Welly, but it had been worth it. The entire expanse of white twinkled and sparkled, including the light tower on the lake side of the building. I was certain that if there were any sailors crazy enough to be out on the frigid lake, the sight of the giant candy cane lighthouse would not only light their way, but make them smile as well.

Yet as fulfilling as my lofty exterior illumination plans had been, it was the inside of the lighthouse that had answered the call of the season. All the little touches of Christmas had made it cozy and inviting. All the holiday baking had filled it with the smells of spices I remembered as a child. Clove, orange rind, chocolate, cinnamon, nutmeg, ginger, and the citrusy tang of lemon swirled in the air, mingling with the smells of savory foods and sweet cookies. Tomorrow I'd bake Mom's favorite cardamom coffee cake and add that to the mix. My lighthouse had finally been filled with the laughter of my family and friends, and I was now in the warm embrace of Rory Campbell. I looked into his eyes and smiled.

"I honestly don't know what to think," I told him. "But I do know that with the help of everyone, especially Mrs. Nichols — if that even is her real name — I have just pulled off the perfect Christmas."

"Indeed," Rory said. "Congratulations. Now hush. We're standing alone under a ball of mistletoe. And this time there are no dead bodies."

RECIPES FROM THE BEACON BAKESHOP

One of my favorite holiday traditions is baking Christmas cookies. After all, what is Christmas without a plate full of delectable cookies? Whether you're hosting a cookie exchange, entering a bake-off, or just baking for family and friends, here are a few of the finest Christmas cookie recipes from Beacon Harbor. P.S.: Santa thinks so too!

LINDSEY'S SIGNATURE LEMON-GINGER SANDWICH COOKIES

Preheat oven to 350 degrees F, place rack in middle position.

Prep time: 30 minutes. Cook time: 10 minutes.

Makes 20 1 1/2-inch sandwich cookies.

For the dough:

3/4 cup sugar
1/2 cup (1 stick) cold, unsalted butter
1 tablespoon molasses
1/2 teaspoon baking soda
1 1/2 teaspoons ground ginger
1/2 teaspoon ground cinnamon
1/4 teaspoon ground nutmeg
1/8 teaspoon kosher salt
1 tablespoon lemon zest (from fresh lemon)
1 1/3 cups all-purpose flour
2 tablespoons heavy cream

441

For the filling:

1 1/4 cup powdered sugar
1/3 cup butter
1 tablespoon fresh lemon juice
1 teaspoon pure lemon extract
1/4 teaspoon kosher salt

In the bowl of an electric mixer, combine sugar, butter, molasses, baking soda, ginger, cinnamon, nutmeg, salt, and lemon zest. Mix on low speed for 1 minute, then increase the speed to medium and beat for 5 minutes, until butter mixture is soft and light. Reduce speed to low and add flour and cream. Mix until a nice dough is formed.

Line baking sheets with parchment. Using a teaspoon, scoop rounded portions, dividing dough into roughly 40 equal portions. Cut each portion in half and roll between your hands until smooth. The dough balls will look tiny, but they will spread as they bake. Arrange on baking sheets leaving 1 1/2 inch between each. Bake until cookies are golden brown and firm around the edges, about 10 minutes. Cool to room temperature.

In the bowl of a stand mixer, combine powdered sugar, butter, lemon juice, lemon extract, and salt. Beat until soft and fluffy, about 5 minutes. Transfer filling to a pastry bag fitted with a 1/2-inch pastry tip. (If you don't have a pastry bag, you can use a gallon-sized zip-lock bag and cut one of the bottom corners off enough to make a 1/2-inch hole.)

Since the cookies will be slightly different sizes, match them up in pairs as best as you can. Flip one of the cookies over, pipe a heaping teaspoon of filling in the center, and sandwich with the matching cookie. Cookies can be stored in an airtight container in the refrigerator for up to a month.

LINDSEY'S SCRUMPTIOUS SOUTHERN PECAN COOKIES

Preheat oven to 350 degrees F, place rack in middle position.

Prep time: 20 minutes. Chill time: 30 minutes. Cook time: 10 minutes.

Makes 36 cookies.

For the dough:

1 cup butter, softened
1/2 cup granulated sugar
1/2 cup packed brown sugar
1 large egg
1 teaspoon vanilla
2 cups all-purpose flour
1/2 teaspoon baking soda
1/4 teaspoon salt
1/2 cup finely chopped pecans
36 pecan halves toasted (for top of cookie)

For the frosting:

1 cup packed brown sugar
1/2 cup cream
1 tablespoon butter
1 1/2 to 2 cups sifted powdered sugar

In the bowl of an electric mixer, beat butter and sugars together until fluffy. Add the egg and vanilla and beat until combined. Add flour, baking soda, and salt. Mix until well blended. Stir in chopped pecans. Cover the cookie dough and put in the refrigerator for 30 minutes or longer.

Preheat oven to 350 degrees.

Shape dough into 1-inch balls and place on parchment-lined cookie sheet a couple of inches apart. Bake 10 minutes until set and lightly browned at the edges. Cool on wire rack.

In a medium saucepan, combine brown sugar and cream. Cook over medium heat until mixture boils. Boil for 3 to 4 minutes, stirring constantly. Remove from heat and stir in butter. When butter is melted, stir in 1 1/2 cups of powdered sugar and whisk until smooth (can beat with a mixer as well). Frosting should look smooth and glossy. If frosting looks too thin, add more powdered sugar. However, keep in mind that the frosting firms up fast once it cools.

Place cookies close together. Quickly spread each cookie with about 1 tablespoon of warm frosting and top with a pecan. Let frosting set, then enjoy!

GINGER'S SIGNATURE GERMAN CHOCOLATE SANDWICH COOKIES WITH COCONUT FILLING

Preheat oven to 350 degrees F, place rack in middle position.

Prep time: 25 minutes. Cook time: 10 minutes.

Makes 17 sandwich cookies.

For the dough:

3/4 cup (1 1/2 sticks) butter, softened
1 1/2 cups sugar
2 eggs
2/3 cup cocoa powder
2 tablespoons milk
1 teaspoon vanilla extract
1 3/4 cups all-purpose flour
3/4 teaspoon baking soda
1/2 teaspoon salt
1/2 cup finely chopped pecans

For the filling:

1/2 cup (1 stick) butter
1/2 cup packed light brown sugar
1/4 cup light corn syrup
1 teaspoon vanilla extract
1 cup sweetened coconut flakes
1 cup finely chopped pecans

In the bowl of an electric mixer, beat together butter and sugar until fluffy. Add eggs and mix. Add cocoa powder, milk, and vanilla. Mix until blended. Gradually mix in flour, baking soda, and salt. Mix until blended (batter will be stiff). Stir in chopped pecans.

Form batter into 1-inch balls and place on parchment covered cookie sheet. Flatten slightly. Bake 10 minutes or until almost set. Remove cookies to cooling rack and cool completely.

In a medium saucepan, melt butter. Add brown sugar and corn syrup. Stir continuously until thick and bubbly. Remove from heat and stir in vanilla, coconut, and pecans.

Using the warm coconut-pecan filling, spread 1 heaping tablespoon onto the bottom of one cookie. Top with second cookie to make a sandwich. Repeat until all the cookies are made.

Enjoy!

GINGER'S DELICIOUS
NO-BAKE OREO BALLS

Prep time: 20 minutes. Chill time: 40 minutes.

Makes 24 truffles.

Ingredients:

1 (15.25 oz.) package Oreos
8 ounces cream cheese, softened
12 ounces white melting chocolate (use a
   high-quality brand, like Baker's)
6 ounces semisweet melting chocolate, for
   topping

Place the Oreos in a food processor and blend until fine crumbs are formed. Mix in the softened cream cheese until a sticky dough has formed. Roll dough into 1-inch balls and set on a wax paper–lined cookie sheet (or a container you can stick in the freezer). Freeze balls for at least 30 minutes.
When the Oreo balls have been chilled,

break white chocolate into pieces and put into a microwave-safe bowl. Heat for 30 seconds at a time, stirring between each trip to the microwave until melted.

Cover a baking sheet with wax paper. Remove Oreo balls from the freezer and drop them one at a time into the white chocolate. Using a fork, roll them carefully until coated in chocolate. Lift with fork and let excess chocolate drip back into the bowl. Place the Oreo ball on the wax paper. Continue until all the Oreo balls are covered with white chocolate. Place in freezer for 10 minutes or until chocolate is set.

Melt the semisweet chocolate in a small, microwave safe bowl. Dip a fork into the melted chocolate and drizzle it over the Oreo balls, creating a chocolate garnish. Let the Oreo balls rest until chocolate is set. Enjoy!

BRADLEY'S SIGNATURE BROWN BUTTER SHORTBREAD COOKIES

Preheat oven to 300 degrees F, place rack in middle position.

Prep time: 40 minutes. Cook time: 50 minutes.

Makes one 9x9 pan of cookies.

For the dough:

1 cup, plus 2 tablespoons salted butter (Irish butter is recommended, but not necessary)
2 tablespoons low-fat milk (I use 2%)
1 cup powdered sugar, sifted
1 teaspoon vanilla extract
2 cups all-purpose flour

For the topping:

6 ounces milk chocolate (may use dark chocolate if you prefer)

To brown the butter: Prepare an ice-water bath with a medium metal bowl set inside. Put butter in a medium saucepan and cook over medium heat, stirring constantly. The butter will start to foam and turn brown. Continue stirring and cooking until the butter turns a nice deep golden brown. Be careful not to cook the butter too far or it will burn. Remove butter mixture from heat and pour into bowl in the ice-water bath. Whisk in milk. Using a rubber spatula, stir continuously while scraping sides. The brown butter will start to thicken. When butter is thick and stiff, remove from ice-water bath and set aside. Allow butter to rest 15 to 20 minutes until it reaches room temperature.

In the bowl of an electric mixer, beat brown butter until fluffy, about 2 minutes. Gradually beat in powdered sugar and vanilla. Reduce speed and beat in flour.

Line 9x9 pan with parchment paper. Press dough evenly in the bottom of the pan. Using a knife, score dough, creating even lines every 2 1/4 inches (to make 16 square cookies). Using a fork, prick dough twice on every square.

Bake in preheated 300-degree oven for 50 minutes, or until golden brown. Remove from heat and let cool in pan for 5 minutes. Using parchment paper, remove from pan and cut score marks with knife. Place on cooling rack and cool completely.

When cookies are completely cooled, make the chocolate drizzle. Break chocolate into chunks and place in a microwave safe bowl. Microwave for 30 seconds and stir well. If chocolate isn't melted, repeat. Dip a fork into the melted chocolate and drizzle over each cookie. Create your own drizzle pattern, or you can dip part of the cookie into the chocolate if you prefer. Let cool on wire rack. Enjoy!

Note: If you don't want chocolate on your shortbread cookies, try dusting them with powdered sugar before serving.

BRADLEY'S AMAZING TURTLE-TOPPED SHORTBREAD COOKIES

Preheat oven to 350 degrees F, place rack in middle position.

Prep time: 40 minutes. Chill time: 2 hours. Cook time: 20 minutes.

Makes 48 cookies.

For the shortbread:

3/4 cup (1 1/2 sticks) salted butter, at
    room temperature
1/2 cup powdered sugar
2 cups all-purpose flour
1 tablespoon cold water

For the caramel:

1 cup (2 sticks) salted butter
2 cups light brown sugar
1/4 cup Ole Smoky Salted Caramel
    Whiskey (you can use regular whiskey if
    you can't find this)

1 1/4 cup whipping cream
1 teaspoon vanilla extract

For the topping:

1/2 cup toasted pecans, chopped
12 ounces quality dark chocolate (you can
  use milk chocolate if you prefer)
2 tablespoons unsalted butter

Preheat oven to 350 degrees. Grease a 9x13 baking pan with butter. In the bowl of an electric mixer, cream butter and powdered sugar together. Add flour and the tablespoon of water and mix well. Press dough in the bottom of the pan. Prick all over with a fork, then put into the oven and bake for 20 minutes or until golden brown. Remove from oven and let cool.

Place pecans on a cookie sheet and bake in the 350-degree oven for 10 minutes. Remove from heat and cool.

To make the caramel, place butter, brown sugar, whiskey, and whipping cream in a medium saucepan. Cook over medium heat and bring to a boil, stirring regularly. Reduce heat and let the mixture bubble for 20 minutes, stirring occasionally. Check temperature with a candy thermometer. You want it to reach 240 degrees. I like to use the firm ball method by dropping little bits of the mixture into ice water. The caramel should form a firm ball. Once the firm ball stage has been reached, remove caramel from heat and stir in the vanilla. Pour caramel over shortbread base and chill in the refrigerator for 2 hours.

Once caramel is firm, break chocolate into chunks and place in a microwave-safe bowl with the butter. Melt the chocolate and butter in the microwave, stirring every 30 seconds until melted. Pour over caramel, making sure all the caramel has been covered. Sprinkle with chopped, toasted pecans. Cool until chocolate has set. Remove entire cookie to a cutting board. Using a warm knife (dip blade into hot water), slice into 1 1/2-inch squares. Enjoy!

FELICITY'S FABULOUS SUGAR COOKIES

Preheat oven to 375 degrees F, place rack in the middle position.

Prep time: 20 minutes. Chill time: 20 minutes. Cook time: 12–15 minutes.

For the dough:

2 1/2 cups all-purpose flour
1 teaspoon baking powder
1/4 teaspoon salt
1 cup sugar
1/2 cup vegetable shortening
1 egg
3 tablespoons milk

TWO TYPES OF FROSTING:

Butter Cream Frosting:
This one tastes amazing but won't have a
  glossy icing look.

1/2 cup butter, softened
3 cups powdered sugar
1 or more tablespoons whole milk
Gel food coloring (in desired colors)

Decorator Icing:

6 cups powdered sugar
1/4–1/2 cup whole milk
1/4 cup light corn syrup
2 teaspoons vanilla extract
Gel food coloring (in desired colors)

In a medium bowl, combine the flour, baking powder, and salt. Set aside. In the bowl of an electric mixer, cream together the sugar and vegetable shortening. Add the egg and the 3 tablespoons of milk and mix well. Slowly add the dry ingredients and mix well. Remove dough from mixing bowl and place on floured surface. Roll into a ball and cover in plastic wrap. Refrigerate for 20 minutes.

Remove dough from refrigerator and place on a floured surface. Cut dough in half. Set one half aside. Roll out dough until it is 1/4 inch thick. Using your favorite Christmas cookie cutters, cut out desired shapes and place on parchment-lined cookie sheets. Bake in 375-degree oven for 12–15 minutes, or until edges just begin to turn light brown. Remove from oven and let cool on a wire cooling rack.

Butter Cream Frosting: In the bowl of an electric mixer, cream butter and powdered sugar until fluffy. Add milk slowly, one tablespoon at a time, until the frosting is the right spreading consistency. Divide frosting into smaller bowls and color with gel food coloring. Frost and decorate cookies as desired. These cookies taste delicious the moment they are frosted. Enjoy!

Decorator Icing: In the bowl of an electric mixer, beat together the sugar and 1/4 cup of milk. Beat until smooth. Add the corn syrup and vanilla extract and mix well.

For this method, you will need a thicker, outlining icing and a thinner flood icing. The outlining icing should be the consistency of toothpaste and will be piped around the shape of the cookie. Remove half of the thicker icing from the bowl and color with gel food coloring as desired. Put into piping bags.

Add more milk as needed to the other half of the icing to make the thinner flood icing. This should be the consistency of corn syrup. When this icing is ready, divide into separate bowls and color as desired. Outline the cookies with the outlining icing, then pipe in the flood icing. Have fun and be creative. Once cookies are decorated, place on wax paper until icing is completely dry. Enjoy!

FELICITY'S FIGGY BARS WITH HARD-SAUCE GLAZE

These cookies are reminiscent of an English steamed pudding.

Preheat oven to 350 degrees F, place rack in middle position.

Prep time: 25 minutes. Cook time: 20–25 minutes per pan.

Makes 96 bar cookies.

For the Bars:

10 ounces dried black figs (scant 2 cups)
1 cup water
2 cups quick-cooking oats, uncooked
1 1/2 cups brown sugar
2/3 cup dark molasses
6 tablespoons butter
2 large eggs
1 cup all-purpose flour
1 cup toasted wheat germ
2 teaspoons pumpkin pie spice
2 teaspoons freshly grated orange peel

1 teaspoon salt
1 teaspoon baking soda
1 teaspoon baking powder
Non-stick cooking spray

Hard-Sauce Glaze

2 cups powdered sugar
1/3 cup brandy
2 tablespoons warm water

While oven is preheating to 350 degrees, spray two 13x9-inch pans with non-stick cooking spray. Line both pans with parchment, extending parchment 2 inches up the sides of pans.

In large saucepan, combine figs and water. Heat over high heat until water boils. Remove saucepan from heat and stir in oats. Place warm mixture in mixing bowl and stir in sugar, molasses, and butter until well-blended. Next, stir in eggs. Add flour, wheat germ, pumpkin pie spice, orange peel, salt, baking soda, and baking powder. Stir until batter is well-blended. Divide mixture evenly between the two pans.

Bake for 20 to 25 minutes or until knife inserted into center comes out clean. Let cool for 10 minutes.

While the pans are cooling, make the

glaze. Place powdered sugar in a small bowl. Stir in brandy and water until blended.

Using parchment paper, remove the warm pastry and place on a cutting board or a firm surface. Brush each generously with the hard-sauce glaze and cool completely.

Cut each rectangle into 4 even lengthwise strips. Then cut each strip into 6 rectangles. Cut each rectangle on a diagonal to make 2 triangles. Enjoy!

LINDSEY'S SCRUMPTIOUS GIANT GINGERBREAD MUFFINS

Preheat oven to 400 degrees F. (Heat will be reduced to 375 degrees F.)

Prep time: 25 minutes. Cook time: 16–20 minutes.

Makes 8 giant muffins or 12 regular-sized muffins.

Ingredients:

2 1/4 cups all-purpose flour
1 teaspoon baking powder
1/2 teaspoon baking soda
3/4 teaspoon kosher salt
1 teaspoon ground ginger
1/2 teaspoon ground nutmeg
1/4 teaspoon ground cloves
2 teaspoons ground cinnamon
1/2 cup brown sugar
1/2 cup granulated sugar
1/2 cup (one stick) butter, melted and
  cooled

1/2 cup molasses

1 large egg

1/2 cup applesauce

1 rounded teaspoon fresh ginger, grated

1/2 cup whole milk

Sugar to sprinkle on top before baking

1 tablespoon melted butter, or non-stick cooking spray

In a medium bowl, combine flour, baking powder, baking soda, kosher salt, ground ginger, nutmeg, cloves, and cinnamon.

In the bowl of an electric mixer, combine both sugars, butter, molasses, egg, and applesauce. Mix until well-blended. Add in fresh ginger and stir until blended.

Gently stir in dry ingredients a little at a time, adding the whole milk between additions. Be careful not to over-mix the batter.

Generously grease muffin cups using melted butter or cooking spray. Pour batter into muffin cups and sprinkle tops with extra sugar. This will give a crispy top to the muffins while baking. Place muffins in a 400-degree oven and bake for 10 minutes. Reduce heat to 375 degrees and continue baking for 6–8 minutes longer, being careful not to overbake. Larger muffins will take longer. When muffin tops are crisp but springy, remove from oven and cool. Enjoy!

For more recipes, baking tips, and information on the Beacon Bakeshop Mystery Series, please visit: www.darcihannah.com

ABOUT THE AUTHOR

Darci Hannah grew up in the northwest suburbs of a Chicago, is a graduate of Indiana University, and currently lives in a small town in Michigan with her husband, three sons and two dogs. She has lived around the Great Lakes all her life and considers them a source of inspiration. When she's not engaged in a rollicking family adventure, walking her dogs, or working at the historic Howell Carnegie District Library, she's either baking up a storm or hard at work on her next Beacon Bakeshop Mystery. Visit her at DarciHannah.com.

The employees of Thorndike Press hope you have enjoyed this Large Print book. All our Thorndike, Wheeler, and Kennebec Large Print titles are designed for easy reading, and all our books are made to last. Other Thorndike Press Large Print books are available at your library, through selected bookstores, or directly from us.

For information about titles, please call:

(800) 223-1244

or visit our website at:

gale.com/thorndike

To share your comments, please write:

Publisher
Thorndike Press
10 Water St., Suite 310
Waterville, ME 04901